Spherical Harmonic

Tor Books by Catherine Asaro

THE SAGA OF THE SKOLIAN EMPIRE
Primary Inversion
Catch the Lightning
The Last Hawk
The Radiant Seas
Ascendant Sun
The Quantum Rose
Spherical Harmonic
*The Moon's Shadow**
*Skyfall**

*forthcoming

Spherical Harmonic

Catherine Asaro

TOR®

A TOM DOHERTY ASSOCIATES BOOK
NEW YORK

This is a work of fiction. All the characters and events portrayed in this book are either products of the author's imagination or are used fictitiously.

SPHERICAL HARMONIC

Copyright © 2001 by Catherine Asaro

Edited by David G. Hartwell

A Tor Book
Published by Tom Doherty Associates, LLC
175 Fifth Avenue
New York, NY 10010

www.tor.com

Tor® is a registered trademark of Tom Doherty Associates, LLC.

ISBN 0-812-56882-6
Library of Congress Catalog Card Number: 2001041534

First edition: November 2001
First mass market edition: August 2002

Printed in the United States of America

0 9 8 7 6 5 4 3 2 1

In memory of Melinda Helfer

March 14, 1943, to August 24, 2000.

Her extraordinary glow

warmed our lives.

Table of Contents

Contents

Acknowledgments

I would like to express my gratitude to the people who gave me comments on *Spherical Harmonic*. Their comments greatly helped the book. Any errors that remain are mine alone.

To Michael La Violette, Bud Sparhawk, Jeri Smith-Ready, and Michelle Monkou for much appreciated readings of the manuscript; to the writers who critiqued scenes: Tricia Schwaab, and Aly's Writing Group, including Aly Parsons, Simcha Kuritzky, Connie Warner, Al Carroll, Paula Jordon, George Williams, and J. G. Huckenpöler; to all those who answered my questions, including Yoji Kondo (aka Eric Kotani), Joan Slonczewski, and G. David Nordley; to Richard Drachman for double-checking the essay. I would like to thank Dean Dauger of Dauger Research for the orbital images and Ray Wilson of Illinois Wesleyan University for his image of the diffraction pattern.

Special thanks to my editors Jim Minz and David Hartwell for their excellent insights; to the publisher, Tom Doherty, and to all the fine people at Tor and St. Martin's Press who made this book possible; to my much appreciated agent, Eleanor Wood, of Spectrum Literary Agency; and to Binnie Syril Braunstein for her enthusiasm and hard work on my behalf.

A most heartfelt thanks to the shining lights of my life, my husband, John Kendall Cannizzo, and my daughter, Cathy, whose constant love and support make it all worthwhile.

BOOK ONE

Opalite

1
Partial Waves

?
Loam.
Looming up.
Looming shadow.
Encircled by shadows.
Wave by wave coalescing.
Waves coalescing in the night.
Flowing in from infinity; waves.
Gathering, coming out of nothing.
Flowing in from infinity; waves.
Waves coalescing in the night.
Wave by wave coalescing.
Encircled by shadows.
Looming shadow.
Looming up.
Loam.
?

Loam.
Looming up.
Looming shadow.
Encircled by shadows.
Wave by wave coalescing.
Waves coalescing in the night.
Flowing in from infinity; waves.
Gathering, coming out of nothing.
Flowing in from infinity; waves.
Waves coalescing in the night.
Wave by wave coalescing.
Encircled by shadows.
Looming shadow.
Looming up.
Loam.
?

I began to exist.

A patch of night sky brooded far overhead. Dark red sky. Shadows loomed around me, their distant tops circling that ruddy patch. I lay on my back and gazed up a ragged tunnel of shadows to a smoldering night.

Sounds crinkled the night: clicks, rustles, whispers. The dark rumbled.

A mistake had occurred.
I shouldn't be here.
I was . . .
?

I felt myself. Arms. Long hair. Breasts. Human.
I was human.
So I lay, dreaming, as my body became solid.
I became aware of an emotion. Fear. It soaked my thoughts. My teeth clenched. Sweat beaded my forehead.

Sweet-smelling moss cushioned my body, bumpy and damp, and a cornucopia of smells tickled my nose. As I stood up, the clicks and clacks went silent. A breeze ruffled my shift, which was a gauzy sleep shirt that came to midthigh. Night turned the cloth dark, but my memory stirred: the shift was blue. I recalled nothing else, though. I clenched my fist in the cloth, my heart beating hard.

Despite the night's warmth, I shivered. My disorientation went deeper than memory loss. Urgency pulled at me, I didn't know why. Nothing here had familiarity. I took a step—and ran into a wall. Wincing, I rubbed my elbow where it had hit. As my eyes adjusted to the light, I saw that the "wall" was a root buckling out of the ground. A large root. Here, it came as high as my shoulders. To my right it sloped downward, and to my left it rose in shadowed bumps, higher and higher, until the shadows of night swallowed its curve.

I dragged my hand through my hair, then stopped when I realized my arm was trembling. *Never show fear, never let anyone see your vulnerabilities.* As soon as that thought formed, I knew it well though I wasn't sure why. I tried to push down my apprehension. I had to find out what had happened.

Seeking a vantage point to look around, I climbed the root, digging my toes into the wet, crumbly moss that covered it. I reached the top, but then I slipped and tumbled down the other side. Although the low gravity tempered my fall, I flipped over and landed on my stomach, knocking out my breath. My hip smacked a small root jutting out of the ground.

Ai! I bit my lip, wincing. *Keep the fear at bay. Think.* The low gravity probably meant this was a small world, or a spongy one, or maybe a space habitat. I climbed to my feet, rubbing my hip. Then I took a look at myself. Although I didn't consciously recall my appearance, what I saw came as no surprise: slender arms, soft palms, clipped nails, slight build, firm breasts, small waist, long legs, delicate feet. My hair fell to below my hips, glossy and black. A healthy body. Youthful. But youth and I had long ago parted.

I had lived 158 years.

Despite its length, the span of years felt natural. It was a start; I knew my appearance and age. Now if I could just figure out this place. Peering into the dark, I saw more roots. Some were small; others were monstrous, bigger than the one I had climbed. They twisted in eerie shadows, evoking in me a primal urge to seek protection from the dark and the unknown.

Dark and unknown . . .
And unknown . . .
Unknown . . .
Warm . . .
?

> ?
> Why?
> Walking now.
> Climb? Climb now.
> Tumbled down the chute.
> Tumbling down, down a chute.
> Tumbling down and down a chute.
> Ground falls away from under my feet.
> I stand up and walk forward a few steps.
> I stand up and walk forward a few steps.
> Ground falls away from under my feet.
> Tumbling down and down a chute.
> Tumbling down, down a chute.
> Tumbled down the chute.
> Climb? Climb now.
> Walking now.
> Why?
> ?

Warmth bathed my cheek. Coppery sunlight filtered through translucent walls.

Walls? Sunlight?

I sat up groggily. What the—? Seconds ago it had been night. A reddish night, yes, but dark. I had been outside. Now I was in an irregular cavity roughly twice my length. Across from me, a chute led upward, twisting out of sight. It looked like I had fallen into a gnarled mass of large roots. In thinner areas, light from outside shone through them, coppery and diffuse.

Disquieted, I put my palms on my cheeks, reassuring myself I was solid. Had I passed out? I crossed my arms across my torso, as if that could ward off this inexplicable situation. I couldn't let this shake me up. I would find help.

It wasn't hard to climb the chute. My knees scraped off moss, and the root underneath rubbed smoothly against my skin. I came out into a sunlit place surrounded by dark green foliage. Each plant had a tripod base, three legs that came together into a stalk, which rose straight up. The plants were all sizes, from tender sprouts smaller than my thumb to growths so large I could see only their tripod bases. I tilted back my head to look up—

And up—

And up—

"Gods," I whispered. Just the bases alone of the largest plants stood ten to twenty meters tall. The three legs joined into a gigantic column that rose hundreds of meters, so high I nearly lost my balance craning back my head to see their crowns. The sheer magnitude of their height thrilled me. Plants didn't grow this large on heavier gravity worlds. Clouds could easily have hidden the tops of these mammoths.

Dizzy from staring, I lowered my head and rubbed my neck. Such strange foliage. Overlapping plates covered everything, supple on smaller plants, thickened into armor on the larger. Flags made from a similar material unfurled from the stalks, spread flat to the sky. They grew huge on the trees, supported by struts, facing the sky like giant hands extended in a plea for money, as if each photon they caught was a beggared coin.

The flags were spaced far enough apart for me to see a patch of sky, possibly the same one I had gazed at last night. Centered in it, a tiny sun shone like a sharp white bead. It was hard to see how that measly orb could provide the light that saturated this forest. As soon as I had that thought, lenses in my eyes recorded the spectrum of the star, and my brain toggled one of its analysis nodes.

Lenses? Nodes?

Until that moment, I hadn't known I had enhanced eyesight or nodes in my brain. But yes, I remembered. The nodes were biochips that augmented my thoughts. Apparently something had disrupted the neural pathways in my brain. As my neurons reconnected, my memories seemed to be returning.

I touched my face, wondering. What color were my eyes? Green. Yes, they were green. The lens enhancements made a translucent film on my eyes, the palest rose and gold. *Sunrise eyes.* My father had called them that. I couldn't remember him, except for a sense of love that transcended details.

According to my lenses and nodes, that "tiny" sun overhead was actually a large star. It looked small because this planet orbited at a great distance. But that made this world even more of a puzzle. From so far away, that star couldn't provide enough irradiation to nurture this fertile biosphere. The planet ought to be a ball of ice.

Besides, sunshine from a star of that spectral class should be white, possibly blue-tinged, but not the smoldering red that bathed this forest. Although the air had an unfamiliar tang on my tongue, I could breathe it well enough. Such an atmosphere would scatter longer wavelengths of light everywhere, making the sky blue. Instead it glowed lurid red-purple, lightened only in a halo around the sun, which shone off to one side overhead.

To one side?

I blinked. In the few moments I had been staring upward, the sun had moved. A chronometer in my brain recorded how long the shift had taken. My lenses marked how it had shifted. My nodes estimated that it took this world 240 minutes to rotate, probably about two hours of light and two hours of dark. The planet had a four-hour cycle.

Pah. That knowledge left me no less bewildered. The short day didn't explain why the night had just switched off earlier. Even with only two hours of night, dawn wouldn't come that fast. I had lost at least an hour, maybe more.

I wrapped my arms around my body, chilled from inside. Mist steamed off the dark plants. Roots buckled in curves and rolls, my height and more. Cavities within them showed everywhere, above and below ground, a network of living caves. As the sun moved out of the patch of sky, shadows filled the forest.

My hunger stirred. I hadn't eaten since . . . I wasn't sure. Could I eat the plants? Their green color suggested they used photosynthesis. But no, that would make them a much brighter green: These were almost black. Perhaps they had an unusual chemistry that let them absorb more light. It would explain their dark color. Unfortunately, it also increased the chance that they might poison me.

The rich, bittersweet smell of the forest saturated my senses. The curving roots resembled waves, green swells in a surreal ocean, breakers rising, rising in great crests . . .

Rising . . .
Undulating . . .
Out to infinity . . .
Rippling out to infinity . . .

With a conscious effort, I pulled back into my body. What the hell? Part of me was here. But another part was *there*. Where? What nightmare had caught me?

Ah, no . . .

2

The Promontory

?
In trouble
Must remain solid
Bring more partial waves.
Can see right through body.
Body has become translucent.
Can see right through body.
Bring more partial waves.
Must remain solid.
In trouble.
?

Awareness returned like waves washing the shore of my mind—and I understood that I had almost ceased to exist. With shaking hands, I pressed my palms against a tripod tree, assuring myself I was solid. Is that what had happened when night jumped into day? Had I just stopped *existing*?

I straightened up and touched my face, my shoulders, my stomach. Solid. I took a long breath. I had to take action. But before I could go anywhere, I needed to see where I was. The large root next to me looked familiar. I clambered to the top and sat with my legs dangling over the other side. The clearing where I had awoken last night lay below. A human-sized dent flattened the moss and footprints led to this root. But I saw no indication I had entered the clearing. Either something had lowered me from the air or else I had come into existence here. How? And from *where*?

I rubbed my arms, trying to warm them. My shift had no sleeves, just ribbons tied over the shoulders. Mist curled around my legs, damp on the skin. The heavy foliage made it difficult to see, but in one direction the land appeared to slope upward. If I hiked to higher ground, I might get a better idea about the area. That gave me a surge of hope. I might find a landmark I recognized or an outpost with people.

So I set off into the forest. My optimism soon faltered. The buckled terrain made the hike painfully difficult. Hidden twigs poked my feet through the moss, making me limp, and underbrush scratched my legs. Apparently I wasn't used to the gravity; I had trouble timing my steps and stumbled often.

A green beetle-thing the size of a handball flew in my face. Startled, I knocked it away. It threatened battle with frenzied clicks of its little lobster claws. Then it flew off. Other more graceful creatures softened the evening. Diaphanous flyers soared through the air, their gauzy black wings edged in gold. They clung to my hair, covering it like a gilded scarf that lay over my shoulders and hung to my hips. When I waved them off, their wings tangled in my fingers and crushed. I felt like an ogre leaving them crippled on the ground, prey to the red beetle-tanks that lumbered along with chopping claws. So after that I let them stay in my hair. They covered it like a sheen of liquid.

The life here had beauty, shiny and vibrant. In some ways the creatures resembled large insects, but they looked stylized, as if they were made from delicate china and enameled in glossy colors. Some had iridescent wings. In human-standard gravity they would have been too heavy to fly. A few evoked crustaceans, their antennae and carapaces glimmering with jeweled colors. Airborne lobsters.

A skinny creature darted out of the trees, aloft on diaphanous blue wings, its segmented body as long as my arm. It came straight at me and I jumped aside, my pulse ratcheting up. It went on with no more than a high-pitched whine. After that I walked even more carefully. The next one might not be so tolerant.

I christened the animals "arthrops," after the Earth phylum Arthropoda, which included insects and crustaceans. These creatures probably defined their own phylum, though, one unlike any human classification. I chose Earth because hu-

man life had developed there, though many of us had long
been separated from our mother world.

Yes. Earth.

My memories returned gently, awaking like bubbles adrift
in the air, their surfaces thinning, spinning, waning, until finally their contents dispersed in a mist of recollections. I had
never considered Earth home, nor had my ancestors. We had
been separated from our mother world for six millennia,
through the rise and fall of empires, and then their rise again.

I hiked in a daze, my feet and skin burning from scratches.
I tried to numb my mind so I wouldn't think about how much
it hurt. The sky turned scarlet and red shadows darkened the
trees. Nanomeds in my body measured the gases dissolving
in my blood.

Nanomeds?

Yes, nanomeds. They cruised my body, little labs the size
of molecules. Different types performed different functions,
such as catalyzing reactions, repairing bonds, or ferrying nutrients. They also analyzed the atmosphere. It had a low oxygen content, but enough for survival. I doubted this place just
happened to fit human life so well. Biosculptors, those gentler cousins of terraformers, had probably fine-tuned it. If so,
surely people lived here. Somewhere. If I could just find
them.

The night never truly became dark. The sky turned the
color of dark bricks. Accompanied by the percussive songs of
clicking, clacking arthrops, I clambered over ridges and
mossy knolls. My neural compass kept me going in roughly a
straight line.

The trees breathed hostility.

Startled, I came to a halt. I turned in a circle, straining to
see. Only arthrops moved in the shadows. Was my mind in-
terpreting this bizarre place as a hostile emotion? Saints
knew, I was in trouble. I needed shelter, water, and food. Although this forest surely required vast amounts of water, I
had found none, and my attempts to dig had brought up no
more than a loam so rich its scent overpowered me. The water these huge roots tapped might be buried too deep to reach.

The prospect of catching arthrops and drinking whatever fluids kept them alive made my stomach lurch, but soon I might have no choice.

Plunging on, I sought to leave this place of undefined anger. I pushed through a tangle of stalks, flags, and tripods—and ran smack into a gargantuan root three times my height. I couldn't go around it; the ridge extended in both directions, plunging into masses of tripod bush. Dismayed, I stared up at its shadowed bulk. Did this forest have no end? My muscles ached. Gouges covered my arms and legs. Bruises purpled my knees. My feet were bleeding. But if I intended to live, I either had to backtrack or climb.

I exhaled. Then I dug my fingers into the moss-covered ridge and climbed, fleeing the antagonism that saturated the forest. Almost immediately, I lost my grip and slid to the ground. Steeling myself, I tried again. This time I made it halfway, higher, almost at the top—and the moss fell apart in my hands.

"Ai!" I tumbled down, languid in the low gravity, and hit the ground with a thud.

I bit the inside of my cheek to hold back my groan. *Keep going.* Drawing in a ragged breath, I climbed to my feet. Then I swayed. So tired. I looked for a better route, but the underbrush made too much of a tangle. With blurred vision, I peered at the root. It twisted through the trees, curving like the Fourier analysis of a complicated waveform, rippling, flowing, ebbing, swirling . . .

Rippling . . .
Riiiiippliiiing . . .

I wrenched back to reality. What was wrong with me? I felt as if I were coalescing, that if I didn't hang on to reality, I would disperse back into nothing. As I was reforming, refinements added to my body and mind like translucent layers of watercolor paint laid over a picture. Or waves, ebbing in from Elsewhere. But waves of what? Existence? I didn't understand. Yes, sure, quantum theory said all matter was waves, including human beings. But it didn't work like this. People were *solid*. I felt tenuous. Insubstantial. So sorry, I seem to have misplaced the J=236 partial wave of an electron in my eyelash.

Pah. I rubbed my eyes. I needed to sleep.

The air vibrated with hostility.

I took a sharp breath. *Stop it*. Air consisted of gas molecules. It had no emotions.

I tackled the root again, and this time I made it to the top. Hooking my arms over its edge, I stared out at the other side.

More trees.

"Shit," I muttered.

I heaved myself over the top. Halfway down the other side, my fingers tired. I slid the rest of the way and crumpled into a heap on the ground. So weary. But I couldn't stop, not now. I hauled myself to my feet and trudged off again, pushing through the brush, escaping that undefined menace. The shadows lightened into a ruddy predawn. I stumbled through a mass of tripods—

Saints almighty.

I had come out on a promontory of rock. The shelf extended for about ten steps in front of me and two on either side. Its sides fell away in vertical cliffs, far down to a lake. The water glittered in the crimson light as if its swells were lit with spectral fire. Forest surrounded the lake down there, dark and primitive, almost black. Nothing but forest. Tripod trees covered the world. But what stole my breath, what made me stare, had nothing to do with lakes or trees.

I wasn't on a world. This was the moon of a planet.

A huge planet.

It dominated the view. Even with only half that giant orb showing above the forest, it spanned the horizon. The topmost edge of the disk reached a third of the way up the sky. It smoldered. Bronze bands striped it, their turbulence visible as storms wracked its atmosphere. It had to be a superjovian planet, almost massive enough to be a star. It glowed only with its heat of formation, but that was plenty. It lavished fiery light on this moon.

Planet and moon were almost certainly locked face to face, which meant that monstrous, glowering world would always stay on the horizon, forever setting. The planet was probably mostly gas; otherwise, its tidal forces would have ripped this moon apart. Given the moon's small size, it had to be dense to have even this low gravity. The horizon was so close, I could see its downward curve. The trees looked like they were falling off.

Day came fast. A halo appeared at the edge of the gas giant. Suddenly the tiny parent star rose past the planet, a bead of white studded like a diamond into the lurid sky.

" 'So is the splendor of what nature has wrought,' " I murmured, quoting a poet I had long admired, though I only just now remembered. Splendor or no splendor, I wanted to be away from this place and its undefined hostility.

The lake reminded me of my thirst. Could I drink the water? Another memory stirred; the nanomeds in my body had a limited ability to make antidotes. I could further improve my chances by boiling the water. I knew how to make a fire. Well, in theory, I knew. It required friction, enough to ignite flammable matter. Whether I could actually manage it was another question. Nor would the moisture-laden plants here burn well, particularly with the low oxygen atmosphere. But if I could make a torch, it could also serve as a weapon.

All right. I had a plan: start fire, make torch, boil water, drink, cook arthrops, eat the nasty things, find people.

Rustles came from the forest.

I spun around, my hair swinging around my body, covered with glistening black and gold flyers. Shadows cloaked the forest, but light still touched its top. Clouds drifted among the luminous crowns, and mist curled around the shadowed trunks. It looked surreal, as if the tree tops floated in a world separate from the shadowed forest below.

Hatred!

I almost stumbled back off the precipice.

The arthrop clicks stopped. The world went silent. Waiting. Again I saw ghostly waves; back in the forest, they coalesced around a tripod tree, forming a human shape. It detached from the tree and moved through the dusk, gnarled arms hanging at its sides. I couldn't see it well, but I felt its seething anger. I vibrated with it. My mind recoiled and then overextended, spreading too thin, ebbing . . .

Ebbing . . .

Ebbing . . .

Dismayed, I struggled to focus. Had the world gone crazy? My mind slammed down a barrier, muting the rage of the approaching creature. Until this moment, I hadn't even known I could protect my mind that way.

It kept coming, tangled in its rage. As it left the forest, I saw it more clearly. Its shape was humanoid, but its torso was an armored trunk, its legs narrower trunks, its arms a tangle of long roots. Its face resembled tree bark, and its hair hung in a snarl of moss. With the cliff at my back, I had no place to retreat. My stomach churned.

The creature emanated fury. It came forward, closer and closer, until it stopped in front of me, its moss eyes staring down at my face.

"What do you want?" My voice rasped, low and husky.

It didn't answer. Instead it grasped my upper arm and closed its other hand around my neck. My heartbeat hammered. With clenched fists, I pounded its shoulders and chest. Although it jerked, it kept bearing down on my neck, cutting off the blood flow. I clawed at its arms. As spots danced in my vision, I knew I had no time left. I was going to die.

No.

I saw only one chance. I stepped back—off the cliff.

The creature had one instant to decide; release me or go over the edge. Whether it actually chose or simply had too little time to act, I didn't know. But we fell together through a chasm of air. I had a strange sense of suspension, as if we were drifting, undulating in this slow-mode gravity while we dropped past the cliff face.

Then I hit water, cold water. The impact tore me away from my attacker, and I plunged deep into the lake. With a hard kick, I slowed my descent. More kicks sent me upward through skirling, swirling water, but it wasn't fast enough. *I needed air.* In reflex, I gasped, sucking in cold water—

Suddenly I broke the surface, choking and coughing. Before I could catch my breath, arms grabbed me from behind. Thrashing in that air-stealing grip, I twisted around—and came face to face with a very living, very human man. No creature, this. The shock of hitting the lake had pulled my mind back from its limbo and thrust me into cold, human reality.

Water cascaded off his head. He had green eyes and dark hair that brushed his shoulders. His skin wasn't bark, but he held his face as stiff and implacable as the armor on the tripod trees.

Then he shoved my head under the water.

Thrashing in his grip, I kicked his legs and arms. But I had too little strength to escape. Desperate, I planted my feet against his torso and pushed. It sent me upward even as it thrust him deeper into the lake. I just barely managed to break the surface, amid slow sprays of water.

The treeman exploded out of the water next to me. He grabbed my hair and jerked me forward, making me gasp. As we fought, water whipped around us, turned red by the sunset. The liquid sprayed up in great arcs, then fragmented into a rain of fat spheres, glittering like slow rubies. I choked, unable to gulp in air. Ai! I had to *breathe.* But again he pushed me under. Frenzied now, I twisted in his hold . . . needed air . . . lungs hurt . . . don't want to die . . .

Suddenly I sagged, as if I had passed out. My act almost became reality, as I began to black out. Then, mercifully, his grip loosened. With a last surge of energy, I set my feet against his thighs and launched upward. This time I shot through the surface in a wild spray of water, coming out of the lake all the way to my chest, sputtering. *Air.*

As I fell back, the treeman caught me in a deadly embrace that crushed out what little air I had managed to inhale. His muscular arms circled my torso. I tried to keep fighting, but my body wouldn't respond, drained by too many hours of hiking with no food, water, or rest. My fists uncurled and my palms slapped the water. My legs dangled. I tried to kick free and my foot grazed his leg.

We stared at each other, our faces separated by a hand-span.

I felt his reaction, just as I had felt his hostility before. Seeing me this close forced him to acknowledge he was murdering a human being, one less protected than himself. He treaded water and we floated, staring. What he expected to find, I had no idea, but this much I picked up, as sharp as the chime of a crystal bell: he hadn't expected the humanity he saw in my face.

My mind couldn't absorb that I was about to die. The situation took on a diamond clarity, as if it were etched in glass, disconnected from me. I watched from beyond the glass, protected from the full impact of the events.

With no warning, he rolled me onto his hip. My trance broke and I gasped in misty air. My hip scraped against the rough cloth of his soaked trousers. He swam with a sidekick, holding me in a cross-chest carry I had learned long ago. No, learned *about,* in a holo on water safety. I knew many things, but only in theory. My life had been protected with almost fanatical thoroughness. Why?

Our legs dragged through the muddy lake bottom. The treeman heaved me to my feet and we stood in the shallows near the shore, the water lapping in low gravity breakers that swelled to our knees. As I gulped in air, a stitch of pain jabbed my side. My whole body felt the pounding of my heart. The treeman stared at my face, his hands clenched on my upper arms. Whatever he saw, it stirred in him a disquieting mixture of fury, desire, and confusion.

Twisting hard, I jerked free and sprinted for the beach, a thin strip of eroded rock next to the promontory. The lake whipped around me in languorous swaths, swirling up to my head and drifting through the air in sparkling lassos of water.

The treeman caught up in two steps. As he yanked me to a stop, I socked his jaw. He dodged the blow, but lost his balance in the process. In a surreal silence, we toppled to the beach, only half out of the lake. The slow fall kept my head from cracking open when it hit the rocky ground, but it still struck hard. My ears rang with a hollow clang, like a cry of desperation. I didn't feel pain yet; I couldn't take in the sensations flooding me, all tangled in fear.

The treeman pinned me on my back, my legs and hips in the water. He held my arms clamped to the ground, kneeling over me, straddling my hips, his body silhouetted against the gas giant that smoldered in the sky behind him.

He had such a strong reaction to what he saw that the image burst from his mind into mine. I lay below him, breathing rapidly, my eyes huge from terror, my skin pale. Rips showed in my shift where the cloth had snagged on plants in the forest. One of my nipples poked through a ragged hole. Soaked with water, the cloth had become translucent. I didn't need the empathic skills I apparently possessed to know what he intended next.

Except he didn't move. I caught only threads of emotion from his mental turmoil; the barriers that protected his mind were even stronger than those that most people instinctively raised to shield their thoughts. But I picked up enough. He couldn't go through with it, neither the assault nor the murder. He longed for vengeance with an intensity that burned. I had no idea what he thought I had done, but even now, when he believed he had a long-desired revenge within his grasp, he could go no further.

I swallowed. "Don't kill me."

He answered in a language I almost understood. It resembled—what? Chays. Chay? Shay. Yes, Shay, an obscure tongue used on a few frontier worlds. The name came from *tza,* an ancient Iotic word that meant cleverness.

Clever or not, right now this Shay wanted to kill me. I searched my nodes for Shay words and came up with, "Understand not." Less than scintillating, but it would do.

He spoke again. "****."

"Understand not," I repeated.

"**** Manq?" he asked.

"Again?"

He spoke more slowly. "Manq, are you?"

"No." I had never heard the word before.

"Who, then?"

With him holding my arms, I couldn't point at the sky. So I indicated it with my chin. "Out there. Skolian." It was true, I realized. I was a citizen of the Skolian Imperialate.

"**** Skolia," he said.

I felt like a computer trying to access data in the wrong format. "Understand not."

He shortened his sentences. "Lying, you. Here Skolians never come. Hunter, you are."

I had no idea what he meant. "Me no hunter."

He shook my arms. *"Liar."*

"Not lies!" My voice vibrated with his shaking.

His anger mixed with another emotion, one harder to define. Grief? "Kill you, I need not. Just tie you here." He gestured to our surroundings. "Opalite, she will finish."

Attuned to his mind, I understood what he meant—and wished I didn't. *Opalite* was this moon. If he left me bound here on the beach, I would die from starvation and exposure. I didn't see how someone his size could perceive me as a threat. Low gravity grew big people and he was no exception. If he found me strange, I had no argument with that, given this bizarre situation. But why the hatred? Despite the many gaps in my memories, I had no doubt I had never seen him before this day.

His rage was mutating into a new anger, this time at himself. He had no wish to feel sympathy for his intended victim. But he felt it. He didn't want to suffer remorse for an act he had yet to commit, but his guilt gnawed. He had no wish to desire a stranger, but his arousal refused to abate. What finally decided him—compassion, remorse, or lust—I had no idea. But he made a choice. Standing up, he hauled me to my feet and jerked his hand toward the forest.

"Walk," he said.

So I walked.

It was better than dying.

3

Hajune

?
??
Fall.
Falling.
Treeman.
The promontory.
Then . . . remember what?
No memory, none of coming here.

Dizziness made my thoughts sluggish. I slowly became aware of my surroundings. I was sitting sideways against a wall, my legs curled under my body. This cavity resembled the one I had fallen into my first night, mossy and green. This time, however, a net of cord-like roots held my body from shoulder to midthigh, as if I had sat here until the forest grew over and around me. But this was no random growth; someone had set these cords with deliberate intent. My wrists were bound together by a looping root that buckled out from the wall. It held my hands by my shoulder, palms inward. I had heard that tying a prisoner's wrists in front of the body was ineffective, but for me, right now, it worked all too frighteningly well.

I bit my lip. I couldn't show vulnerability, not even to myself. Never give in to fear. But gods, I didn't want to die. I drew in a long breath, my chest rising with the effort. A circular opening in the opposite wall taunted me with a promise of freedom. It had no door, not even a gate. If I could only reach it. Beyond that opening, the forest brooded in bright, midday sunlight . . .

Midday . . .

No memory, none of coming here.
Then . . . remember what?
The promontory
Treeman.
Falling.
Fall.
??
?
.

Dawn showed beyond the entrance. I struggled to focus.
Had I faded again? I couldn't stop shuddering. Saints only
knew what the treeman had thought if I turned into a ghost in
front of him. Maybe he believed this web of roots could hold
a specter. If so, he was apparently right, unfortunately, in my
case.

A fire smoldered in the center of the cavity, in a depression
lined with rock and bordered by wet moss. Smoke curled
through a hole in the roof. The heat and humidity made the
place like a sauna. A scrap of cloth lay among the coals.
Charred cloth. Blue. It was all that remained of my clothes.
Embarrassed, I tugged on my bonds, trying to cover myself.
The roots flexed but showed no sign of loosening. If anything, they tightened. I quit fighting and concentrated on
breathing, which had suddenly become a challenge.

After a moment, the roots loosened. "Come on," I muttered. "You can get out of this." I surveyed the cavity. It didn't
contain much: a dish and cup by the fire, both red clay, and a
pitcher with a spout. The pitcher smelled of water. Did the
treeman intend to drink it? If he could, chances were I could
too. I had to risk it; my thirst had become excruciating.

Moving with care, I straightened my leg. The roots pulled
tight, until I struggled to breathe. I waited for them to loosen.
They were curled around my torso, hips, and upper thighs,
but their tangle didn't extend farther down my body. When I
could breathe again, I stretched my leg to the fire pit. It took
several stops and starts to deal with the tightening cords, but
I managed to hook the pot with my foot. I pulled it toward

me, first using my foot, then my knee, slowly so it didn't tip over. With all the pauses, it seemed to take forever. But finally I brought it to my body.

I bent my head between my arms, an awkward position with my hands bound. Straining downward, I managed to grab the pitcher with my teeth. As I straightened, the pot slipped, but before it fell, I caught it with my elbows. Frantic with thirst, I worked it up into my hands and tipped it to my mouth, not even waiting for the roots to loosen.

Water ran down my throat, warm and welcome. According to my nanomeds, it contained bacteria my stomach wouldn't appreciate, but nothing it couldn't handle. However, this water wasn't the same as that in the lake. It had probably been boiled . . .

". . . are you?" a deep voice asked.

I jerked. The treeman was sitting against a wall. Outside, night had fallen. Fear constricted my chest. Where had he come from?

He almost looked human. He wore green trousers woven with softened threads, perhaps spun from the plants. Vine designs lined their seams, flecks of bright green and blue beetle carapaces sewn into the cloth. Similar designs bordered the well-formed collar and cuffs of his tunic, and the lower hem that lay against his thighs. His belt looked like cured plates of plant armor, also inlaid with vine designs in red, blue, violet, and gold. His boots wrapped around his muscular legs, with thongs crisscrossing them from foot to knee. Other thongs ornamented with violet and red carapace-enamel hung from their upper edges, their tassels braided with red beads. His hair resembled moss again, curling to his shoulders, as if he had turned partially back into a forest creation.

"Cold, are you?" he repeated.

"Hot." My voice rasped. "Too much—" I searched my memory for the right Shay word. "Too much steam."

He remained silent, sitting by the wall, one of his long legs stretched out, the other bent at the knee with his elbow resting on it.

Despite the strange circumstances, this felt familiar. A memory came to me. A cold place. Freezing. A huge guard held me wrapped in his jacket, trying to keep me warm, though he shook with cold. All moisture had frozen out of the air. We were in a hovercar. The driver was dead, killed by the avalanche that had engulfed the car. The weight of snow would have crushed us all had the driver not braced himself against the roof, adding the final support that kept the craft from collapsing. He had given his life to save mine. My heart wrenched with the memory. What had I done, that they would make such a sacrifice?

A clue: both men had worn uniforms. Military. Imperial Space Command. ISC. They were my bodyguards. Why I, a civilian, had military bodyguards I didn't recall. And I was a civilian, I was certain. I had long mourned the man who died. My other guard had almost died as well, from hypothermia, before a rescue team dug us out of the snow.

I could see now why that situation recalled this one. It wasn't only the fear. Both times I had been trapped in a small place with someone I didn't know well. It was an occurrence so rare, it brought on the memory despite the otherwise different circumstances.

"Why stare you at me?" the treeman asked.

I swallowed. "I'm scared."

"Should be." He used a matter-of-fact tone.

"What you—" I stumbled over the idiosyncratic Shay grammar. "What you me do?"

"Say again?"

"What do you to me?"

"Tithe, to me, you with yourself pay."

Even understanding his words, I couldn't follow them. So I sent a thought to my language libraries: *change his Shay grammar to a form I understand.* It translated his words as, "You are the tithe."

Did he mean a tax? Or *tyth,* the Shay word for thief? My memory said *tyth* derived from the Iotic verb *ti`.* Ancient Iotic was a precursor to most of our languages, including the modern Iotic I spoke. In ancient Iotic, *ti`* meant "eat plants or the meat of animals," but in Shay it had come to mean "feed oneself by stealing food." Did he believe I had filched his dinner?

"I rob not," I said, trying to sound trustworthy.

He said something about my life. A loan? It wasn't clear. "I owe a debt?" I asked. "This debt to you?"

"Manq owe." The intensity of his gaze burned. "Your life pays this debt."

I didn't like the direction our conversations kept taking. "No kill me."

"Then tithe." As he spoke, one of his memories broke past his guarded thoughts. Normally I had trouble picking up clear images from his mind, but this one exploded with painful clarity. *Rugged stick figures were destroying the forest, mutilating roots.* I had to fortify my barriers, muting the brutal intensity of that image. This memory had great power over him. His grief filled the cavity. Stick figures maiming roots. Did he see that as a form of murder? I questioned my perception of his memory, though. It could be skewed, like my perception of him. Sometimes I saw him as human and other times as a treeman, a creature created by the forest to exact its revenge.

Then I realized both were true. His human body matched his physical appearance. His treeman aspect was how my mind interpreted his self-image, at least what I managed to pick up from his guarded thoughts. Yes, I remembered. I had long seen this way, in more than one mode. Normally I had a better ability to process my perceptions, but right now I was incomplete. Partial waves continued to come in from another reality and fine-tune my existence.

Fatigue, dazing, hazing, dazing . . .
Fatigue and hunger, dazing, hazing, dazing . . .
Untether my mind, drift, drifting into psiberspace . . .
Or what had been psiberspace, before the implosion . . .
Untether my mind, drift, drifting into psiberspace . . .
Afloat, afloat, afloat, floating in a forever sea . . .
Floating, dazing, hazing, dazing . . .

"—speak!" He sounded frightened.

Fade away . . .

". . . *come back!*"

With an effort, I pulled into focus. The treeman was crouched in front of me, his body rippling. No, he wasn't rippling; reality was rippling. The cavity ebbed and flowed.

"Say again?" My voice sounded like distant leaves blowing over a plain.

He blanched. "What ****?"

"Understand not," I whispered.

"You started to *vanish*." Sweat trickled down his temple. "Manq trick."

"No trick." My voice was a lost wind.

"Manq cruelty." He stated it flat and hard, as if to fend off whatever I had become.

"Not Manq."

"Did the Manq tell you?" His voice cracked. "Did it make a good telling?"

"Tell me what?"

Again that image came into my mind, sticks destroying roots.

"Stick people?" I asked, bewildered.

"You ****."

"Understand not." The cavity was solidifying. The treeman looked almost human now, though his eyes still resembled moss. I could feel my breath, fast and hard.

His disquiet seeped into my mind. To him, I looked young, unprotected, and frightened. It bothered him.

He spoke again. "You claim Skolians live above Slowcoal?"

"Slowcoal?" I asked.

"The huge coal that broods in the sky."

So that was what they called the gas giant. "Yes. Skolians live on many worlds."

He snorted. "I have never seen a Skolian. I have no belief they exist."

"I exist." At least I thought I did. "You are Skolian, too."

"I am not Skolian."

"Is true." My language libraries supplied the information. "Opalite and Slowcoal are part of Skolia."

Despite his frown, he didn't object again, which made me suspect he had heard it before.

Exhausted, I closed my eyes. It was only an instant. But when I opened them, sunlight was filtering into the cavity, though a second ago it had been night. A gauzy arthrop hung from the ceiling, its wings like lace spun into a spiral, going around, *round, round* . . .

Round . . .
Round . . .

"—dying, are you?" He sounded closer now. Urgent. Apprehensive.

My eyes were closed. Closed? I opened them. Night had fallen, but Slowcoal light filled the cavity, augmented by embers in the fire pit. Disoriented and dizzy, I didn't try to speak. The treeman was kneeling in front of me, holding the pitcher of water to my lips. I drank, gulping, and the precious liquid soothed my throat. After I drank my fill, I bent my head over my bound hands and wiped the moisture from my lips. My arms shook.

He paled. "What are you?"

"I know not." My answer was almost inaudible, like wind over water in a far away place. "Go home . . . I must."

His voice hardened. "You stay."

"No."

"Yes. Manq lost you. I found."

"Not Manq. Skolian."

"You look Manq."

How did Manq look? I thought of his memory. Stick figures. I didn't look that way to him. He considered the Manq human, but his subconscious thought of them as dead sticks with no humanity at all.

"**** the sun?" he said

"Again?" I asked.

He said something about the sun and my hair. With a

wrench of dismay, I recalled who else had hair like mine. An image came to my mind, a man in dark trousers and a rumpled gray sweater sitting at a console. Gleaming hardware surrounded him, lights flashing as he peered at a graph that rotated in the air. He had tousled hair, glossy and black with gray dusted at the temples.

My son.

My son.

The treeman gestured at my hair. "**** Manq is."

I tried to concentrate, but the memory of my son brought a gut-twisting dread. Something was wrong. Very wrong.

The treeman shook a length of my hair and repeated his indecipherable question. Anger leaked into his voice. And unease. He hid his apprehension well, but I felt it. He wondered if he had caught a supernatural being.

Fearing he would decide that my apparent spectral state gave him more reason to end my life, I tried to answer. "Manq hair black?"

He let go of my hair. "Yes."

"What else is Manq?"

The treeman tapped his finger next to his eye, then indicated the pitcher he held and spoke a word. He touched a copper ornament on his tunic and repeated the word.

The only similarity I could see between the pot and ornament was color. "Manq eyes brown?" That wasn't the Shay word he had used, though.

"Not brown. Some red." He repeated the other word. "Like metal."

I stored his word in my memory. "Copper?"

"Yes. Copper."

"Not copper, my eyes."

"True this is." He motioned at the walls and said another word. "Yours are like that."

I repeated the word. "Green?"

"Yes. Manq are also tall."

"I am small."

He answered grudgingly. "Yes. Your hair, too, is different. In the sun, it looked Manq. But now, what I see, this hair of yours isn't Manq." He indicated the tiny, curled spears of moss clinging to the wall. "Manq hair is like that."

"Green hair?" Maybe they had altered it to incorporate chlorophyll.

"No. Black."

Puzzled, I glanced at the moss he indicated, then at him.

"Like the water." He brushed his finger through the sheen of moisture on the moss.

"Manq hair liquid?" Apprehension surged over me, but my mind shied away from any memories his words might have evoked. I didn't want to know.

"Did the Manq leave you here?" he asked. "Abandon you?"

Did they? "Know not."

"Why know you not?"

"Thinking gone."

"They think not?" He made a grimace of a smile, as if he found bitter humor in that.

"Not them," I said. "Me. Bad memory."

"You have unpleasant memories?"

"No bad. Gone."

"You forget?"

"Yes."

"Did the Manq do that to you?"

"Know not."

"Fables you tell." His hand curled into a fist on his knee. "With the Manq, you live."

I had no idea where I lived, when I wasn't dispersing into who-knew-where, but I was almost certain no one I knew called themselves Manq. "No. Not Manq. I am Skolian."

He scowled. " 'Skolia' is many places. Which do you come from?"

"Know not."

"I don't believe you."

I shook my head, too drained for the verbal combat.

"If you are not Manq," he said, "why are you here?"

"Know not."

"Did they leave you to die?"

Had they? It made more sense than I wanted to admit. "Is possible."

The treeman considered me, first my face, then the rest. He folded his large hand around my breast and stroked my nipple with his thumb. "You are pretty. You will be the tithe."

"No touch!" My voice came out clear that time. "You got that? No touch."

Watching my face, he withdrew his hand. I tried to hide my alarm, but I knew he saw. It didn't gratify him, though. The prospect of force held no excitement for him. I tightened my muscles to keep my arms from trembling.

"Are you a priestess?" he asked. "This is why no touching?"

"No priestess. Mathematician." I hadn't recalled that until I said it. But, yes. Like a song with endless variety, its melodies intertwined in exquisite threads, so the equations I solved seemed to me.

"No mathematics here," he pointed out.

"Is true."

"Find you other job."

"I must go home."

He brushed a lock of hair out of my face. "No."

A memory came with ringing clarity: *Eldrin stroked a tendril of hair off my cheek.* For all that many people found his coloring odd, the mismatched result of genetic drift in altered populations, he looked handsome to me, his hair the hue of burgundy wine, his metallic gold lashes long and thick, his eyes a vivid purple. A sprinkle of freckles scattered across his nose. His coloring bore little resemblance to our son's, who had my darker hues, but their classic features were the same.

"No touch." I pulled my head away from the treeman. "Husband I have." The importance of those words went beyond the relationship. Something had happened to Eldrin, a devastating crime. And I couldn't flaming *remember.* I yanked at my bonds, my eyes burning with tears I refused to shed. Instead I swore.

"****?" the treeman asked.

I clenched my fists. "I don't *understand* you."

He spoke slowly. "Your husband. Did he leave you to die?"

"No." I had no doubt about that. Another memory came: Eldrin facing me, pushing me backward. Behind him, armored giants strode toward us down a pillared corridor, nightmare monstrosities of mirrored metal with no faces, human in shape but over two meters tall. Gods only knew what lived under that armor. Manq?

"Husband," I said. "Take Manq."

"He took the Manq?"

"No. They took him. My son—" My son *what*?

"You have a boy?"

"Yes. No. Adult. Grown-up."

His eyebrows went up. "A young mother you were."

"No. Old." I pulled angrily against the roots holding my wrists. "My *son*. Where?"

"I have seen only you."

"Cut me free. Please. Help me find my family."

He made a derisive noise. "Why ****?"

I felt his reaction more than I understood his words. If I was Manq, then as far as he was concerned my family could rot in perdition. If the Manq had captured or killed them and wanted me, it gave him all the more reason to deny them what they sought. They owed him reparations and I had appeared. For him, that was enough.

I blinked . . .

Night had become day. Only embers remained of the fire.

I groaned. Not again. How long had I lost this time? Unlike before, however, this last transition was softer, filled in with vague memories. I hadn't become as much of a ghost, at least not enough to work free of my bonds. During that strange, half-real time, the treeman had made soup. I recalled his disquiet as he gave me a bowl. My hands had been translucent. He had hoped the food would make me solid again.

The cavity was empty now. Beyond the entrance, day was darkening into night. Iridescent arthrops flitted around the fire. They must have been coming in for a while, because some hung on my hair, giving it a sheen. The effect created a sense of familiarity—one I hated.

Aversion surged through my mind. *Pain.* My thoughts recoiled. Frustrated, I turned my concentration to the now absent treeman. What did he want? His mind had roiled with conflicted emotions: the urge for revenge that prodded violence; the compassion that stayed his hand; the desire that urged him on; the kindness that counseled restraint; the fear that gave him pause; the loneliness that sought company; and his growing doubt I was Manq. Unfortunately, no matter which emotions won out, none of the likely results involved him letting me go.

How to leave? Cut the cords? With what? Yell for help? To whom? Those hordes of people I had seen roaming the forest? Even if anyone else lived here, I had no reason to believe they would help. My struggles so far had succeeded only in tightening the cords. I suspected the plant grew these "roots" to feed itself by holding its captured prey until it died, after which the decomposing body provided nutrients. Being plant mulch wasn't on my list of useful pastimes.

I needed a new approach, an escape too quirky for the treeman to foresee. It would help if I understood why I had ended up here. But when I concentrated, the memories fled. So I let my mind wander. Math swirled in my thoughts: Fourier sums, Laplace transforms, Bessel integrals, Airy functions, beautiful, fascinating . . .

Selei transforms.

Selei?

Like my name.

My name.

Dyhianna Selei. That was my name. Hah! I was getting somewhere.

I had invented the Selei transform at age ten. A strange pastime for a child, but I had enjoyed it. It was a game, really, one that interested only a handful of scholars. The transform defined a universe outside our spacetime. That itself wasn't dramatic; many math theories described *spaces* that were unusual compared to our own. They weren't real in a physical sense. You couldn't visit them. They were just math. But the Selei universe had a difference.

We had found a way to visit.

Academicians had a catchy phrase for it: *a Hilbert space spanned by an infinite set of orthonormal Selei eigenfunctions.* Everyone else just called it *psiberspace,* or *Kyle space.* Matter couldn't move from our universe into Kyle space. Only thoughts. *People* couldn't enter that universe any more than they could physically enter their own mind.

Except somehow my son and I had done that. We had become thoughts. I had almost dispersed in psiberspace, my mind spreading like ripples in a pond. Coming back to this universe was difficult. I was doing it now, wave by partial wave, but a void existed where I should have sensed my son. Taquinil. Taquinil Selei.

He was gone.

The treeman left me to brood, alone in the cavity, caught tight by the roots. Or maybe he left me die. I had no intention of doing either.

I practiced shifting reality.

First I relaxed my mind. Drifted. I became an infinite sum of partial waves. Spherical harmonics. Why I had fragmented into spherical harmonics instead of some other functions, I had no idea, but it had a certain poetry. Harmonics of thought.

I focused on a purpose: leave. Could I enter psiberspace and come out in a new place? In math, if you took a function from one "space" to another and then changed its shape, it would also have a new shape when you took it back to the first space. Engineers did it all the time with Fourier transforms, going from a space where time varied to one where energy varied. For Selei transforms, spacetime defined the first "space" and thoughts defined the second. If I went into psiberspace, altered my thoughts, and came back, it ought to change my position and time here.

Closing my eyes, I tried to fade. Except it wouldn't work.

After all the shifting in and out of this universe that had bedeviled me, now I couldn't do it. If I hadn't known better, I would have thought Kyle space had vanished, imploded like a contracting universe collapsing at the end of time.

Pah. Psiberspace couldn't implode. I thought of the Fourier analogy. If time existed, so did energy. You couldn't have one without the other. The same held true for Kyle space; as long as people could think, it existed.

But that didn't mean we could reach it. We accessed it through the psiberweb, a network of specialized computers. In Kyle space, a thought could exist everywhere, like a peaked wave. Similar thoughts peaked close together; dissimilar thoughts peaked far apart. As soon as a telop, a telepathic operator, transmitted a thought, it existed throughout the web. Other telops could immediately pick it up whether they were in the next building or across the galaxy. The web gave us instantaneous communication—and so provided the glue that held together interstellar civilization.

If I were a telop, that could explain my military bodyguards. True telepaths were rare; the strongest of us were less common than one in a trillion. You needed telops to use the psiberweb, and the web offered immense strategic advantage to whoever controlled it, so the military recruited many of us.

Had the war torn apart the web? No wonder I had so little control in Kyle space. I needed a new web node. But making such a node required extensive technological support, none of which I had here.

I clasped my bound hands and leaned my head against my knuckles. My arms ached from being in the same position for so long. But I couldn't let myself become disheartened. Surely if I concentrated enough, I could affect some change in psiberspace. I probably couldn't do much, which meant I wouldn't alter my position here more than a small amount. Nor would I have much control. It was a risk, but it was better than waiting for whatever the treeman intended.

A scraping noise broke the quiet. I opened my eyes. Across the cavity, two legs sheathed in boots showed in the entrance. Red light bathed them, the fast changing luminance of either dawn or sunset. The treeman crouched down and ducked through the opening. He carried a cord strung with giant beetles, one iridescent green, one brilliant red, and one vivid blue.

He glanced at me, then looked away as if to avert danger. Settling by the fire pit, he laid down his dead beetles. Then he set about remaking the fire, using plant flags for fuel. To start the flame, he used a flint—and that one object spoke volumes.

I recognized the markings on that flint. Its design came from a well-known interstellar merchant who sold through the web marketplace, often called the cyber-nexus. Someone here had access to an off-planet network. It was the only way the treeman could have that flint. Its purchase order had to have gone through the psiberweb. I had often seen such orders flitting along its conduits. Relief trickled over me. Perhaps a safer escape existed than dispersing back into limbo.

The treeman worked on gutting his beetles, never glancing up. But I felt his awareness of my presence. He wanted sex. Why he held back I wasn't sure, but from his mind I sensed that a gentle person hid behind that implacable exterior. The Manq's destruction of the forest had scarred his emotions.

It came to me then, crashing like a wave heavy with storm foam.

I spoke softly. "Was she your wife?"

He jerked as if I had hit him, and froze in the process of setting a flag-leaf on the fire. Then he looked at me. "They made me watch." Even more than the grate of his voice, his grammar told of his agony. My translation nodes didn't have to alter it. Shay sentence structure changed when the speaker was upset, becoming akin to more widely spoken Skolian languages. It was why many of us sounded distraught to the Shay even when we were perfectly calm.

"They tied me to a tripod," he said. "Then they made me watch."

"I'm sorry." Gods, what had I stumbled into? Had the people he called Manq forced him to watch while they murdered his wife? No wonder rage drove him.

He dropped the flag into the fire. Sparks jumped into the air and floated down, turning into tiny embers. One hit the wet moss and sizzled.

"They were Traders," I told him. Just saying the name made me queasy. Sweat trickled down my neck.

He poked the flames with a green stick. "Who trades?" Strain crackled in his voice.

"The Manq. We call them Traders. Aristo Traders." They had red eyes instead of copper, but everything else he had said fit. "Their hair glistens like water." I sifted through my language modes for a Shay word. "Manq hair glitters."

His face became more drawn. "Yes."

I did a search for words that resembled *manq* and came up with *maana*. That didn't help much, given that it meant "with one's nose cut off." Then I found *mankatuul,* for "trades pain." It derived from the ancient Iotic word *ma'tuul,* meaning "base" or "vile."

"Mankatuul," I said.

Gazing at the fire, he repeated it in his own dialect. "Manqatile."

"They took my husband." Pain saturated that realization.

"I don't believe." He fixed me with a hostile stare. "You are they."

"I am their enemy." I understood him now. Dying was a better fate than capture by Aristos.

But my husband? Eldrin? *What had happened?*

The memory crashed in like mental thunder. Eldrin had pushed me and Taquinil through a "door" from our universe into Kyle space. My last sight had been of Eldrin standing unprotected, in his sleep trousers and robe, his arms outstretched from shoving his wife and son. Our bodyguards lay dead around him. They had striven until the very end to protect us. A Trader warrior had reached Eldrin, eight feet tall in its mirrored body armor. It loomed behind him, its massive arm clamping around his waist.

Nausea swept over me. "They *took* him."

"Say again?" the treeman asked.

My voice shook. "My husband. The Manq took him." And

our son? Both Taquinil and I had fallen out of our universe. But he had never come back.

I struggled to stay calm, though I wanted to shout. "Untie me. I must find help."

He lifted the line of beetles into his lap. "You are lying."

"No! Is truth."

He drew a knife out of its sheath on his belt, a blade sharp and modern, with a cyber-nexus trademark on its hilt. It glittered in the red light. Did he intend to cut me free? Or kill me?

"Let me go," I said. "Please." I wasn't used to asking. Usually people asked me to do for them.

"You tell this story to make me feel sorry." He cut open the red beetle and shook its liquid innards into a clay pot. "It will not work."

Despite his unyielding pose, I felt his doubts. "Is truth." I labored with the language. "Much is at stake. Thousands of colonies. Do you want the Manq to control it all?"

"I understand you not." He opened the green beetle as if he were cracking an egg, then emptied it into the pot and dropped its carapace on the ground. "You talk too fast." He picked up the blue beetle. "And you say words oddly."

"Try, I do. But my Shay is small."

He gave me a startled glance. "Hai! You speak Shay. Not Hajune Shay."

"What is Hajune Shay?"

"My speak."

Hajune. It might derive from *Ha'te june,* which in ancient Iotic meant "the other." "Hajune is another form of Shay?"

"Shay, city language. Hajune, forest language."

My hope jumped. "A city is here?"

"Thirty klicks west, in the land under the full coal."

Klicks. Nowadays that terminology was mostly used by spacers, another indication the treeman didn't live in isolation. "What is the full coal?"

He motioned upward with the blue beetle. "Slowcoal. The planet."

I spoke carefully, drawing on language routines that continually updated as we conversed. "If we go to where Slow-coal fills more of the sky, will we find this city?"

"Of course. You know this not? You talk like them." He studied me. "City Shay are not Manq. City Shay hate Manq."

"As do I." We were finally getting somewhere.

"Then you are from the city?"

"Even farther."

"The starport." He made it a statement.

My hope jumped. "Yes. The port." It was true in the sense I thought he meant, that I came from beyond Opalite.

He showed me his knife, a diamond-edged steel blade. "At the docks, I traded for this. That docker, he wanted nothing more than a shirt I made. For that nothing shirt, he gave me this."

"A fine knife," I agreed. As long as he used it on beetles and not me.

"Where is your home?" he asked.

I started to say I didn't know. Then I realized I did. It was on a space habitat called the Orbiter. Eldrin and I lived there together. I served as liaison between the Skolian government and psiberweb. Eldrin was a singer, a glorious baritone. He wrote folk ballads. I had always loved his music, fascinated by the mathematical intricacies within its melodies. Our son Taquinil was an economics professor at Imperial University on the planet Parthonia. He had been visiting us when the Traders attacked.

"I live in a space station," I said.

He gutted the last beetle, dumping its insides into the pot. "A strange place, without trees."

"Many trees are there."

"It is hard to imagine." He set the pot in a tripod of wet green sticks and placed it over the fire.

"Treeman, have you a name?"

He glanced at me. "What say?"

"Your name, I know it not."

"Why call me 'treeman'?"

"The first time I saw you, it looked like you came out of a tree."

His expression lightened, gentling his face. "Tripodman is better, then. I am like that." Although it was the first time I had seen him smile, he obviously did it often; it creased well-worn lines around his eyes.

Curious now, I asked, "Other names have you, Tripodman?"

"Hajune Tailor."

"Tailor? You sew clothes?"

Hajune reddened. "The city Shay trade many fine goods for these nothing clothes I make." He stirred the liquid in the pot, and an aroma filled the cavity, tangy and rich, like exotic spices mixed with bittersweet fruit. "But I prefer Hajune. It means 'the Other Man.' Forest man, not city man."

I felt his love for the forest. And he enjoyed his profession. If the clothes he wore were any indication, he undervalued his abilities a great deal. Few people even knew how to tailor anymore, let alone with such finesse. Rich offworlders would pay a fortune for his work. He needed an agent. He could get a lot more for those clothes than a knife, even one as expensive as his diamond-steel blade.

"Impressive they are, your tailor-things," I said.

"I use only dead plants. Never living." He swept out his arm. "This forest is home. Here we loved—" He stopped, his animation vanishing like a doused light. He lowered his arm. "Here I prefer to live."

His loneliness filled the cavity. Tears gathered in my eyes, from both his grief and my response to his pain. His anguish didn't show on his face, but I absorbed it from his mind. He had cherished his wife, wanting nothing more than to live with her among the trees and lakes.

This time when his memory came, I saw the assault in gruesome detail. The images shattered. His wife's copper-eyed attackers weren't Aristos. These were Razers, the secret police created by the Aristos. Half Aristo and half slave, Razers occupied the top level of the Trader slave hierarchies, which meant they had considerable wealth and authority themselves.

Aristo genes dominated their makeup.

Two of them held a woman on the ground, a female version of Hajune, tall and lovely. Hajune's memory didn't include a full image of himself, only as much as he could see with his own vision. He fought like a madman, crazed with desperation, while two other Razers bound him to the leg of a giant tripod. His wife's screams filled the universe. Her terror infused my mind, as it had filled Hajune's; I experienced it as he had felt it, through her mind.

Here in the cavity, Hajune gave a strangled cry. Leaning over, he wrapped his arms around his body. Then he lurched to his feet and left the cavity. He strode off into the forest.

Gods. How did he live with that emotional earthquake of a memory? Nor could I understand how such an atrocity could have happened here. This was a Skolian world. Razers couldn't brutalize our citizens. Trader secret police became war criminals the moment they entered Skolian space.

I had to do something. For Hajune. *For Eldrin.* I couldn't stay on this far-placed moon while Aristos imprisoned my husband, who had given up his freedom, possibly his life, to prevent my suffering a fate similar to Hajune's wife's. This much I knew, at an instinctual level: if the Traders caught Eldrin, Taquinil, or me, they would never let us escape, not even through death.

Outside the shadows had switched direction and evening was falling. The fire continued to smolder. It made me uneasy. A forest fire was unlikely in this wet, low-oxygen climate, but not impossible. Bound as I was, I could do nothing if a spark ignited the moss that carpeted this cavity.

Closing my eyes, I tried to settle my mind. It didn't work. My thoughts contracted into knots and my concentration broke every time a beetle clacked.

It took a long time to reach a meditative state. But finally I spread into a sea of thoughts, calm and serene. Opening my eyes, I saw the cavity ripple like a viscous sea. It wasn't truly bending; it took immense energies to curve spacetime, enough to destroy this moon. I was seeing another reality superimposed on this one, as I transformed . . .

?
Go.
Lets go.
Letting go.
Transforming.
Mind dissolving.
Going elsewhere.
Mind dissolving.
Transforming.
Letting go.
Lets go.
Go.
?

Taquinil

?
???
Coming.
Struggling.
Mind reforms.
Mind reforming.
Coming elsewhen.
Mind reforming.
Mind reforms.
Struggling.
Coming.
???
?

Gradually I became aware again. A tiny pink flower gleamed in the moss near my eyes, a drop of water on one petal. The aroma of bubbling soup filled the air. Heat from the fire warmed the front of my torso, and my limbs ached with returning circulation. Bizarrely, I had on the blue shift again; I must have gathered more of it in psiberspace. It had a hazy translucence, though. Ghost shift.

I sat up stiffly. Gazing across the fire, I saw the tangle of roots where I had been bound. My chronometer said only seconds had passed since Hajune left. Before I made my own escape, I needed food, lest hunger stop me where roots had failed. I used the carapace of a gutted beetle to spoon down half the soup. It was tangy and bitter, with a sweet aftertaste, more palatable than I expected. If I hadn't seen Hajune make it, I would have never dreamed it came from over-sized-bug innards. After I ate, I doused the flames with the last of the water in the pitcher.

Then I left.

Outside, tripod trees loomed in a red night. I smelled water in one direction. The lake? I headed that way. The purported city was only thirty kilometers away, "under" Slowcoal. Normally, I could easily walk that far, but here it would be harder. I paused to fashion rough shoes out of plant flags. They weren't the most comfortable footwear, but they made it easier to hike.

Then I set off again. As I pushed through the underbrush, I pondered this last time I had faded. An odd sense tugged my mind. What? The memory hovered at the edges of my thoughts. Frustrated, I finally gave up trying to catch it and let my mind wander.

Suddenly the memory jumped into focus. Taquinil! I had sensed him in psiberspace. Perhaps it was wishful thinking, but I felt certain he had been real. A mother's joy flowed over me, tempered by the knowledge that it had only been a trace, nothing more concrete.

As hope buoyed my thoughts, spherical harmonic wave-functions evolved in my mind. I saw them as shimmering orbs in lavender, rose, and blue. Some resembled symmetrical flowers; others were rings and teardrops. They rotated against a silver atmosphere.

It had always been this way, my mind forming vivid mathematical images to accompany intense emotions. When I was ten, even before I had any neural augmentation, the doctors told my parents that my intellectual potential was beyond what their tests could measure with accuracy. That didn't stop them from doing test after test, though. I seemed to fascinate them. They ascribed my increased intellect to the extra neural structures that made me a telepath, as well as to genetic and environmental factors. Over the decades, as neural surgeons augmented my brain, its capacity increased.

Eventually, to support it, I created the psiberweb.

It had formed around me in Kyle space, a tangle of threads, gold, silver, palest rose, and vivid blue, all shot through with strands the color of a deep forest, rough here, smooth there, knobbed in places, glossy in others. I untangled the threads, creating pipelines where thoughts flowed, darted, and vibrated. Electric blue light pulsed along the strands, leaving swirls of color in their wake, like the rainbows on an oil slick.

A few decades after I created the web, the evolution of my mind had reached a critical point. Then I changed. I underwent a mental phase transition the way liquid changes to gas. My mind became something else. What? I couldn't say. But after it happened, Eldrin was my anchor more than ever. Lover and beloved: he kept me at least partway human, where I might otherwise have faded from reality altogether.

Now the Traders had Eldrin. And Taquinil was gone.

More memories: doctors speaking in low voices, unsure how Eldrin and I would take their news. Someday our son would make the same mental transition I had experienced. Taquinil and I had a great deal of use to our people, enough to make the ruling Assembly define us as "invaluable resources." But we also frightened them, everyone—except Eldrin. Year by year, decade by decade, he had watched our son's intellect grow, a proud father bemused by the luminous genius he had sired. Only Eldrin truly accepted us as we were. Our intellects neither overawed nor put him off. He simply loved us. And so we loved him back, unconditionally, with all our hearts.

Eldrin, love, where are you? Now that the memories had begun, I couldn't stop the harrowing images. Taquinil and I were facing Eldrin inside an octagonal chamber. Behind Eldrin, waroids approached, Trader commandos in body armor.

Walking fortresses. Taquinil shouted a warning to his father, but his words stretched out in the slow-time around the singularity.

Singularity?

Yes. It punctured spacetime in an incandescent column, coming out of Kyle space, existing within that octagonal chamber, then returning to the netherworld from whence it came. That last moment seared into my mind: Eldrin staring at us, caught around the waist by the waroid behind him, his left foot lifted, his arms outstretched, his body straining against his captor's armored limb. Desperation filled his gaze. And love. Terror and love.

A tear ran down my cheek. Had I lost them both? But I *had* sensed Taquinil in psiberspace. I had to believe we could recover him. All those extra neural structures crammed in my skull had to be worth something. The thought that Eldrin's sacrifice would be in vain was too painful to endure.

I swept aside more brush and stumbled forward. With no warning, I came out onto the promontory above the lake. I felt as if I were repeating history, like a wave, coming here over and over, ebbing and flowing against the shores of reality. Except now I knew what to do: find the starport in the brooding land beneath Slowcoal.

Dawn reddened the sky and Slowcoal spanned on the horizon. Walking to the edge of the cliff, I looked around for a path down to the lake. My steps knocked chunky rocks off the promontory, and they slowly dropped to the water far below. When they hit, swells rolled across the lake, rising high in the low gravity. Their slow crests caught sparks of red light and glinted like rubies.

A presence stirred in the forest, distant but closing fast. Hajune.

I dove off the promontory. As I sailed away from the cliff, my mind stretched out and beyond, seeing all my surroundings, even myself arching through the air, a translucent figure silhouetted against the scarlet sky and the great disk of Slowcoal.

4

Slowcoal

Go
Sluicing
Swimming
Water sluicing
Swelling wave
Water sluicing
Swimming
Sluicing
Go
•
Go
Sluicing
Swimming
Water sluicing
Swelling wave
Water sluicing
Swimming
Sluicing
Go

I broke the surface and gulped in air. Drops of water rained lazily over me in fat spheres. No, not spheres. Spheres were hollow. These were balls. Elongated balls. They weren't perfectly round even in this gravity. Another memory came, my father-in-law saying, *You spend too much time with your equations.* But his tone had been fond.

I swam smoothly to the shore. As I waded onto the pebbly beach, a green bulldozer-bug the size of my foot scuttled into the forest. My shift was plastered to my body, almost transparent, but at least it hadn't dissolved.

The forest resumed a few steps up the beach. I made my way into that surreal landscape of giant roots and tripods. Nausea plagued me. According to my internal sensors, it came from lack of food and sleep, exposure to the elements, unfriendly bacteria, and impurities in the air. It didn't bode well: none of that was likely to improve unless I found help. Even if I did locate people, they might not like me any more than Hajune did.

After about an hour, I had to stop. My stomach felt like it was turning inside out. Sitting on a root, I bent over and held my abdomen. Sweat beaded my forehead.

What had gone wrong? I shouldn't have ended up alone, without recourse, poisoned and hurt. Taquinil and I should have come out in a controlled environment designed to help us recover. We couldn't have gone into that singularity without preparation. Shoving people into a hole in spacetime wasn't something you did on the spur of the moment. Either our plans hadn't been complete or we had been too rushed to do it right. But chances were I had come out near my intended target. If a city did exist where Hajune claimed, I might have contacts there. If I could just reach them.

Unfortunately, right now I was going nowhere. I slid off the root and curled up on the moss, too sick to move any farther.

A rustle came from the undergrowth. I groaned, envisioning a beetle-tank bearing down on me. Although none had attacked so far, those lobster claws of theirs deserved respect. I knew I should move, but just the thought made my stomach lurch.

No. Wait! Not a beetle. I rolled onto my back—

—and looked up at four people. They stood over me, dressed in black uniforms with red braid on the cuffs, three men and a woman, their black hair shimmering, their eyes the color of dark, discolored copper.

Manq.

I scrambled to get up, but the Manq dropped into crouches, blocking my escape. The largest one knelt back, sitting on his feet, and hoisted me over his legs, shoving me so I lay across his thighs, facedown.

They were Razers. I had seen them hundreds of times on

news holos, the secret police who guarded Trader Aristos and terrorized Trader citizens. It said a lot about my diminished condition that it had taken me so long to sense their approach. But I felt them now. Their minds opened like cavities, hungry for prey. For empaths.

As I struggled, one of the Razers laughed. They didn't even bother to draw the EM pulse guns they wore in holsters on their hips. My neural nodes helpfully calculated that it was impossible for me to fight four armed and trained guards, each with at least twice my body weight in muscle.

"Someone left us a present," the woman said in the elegant language of the Highton Aristos. Her throaty burr made the words deceptively beautiful, a jarring contrast to the ugly images that flowed from her mind as she envisioned what they would do with me. They had a new plaything and what they intended wasn't pretty.

Lights flickered on a gauntlet worn by another of the Razers. With a jolt of memory, I recognized the pattern. He was monitoring the area, probably on guard against discovery. Even with that precaution, it spoke volumes about their arrogance that they so casually attacked a stranger while in hostile territory. Their assumption of superiority scraped against my mind, their conviction that they had every right to indulge their Aristo-bred urge to brutality against an empath.

I tried to flip off the Razer, and surprised myself with my enhanced speed. Apparently I had more augmentation than I had realized. But the Razer moved faster. He held me down with one hand while he pushed up my shift with the other. I rammed my elbow back, aiming for his crotch. It caught his stomach instead, but at least he quit laughing. Anger surged in him, inflaming the urge to violence already in his thoughts. His mental images scared the hell out of me.

The other three Razers pulled away my shift, which fell apart with the least tug. I tried to blanket my memory of Hajune's wife, but it hunkered in my mind, spurring terror. One of the Razers lifted his hand and pulled off a black leather glove. He clenched his fist, then flexed his fingers. I wanted to vomit, from both fear and my upset stomach. Well, good. I stuck my finger down my throat. It didn't take much; I gagged immediately—and upchucked all over them.

The large one gave a disgusted shout and threw me off his lap. I swung my head around, my still-spewing lunch deluging the others with half-digested beetle innards. They reacted like the first, jerking back with revulsion. That slight break in their ranks was all I needed. Energized by adrenalin, I lurched to my feet and *RAN*.

I plunged through the plants, uncaring that brambles tore my skin or roots gouged my feet. The path I chose cut under the bush-clogged base of a tripod tree. Huge roots blocked either side, extending to the left and right. I barely had room to scrape through, which meant the Razers would have even more trouble. I heard the hum of an EM pulse gun and the crackle of shredded foliage. The shooter may have mistimed the shot due to the low gravity, but I suspected he missed because he fired to frighten rather than kill.

On the other side of the tree, I took off, headed for a city I had never seen, with only Hajune's sketchy description and my neural compass to set a direction. If the situation became desperate, I could try fading out of reality again. But in my depleted state, I doubted I could achieve even the minimal control I had managed before. I might come back inside a tree, up in the air, under water, or I might never make it back at all.

Time seemed to stretch as I raced in a surreal daze. My steps elongated whenever I had an open area to run in, and I sailed over the ground. Soon I reached a small lake. The sunset caught red sparks on its big, slow swells. I swam hard, relieved as the water cleaned me off. The cold numbed my cuts and scratches; I didn't realize how much they had hurt until the pain faded. I hoped my nanomeds could deal with the influx of bacteria and who-knew-what-else from the water into my body.

I neither heard nor felt pursuit, but that didn't mean the Razers had given up. It all depended on how much effort they felt like expending to retrieve their toy. Given my vomiting, they might have lost interest. I hoped so. But I kept up my speed.

Fleeting night swept the moon. I reached the opposite shore and plunged back into the forest. Part of my mind concentrated on finding the best path. The rest of me thought about how much I loathed this place. In my short time here, someone had tried to murder me, threatened violence, and tied me up. Razers intended a gang assault with torture. I could barely eat the food or drink the water. I couldn't even keep my blasted clothes on.

My being alone this way made no sense. I was never alone. A lack of privacy had plagued my life, constrained it until I wanted to tear away the layers of protection the way a shimmerfly would burst free of its cocoon. But why? For what reason had I lived such a controlled life?

Oh. Yes. I remembered.

I was the Ruby Pharaoh.

Slowcoal dominated the sky, shedding angry light across Opalite. Its clouds boiled in great bands. I staggered beneath the world, holding my side, gasping as I clambered over low roots. They buckled in a twisted landscape, making strange hollows. Mist drifted in streamers, haunting the monstrous tripods. I could only see the giant bases of the trees; the rest stretched up into fog. Who had designed this manic biosphere? I would bet anything that it had gone wrong, that their simulations hadn't predicted the plants would grow this big.

My thoughts beat in time with my labored pulse, pouring memories into my mind. Ruby Pharaoh. It was a titular position. The Ruby Dynasty no longer ruled. We hadn't for thousands of years. That honor went to the modern Skolian government, an Assembly of representatives elected from the more powerful worlds of our civilization. But I ran the psiberweb—and the web made interstellar civilization possible. To control the web, the Assembly had to control me; hence, our constant, invisible struggle for power.

We had set that aside, however, for a much bigger struggle, one far beyond those political games.

The Radiance War.

Skolia had gone to war with the Traders. We destroyed

their capital. They killed or captured our leaders. We broke their fleet. They crushed our largest military complex. We hurled our desperate armies against each other until the star-spanning battles exploded in a furious climax. It was a war unmatched in human history.

I had no idea who had won.

My neck prickled. Up until now, I hadn't believed Kyle space could actually have imploded. I had assumed my impression of such a catastrophe was an artifact of my strange condition. Now a growing disquiet ate away at that conviction. What if the implosion had been real? It couldn't stay that way; as long as human thought existed, Kyle space would recreate itself. But it would reform as a new universe with no trace of the psiberweb.

The magnitude of it stunned me. The networks that linked into psiberspace also linked to uncounted optical, electronic, biological, quantum, and neural networks. If Kyle space imploded, that would pull down many of the nets linked into it, which would disrupt networks linked to those, which would disrupt others, and so on, the failure spreading like a tidal wave. The nets used by humanity were interwoven, all of them, for all of us, regardless of where our allegiances lay. It could end up in one huge, star-spanning collapse, a disaster of almost unimaginable proportions.

It could never happen. Fine. Why couldn't I detect a hint of the web?

Then it hit me. The Traders could have precipitated an implosion if they had tried to follow Taquinil and me into Kyle Space when we escaped. That could have collapsed the singularity. But if psiberspace had collapsed and I hadn't vanished, I must have recreated a bubble of it, a tiny universe in the birth throes of its metaphysical big bang. Which was impossible. Supposedly. Yet I existed.

As my burst of energy faded, I became aware of my nausea, thirst, and exhaustion. I slowed to a walk, and my hair stopped flying around, hanging instead to my knees. One hundred fifty-eight years is a long time to let the protein on your head grow, even if you remember to cut it every few decades. Many cultures had tales about a person who wore his or her hair as clothes. Well, it didn't work. Mine wouldn't cover the front of my body even when I held it in place. It shifted all the time and kept uncovering my backside as well. It was better than nothing, though.

I heard the city before I saw it. It rumbled like a heartbeat. The green-black forest ended abruptly, and I walked out onto another promontory, a giant step in the land. Slowcoal dominated the sky, making the night almost as bright as day. Its red light bathed the scene.

I went to the edge of the cliff. No lake rolled at its bottom. A city nestled down there, penned on one side by this cliff and on the other three by forest. Rounded and natural, the buildings resembled the blue, green, and aqua beetle-tanks. Paths wound among them. I saw no machines, but I suspected the city dwellers had plenty of technology. It probably wasn't possible to make a permanent home here without the benefit of modern advances.

I felt rather than heard Hajune emerge from the forest, an eerie repetition of how I had first met him. This time, however, he emanated no hostility.

His footsteps rustled behind me. "I thought you would come here."

I turned, pulling my hair across my body. He stood several paces away, his pack slung over one shoulder and an axe lashed on his back.

"I won't go back with you," I said.

His forehead furrowed. "Understand you, I do not."

"Go back with you, I will not."

"I know."

"Then why you come?"

"It isn't safe for you to roam." He gaze traveled down my body and he reddened, then looked back at my face. "Especially like that. Manq take."

I grimaced. "I met them."

He stared at me. "They *caught* you?"

"No. I ran away."

"Smart. Smarter still for you to have a guard."

"You offer protection?" I couldn't hold back my incredulity.

"Yes."

"Why?" I scowled. "You wanted to kill me before."

"I thought you were Manq."

"Not Manq."

"I know."

"How know you?"

"Talk. Listen. Watch."

"Why leave me tied, then?"

"I did not want you to run away."

"Why?"

"Beautiful you are." Softly he added, "Lonely I am."

His undisguised pain caught me off guard. I was used to the Assembly and Imperial court, which were both saturated in the protective discourse of politics. An admission of vulnerability would bring in the predators faster than an eye blink—and given the power we dealt with, that could ruin a life. Pah. No wonder I spent so much time in the web, hidden from all but my family. My people didn't have the brutality of the Traders, but we weren't angels either.

I spoke more gently. "Married, I am."

"No husband here."

"Told you. Manq take."

He exhaled. "Then he is dead."

I shook my head. "He is more valuable alive."

"Why?"

Good question. He was my consort, but it was more that that.

Rhon.

Eldrin and I were Rhon psions. Empaths. Telepaths. Our family had been bred for the traits. Rhon had a specific meaning: we were the strongest psions human DNA could produce. And the rarest. Rhon also meant we were members of the Ruby Dynasty. Eldrin and I were part of the same extended family. Anger shot through me, but I didn't know yet what caused it.

How much did Hajune understand the Manq? Trader Aristos were anti-empaths, the result of an attempt to make humans resistant to pain. But the project hadn't worked; instead it produced mutated empaths. When an Aristo picked up another person's pain, the Aristo's brain sent the signals to its pleasure centers. The more another person hurt, the more the Aristo experienced pleasure.

My heart lurched. Psions projected their emotional responses more than normal humans, making us highly sought by Aristos. Eldrin was their ultimate prize: both a priceless political prisoner and an empath as powerful as the human mind could produce.

I stared numbly at Hajune. To his question I said, simply, "Psion."

His face revealed his dismay. "The Manq will hurt him."

I felt ill. "Yes."

"My wife was also an empath."

Softly I said, "My sorrow."

His grief rippled. "Mine also."

I sorted through my Shay libraries for the appropriate phrase. "I offer grace to her time and space of burial."

When he stiffened, I feared I had misspoken. But then he said, "We had no burial. The Manq took her body."

I shuddered, wondering why they wanted her body. She could no longer project the emotions they craved. "Are you sure?"

The pain on his face made me wish I hadn't asked. "I saw her die. I saw them take her."

It was beyond my ability to understand how they could inflict such cruelty. "I am so very sorry, Hajune. This is too much hurt."

His jaw worked. "Yes."

"How long since it happened?"

"Two ****"

I tried to decipher the word. "Decadar?"

"Ten risings of sun."

Twenty Opalite days had passed since the murder. Eighty hours. Saints almighty, it had just happened. He must be raw with shock. No wonder he had attacked me when I came through his territory, my hair lustrous with hanging flyers, resembling Aristo hair.

"Go you to the authorities?" I asked. "Report what happen?"

His shoulders hunched. "No authorities on Opalite. Only city Shay."

"Go you to city?"

"I am Hajune. Other Shay. Not city."

I had only a few files on the Shay, but my scant library suggested they formed insular societies. Apparently a demarcation existed here between forest and city dwellers. But we had to warn the city Shay about the Razers. And Hajune needed help to deal with his grief. His heartache filled his thoughts.

"How many Manq are here?" I asked.

He spit to the side. "Four have I seen."

"I also." I wondered at their behavior. They had to know they faced interrogation and execution if they were caught. They should never have touched Hajune's wife. Then they had let Hajune, a witness, survive. Even if they had guessed about his antipathy to the city, they couldn't count on his silence.

The implications of their choices hit me like ice. Hajune was also an empath. It made sense; psions tended to seek each other as mates. I picked up his moods more easily than I did with normal humans. The Razers had probably fed off his emotional pain. He had far more value to them alive; empaths brought high prices on the Trader slave markets. They probably hadn't expected his wife to die and would have been more careful with him if they meant to take him later. It could also explain why they hadn't shot me.

But that implied they expected rescue.

The prospect of more Traders arriving, probably with an Aristo warlord, chilled me. I wanted to run and run, to find the deepest hole possible. But if they decided to look for us, there was nowhere we could hide from the sensors of their warships.

We had to bring in help. I spoke gently. "Did you tell the city Shay about the Manq?"

"Why? It is no use. My wife is dead." He clenched his fist. "Thinking of them—of her—I *cannot*."

I softened my voice. "Must tell, Hajune Tailor. To give warning."

"City Shay have never helped forest Shay."

"Even so. You must tell them. It is right."

He crossed his arms, their well-developed muscles bulging under his clothes. "No."

"Must."

"To city, I take you. What you tell city Shay, I care not."

It was a good solution. He knew I would go to the authorities. By escorting me to the city and providing protection, he ensured its people received warning, but without admitting his intent.

"Your proposal is fair." I wished I could as easily find a way to assuage his grief.

"We go, then."

I spoke awkwardly, still holding my hair in front of myself. "My clothes are gone."

A blush touched his cheeks. "Nice it is."

I glared. "Embarrassing it is."

His expression softened. He pulled off his axe and shrugged out of his pack. After setting them on the ground, he took off his jacket and gave it to me.

"My thanks." Relieved, I fastened up the big jacket. It hung almost to my knees.

Still stolid, he put on his pack and took up his axe. "We go now."

So we set off, Hajune leading the way down a switchback path cut into the side of the promontory.

The city waited.

5
City Shay

The city simmered in the dawn. From above, it had looked small, only a few hundred square meters. Down here, its extent became clearer. The Shay built up among the trees rather than out along the ground. They cut stairs into the massive trunks and strung bridges between the columns far above the ground. As a result, they lived on many levels.

We encountered no one on the winding paths. I soon realized people were peering at us from homes within the trees, hidden in foliage. Hajune projected a confident lack of concern, but beneath that his tension thrummed, as tight as a vibrating drum skin. He disliked the city; it constrained him, both physically and mentally. I understood. I too had trouble with large groups of people. Even when I buffered my mind, their emotions surged against it in waves, until I had to escape that mental pressure.

I also felt Hajune. His emptiness at the loss of his wife hollowed his heart. Psions responded strongly to each other. Eldrin and I had also felt it. When we loved, we felt the pleasure it gave our partner as well as our own. It created a two-way exchange, as our partner's contentment became our own. Hajune had lost half of himself.

As had I.

Another memory came: once Eldrin and I had climbed the Sky, the inner surface of the spherical Orbiter. Sky glowed like a blue glaze in a gigantic bowl. Such a waste of space, to give half the surface area of the station to a human-made sky. But the Orbiter was designed for beauty, not efficiency. Ground had an even more compelling splendor: mountains, trees, valleys, parks, and an ethereal city, all idyllic.

Holding hands, Eldrin and I had strolled to the sun and sat on the edge of that great lamp. We looked "up" at the ground hemisphere several kilometers above our heads. And we talked, sharing thoughts, reminiscing, enjoying each other's company even after decades of marriage. He and I were two parts of a whole.

The knowledge of his capture burned in my mind. He had given his freedom, maybe his sanity, to protect Taquinil and me. I wouldn't let that sacrifice go for naught. I would make it home and I would find Taquinil. If only I could remember what should have happened here.

J'chabi Na.

My steps faltered. A name. In my Iotic accent, I had trouble with the glottal stop in J'chabi and pronounced it as "Jaichabi." It translated as "watcher." J'chabi Na played a role in this.

"Hajune Tailor." I glanced up at him, aware of his height and powerful build. "Know you a man named Jaichabi Na?"

His face became even more closed. "City Shay, he is."

"He lives here?"

"Yes."

A rush of emotion hit me, so powerful it felt visceral. What? Fear? But without threat. J'chabi Na had importance. I didn't know what provoked the fear, but I needed to see him. I trusted my intuition; it had always proved solid, and now it was also augmented by analyses my neural nodes performed at an almost subconscious level.

"I must find him," I said.

Hajune clenched his fist. "Why?"

"He may have answers about my husband." I hoped.

"J'chabi Na is city Shay."

"Yes. City Shay."

He stopped and stood, large and forbidding, staring off into the trees. I waited with him. Just when I felt certain he would leave me here and return to the forest, he brought his gaze back to me. "Come, then. I will take you."

As the sun passed overhead, Hajune led me up dark green steps carved in the tripod leg of a tree. At the place where the legs joined into a massive trunk, the stair became a spiral that

wound around the tree. Fifteen large people could have circled that trunk, holding hands, their arms outstretched. And it
was only moderate in size compared to the other trees.

We climbed about a hundred more meters, passing several
levels of the city. People peered out at us from houses within
the trunk. Apparently the tree could go on living after having
parts of its column hollowed out. Perhaps nutrients traveled in
the outer layers, making the core less necessary for survival. It
didn't even need all of its outer portions; the houses had many
windows. It intrigued me that the Shay chose to build here,
where Slowcoal saturated the city with ruddy light.

Far above the ground, Hajune led me across a bridge made
from vines and solidified pulp. It hung between two giant
trees, narrow and supple. The bridge swayed with his weight
and long-legged stride. It provided the only access to the
trunk we were approaching.

"No stairs?" I asked.

"No stairs," Hajune agreed.

I tried again. "What if this bridge breaks?"

"Build another."

The tree we were approaching had no stairs. "What happens to the people on that tree when the bridge is out?"

"They get hungry." Hajune stopped and turned back to me.
"Only wing-things up here to eat." He touched my hair,
which had acquired a covering of gauzy black and gold fliers.
"Like these."

My stomach flipped-flopped. "People eat these?"

"They do not taste so terrible." He turned and set off again.

I followed, glad I didn't live on Opalite. I had my doubts
about the cuisine.

At the end of the bridge, Hajune stepped onto a narrow
deck that circled the tree. As we walked around the trunk, I
glanced at the windows above us. Shutters covered most, but
I thought someone looked at us from the darkness beyond
one portal.

On the far side we came to a short stairway that penetrated
into the trunk. Climbing the stairs, we entered a tunnel of
dark green walls. At the top, Hajune halted before a rounded

door. Then he stepped aside for me. "Home this is, to J'chabi Na."

I wiped the back of my hand across my forehead. I still couldn't remember J'chabi Na. Many reasons existed for his name to stay in my mind; he might be my contact, or he could be a traitor, the reason my escape route had partially failed. I might be about to greet an enemy. But I became more agitated when I considered leaving this place than when I thought of staying.

"How do we let him know we are here?" I asked.

Hajune indicated a loop of vine hanging by the door. "Pull."

So I pulled. A vibration shivered the ground under my bare feet and a bittersweet fragrance drifted in the air. After several seconds, both faded.

We waited. Shadows of evening filled this tunnel. The brooding light turned the air red and walls black.

"Do you think he is gone?" I asked. I couldn't be sure I had seen someone in the window.

Hajune snorted and said, "City Shay," as if that explained everything.

The door slowly split down the middle. A man stood there, his face closed and wary. He wore gray-green trousers, a dark shirt, and dark ankle boots. His iridescent blue belt gleamed with inlaid shells from beetle-tanks. He narrowed his gaze at Hajune. "Why come here, you?"

Hajune jerked his head toward me. "She ask."

The man looked me over, taking in my apparel, or lack thereof. "What want you?"

Good question. I wished I knew the answer. "Are you Jaichabi Na?" I almost winced at the way my pronunciation of his name revealed my Iotic accent.

"Asks who?" he responded.

"Dyhianna Selei."

The color drained from his face. His surging emotions were too complex to separate, but his agitation came through like a jolt of electricity. Whatever my name meant to him, it went deep.

He turned sideways, revealing a green, rounded hall, and raised his hand in an invitation to enter. I didn't want to go alone. When I glanced at Hajune, he tilted his head to me. Then he drew the axe from his back. Pulling a weapon was hardly a gracious response to hospitality, if that was what J'chabi Na offered, but even so I was glad for Hajune's axe.

I detected no recognition from Hajune, neither in his body language nor his mind. He didn't know my name. I wasn't sure whether to be relieved or unsettled that he had no idea he accompanied the Ruby Pharaoh. It all depended on what that title meant to him.

J'chabi Na made no protest about the axe. He didn't seem surprised that I came with an armed guard. As we entered the hall, he stepped back, his posture indicating reserve and caution. He resembled Hajune, having the same large build, broad shoulders, brown hair and eyes, and strong face. He kept close control over his facial responses though. I couldn't pick up his mood as well as with Hajune, but I could tell he didn't know whether to offer welcome or denounce me as a fraud.

The hall ended in a circular room about twenty steps across. It extended many stories above us, with balconies circling each level, giving a tiered effect to J'chabi Na's living space. Moss carpeted the floor, the same type that had grown in the cavity where Hajune had confined me. Although Hajune still made me uneasy, I understood now what had motivated him. My fear for Eldrin tormented my thoughts, unrelenting.

J'chabi courteously indicated a mossy ridge. "Sit, please, if you will."

With a formal nod, I settled on the ridge. Hajune stayed on his feet, at my side, his axe gripped in his large hands.

"Care you for nourishment?" J'chabi asked, his voice guarded.

I thought of my reaction to my last meal here. "My thanks, but no." Hajune didn't answer.

I wasn't sure what to think of this strained tableau. Rather than risk revealing my vulnerable situation, I waited for J'chabi Na to make the first move. He stood awkwardly, a few feet away, watching me. I grew uncomfortable sitting while they stood, so I rose again, aware of Hajune at my side. I wanted to ask J'chabi what he knew about me, but I didn't want him to see my disorientation. Outside, night had fallen, though it had been noon when Hajune and I entered this unnamed city. Discreet light panels set around the room softened the red light that poured in the windows, giving it a gold cast.

"Sorry I am," J'chabi finally began, his discomfort obvious. "Very sorry. But I must ask you to take a DNA test."

That came as no surprise. Mine was no small assertion. Impersonating the Ruby Pharaoh carried penalties, anything from imprisonment to execution, depending on the circumstances. But what would he do with proof of my identity? My genetic records were closely guarded. If a Shay native in the hinterlands had them, then either I or Imperial Space Command had provided the records, or else he had stolen them. I doubted ISC would have released such secured information.

"How know you my DNA?" I asked.

In a careful voice, he said, "Before I answer, I must do the test."

I rubbed my throbbing temples, pressing with my fingertips. Even aided by translation nodes, I struggled with the convoluted Shay grammar. The language had so many declensions, it took an entire mod to keep track of them.

Hajune glanced from me to J'chabi Na. "Why test?"

J'chabi didn't answer, he simply waited.

"How far is the starport from here?" I knew I hadn't said it right, but fatigue weighted my responses. It had been too long since I had eaten food that stayed down. The rapid change of day and night confused the diurnal clocks of my body, leaving me tired all the time.

"Say again?" J'chabi asked me.

"The starport. From here, how far is it?"

"The starport is closed."

My disquiet grew. I glanced at Hajune and he tilted his head to the right, a Shay gesture that indicated lack of knowledge. Turning back to J'chabi, I said, "Closed why?"

"The Traders, ****"

"The Traders destroyed the port?"

"Yes."

"Why?"

He spoke again, but I shook my head. Then, realizing he might not recognize the gesture, I tilted my head as Hajune had done.

J'chabi Na suddenly switched into Iotic, my native language. "One of our ISC squadrons engaged a pack of Trader ships that came into this star system. The ISC squad stopped the Trader attack on Opalite, but in the battle, the Traders destroyed our starport."

I stared at him. His fluency stunned me. Although he had a strong accent, his Iotic was otherwise perfect. Yet it took years to master, even with neural augmentation. Almost no one learned Iotic as a first language, only the Ruby Dynasty and the noble Houses. We were anachronisms in modern Skolia. People didn't usually know my language so well unless they were scholars of the classics or expected to interact with my family. His Iotic offered another reason to believe he was my contact, but it didn't tell me whether or not he had a connection to my difficulties. He guarded his mind well, obviously trained to build barriers against telepaths.

I spoke cautiously. "Did any of the Trader ships land?"

J'chabi shook his head, a gesture from my culture, not his. "One of their vessels crashed here, but we found no survivors."

I spoke quietly. "Some may have survived. At least four Razers are hiding in the forest."

He looked uncomfortable. "The ISC ships had to leave. They were needed elsewhere."

Hajune was watching us intently. He spoke in Shay. "Talk you what language?"

"Iotic," J'chabi said.

Hajune blinked. "I know it not."

I answered in Shay. "It is my tongue." I suspected Hajune had little or no formal education. Although few schools taught Iotic, it was almost impossible to study the history, cultures, or sociology of Skolia without learning about the language.

"What say you to J'chabi Na?" Hajune asked.

"I need a ship to go offworld."

J'chabi answered. "No ships."

I glanced at him. "Then I must send a message."

"No communications."

My unease deepened. "Why not?"

"Psiberspace gone."

So my impression of a collapse had been right. Gods, it must have been an interstellar catastrophe. "How did it happen? Why?"

He tilted his head to the right. "Nothing yet do we know."

This sounded worse and worse. With neither a port nor communications, I had no way to call in help. But I might have another option. To escape the roots Hajune had used to confine me, I had operated in Kyle space without technological support. By myself, I had too little control to contact anyone offworld, but with the support of a console I might achieve more.

"The comm equipment may still help," I told J'chabi. "Will you take me to it?"

He responded in a guarded tone. "Test, I must."

That blasted test again. If I wanted his help, I had to prove my claim. I didn't like it, but he had good reason for his refusal. If I was an imposter and he took my word, he could create a lot of trouble for himself and ISC.

I spoke stiffly. "Very well. Do the test."

He bowed from the waist, another behavior never seen among the Shay, but familiar in the Imperial court and Assembly. Then he strode to a staircase that spiraled around the living area. When he reached the balcony above us, he walked halfway around it and went through a rounded doorway.

Hajune turned to me. "Why does he speak your language?"

"I'm not sure." I rubbed my hands on my arms, my palms sliding over the leathery jacket. I felt at risk here, open to attack.

J'chabi soon came back down. He held a black box about

two hand-spans long. It stirred my memories: the medics who monitored my health had those boxes. I took good care of myself, but they were always checking me anyway. At the slightest hint of a problem, they became agitated and put me on a strict regimen until whatever had perturbed them came back into balance. It irked me no end. But if I sent them away, ISC Security sent them back. Security reacted the same when I tried to send away my human bodyguards. I had mechanical guards too, but it was easier to deal with their constant presence. They had no emotions.

I sat again on the mossy ridge. Hajune stood guard while J'chabi set down his box. The silence in the trunk house settled over us. Everything seemed muted.

From his box, J'chabi removed a spatula the size of his index finger. Knowing what he wanted, I opened my mouth. He scraped the inside my cheek. A person's cells all had the same DNA, but modern disguise artists found it easier to mask the DNA of exterior skin and hair cells than those inside of the mouth.

He slid the spatula into a slot in the box and watched data flow across its screens. Holos of a woman's body formed above the box. My body.

The test took only a few moments. When it finished, J'chabi continued to stare at the screens, his face strained, his gaze averted. I feared something had gone wrong. Then I realized he was struggling to control himself. His mental turmoil broke past his barriers and saturated the room. Shock. Disbelief.

Hope.

J'chabi shifted position, bending on one knee in front of me. He rested his elbow across his other knee and bowed his head. Then he spoke in Iotic, with a reverence that bordered on awe. "It is my honor to serve you, esteemed Pharaoh Dyhianna."

I touched his shoulder. "Do not kneel, Jaichabi Na."

He raised his head, then stood. His voice shook. "Rumor claims you died."

I smiled. "Rumor is wrong, I think."

As his wariness eased, his mental defenses lowered. His mind revealed nothing about him having a a link to my difficulties here. Nor did he hide his joy that I lived. Although the Shay spoke little, they seemed to show their emotions easily, without guile or hidden agendas. It was like fresh, cool air gusting through the room.

"How can I help?" J'chabi asked.

I gave him a rueful look. "I could use some clothes. Also food and water. Hajune tried to give me some, but it made me sick." I didn't reveal what else Hajune had done. It would lead to his arrest, possibly his execution, if ISC came for me. That "if" carried a lot of weight, with the port destroyed, the web dead, and who knew what else.

"It is my honor. I have kept the recovery chamber readied in the hope that—" J'chabi's voice caught. "But I never believed my hope would be answered."

I rose to my feet. "I thank you for your support, honored Jaichabi Na."

He bowed and withdrew then, going up the spiral stairs. Watching him spurred my memories. He belonged to an elite group of watchers I had set up on outposts, in case my family ever needed an escape route. Taquinil and I should have coalesced here, under J'chabi's care, in a chamber designed to facilitate our transition from Kyle space to here.

Hajune spoke. "Your words with J'chabi Na, I understand them not." Disquiet flooded his mind. He knew his earlier actions could have far-reaching consequences. Remorse had prompted him to offer his services as a bodyguard, but now he feared for his life.

I thought of his wife. "What happened before, with you and me—it is of no consequence." Grim memories flooded my mind, and I lost my grip on the grammar. "The Manq have decimated my family, through death, capture, and torture. Had I found one of them in this forest, I too would have wished them dead."

"Who is your family?"

I didn't lie to him. "Skolia. I am the eldest."

Hajune stared at me for a long moment. Then he went

down on one knee and bent his head, holding his axe across his thigh. In a low voice, he said, "My honor in your presence, great Pharaoh."

This was embarrassing. I went over and touched his shoulder. "Please don't do that."

He rose to his feet. "I am glad I did not kill you."

I managed a smile. "So am I."

"Small you are. I had thought all in the Ruby Dynasty were giants."

"Many are. I am the smallest."

"Small in size." He spoke softly. "Not in self."

A rustle made us look up. J'chabi was coming down with an armload of clothes: gray trousers, a blue shirt, a bodysuit to wear under them, and dark blue ankle boots. They looked like exactly my size and preferred style.

Another memory: I had known I might coalesce on Opalite. I had spent years designing mathematical models to predict the future. They rarely gave reliable results, though. Too many variables existed. The predictions became vague, bizarre, or nonsensical when taken more than a short time into the future. But I had worked endlessly, until a few patterns repeated. They had said I would cease to exist. Not die. Simply *cease*.

So I had taken steps to ensure I resumed existing. Those steps had almost failed. Even now, I wasn't fully here. We hadn't had time to prepare our escape; that was probably why I had coalesced in the wrong place. But it had worked well enough. I was still alive.

For now.

6

Search Beneath a Crimson Sky

"Four Manq prowl the middle forest," Hajune continued. He sat with J'chabi and three city officers on the ridged floor of J'chabi's home. A reluctant Hajune had finally agreed to answer their questions.

The newcomers, two women and a man, recorded his words on holosheets. The women looked like sisters, just as the Shay men resembled brothers. They were a striking people, tall and well built, with hair the color of rich loam and skin a smooth, even brown. I wondered if the city and forest Shay realized how similar they appeared to outsiders, or if like Hajune, they all perceived great differences among themselves.

I stood by the wall, silent. They seemed to have forgotten my presence. I had become good at listening without being noticed even among my own people, who had some idea of my abilities. Here, where only Hajune and J'chabi Na knew the truth, it became that much easier to be invisible.

"We must find the Manq," the taller woman said.

"Soon," the new man said.

"Capture or kill?" J'chabi asked.

I remembered Eldrin. *Kill,* I thought.

"Capture," the shorter woman said.

"Kill." The submerged hatred in Hajune's voice did nothing to lessen its impact. The other Shay shifted their weight.

"They may have important information," the new man pointed out.

J'chabi glanced in my direction, his gaze discreet. His mood suffused my mind. He wanted the Razers to die because he feared they would hurt or capture me. Yet as much as a part of me wished to avenge Eldrin, I knew they might give us valuable information. With reluctance, I focused on J'chabi: *Let them live. Intelligence. Information. Interrogation.*

His forehead furrowed as if he were hearing a distant, almost inaudible conversation. Then he addressed the others. "I agree, in principle, with Hajune Tailor. We must ensure the safety of this city. But knowledge also brings safety. First we question the Manq. Then we execute."

The taller woman spoke firmly. "Trial we must have."

Hajune's fist clenched around the handle of the axe on his knees. "No trial do we need. I witnessed their crimes."

Her voice changed, offering comfort. "To the time and space of your wife's death, Hajune Tailor, we offer grace. But we must have a trial. It would be wrong to do otherwise."

He said nothing. It was fortunate she had a strong sense of self; otherwise his stare might have disintegrated her, it was so intense. His pain filled the room, undisguised. I wondered that the others didn't crumble under its weight. Tears gathered in my eyes and I let them fall, in respect for his loss.

"You must not," J'chabi told me in Shay. Again.

"I must." I stood with him and the others in the entrance of his house.

He switched to Iotic. "We cannot risk you coming with us to hunt the Manq. It is an incredible fortune you have survived. Your life is our most precious resource. We must protect it."

He sounded like ISC Security. I loathed being treated like priceless china. It had been this way since my birth. I looked vulnerable to people. Young. My aging had been delayed by genetics, good health, and the cell repairs performed by nanomeds in my body. Faint lines showed around my eyes and traces of gray in my hair, but my face looked waif-like, "pretty" Eldrin used to say. And compared to the Shay, I was small.

I crossed my arms. "I'm going with you." Whether I stayed here or went into the forest, the level of protection I had was about the same, minimal compared to what ISC maintained over me. In the greater scheme of existence, it mattered little whether Hajune and I stayed or went—but to us it made a big difference.

Hajune spoke to me in Shay. "Why fight you with J'chabi Na?"

"I want for you and I to go with the searchers," I said.

"Yes." Hajune raised his hand, indicating agreement. "Guard you, I shall."

J'chabi put his hands on his hips. "Guard her *here*. Come not."

"Stay not," Hajune told him. "With Manq, we have business."

"Here stay," J'chabi said. "We must protect Lady Dehya."

The city security team was listening with avid curiosity. The taller woman spoke. "J'chabi Na, why say you 'Lady Dehya'?"

Good question. I had asked him to say Dehya, but he seemed unable to drop my title completely. Until I knew more about the situation I faced, I preferred to keep my identity concealed.

"It means a female relative," I said.

"Why want you to come with us?" she asked.

My fist clenched at my side. "Manq take my husband. Son. Niece. Nephews. Kill my family. Make our lives hell. I want to see them caught."

The male city officer asked, "Know you how to shoot a gun?"

"Yes." I knew in theory, anyway.

"Come then, Lady," the tall woman said.

"Dehya," I said.

"Eh?"

"Dehya. It is my name."

"I am Natil." She introduced the shorter woman as Komoj and the man as Xink'ok, with a glottal stop that made me want to say "zinc oxide" in Earth English. All the languages we spoke now had their roots in ancient cultures on Earth, primarily from North Africa, the Near East, and Mesoamerica, but the glottal stops had fallen out of use in most modern tongues.

J'chabi looked ready to explode. "I protest."

"Why?" Natil asked.

"We must not endanger the lady."

"She is an adult," Zinc said. "She makes her own decisions."

Good answer. If I escaped this place, I might hire Shay for bodyguards. Then again, after ISC finished training them, they would probably be just as fanatically protective as all my other bodyguards.

J'chabi spoke to me in Iotic. "Please, Pharaoh Dyhianna. Do not endanger yourself this way."

"I'm not helpless. And the risk is small."

"*Any* risk is unacceptable. The Razers might recognize you."

"How?" I was probably the least imaged potentate in human history. I had eradicated every picture of myself on the webs, and I had access to parts of the networks most people didn't even know existed. The Assembly had made it a crime to take holos of me. They even thought that law was their idea.

"I don't know," J'chabi said. "But the possibility exists."

I knew if I gave him a direct order to stop his protests, he would do so. But was it worth making the person entrusted with my life feel he had failed his duty? More mattered here than my need for vengeance. A leader didn't just give orders, she chose the path that offered the most benefit to her people.

"Very well." I forced out the words. "Hajune and I will wait here."

J'chabi's shoulders relaxed. Then, forgetting he was supposed to treat me like a relative rather than a Pharaoh, he bowed.

The others were watching us intently. Their moods suggested they didn't understand Iotic. They made no attempt to hide their interest, obviously having guessed I was more than an "aunt."

I spoke in Shay to Natil, the taller woman. "Hajune Tailor and I will stay here."

Hajune's protest burst into his mind. But he remained silent, standing like a wall at my side.

"You are sure?" Natil asked.

"Yes." I wanted to strangle the Manq. Slowly. No, it wasn't noble. It wasn't high-minded. But gods, I wanted it. Lacking that opportunity, I would settle for staying alive so I could regain power and gather our ISC forces against the Traders.

Hajune stood like a statue while I ate nutrient sticks from the food stored here. Experts had designed them specifically for my metabolism and body chemistry, so they not only appeased my hunger, they also settled my stomach. I sat against the wall, my legs stretched out on the designer moss, my body warm, and my thirst quenched. Ruddy sunlight poured through the portals above my head. After the last few days, this would have been heaven if Hajune hadn't been staring at me.

Had J'chabi known the full story, he would never have left me alone with Hajune. As a Rhon empath, I knew Hajune wouldn't attack me again. But convincing J'chabi would have been difficult, and I had no wish to argue the matter.

I considered Hajune. "Does it make you tired, standing so much? Please be comfortable."

"I watch." An edge came into his voice. "Always now, I will watch."

My contentment vanished. The Traders had left him that legacy: constant fear.

Vibrations shuddered the floor. A door scraped and footsteps rustled in the entrance tunnel. As I stood, Hajune moved between me and the entrance to this room, his weapon ready in his hands. He no longer carried his axe; J'chabi had given him a Lenard K16 laser carbine.

"Hajune Tailor," a voice said from the doorway. Looking past Hajune, I saw J'chabi with Natil. Their mood was sober.

"It pleases us to see you safe," I said. Then I winced. It pleases us? Talking that way wouldn't help hide my identity. It did relieve me that they were back, though.

Natil watched me with close scrutiny. "Your Shay is hard to understand. Strong is your Iotic accent."

Ach. So they knew. I said, "I regret the difficulty," but offered no other explanations.

"Have you news?" Hajune asked them.

J'chabi took a deep breath. "We found the Manq."

Hajune went very still. "Did you capture them?"

Natil answered. "Two." After a pause that went on too long, she added, "The other two killed themselves before we could take them."

A muscle twitched in Hajune's cheek. "So."

Sorrow softened J'chabi's voice. "Hajune Tailor—we found your wife."

7
Skyhold

Green and round, the hospital was part of the forest. It spanned the gigantic tripod bases of four trees. Inside, it had a small but modern facility. The doctor led Natil, J'chabi, Hajune, and me to a rounded chamber. Two small globes in one corner shed muted light over a bed against the far wall. A woman lay there with a pale green sheet pulled up to her shoulders. I barely recognized her as the person in Hajune's memories; this woman was wasted and still, her body gaunt under the sheet.

She was also alive.

Hajune made a strangled noise and strode past the doctor. But he froze when he reached the bed, as if he feared to extinguish the faint breath that clung to his wife's dying body.

The doctor, another tall Shay woman, joined him. "She has been in a coma."

His words were almost a whisper. "I saw her die."

The doctor's voice was infinitely gentle. "Her state mimics death. It is a defense against the unbearable." She started to lay her hand on his arm, then hesitated as if unsure how he would respond. Softly she said, "Sorry I am, so sorry."

My sadness deepened. Although I hadn't realized the Shay could go into a death trance, I knew other humanoid races that used such a defensive mechanism. The Razers must have taken her in the hope that she would revive. But it didn't work that way. The person died within a few days.

We withdrew then, not wanting to intrude on Hajune's final moments with his wife.

J'chabi spoke in Iotic. "No one uses our telop console now. We've tried to reconnect with the offworld nets, but we find no trace of the psiberweb. Without any means to leave Opalite, we have no idea what happened."

J'chabi, Natil, and I were in an alcove of the hospital. We

sat on a wall bench, a ledge covered by engineered moss with cleansing properties that made it sterile. J'chabi balanced the laser carbine on his knees, guarding me while Hajune stayed with his wife. Natil watched us with her keen gaze. The room had several entrances, and medics passed through now and then, absorbed in their own affairs.

"Are any planetary computer networks working?" I asked.

J'chabi made an affirmative wave with his hand. "The city net failed when everything else collapsed, but we had it working within an hour." He paused. "The Traders who destroyed our port told us that you had died in the war."

Dryly I said, "I'm sure they wanted that to be true."

"I wish I could offer you offworld access. But we're an inconsequential settlement, one with low priority for repairs."

"Don't you, personally, have a top-priority link to ISC?" I had set it up myself, so he could reach Imperial Space Command no matter what.

"It is down also."

That finished off my last hope that some fragment of the psiberweb might still survive.

Footsteps padded nearby. Turning, I saw the doctor. She came over and sat next to J'chabi, her face weary. "Hajune Tailor is still with her. I think he could use some support." Softly she added, "He hurts so much."

So we went with her. Hajune's pain filled the hospital in a fog, one I had trouble moving through. Yet no one else seemed affected. My empath's mind was a curse now. It tore at me to feel his anguish and be unable to help. The injustice of it struck like a blow. He had recovered his wife only to lose her again.

We found him sitting on the bed holding his wife's hand. He glanced up as we entered, then went back to watching her face. J'chabi and I stood with him, and Natil stayed back, apparently assuming we knew him better. But none of us could really call him friend.

I laid my hand on his shoulder. "My sorry, Hajune Tailor."

He nodded, still looking at his wife. Her thoughts slumbered at the edges of my awareness. My mind skirted hers like a soft-footed animal searching for an entrance to a fortress.

I acted in pure instinct; my mental barriers dropped and my mind opened. *Come back,* I thought to her. *Hajune needs you. He loves you.*

It wasn't until I started using biofeedback on myself that I realized what I was doing. Yes, I remembered. I had a talent for this. Humans had long known how to use biofeedback. Some empaths could turn that concentration outward, affecting others as well as themselves. I reached my mind out to Hajune's wife, my efforts aided by the biomech that enhanced my brain. But I still couldn't connect. Not alone. Instinctively, I drew Hajune into our link.

Skyhold, come back, he thought. *Without you, I am nothing.*

No response. His wife continued to fade.

Skyhold, truly do I need you.

Nothing.

Please. His thoughts ached. *I would like to say good-bye.*

Still nothing. Hajune bent his head and tears slid down his face.

I gently withdrew my mind. It was just him and Skyhold now. I didn't think he realized we had all been in a link. Although I could open the mental door, only he could truly reach her. She probably had too little of her conscious mind left to sense him, but perhaps this would give him a small portion of closeness with her in their final hours together.

J'chabi, Natil, and I stayed in the room, seated on a wall bench. The doctor was at a console, monitoring her patient. Although Hajune seemed to want us there, he never spoke, only sat on the bed holding his wife's hand. Silence filled the room, but it wasn't complete. A faint hum came from the walls, a vibration of the life within the hospital, the sound carried by the trees that cradled this building within their great bases.

Hajune suddenly spoke. "Skyhold?"

I raised my head, stirred out of my doze.

"Skyhold?" His voice was urgent.

"Hai!" The doctor jumped up from her console and strode to the bed.

I froze. No. Not now. Skyhold couldn't be dead already.

"Sweet gods," Hajune whispered. The doctor was leaning over Skyhold now.

Then, in a husky voice almost too soft to hear, a woman said, "Hajune Tailor? Why cry you, Husband?"

He made a choked sound.

The doctor spoke kindly. "Rest you must, Skyhold. Sleep."

"Rest I will . . ." Skyhold murmured.

Hajune spoke softly to the doctor. "What happened?"

Her voice caught. "Apparently she is stronger than we knew."

Tears wet his cheeks. "Thank you." He glanced at me. "And you."

"It is you who brought her back," I said.

He bowed his head, then turned to his wife. His joy filled the chamber.

Yet pain still existed here. It didn't come from Hajune.

Then I knew; it ached within me. I had many memories now: Eldrin laughing, Eldrin in my arms, Eldrin swinging a young Taquinil into the air, Eldrin beaming with pride at his son.

Eldrin.

The Web Chamber resembled others I had used, except this one was round, as were most rooms in this city. Such geometries fit better within the trees. The white walls glowed with subdued lighting. The room contained a few small consoles. Only one had a telop chair, and it was a pale copy of the Triad Command Chair I usually used to access the psiberweb. Triad Chairs thundered with power: this one whispered. But a whisper would be all we needed, if the right people heard.

The Web Keeper insisted on installing me in the chair. I had designed its prototype a century before her birth, but I let her help me out of my clothes and into the telop skin anyway. The bodysuit had small holes at the wrists and ankles, neck, and base of the spine. Prongs from the chair snapped easily through those holes into sockets in my body, and biothreads linked the sockets to my neural nodes. The chair's exoskeleton folded around my body, sheathing me in a silver mesh.

This chair was a stranger, with unfamiliar smells and textures. Closing my eyes, I went through a series of relaxation exercises. Then I let signals from the console "shake hands" with the biomech in my body. When my neural nodes and the console had become acquainted, my mind diffused outward, reaching for the web—

And found nothing.

I felt as if I had dropped into a cold void. The gateway created by the console should have boosted my thoughts into psiberspace. But this gate went nowhere. The Kyle space it had linked to no longer existed.

I turned my concentration inward. With the support of the chair, I had better focus and control. I entered a netherworld, unformed and dark . . .

darkness   darkness

drifting mind mists   drifting mind mists

drifting mists of the mind   drifting mists of the mind

drifting mist of foaming bubbles   drifting mist of foaming bubbles

drifting mists of the mind   drifting mists of the mind

drifting mind mists   drifting mind mists

darkness   darkness

Taquinil
Kelric
Eldrinson

The universe existed as a green blur.

Gradually, the blur resolved into a low ceiling. I was lying on my back, covered by a sheet. Moss made a pleasant cushion under my body.

Some time later I turned my head. This chamber resembled the main living area of J'chabi's home. Someone was sitting on a ridge across the room, reading a holobook.

"My greetings, J'chabi." My voice came out rusty. I sat up slowly. I still wore the telop skin, so I let the sheet fall.

He looked up with a start. "Greetings, Pharaoh Dyhianna." He spoke in Iotic, with relief. "You look well now."

"Thank you." I hesitated. "I don't remember coming here."

He didn't seem surprised. "You have slept for three days."

"Opalite days?"

"Yes."

That meant twelve hours. I was losing track of time. Nor did I have any idea how much time had passed between when Eldrin pushed us into Kyle space and I coalesced on Opalite. "J'chabi, do you know the date by the Skolian calendar?"

"Not exactly." He came over and sat by the bed on a mossy ridge. "We don't use ASC dates here."

It didn't surprise me. Opalite's residents had little reason to use the ASC dates of the Skolian calendar. Computers here could convert to ASC, to provide a baseline for a comparison with the standard timeline. But from the solitary nature of the community I had so far seen, I doubted much demand existed for such a service.

"Do you have an idea of the Skolian date?" I asked.

He considered. "The web collapse came toward the end of 374 ASC. It has been over a standard month since then, I think. Perhaps two."

That meant I had been stranded in a mathematical limbo for over a month before I reformed on Opalite. So long? That time span fit J'chabi's attitude, though. The web collapse must have sent shock waves through all the settlements of humanity. Yet the Shay seemed relatively blasé about it now, which suggested they had grown used to the situation. Given how long I had spent in a nascent psiberspace, it astonished me that I had come out again.

But wait. Someone had called me there.

I strained to catch the elusive memory. I had sensed Taquinil this last time, but I had no idea when or where he existed; neither time nor space had meaning in Kyle space. It was more than Taquinil, though. I had been aware of two other minds.

Eldrinson.

Yes. Eldrin's father. My father-in-law. It had always bemused me that the father was called Eldrinson and the son
was Eldrin. Eldrinson had probably decided that naming his
firstborn Eldrinsonson was overdoing matters. It didn't surprise me that I sensed my father-in-law. He, Soz, and I
formed the Triad that made the psiberweb possible. I created
the net, Eldrinson supported it, and Soz used it to direct ISC.
Together, we made a formidable force.

Had made a formidable force.

Soz was gone.

I sat in silence, stunned with this new realization. Soz no
longer formed part of the Triad. But it was impossible to dis-
engage from it without damaging your brain beyond repair.
The only way to leave the Triad was to die.

Nausea spread through me. I folded my arms across my
stomach while my eyes burned with tears I couldn't shed.
Damn the Traders. Damn them all. I rocked back and forth.
Soz. *Soz.*

Gradually another tendril of memory curled past my up-
welling of grief. I *had* felt a third mind in that nether universe. Who?

Kelric?

He was my nephew, the youngest child of my sister Roca.
Kelric had died eighteen years ago, a casualty of war. I had
long grieved for him. Physically, he and I were as different as
possible; he was huge and muscular, a military officer, gold
rather than dark. But I had more in common with him than
other members of the Ruby Dynasty. A gifted mathematician,
he shared my love of equations.

But he was *dead.*

The blurred memory of a conversation in psiberspace
came to me . . .

Aunt Dehya?

Kelric?

Where are you?

Gone . . .

Have you died?
I exist.
Come home. Our people need their Pharoah. Your family needs you.
I will try . . .

"Pharaoh Dyhianna?" J'chabi was watching me intently.

I refocused on him. "I'm here."

He regarded me curiously. "Even when you are present, rather than faded away, you are not always here."

I gave a wan laugh. "You put that far more politely than the Assembly does."

He flushed. "My sorry. I meant no offense."

"You gave none." I rubbed the back of my neck, working out kinks. "Did I fade away in the telop chair?"

"Your body became translucent." He blinked rather rapidly. "We feared to touch you, lest it do damage. Your body overlapped the chair, like a holo superimposed on a solid object."

Such a strange image. "I wonder if that's where ghost tales come from. Maybe ghosts are people partially transformed into an alternate reality." Seeing J'chabi's alarmed expression, I gave him a rueful look. "This must all seem bizarre to you."

"It is my honor to serve the Ruby Pharaoh."

That was tactful. "It is my honor to have your loyalty."

He actually blushed at that. "What will you do now?"

"I'm not sure. It depends on whether or not I contacted anyone."

"Don't you know?"

I sifted through my memories. "I recall a vague sense of Eldrinson Valdoria, the Web Key. Perhaps other family members."

"Can they send help?"

"I'm afraid not." Eldrinson and my sister Roca were still on Earth. ISC had sent them there during the war, for protection, because the Allied Worlds of Earth had remained neutral, too small a power to pose a threat, but big enough that neither we nor the Traders could easily conquer them.

Conquer. I winced. But I couldn't deny we called ourselves the Skolian *Imperialate* for a reason. Unlike the Traders, we didn't blatantly subjugate worlds, but ISC had been known to occupy settlements without their agreement. Supposedly Skolia was a democracy, like the Allied Worlds, with an elected Assembly, but we stretched the definition to breaking.

The constant political maneuvering of the Ruby Dynasty with the Assembly wore me down. I resented the clenched control they exerted over our lives—

Anger surged over me, and a rush of memories. Control, hell. They were maniacs. Eldrin was my *nephew*. The son of Eldrinson and Roca. The Assembly had forced our marriage and demanded we have children. Rhon psions were almost impossible to produce in the lab, which made the Ruby Dynasty the only known source. Without us, the psiberweb couldn't exist. Any telop could use the web, but only we could power it. Desperate to ensure their supply of Rhon psions, the Assembly had given Eldrin and me no choice. Never mind that it threatened to tear apart our family. No price was too great.

J'chabi was waiting patiently. Seeing me focus on him, he continued. "Could you have contacted anyone in Kyle space but not remember?"

Hard as it was to do, I made myself switch gears. Brooding about the Assembly would do me no good right now. "It's possible. I tried to project an impression of my location and situation, but even if I reached someone, it might not register enough for me to remember."

He spoke with a hope that sounded forced. "If anyone can make contact, it is you."

"I hope you're right." Eventually someone would find out we had been here.

I just prayed we were still free and alive then.

Natil stood in the doorway of J'chabi Na's home. "Come in, may I?"

J'chabi moved aside, inviting her to enter.

I was waiting a few steps back in the hall. "Have you news of Hajune and Skyhold?"

Natil walked into the hall. "Skyhold recovers slowly." The taciturn officer actually cracked a smile. "But recover she does."

"This is good," J'chabi said.

Natil seemed distracted. "Another problem we have."

J'chabi ushered us into the main living area. "Problem?"

"A ship in orbit."

My hope surged. "Skolian?"

Natil turned her dark gaze on me. "Lady, I hope this ship comes not for you."

I regarded her uneasily. "Why?"

She answered flatly. "Trader."

Ah, no. We were fast running out of options. "Are they looking for the crashed Aristo ship?"

"Yes. We gave them the two Razers." Natil grimaced. "Still the Traders say, 'We punish.' "

Her words cut like honed steel. I had seen how the Traders punished worlds. How far they took it would depend on the importance of the Aristo who had died, how close their kinship ties were to his family, and what they thought they could get away with. Their retaliation could range from kidnapping Shay natives to slagging this entire moon. Most likely they would abduct whatever Shay they could sell for a good price in their slave markets and then destroy this city.

"This is a Skolian world," I said. "They're breaking so many treaties by coming here, I can't count them." I could, actually. They were violating four clauses in the Halstaad Code of War. We could take them to trial on any one and win—which right now meant about as much as nits in a nova.

"What can we do?" Natil asked.

Good question. "Are any starport defenses still operable?"

J'chabi answered. "All were destroyed."

I stood thinking. "Tell them this: our ISC backup forces have the Aristo and crew from the Trader ship that crashed."

"No ISC backup here," Natil pointed out.

"We know that. They don't." I was mangling the Shay syntax, but it didn't matter. The tension indicated by my "inverted" sentences fit the situation. "Remind them about the Halstaad Code. They know they're violating it."

J'chabi frowned. "I doubt that will stop them. It won't be hard to verify that we have no ISC support."

"But it will stall them. I'll keep trying to reach ISC." If I could bring in armed ships, it would put teeth into our bluff. Otherwise, the Traders would discover that they had chanced upon a far greater prize than they expected: the Ruby Pharaoh.

8
The Brooding Night

Waveform
Waves forming here
Forming from term after term
Waves forming, term after term
Waves spreading, ripples spreading
Waves spreading, ripples spreading
Waves forming, term after term
Forming from term after term
Waves forming here
Waveform

. . . Again I awoke in J'chabi's home. This time I was alone. As I sat up, my arms became translucent. Alarmed, I concentrated until they solidified.

J'chabi appeared in the doorway, holding the laser carbine. "You are back."

I spoke in a rasp, my throat dry. "How long this time?"

Concern shaded his face. "You were gone half a decadar."

Five Opalite days. Twenty hours. It was taking longer and longer to re-form. "The Traders?"

"We sent your message to them." He entered the room, moving with the careful courtesy he always used around me. "They have made no more hostile moves. But they haven't left either. They seem to be waiting."

I could guess why. They had probably surmised that ISC had little presence here aside from its orbital defense system, which was in tatters now. With the destruction of the port, no functional base remained on the moon. And apparently Opalite had only this one city, an outpost intended for scientific research. Soon the Traders would call our bluff.

"Did you reach anyone?" J'chabi asked.

"I don't recall any contact." I wished I had a more encouraging answer. Desperation suffused his mind. Without ISC intervention, we would become slaves or die. And more was at stake than most anyone knew. For the Traders to capture any member of the Ruby Dynasty would create a crisis. If they seized the Pharaoh, it would be a disaster.

I shuddered, trying not to think of pain and fear. My brain had neurological defenses. They blocked me from answering questions that would compromise ISC security or hurt my family. If interrogation became impossible to bear, the implants would erase my memories by disrupting neural links. But no defenses were foolproof. The Traders could learn enough from me to cripple Skolia. I would rather die than betray the people and family I loved.

J'chabi was watching my face. "What do you want me to do?"

I took a steadying breath. Then I indicated his carbine. "If the Traders come . . . I mustn't go with them."

His face paled, but he didn't look surprised. "I understand."

Gods willing, he wouldn't have to kill me. The longer this standoff continued, the greater the chance that help would reach us.

A more optimistic thought came to me. "I have another idea."

His face brightened. "Yes?"

I grinned. "It's time to confuse our Trader guests."

Natil scratched her chin. "Why do you want to send pretend messages?"

We were standing in an alcove off the city's web room. Two of the security officers, Natil and the man Zinc, had joined Hajune, J'chabi, and me. With the starport destroyed, the communication console in this alcove offered the only way for us to talk with ships in orbit.

Today J'chabi translated my Iotic into Shay for the others, and their Shay in Iotic for me. Although I was learning the language, right now I couldn't risk a mistake due to my stumbles with its nuances.

"I will make the messages sound like ISC chatter," I said.

"Both outgoing and incoming. It will all be in ISC code. But I'll use a code the Traders have broken. If this works, then when they pick up the messages, they will believe ISC ships are on approach to this system."

"But they are not," Zinc pointed out. "Obvious this soon will be."

I paused, considering what to reveal. During the war, our naval research labs had figured out how to hide ships in giant antimatter fuel bottles. They weren't "bottles" in a physical sense, but rather containment fields in the shape of a Klein bottle. A normal bottle twisted the fuel out of normal space; a giant bottle could twist out an entire ship. Soz had used it to sneak an invasion fleet into Trader territory, so by now the Traders probably knew we could hide ships. That might fool these into thinking ISC forces lurked nearby, at least until they began to question why these concealed forces did nothing to assert their presence.

If, if, if. I wished I knew what was going on out there. I couldn't tell the Shay too much, lest the Traders capture them.

I spoke carefully. "I can make it sound like ISC has new stealth tech."

Natil didn't look convinced. "That won't fool anyone long."

"Any time it can give will help," I said.

Zinc shook his head. "We don't know ISC codes. Nor do we know military protocols. But the Traders do. We can't fool them."

J'chabi watched me closely as he translated. I answered quietly. "I know the codes and protocols."

Silence greeted my words. Then Natil said, "Very few people have such information."

"Yes." I left it at that.

Natil and Zinc appraised me for a long moment. Finally Natil set her hand on the high back of the comm console. "Shall we start, then?"

I exhaled, trying to release tension. "An excellent idea."

Then I went to work.

"We demand reparations for our destroyed ship." The voice of the Trader commander crackled on the comm. He spoke in Eubic, a standardized language used by their slave castes. It left little doubt about how he viewed us.

I wanted to answer in Highton, the language of their aristocracy, just to defy his assumptions of our inferiority. Given how few people knew Highton, though, it would make him suspicious. So I used Eubic, keeping my voice cool. "You can address these issues with Colonel Stonemason." I used the name of a real person. Stonemason was an officer renowned—the Traders might say infamous—for his military prowess. He supposedly commanded the ships en route to Opalite. But I knew our bluff wouldn't hold much longer.

"We await his arrival." The commander's tone had more bite than the last time we had spoken, a few hours ago.

After we finished, I leaned my elbows on the console and rested my forehead on my palms, disheartened. Natil, Zinc, and J'chabi waited, standing around the console.

Natil touched my shoulder. "Lady?"

Looking up, I spoke tiredly. "You need to evacuate the city."

"If the Traders want to find us," she said, "no place on Opalite will be safe."

"True. But perhaps if we make it inconvenient enough, they will decide it isn't worth the effort." I pushed my hand through my hair. "They will probably destroy the city in retaliation for the ship they lost. But they might consider it a waste of time to hunt down your people. They have trillions of slaves on thousands of worlds. They don't need more, except psions."

J'chabi blanched as he looked at me. Natil considered him, then me. "I understand that Hajune Tailor and his wife are empaths."

"Yes." My thoughts lurched at the memory of Skyhold. "The Razers found him in the upper forest, so he and Skyhold should flee into the lower forest. But evacuate the city in all directions. It will help confuse matters. The Traders may not consider Hajune worth a lengthy search. They must have far more pressing concerns right now, after the Radiance War."

Natil spoke quietly. "I think you too should evacuate into the lower forest."

I swallowed. Then I gave an affirmative lift of my hand. Even that slight motion felt heavy.

For now the Traders were holding off. But their commander was becoming impatient.

"Lady Dehya." Urgency filled J'chabi's words. "We must go."

I snapped awake, sitting up even before the sleep cleared from my mind. J'chabi was kneeling next to me, with Natil and Zinc looming behind him.

"What is it?" I asked, pulling on my boots.

"The Traders are sending down shuttles." He spoke in a low voice, as if they could hear us even here, despite the aural shields that shrouded his home. He handed me a pulse gun. As I strapped its belt around my hips, I saw he had a similar gun at his side. Anyone he shot would die instantly, their body torn apart by serrated projectiles that moved at hypersonic speeds.

Including me.

We fled his home during the brooding night, beneath the great banded orb of Slowcoal. Bathed in its red light, we ran for our lives and our freedom.

Ridges, tripods, beetle-tanks. Forest surrounded us. Natil and Zinc walked ahead, and J'chabi came with me. Behind us, Hajune supported Skyhold, helping her keep our pace. His bittersweet love suffused the night. For all his joy at her survival, he knew that if they became slaves, they both faced a lifetime of what she had already endured. Aristos lavished care on their pleasure slaves, far better than the Razers had treated Skyhold, but it was only because they wanted their valuable property in good shape. It didn't make them any less sadistic, only more accomplished in what they inflicted.

I tried not to dwell on the future. Instead, I sought memories of good times, knowing they might soon be all that remained of what I cherished. Once, in his youth, Eldrin had set up a surprise for me. I had worked a grueling day in the web. That evening, exhausted, I had gone home to my new husband, a man I hardly knew. I opened the door into an empty living room dimly lit from an orb in one corner. Suddenly a slew of small holos had run into the room: soldiers, dancers, jugglers, mimes, drummers, revelers—all one hand-span high. They whirled around me and I stopped, dumbfounded.

A deep laugh came from the archway across the room. Eldrin stood there, mischief in his gaze. *Like my friends?* he asked. *They're for you.*

Later that evening, I had shown him how much I appreciated his greeting. Taquinil had been born nine months later.

Up ahead, Natil froze, holding up her hand. We all stopped, listening.

Voices. They spoke Eubic.

My stomach felt as if it dropped. The Traders were off to our left, closing on our location.

J'chabi spoke in a low voice. "Dehya and I should separate from the rest of you."

"Go," Natil said urgently. "We will draw their attention."

I glanced at Hajune and Skyhold, he with his arm around her waist. The color had drained from their faces, making them ghostly in the red light.

"Be well," I said in Shay. Then J'chabi and I took off, going west.

After several minutes, we came out of the trees on the shore of a lake. We dove in and swam hard. Large swells roiled the surface. Even soaking wet, my clothes caused little problem; I had the same strength as always, but less weight to move through the water. My body displaced just as much liquid as it would on a heavier gravity world, though. I felt as if I were floating in a heavy mist.

On the far shore, we waded out onto a gravel beach. As an armored crab-creature scuttled in front of us, we surveyed the area, looking and listening. The forest started twenty paces up the beach.

J'chabi said, "I think it is all ri—"

Then he froze, his sentence lost.

Trader soldiers were striding out of the forest.

9
Vazar

They came like specters through the mist, eight of them, all in gray flex-armor. Helmets hid their faces. Some had pulse rifles, deadly silver mammoths that caught glints of red from the ruddy night.

I had no time for fear. Whirling around, I sprinted away from them, my hand dropping to my gun. Before I had gone more than a few steps, a projectile hit my back. It didn't explode, rip me up, shake apart my insides, or otherwise commit mayhem. It just knocked me over. Even as I fell, I yanked out my weapon. Twisting in the air, I landed on my back, already firing, my body toggled into an enhanced speed mode.

Something thunked my wrist, and a loud crack split the air. As my hand spasmed, my gun went flying. Still moving, not even pausing to breathe, I scrambled to my feet. Jaichabi was already up to his knees, his gun out and aimed. But against this many soldiers we had less chance of escape than an ice cube in hell.

My sense of time changed, slowing, though my nodes claimed I was still in an accelerated mode. "Jaichabi." My voice sounded deathly in the thick air. "Now."

He turned, bringing his gun to bear on me. Grief etched his face, but he never wavered. We both knew the price of my capture by the Traders. With a dream-like calm, I watched his thumb press the firing stud. Thunder echoed in the forest.

Yet even as he fired, his gun snapped out of his hand as if a giant had tapped it. The weapon sailed in a slow arc toward the lake. The bullet he had fired whipped past my head, close enough for its serrated edges to slice off a tendril of my hair. The lock wisped across my cheek and fell down my front.

Still caught in a slowed time sense, I turned my head. New commandos were broiling out of the forest, these in black armor instead of gray, their dark forms vivid against the backdrop of foggy trees. Their black visors glinted, probably giving them heads-down displays. Conduits on their armor glittered with a hard-edged sheen. I had no doubt that the techno-warriors inside that armor had the enhanced speed, strength, and neural augmentation of lethal combat machines. They ran across the beach, six of them, like shadows come to life, deadly shades.

The Traders turned their attack on the newcomers. Both groups were firing now, using weapons far more fatal than whatever had hit my wrist. Bursts of light jumped in the misty air. The armor they all wore offered some protection, but it couldn't stop pulse weapons and lasers.

The battle ended in seconds. The three surviving Traders threw down their weapons and raised their arms. The remains of four others lay crumpled in fused piles of gray armor. One of the Traders had run, but I doubted he could outpace the black-armored commandos.

Then the leader of the commandos removed her helmet. Her hair fell free, dark as a moonless night, wild around her face and shoulders. Towering on the beach, long-legged and muscular, all in black, she stood with her booted feet planted wide and her laser carbine trained on J'chabi. The gigantic weapon glittered red. Fierce exultation flushed her face, as if she were the incarnation of an avenging goddess descended to scourge the world.

My sister-in-law had arrived.

10
Majda Prime

Vazar?" I gaped at her. Time snapped back to normal and nausea rolled over me, a delayed reaction to the carnage on the beach. Pain stabbed my wrist, then receded, probably as my nanomeds numbed the area.

Vazar strode forward, her gun trained on J'chabi. With eloquence, she said, "Shoot at her again, you scum on a slime-mold, and you're fucking dead."

"Vaz, wait," I said.

She directed one of her warriors to J'chabi. "Watch him."

"Vaz, listen to me," I said. "This is Jaichabi Na, my contact here. He gave me shelter and aid. He was following *my* orders to shoot, so the Traders wouldn't capture me. I don't want him hurt. Understand?"

Vazar stopped in front of me. My head barely came to her shoulder. Her fierce gaze was even more disconcerting up close. She motioned over two of her commandos, giants in black body-armor. "Don't let anyone near the Pharaoh. If anyone threatens Her Highness, slag the worm-eating vermin."

I tried again. "Vazar, answer me."

She finally focused on my face. "My honor at your exalted presence, Pharaoh Dyhianna."

"I'm glad to see you." That was certainly an understatement. I could have hugged her, if I hadn't been afraid her return embrace would crack me in half. "But I don't want you killing everything that moves." In all the years I had known her, I had seen her like this only one other time. But then, I had never seen her in battle before.

"I will protect you," she assured me. "I'll annihilate any putrescent spawn of a toadstool that blinks." Then she strode off to where her people were manacling the three Traders. Two more of her team emerged from the forest, dragging the Trader who had run. Given the damage to the armor, I doubted the person inside still lived.

Bile rose in my throat. My wrist throbbed. I didn't want to show vulnerability in front of these warriors, but I couldn't stop my response. I folded my arms around my stomach and leaned over. It felt as if all the shock would surge up and empty out of me, along with my last meal. I struggled to hold back, to keep it all inside.

It took me several moments to regain control, but I managed. One of the Jagernauts was hovering next to me. He had removed his helmet, revealing a youth with light brown hair and blue eyes.

"Are you all right, Your Highness?" he asked.

"Yes, thank you." My voice rasped.

Vazar was overseeing the cleanup on the beach. Her implacable anger felt like a tangible presence. I had seen her this way two years ago, when the Traders captured her cospouse, Althor. Eldrin's brother: my brother-in-law. She had changed completely from the vibrant extrovert who thrived on life, laughed with ease, and loved both Althor and their co-spouse Coop to distraction. Her fury had been ice.

Over the past two years, she had learned to cope with her anger and grief. I didn't know what drove her now, but I dreaded the answer. Had something happened to Coop, or to his and Vazar's son? Both Coop and the boy had been on the Orbiter when the Traders attacked. The raiders had come for my family, but they might have taken others as well.

Please, I thought. Don't let any more be dead or captured.

My youthful bodyguard indicated one of the ISC commandos moving among the injured combatants. "I'll call the medic over."

"No." I spoke numbly. "Don't. I'm fine." Vazar's people needed him more.

My guard was clearly unhappy with my response. I could almost feel his urge to call the doctor anyway. As a Skolian civilian, I couldn't give him orders, but for him to go against the wishes of even a titular Ruby Pharaoh was no small matter.

Seeing all these Jagernauts made me think of Soz, my niece, formerly a Jagernaut, now the Imperator. Except Soz was gone. I felt her absence. I knew all I had to do was ask.

Just a simple, *How fares Imperator Skolia?* But I couldn't bear to hear the answer. As long as no one verified her death, a part of me could go on believing she lived.

I walked over to J'chabi, accompanied by my hulking guards. Another of the commandos was keeping watch on J'chabi, but he seemed more concerned than hostile. I suspected he had heard me speak to Vazar about the role J'chabi played in my rescue.

I spoke to J'chabi in Iotic. "How are you?"

"I am fine, Your Highness." He motioned at my arm. "You should have that tended."

Startled, I looked down. What—? My wrist was bent at an odd angle. With a surge of vertigo, I remembered the crack I had heard when I lost my gun. Spots danced in my vision. Someone caught my uninjured arm and spoke, but a roaring had started and I couldn't hear.

Suddenly Vazar was at my side. "Dehya, listen. You must let my medic tend you." She guided me to the edge of the forest, where a large root buckled out of the gravel.

As I sat down on the root, the medic came over. Vazar hadn't called him, and neither she nor the doctor wore a helmet now, but he obviously knew what she wanted. Like Vazar, he and the other commandos were Jagernauts, ISC's elite fighting machines. That meant they were psions. They could form mental links, individually or as a group. They needed neural augmentation to do it, and the strength of the link faded with distance, but it still offered immense advantages when they worked as a team.

When the doctor examined my wrist, I gritted my teeth. My nanomeds could no longer dull the stabbing pain. Then he gave me medication, which made me feel better. I hadn't realized how bad my nausea and pain had become until they went away. He set my wrist and injected me with temporary nanomeds to supplement those already in my body. My neural nodes monitored the invasion of these new meds. My own meds wanted to neutralize the intruders, but the injected meds produced chemicals that sent conciliatory messages, so they all settled down and worked together to repair my wrist.

While the doctor did his magic, Vazar told me what had happened with our people. Even after many weeks, ISC still didn't know why the web had collapsed. Although the initial furor of confusion and disbelief had calmed to a simmer, no one had answers yet. The messages I had sent had managed to reach several ISC telops, but only faintly. It had been hard for the telops to resolve the content, which was why it had taken ISC this long to respond. They had asked Vazar to accompany them in case I needed help as a psion. Although she wasn't Rhon, she was a strong telepath, and she and I also had a close family link.

After we talked, she went to check on her team. They moved over the beach, all in black, their towering figures blurred by the mist. A shuttle landed, misty and dark, and took the three living Traders. Another came for the bodies. The Trader dead would be returned to their ships. That ISC let me stay here, sitting on a root, gave me a good idea how much firepower they had in orbit. They could probably monitor my position to within a millimeter.

Vazar eventually returned and sat next to me. My bodyguards stood like silent monoliths at our backs. We stayed that way for a while, staring at the lake. Layers of mist hovered above the water, which was utterly still, forming a dark surface, like a mirror.

Finally Vazar spoke in a low voice. "When I saw him fire at you—I swear, Dehya, I thought I would explode."

"I told him to fire." I released a long breath. "But I'm glad you all showed up."

"I also."

"Vaz . . ."

"Yes?"

I forced out the words. "My family?"

She turned to me, her face drawn. "The Traders have your husband." Her voice rasped. "I am sorry. So sorry."

I could barely answer. "I too."

"As far as we know, they never caught your son."

"Have you word of him?"

She paused. "Nothing."

The doctor may have worked wonders on my wrist, but nothing could take away this pain. "And my niece? Soz?"

Her husky voice roughened. "The Traders killed her too."

No. Somehow I found my voice. "How did it happen?"

"She went with the drop team that infiltrated the Trader capital. They rescued Althor and captured Jaibriol Qox." Grief edged her voice. "Damn it, Dehya, they *had* him. The Trader *emperor.* But after the shuttle took off, it blew up." Her voice caught. "Althor too."

Ah, no. Not Althor. When would it stop? When the entire Ruby Dynasty was dead? No wonder Vazar had gone crazy. My voice caught like cloth on a rough edge. "At least the Traders can't hurt him anymore."

She spoke softly. "Yes."

My grief snapped, feeling like anger. "What the hell was Soz doing with the drop team? The Imperator doesn't go into combat."

Her expression became guarded. "She went to avenge her brothers."

Although I knew Soz had wanted vengeance, she was too smart to put the herself in danger that way. "That makes no sense."

Vazar started to answer, then fell silent.

"What is it?" I asked.

At first I thought she wouldn't answer, but then she spoke. "Her mind was apparently too much like yours. The Triad power link couldn't survive it. She didn't want to cause your death."

Memories flooded me then, like water freed by an exploding dam. Soz and I had similar minds. It had never mattered until the Triad linked us. Then our minds had threatened to overload the Triad, like a massive short circuit drawing too much power through the same lines.

Only once before had the Triad overloaded. It happened with Kurj, the oldest son of my sister Roca. His father had been Roca's first husband, before Eldrinson. Back then, only

five Rhon psions had existed: my parents, Roca, myself, and
Kurj. Although Roca's husband hadn't been Rhon, he had
carried all of the recessive genes, most of them unpaired. He
and Roca could father a Rhon son. Kurj.

Or so the doctors claimed.

In his thirty-fifth year of life, Kurj had uncovered the truth:
the man he called father couldn't have sired him. He didn't
have the genes. The Assembly had perpetrated a deception.
Determined to create more of the Rhon, they had gone into
the fertility clinic chosen by Roca and her first husband and
switched the sperm used to impregnate Roca. In an unforgiving parody of the Greek myths that had always fascinated
him, Kurj discovered that his grandfather was also his father.

Embittered, coldly furious, and hungry for the authority
the Assembly sought to forbid him, Kurj forced his mind into
the powerlink formed by his grandparents. My parents. He
made their Dyad into a Triad. No one was prepared for the resulting explosion of power. The link couldn't support both
Kurj and my father. When it began to tear apart their minds,
my father gave up his own life to save Kurj, who was both his
son and grandson.

Even now, seventy-three years later, those wounds had yet
to heal fully. The Assembly continued to fight for control
over us, keeping the pain raw beneath the emotional scar tissue. Yes, I understood what had driven Soz, but our interaction hadn't been as dramatic as what Kurj had experienced
with my father. She should have *waited,* damn it, she should
have given me a chance to find a solution.

I pushed my hand through my hair. "The people I loved
have sacrificed too much. I would give my life to have them
back."

"You must live," Vazar said. "We need you."

"We need Soz. Althor. Kurj. Kelric. My parents." My voice
cracked. "Eldrin and Taquinil."

Vazar put her hand on my shoulder. Incredibly, tears
showed on her face—Vazar, who never cried. We leaned together, her head resting against mine.

And we wept.

————

We gathered at the starport: Hajune and Skyhold, J'chabi Na, and myself. Natil and Zinc came too. Jagernauts surrounded me, with Vazar at my side. We stood near an ISC shuttle on the only stretch of tarmac still in one piece. A rare breeze tugged our hair and cleared the mist. We had one of the few long lines of sight on Opalite, several hundred meters in every direction. Debris littered the shattered tarmacs like bits of a porcelain city smashed by a vengeful giant. Ruined buildings showed in the distance, evoking the jagged bones of giant skeletal fingers extended to the sky.

Hajune's emotions roiled. He rejoiced that he had Skyhold, and that ISC would protect Opalite. But remorse saturated his thoughts.

I drew him to one side, away from the others. "It never happened."

He touched his temple. "Know I that it did."

"Hajune Tailor." I tugged down his arm. "Grief can wring a good heart into hatred. Do not castigate yourself."

Although his strain didn't fade, he spoke kindly. "Go you well, Pharaoh Dyhianna. Go with grace."

My voice softened. "And you."

We rejoined the others then, and I said my good-byes. Then I boarded the shuttle with Vazar and the Jagernauts.

The time had come to learn what the Radiance War had cost my people.

BOOK TWO

Night of Strings

11
Nomads

Havyrl's Valor, a Firestorm battle cruiser, had been named for one of my many nephews, Havyrl Valdoria, another child of Eldrinson and my sister Roca. Eldrin had been their firstborn, Althor second, Havyrl fifth, Soz sixth, and Kelric tenth. Gods only knew what it had done to my sister and brother-in-law to lose so many of the children they loved above all else.

As our shuttle approached the cruiser, my memories continued to return and my anger to grow. The Assembly had gone to appalling lengths in making Eldrin become the Ruby consort. First they had drugged us. When that failed, they invoked an ancient law that required Ruby pharaohs to wed their kin. Still we refused. So they used other threats. Eldrin's parents became so incensed by the situation, they withdrew their support of the psiberweb.

The Assembly had negotiated but never relented. They finally imprisoned Eldrin, leaving him one choice: do what they wanted or live in solitude. It would have destroyed him. I could have kept fighting, but Eldrin would have suffered. And by then I had begun to love him. Like knew like. In the end their methods worked, because Eldrin and I cared more about what happened to each other than about wrestling with Assembly politics.

But their desperation still backfired. Yes, we soon had the first of the children they wanted. Taquinil. It was he who paid the harshest price.

The minds of Rhon psions differ greatly. My father-in-law had a deep, nuanced power, but also a subtlety that blunter minds within the Rhon lacked. That subtlety manifested in some of his children, including Eldrin. My own mind was delicacy rather than force, taken to the limit psions can tolerate before they become so sensitive they can no longer function. Or at least, we had thought my mind defined that limit.

Until Taquinil.

The Assembly claimed they chose Eldrin as the Ruby consort, rather than Kurj, because Kurj's blunt mental power would have harmed an empath of my sensitivity. Given that Kurj and I had worked together fine for decades, their reasoning was about as credible as saying people couldn't travel in spaceships because starship drives were dangerous. The concept of Kurj and I united had probably terrified the Assembly. The two of us already had influence; the Assembly didn't want it further concentrated in a marriage. In contrast, Eldrin was young and inexperienced, a farm boy lost in the intrigues of Imperialate politics. They thought it made him malleable.

Perhaps it did. But none of that mattered after Taquinil's birth. Our son inherited a heightened empathic capacity from both of us, with disastrous results. His ability ran so deep, he had no capability to block emotions. They poured into his young mind from a complex, often painful universe. Eldrin and I shielded him in his youth, but we couldn't protect him forever. When he left home, his shields shattered—and his mind splintered into many personalities.

Although it took years, Taquinil did reintegrate his mind. The doctors finally discovered a way to put a biomech web in his body that provided chemicals his brain lacked, the specialized neurotransmitters that let a normal empath "block" emotions. He eventually became an economics professor. People marveled at his genius and accomplishments, but few truly knew the magnitude of what he had achieved.

For years I had hated the Assembly for the hell my son suffered. But Taquinil has always been one of the great joys in my life. He and his father. Despite the anguish, I would never have given up the love we shared.

And now I had lost them both.

Havyrl's Valor rotated in space, majestic. The giant spoked cylinder resembled a space habitat. Seeing it, knowing that it symbolized my return to my people, home, and family, I wanted to jump up with anticipation. I couldn't of course; I had to act with the proper decorum. But joy spread through me like warmth from the sun.

After our shuttle docked in the central tube, we went through the usual decontamination chamber, floating in microgravity. Then Vazar and my bodyguards escorted me through a docking ring of the ship. It had a luminous quality, from the subtly glowing white walls of its corridor to the blue light-bars that ran along at waist height. I inhaled fresh, pure air. It had no scent I could discern, but it filled my lungs like a benediction.

We went to an elevator car that would carry us "down" a spoke to the main body of the cruiser. A group waited for us at the car. At first I saw only a cluster of officers in. Then we floated closer and I recognized the man in the blue admiral's uniform. He was average height for a Skolian, about six feet tall, with a shock of graying hair. His face had regular, chiseled features. I knew that visage well, so very well. Admiral Jon Casestar. A lump seemed to form in my throat and I wondered if I could speak.

As we came up to his group, the drawn lines of his face transformed into a subdued elation that caught me by surprise. Jon had never been one to show emotion, yet now he watched us with open welcome.

Holding a handgrip, Jon bowed from the waist. "I am at your service, Pharaoh Dyhianna." His voice was roughened with that rare, unexpected emotion.

I barely restrained my undignified urge to throw my arms around him. "It pleases me greatly to see you, Admiral." What an understatement.

He indicated the elevator. "Will you do me the honor of boarding my ship, Pharaoh?"

I smiled. "It would be my pleasure."

The elevator was large, which was good, because we had accumulated many people. As the car descended, our weight increased and a Coriolis force nudged us to the side. By the time we reached the "bottom" of the spoke, the gravity was almost human standard. After so long on Opalite, I felt heavy. Disoriented. I had to recalibrate the way I moved. When the elevator door slid open, I paused, readjusting. Everyone waited.

Painfully aware of them all watching, I walked forward. It unsettled me to have an audience. On the Orbiter I tended to stay isolated. With virtual reality, psiber communications, and holo-projections so common now, it was possible even to attend Assembly sessions on the planet Parthonia without ever leaving the Orbiter. My Evolving Intelligence computer programs dealt with the flood of web messages I received. I spent days at a time in the web and had gone for months without seeing anyone in person except my husband.

The Evolving Intelligences, or EIs, were descendants of AIs, also called McCarthy machines for the genius who coined the term artificial intelligence in Earth's twentieth century. Kurj had once told me that some Assembly councilors wondered if I had died and my EI personas just kept simulating me. The rumor tickled my fancy. In part, I avoided people because my mind was too sensitized to emotions. But the main reason I evaded the Assembly was because I was tired of them trying to control my life.

Strong emotions stirred in the people around me: joy, wonder, relief. I appreciated their welcome, but their awe disconcerted me. The Assembly had long claimed the Ruby Dynasty served as symbols, that the titular nature of our positions was offset by the hope we gave the people of Skolia. I had always taken that with a dose of cynicism, knowing they hoped such words would convince us to quit fighting them. But at times like this I wondered. It was also humbling to remember that if I slipped up, all Skolia would know.

A Firestorm battle cruiser was a starfaring metropolis. We followed silver paths through a city of coppery and gold buildings. On a bronzed balcony circling a distant sky needle, armed guards paced. A magtrain hummed on a glowing rail that curved over the buildings.

As we walked, Jon spoke quietly. "Your appearance will encourage our crew. We have had a problem with morale."

"Here on the cruiser?" I asked. "Or more generally?"

"Everywhere. The war created chaos." He paused, the

length of his silence revealing his disquiet. Then he said, "We still don't know why the web collapsed. And we lost the Third Lock."

Foreboding rose in me. I had thought perhaps Taquinil and I had caused the collapse when we went into psiberspace, but the Traders could have done it by trying to use the Third Lock. It took a Rhon psion to create and maintain a psiberweb. We were Keys for the Locks. If the Traders had tried it with telops less powerful than the Rhon, it could have wreaked havoc and killed the telops.

Now they had both a Lock and Eldrin. They could build their own web.

Damn.

The Locks were our history. Six thousand years ago a race of beings had moved Stone Age humans from Earth to the planet Raylicon, then vanished. The bewildered humans developed star travel and built the Ruby Empire. But it collapsed, followed by five millennia of dark ages. When the Raylican people, my ancestors, finally returned to the stars, they found ruins of the Ruby Empire, including the Locks. Those machines baffled our scientists. The ancients had mixed mysticism, science, and mathematics in ways we had yet to unravel. This much we knew: the Locks were portals into Kyle space. Three survived: one in the Orbiter, which we had found abandoned in space; a second in ruins on Raylicon; and a third as a small space station. To protect the Third Lock, ISC had created Onyx Platform, a city of space habitats. But something happened during the war, I didn't know what, only that the Traders captured the Third Lock. They used it to locate the elusive First Lock on the Orbiter, my home. Then they sent commandos after my family.

"What happened to Onyx Platform?" I asked.

"We lost all twenty-three space habitats." Jon cracked his knuckles, one of his rare mannerisms that revealed tension. He wasn't truly a granite monolith; he just kept his emotions to himself. "Admiral Tahota was in command. She and her volunteers rigged antimatter fuel containers throughout the stations. Seven billion bottles."

"Rigged? You mean they fixed the bottles to go unstable?"

Jon nodded. "When the Traders converged on Onyx, the bottles collapsed—and dumped seven hundred billion kilograms of antimatter plasma." He regarded me steadily. "It blew the entire complex."

His words felt like a punch to the stomach. "Two *billion* people lived at Onyx."

"Tahota evacuated them. Refugees from Onyx are pouring into settlements all over space." Grim satisfaction showed on his face. "Tahota and her volunteers didn't die in vain, Your Highness. To break Onyx, the Traders had to send the bulk of their fleet. When Onyx blew, it took the entire invasion force. It broke the Trader military. Pulverized it."

I absorbed that. Tahota had been one of Kurj's top officers and closest friends. If anyone could successfully evacuate Onyx during a battle, it was she. But losing her was another blow. I grasped at a shred of hope. "Are you sure the Traders have the Third Lock? Maybe it was destroyed too."

A shadow came over his face. "Tahota had to let it go. The evacuation hadn't yet finished."

I tried to hold in my disappointment. "How could the Traders miss seven billion bottles collapsing at the same time?" The "bottles" were actually containment fields. The invaders should have detected that many of them going unstable.

The corner of his mouth quirked up, which for him was a sign of great approval. "Tahota used the same trick the Radiance Fleet used to hide its ships. Her people hid the unstable bottles in stable ones."

Memories sparked in my mind: the fuel bottle trick had been Soz's idea. Jon Casestar had headed the project. If we could store antimatter fuel in containment fields that twisted out of this universe, why not ships? It had taken several years to make it work, but in the end they had succeeded. That was now the Radiance Fleet penetrated Trader space; most of its ships were hidden in giant fuel bottles. It was also why our bluff at Opalite worked; the Traders knew we could hide ships.

"What happened with the Radiance Fleet?" I asked.

His expression lightened. The change wouldn't have been much for most people, but for him it made a notable difference. "The invasion destroyed the Trader capital, Your Highness. We crippled their government. Even worse—for them—their emperor died without an heir."

My pulse leapt. Worse, indeed. The Trader emperor served a more important role to his people than the Ruby Dynasty did to ours. For one thing, he actually ruled. No elected Assembly for them; they found the concept ludicrous. They had a caste structure even within their aristocracy. The Aristos considered their emperor the embodiment of their supposed superiority. Without him or his heir, they lost not only their leader, but the symbol that defined their identity. Well, good. It would weaken them.

However, I could tell Jon had left out something. I considered him. "If the Trader government and military is in such trouble, why don't we finish what we started and liberate the worlds they've conquered?" It would free trillions of slaves. We couldn't offer them better lives in a material sense; they already enjoyed prosperity. It was how the Aristos kept so many people subjugated. But we could give them freedom.

Jon cleared his throat. "We have a problem."

"Yes?"

"We lost most of the Radiance Fleet."

I stared at him. "That included almost *all* of our forces."

"Yes." He didn't try to soft-pedal it. "We don't have the military strength to overthrow them. Nor do they have the strength to conquer us."

A stalemate. Wars weren't supposed to end that way. "I suppose they claim they won."

"Of course. As do we." He walked with his hands clasped behind his back, his face drawn. "The truth? I think they're exhausted. No one wants more fighting. But now that they have a Lock and Key, they won't stop."

I suddenly wanted to sit down. "That means we're going to war again."

"Whenever they get organized." He sounded drained. "Your death was the final blow. The morale of our people went so low that some groups began talking about surrender to the Traders." An uncharacteristic bitterness edged his voice. "*Surrender.* After we have fought for centuries to remain free."

"But I'm not dead."

He actually cracked a smile. "You must speak to the people."

"Yes. Of course." The thought unsettled me. I hadn't spoken in public for decades. The Assembly encouraged my solitude. It made me easier to guard. But I had to find words of hope for my people. We could never give in to the Traders. How we would stand against them, I had no idea yet, but we would find a solution.

Somehow.

We stopped at the wide door to the operations bay. Jon Casestar wore his dress uniform, with medals agleam on his chest in red, gold, purple, and white, all bright against the dark blue of his well-pressed tunic. His dark trousers had a holographic stripe of electric blue down the outer seam of each leg. Eight Jagernauts in black dress leathers surrounded us. Vazar stood at my side, a Jagernaut Primary, her rank equivalent to admiral, indicated by the narrow gold holostripe on each leg of her black trousers and around each of her biceps. Her black knee-boots reflected light in their polished surfaces.

When Jon raised his hand, sensors in the door responded and it rolled upward like a great, corrugated scroll made from metal. The entrance was three times my height and wide enough for six people to walk through abreast. My stomach felt as if the proverbial shimmerflies were fluttering there.

Four Jagernauts went in first. Then Jon and Vazar entered. I heard no sound from the bay except the muted, ever-present hum of the ship. Nothing else gave any clue that a major control center lay beyond that entrance. EI brains could run most of this cruiser, but it still needed a human crew. For all that the presence of other minds pressed on mine, I heard no voices. It was as if whoever waited beyond held their breath.

The silence unsettled me. I pulled at the sleeves of my jumpsuit, straightening nonexistent wrinkles. It was made from emerald-green cloth, with a high neck and long sleeves. The belted suit had no other ornamentation except the Imperialate insignia on my right shoulder, a gold sun exploding past a black triangle, all set within a red circle.

Vazar and Jon stopped at the edge of the observation platform, which was bordered by a waist-high rail. The bay below could hold hundreds of people, but from here I could see no one. Jon spoke to the assembled crew, his voice assured. I couldn't discern the words. Then he turned and beckoned me.

My mouth felt dry. I walked forward, aware of the Jagernauts coming with me. As I approached the edge of the platform, Jon and Vazar moved apart, taking positions to either side. I restrained the urge to wipe my sweating palms on my jumpsuit and instead set my hands on the rail. I could see the bay below now. People stood everywhere: by consoles, in aisles on the Luminex floor, even in the circular cars at the ends of giant robot arms that could move anywhere within the bay but right now hung suspended in the air. A swell of emotions washed over me, muted by the natural mental barriers people raised regardless of whether or not they were psions. Uncertain, afraid to hope, unable to recognize me—they didn't know what to think.

Jon said, simply, "The Ruby Pharaoh."

Opalescent globes rotating in the air above us picked up his words and sent them to other globes spinning above the bay. Their colors swirled as they transmitted his voice. No one moved. No one spoke. No one even coughed or cleared their throat. They simply watched me. Their moods blended into a haze; I couldn't discern individual responses. All I knew was that this didn't feel right.

I ran my hand along the rail until I found its latch and clicked it open. As the rail retracted to the side, white steps formed in front of me, leading from the platform down into the bay.

Jon glanced at me, alarm sparking in his thoughts.

Let me do this, I thought, even knowing he couldn't pick it up. Although he wasn't a psion, he had good intuition about people.

After a pause, he gave a slight nod. Then he motioned the Jagernauts forward. Four of them descended the steps, walking with a steady tread. I followed, taking the stairs slow so I could look out at the crew that served this great city in space. Light filled the bay from the Luminex walls. Accents of color showed everywhere, the holos of people put up to remind them of the worlds they called home, green forests and russet plains, seas wild and frothy, splashes of red blossoms or bright purple birds.

They all watched me descend. At the bottom, I started to walk forward. I passed a woman on the right—and she moved with fluid grace, going down on one knee. She bent her head and rested her arm across her thigh.

Caught off guard, I stopped. But the crew didn't. Like a wave swelling through the bay, they knelt, one after another, their heads bent, their gazes averted. Their emotions surged, easier to read now. Hope. I gave them hope.

It humbled me.

"Stand, my people." My voice had the throaty quality it took on when I felt self-conscious. The spinning globes sent my words through the bay and the crew rose to their feet, still watching, waiting for me to continue.

"I am glad to see you all," I said. It was hardly the most dramatic opening, but I had never liked pomp. Besides, it was true. "It gratifies me to see you stand tall. We of Skolia have thrived for six thousand years. We will continue for many more millennia. But today we begin a new era. Let us enter it with new energy, determination, and hope." My lips quirked up. "We're a tenacious bunch, we Skolians. We come from almost every background you can imagine, but we have one thing in common. We never give up. We've triumphed over time, space—and Traders. And we will again."

Their mood was lightening, giving way to cautious optimism, at least for now. Apparently Jon was right; this was what they needed to hear, reassurance from a pharaoh who lived when all had thought she died. So I continued to talk. If

it would help morale, I would do my best to provide inspira-
tion.

I just wished I felt it myself.

Alone, in the dim light of my suite, I reran the news holo.
Again. I sat slouched in a softseat that molded to my every
move, trying to relieve my rigid posture. It did no good. I
played that holo again and again, and as I watched it, I died
inside.

The broadcast showed Corbal Xir, an Aristo with great
power. His mother had been a sister of the first emperor. At
132, Xir was the oldest Trader. His hair had turned white. He
wasn't the oldest living human; that honor went to my ex-
husband, Seth Rockworth, who had reached 176. At 158, I
was the eldest Skolian. But Xir had stopped seeming young
to me long ago. He knew firsthand the never-ending strain of
this conflict that wore us down decade after decade. He was
also the Aristo closest to the Carnelian Throne. Since Jabriol
II had left no heir, Corbal Xir was next in line to become
emperor.

In the holo, Xir stood in the Hall of Circles, the audience
hall in the emperor's palace. The circular chamber had survived the Radiance Fleet invasion, but a great crack ran from
floor to ceiling in its snow-marble walls. Xir towered on the
center dais next to the Carnelian Throne, a chair made from
snow marble, inset with glittering blood-red gems. Rows of
diamond benches ringed the dais with rubies on their high
backs. Aristos sat on those benches, rank upon rank of icy
human perfection. They looked unreal, every one with glistening black hair, ruby-red eyes, and snow-marble skin.
Watching them made my skin crawl. They sat in silent triumph while Xir spoke.

I didn't listen to his grandiose propaganda. I barely looked
at him. I saw only one person—the man who stood next to
Xir. At six-foot-one, he was half a head shorter than the
Aristo lord. Wine-red hair was tousled around his handsome,
haggard face, and dark circles showed under his eyes. The
ripped sleeve of his white shirt revealed bruised skin. His

arms were bound behind his back and a diamond slave collar glittered around his neck.

I knew that shirt. He had been wearing it the last time I saw him.

I knew that man.

It was Eldrin.

My husband.

12

Orbitals

Sleep evaded me like a skulking thief. Every time I dozed, my fears for Eldrin haunted my dreams. I thrashed around until the covers tangled my legs together. The air-bed adjusted to my every move, trying to soothe, but I still felt as if I were sleeping on rocks. Even the satiny sheets offered no comfort.

Finally I flopped onto my back and lay with my arm across my forehead, staring at the ceiling. The only light in the room came from holo panels on the walls. I had set them to show starscapes of nebulas that graced interstellar space like crowns studded with jeweled stars. But tonight those spectacular views only seemed cold.

After a while, I got up and wandered into the living room. I felt the suite's EI turn up the heat, probably to account for my wearing only a sleep shirt. The flimsy material drifted around my body, shifting in the cool air. Dim light from the bedroom filtered through the archway, turning everything a ghostly blue. No sound stirred the night except the distant hum of the ship that always lingered at the edges of my mind.

The pseudogravity from the ship's rotation pulled at me. My weight felt like my thoughts: too heavy. I needed to act, to help Eldrin, to descend on the Traders with guns blazing and bombs exploding. Except Soz had already done that. And died.

Damn it all. Soz should have *waited*. I could have found a solution. Before all this happened, I had been trying to predict the outcome of the war. I had modeled possible scenarios, estimated their chance of occurring, and then used the results to fine-tune the models, hoping to converge on a probable scenario. The more data I had, the better my predictions. I was always adding information, everything from big events to tiny details. You never knew when seemingly unconnected facts or contemplations would cause unexpected correlations.

Ideally, the models would converge on one scenario. But

they never did. The best I could do was estimate a range of vague futures. The further ahead in time I took a model, the more it blurred. Most gave nonsensical results. A few patterns had emerged over time, but Soz's death hadn't been one of them. Some models predicted Eldrinson and Roca would become captives—but not of the Traders.

In others Taquinil died. I hated those models.

Taquinil. Standing in the middle of the room, I closed my eyes and put my face in my hands. If only I could find a prediction that would give me hope. *Try.* I focused my mind and updated my models of Taquinil with everything that had happened since I last saw him. Within moments, I had a new prediction: Taquinil simultaneously existed and didn't exist.

Well, great. That helped. Disheartened, I opened my eyes and lowered my arms. I probably hadn't recovered all the data in my neural nodes yet. The prediction might be nonsense. But I couldn't be *sure*. That was the hardest part, never knowing for certain.

Taquinil? I thought. *Can you reach me?*

An odd sensation came to me, as if a hand brushed my mind. Had the wall across the room rippled? I rubbed my eyes and discovered I was smearing tears across my face. All the equations in the universe couldn't take away the pain of all these losses.

Longing for hope, I started the models evolving again. But every time I tried to see Taquinil's future, other impressions interfered. A vague sense of my ex-husband, Seth Rockworth, kept coming up. I failed to see why, after my decades of contentment with Eldrin, I would predict a Rockworth in our future. Seth and I had never been compatible. Yet these models kept coming back to him.

I let out a long, slow breath. I didn't have enough data to make any definitive predictions. I needed information.

I went to the console by the wall. Its chair molded to my body, pushing my back into good posture, straight instead of slouching. Then I went to work. After so long, it felt odd to look up Seth on the webs. I couldn't help but be curious; I hadn't heard news of him for years. It no longer hurt to think about him; time had eroded the sharp edges of those memories, shading them in softer colors.

The ship's public databases had almost nothing on Seth. So I hacked the secured accounts in the ISC intelligence network onboard. They had a whole dossier on him. ISC used spy programs to monitor the interstellar webs, keeping track of anyone they thought might be of interest, which certainly included William Seth Rockworth III, Allied admiral and former Ruby consort.

Seth still lived in the Appalachian Mountains. He had retired after a long career in the navy and now spent his days reading and gardening. His second wife had passed away fifteen years ago. He had six children, many grandchildren, great-grandchildren, and more, a huge extended family. He also worked with refugees, finding homes for children orphaned in the war. He had taken four into his home and given them his last name: Jay, Lisa, Peter, and Kelly Rockworth.

His refugee work didn't surprise me. Beneath his brash exterior, he had always had a tender heart. His foster children had a Skolian mother and Trader father, both lost in the war. If they went to their Trader relatives, they would become slaves. The Skolians didn't want them. Apparently an Allied relief agency had sent them to Earth.

It took awhile, but I finally located a holo of Seth standing with the children. His appearance startled me. Gray streaked his black hair, lines showed around his eyes and mouth, and he had gained weight. Even so, he still looked like the dashing naval captain I had fallen for all those decades ago.

The foster children were striking. The oldest boy was about sixteen. He had black hair and brown eyes and stood about six-feet-two, with a gangly frame that would fill out into a well-built physique. He was grinning at a toddler he held in his arms, an angelic boy with yellow hair. A girl of about thirteen stood next to them, a beauty, but with odd hair, blond, lavender, and black mixed together. A dark-haired boy of about nine stood in front of them, laughing at whoever was taking the holo.

Despite the obvious good nature of the people in that image, a chill went up my neck. I couldn't mistake the oldest boy's heritage. Aristo. It showed in the classic planes of his face, the high cheekbones, even the way he held himself. I shuddered, wanting to turn off the holo. But he wasn't pure Aristo, not with brown eyes and normal hair. He might have disguised his appearance, but I couldn't imagine Seth taking in an Aristo youth. More likely, one of the boy's progenitors had been an Aristo who had children with a pleasure slave. It was hard to tell with the other children, but they had enough resemblance to one another that they could be related.

That boy, the oldest. What about him caught my attention?

I evolved new models in my mind, trying to explain the children. For some strange reason, a sense of Eldrinson and Soz kept coming up. Odd. The same thing had happened when I had tried to predict outcomes of the Radiance War. I had told Eldrinson, but he could see no reason why he should come up so much. Soz had said the same. Or so they claimed. But they protected their minds with Rhon barriers. I had kept at them about it, until finally Eldrinson told me this: *Put Jaibriol Qox in your equations. Gently.*

That had been the last time I had seen him; it had been only moments before he and Roca had left for Earth.

Well, so. I had already put Jaibriol II in my equations. He was the Trader emperor, after all. He had to be there. But *gently*? Aristos tortured people. I had tried the suggestion anyway, using gentler aspects of the emperor, but the models still hadn't converged. Not then.

What about now?

I added my recent experiences to those models. New patterns began to develop in my mind. Viquara Iquar suddenly appeared. Jaibriol II's mother. She had died in the war, along with her consort, Kryx Quaelen. As the Minister of Trade, Quaelen had wielded a great influence. Some claimed he and Viquara were the true powers behind the throne.

So what did I have? A lot of very powerful, very dead people. Viquara. Quaelen. Jaibriol II. Soz. Althor. What the hell had five major interstellar leaders been doing in the middle of battle? It was crazy.

Even more bizarre, my models suggested these people had some connection to those four refugee children on Earth. Why?

I mulled over possible scenarios. Before Viquara had wed Kryx Quaelen, she had been married to the Trader emperor. He too had died without an heir. Since Viquara had no claim to the throne through blood, it left her marginalized, without power. Then she conveniently produced Jaibriol II, her son, whom everyone thought had been dead for seventeen years. Genetic testing had proved that yes, he was indeed the emperor's son. Apparently they had hidden him away to protect him from assassination. And now, guess what? Here we had a sixteen-year-old-boy with Aristo heritage hidden on Earth.

If that boy was Viquara's son or grandson, what the blazes would Seth be doing with him? And then we had Kryx Quaelen. As Trade Minister he traveled extensively and had probably fathered many children. That didn't explain why Soz kept coming up in my models. Well. So. She had been in exile for seventeen years, pursuing Jaibriol on some planet. We had only her word that she never found him. Could *they* have had children? Gods, what an atrocious prospect. I didn't even want to think about the implications.

It all held a grim fascination, like watching a disaster in slow motion. I ran an analysis on Seth's foster family, asking for a comparison of their appearance with holos of Jaibriol, Viquara, Kryx, Soz, Eldrinson, and Seth.

The results came back fast: *secured.*

Secured? What the hell?

It took me another hour to unravel the tangle of safeguards that blocked my investigation. The security programs were disguised, invisible to anyone with less experience in the webs than myself, which meant most everyone alive. Whoever had hidden them was an expert, someone with close to my ability in unraveling such systems and probably more military knowledge. That meant either Soz or Kelric. Althor had the military experience, but he didn't have that extra flash of brilliance Soz and Kelric possessed. Given that Kelric was dead, that left Soz.

The computer finally gave me the analysis: it was within the realm of possibility that Seth's foster children were offspring of Eldrinson, Soz, Kryx, or Jaibriol. It also gave me a long list of other possible parents, some far more probable than the four on my original list. Neither Seth nor Viquara appeared on either list. Seth's absence made sense; his only relation to the Ruby Dynasty was through marriage. But Viquara was Jaibriol's mother. If he appeared, she ought to be a candidate as well.

I rubbed my chin, baffled. Then I reviewed what I knew. Eighteen years ago ISC had captured Jaibriol II. He escaped and Soz went after him. ISC found the debris of their ships. Two empires grieved for their deaths. No one knew their lifeboats had crashed on a world with no human settlements. They came down on different continents. Survival had been a struggle. Soz searched for Jaibriol, but a world is a big place. Viquara's people found him first, many years later. The sensors that had survived the crash of Soz's lifeboat warned her when the Trader ships came. She found their landing site after they left. Using a transmitter they discarded, she called for help. Then she came home—and went after the Traders with a vengeance.

So. Soz and Jaibriol. Two people stranded for years on a planet with no other humans. Circumstances push them together. They have children. The idea of Soz bearing an Aristo's children seemed as likely as Soz growing a second head, but I couldn't ignore it. Had Qox forced her? I remembered her brooding, fierce moods. Pride could have kept her silent; as Imperator, she would never want it known she had borne Jaibriol Qox's children. It could be explosive. I couldn't imagine Soz abandoning her children, not even if an Aristo had sired them, but she might take them to Seth.

I just didn't see how Jaibriol could force her. It fit no profile I had of Soz's behavior. With her military training, she could have flattened him. The only way she would sleep with him was of her own free will. Gods. What a disagreeable thought. The computer spewed error messages everywhere, more from my outrage than from the prediction.

Maybe Eldrinson had fathered the children with an Aristo woman. Taking them to Seth would make sense if Eldrinson had custody, though how he would have managed that I had no idea. Nor could I imagine him cheating on Roca. Could an Aristo woman have forced him? Possibly. Methods existed. Jaibriol II had briefly held Eldrinson hostage during his escape from ISC eighteen years ago. Hah! Maybe Jaibriol was female. Stranger things had happened. Hell, he could be both male and female.

"Ach." I pushed my hand through my hair. This was getting me nowhere.

A bell chimed. Then the EI said, "You have a visitor. Vazar Majda."

I stretched my arms, working out the kinks. "All right. Let her in."

A graceful horseshoe arch separated my bedroom from the main room of the suite, an unexpected touch of elegance on the battle cruiser. I went through it and found Vazar standing in the living room, surrounded by blue furniture and white walls with floor-to-ceiling holo-panels of radiant nebulae, the fiery nurseries for newly born stars.

"My greetings, Dehya." Against the glittering backdrop, she looked like a warrior goddess of the stars. She wore her regular uniform now, snug black leather studded by silver clasps and picotech conduits. It did nothing to disguise her spectacular figure, which before her marriage had inspired amorous pursuit from numerous men, and some women too. She had the classic black eyes and aquiline nose of Majda. Her glossy dark hair tousled around her shoulders. She had been the perfect choice for Althor's wife, cementing ties between the Ruby Dynasty and House of Majda. Never mind that both she and Althor were actually in love with Coop, their co-husband, a commoner totally unacceptable to the nobility, a lithe blond artist whose angelic beauty left even me breathless.

Vazar put one hand on her hip and regarded me curiously. "Are you going to stare at me all night?"

"Heya, Vaz." I rubbed my hands along my arms, self-conscious in my sleep shift with a fully battle-ready Jagernaut looming in my rooms. Vazar came unarmed of course, but she was a weapon herself, her body enhanced and augmented into a versatile killing machine.

"How are you?" I asked. Her face looked drawn.

She grimaced as if I had asked about hostile troop deployments. "I can't sleep."

I motioned her to a couch against one wall, its blue aircushions strewn with white silken pillows. "Please. Be comfortable."

"Comfortable?" She snorted. "Whenever I'm in your rooms, I feel like I'm going to break something." But she went over and sat, her black uniform a dramatic contrast to the pale blue sofa, her long legs stretched out across my white carpet, her heavy boots digging trenches in the pile.

I crossed the room to a crystal cabinet. "Would you like a drink?"

"If it has some life to it."

I pulled out a bottle that read *Blazer's Starland Ambrosia.* I had never tried it, but I had heard Blazer's Starland was some sort of rowdy amusement-park-cum-space-station. I poured us each a drink, then went over and sat on the sofa. As Vazar took her glass, I tipped my crystal tumbler to my lips and swallowed. The liquid went down my throat as smooth as velvet, caressing my throat.

Then it detonated.

"Good gods!" I gasped, my eyes watering. "What *is* that?"

Vazar downed hers in one swallow. She lowered her glass and made a semi-approving noise. "Not bad."

I blinked at her empty glass. "How do you do that?"

She leaned back on the sofa and stared at the opposite wall. "It's nothing."

"Vaz." I watched her closely. She looked like hell. From experience, I knew she would evade questions about herself, so I used a roundabout approach. "How is Coop?"

"I don't know." She shifted restlessly. "I haven't been able to get a message through to the Orbiter since the war." Vazar suddenly pushed to her feet and strode to the cabinet. She came back with the bottle of Blazer's rocket fuel. When she dropped down onto the sofa, the cushions sunk under her weight. Then she poured herself another glass and handed me the bottle. "It's all yours, Pharaoh."

I watched her drain her glass. She clenched it so tightly, her knuckles had turned white. I gently pried the tumbler out of her fist. Her fingers felt like steel cords. Then I set the glass on the floor and put the bottle of "ambrosia" next to it.

She glared at me. "What did you do that for?"

I spoke softly. "The hurt will still be there tomorrow. You'll just have it with a hangover."

For a moment she simply looked at me, as if she hadn't decided whether to explode or pour herself another drink. Then she sat forward, planted her booted feet wide, rested her elbows on her knees, and leaned her head in her hands. She spoke to the floor. "It's flaming fucked."

"At least it's over for Althor. No more pain."

Vazar lowered her arms so her hands were hanging between her knees. She regarded me with a bleak gaze. "ISC fixes our brains so that interrogation disrupts our neural activity. It's like pressing the delete key. Zap. No more memory. Althor also had his mind set so he couldn't speak about Coop, me, and Ryder."

It didn't surprise me. Vazar and Althor had been friends for decades. They had both wanted Coop. So they had all married. Although I had never fathomed their three-way marriage, I knew Althor would have done anything for them. I hadn't thought Coop had any interest in women, but thirteen years ago Vazar had borne him a child, a boy called Ryder Jalam Majda.

"Althor wanted to protect you all," I said gently.

"I know." She poured herself more Blazer's. "But in the end he probably didn't even remember us."

I touched her arm. "Jon Casestar tells me the evacuation of Onyx Platform succeeded."

Vazar stared into her glass. "Hell of a job."

I watched her vanquish her drink in one long gulp. "The Traders didn't know enough about the Onyx perimeter defenses to stop the evacuation. Two billion people escaped."

"That's right." She frowned at her empty glass.

"Vaz." I leaned forward, trying to get through to her. "Althor set up the Onyx system. If he had broken under interrogation, the Traders would have known our defenses well enough to stop the evacuation." I spoke quietly. "Your husband saved two billion people. He's a war hero."

She fixed me with a stare. "I know what you're doing. It doesn't make him any less dead." After a pause, she added, "But thank you."

I wondered if Eldrin wished he were dead now. Would he forget Taquinil and me? His absence left a vacuum. We had been married for fifty-seven years. On the day Eldrin and I wed, Coop hadn't even been born. Even now, at thirty-eight, Coop looked like a boy. Vazar could pass for thirty, though she was actually in her mid-sixties. The same had been true for Althor, who would have been almost seventy now.

I spoke tiredly. "We're too old." Taking a swallow of my drink, I gulped as its warmth exploded through me. "It doesn't matter how young we look. We've lost the edge of youth."

"Youth is a waste of time," Vazar muttered. "Overrated. When I was young, I was wild and confused."

I smiled. "Now you're wild and opinionated."

She slanted me a wry look. "You sound like my cousin."

By "cousin," I knew she meant General Naaj Majda, Matriarch of the House of Majda. Naaj had a great deal of power. Too much. "Jon Casestar tells me Naaj has taken over the duties of the Imperator." It meant she commanded ISC.

Vazar regarded me uneasily. "You going to throw her in the brig?"

"Now why would I do that?" I asked dryly.

Vazar just said, "Hereditary." We both knew the title of Imperator went only to the Ruby Dynasty.

"A hereditary position with no heirs," I said.

She spoke carefully. "Six of your sister's children are still alive."

"So they are." Vazar was well aware that none of them had the training to lead ISC. Most had never even left their rural home on the planet Lyshriol. Roca would be a better choice for Imperator. Although she was a diplomat rather than a military officer, she had extensive experience with the power structure of Skolia. But no one was going to inherit anything unless they had the freedom to assume that title. And Roca didn't right now.

I set my glass on the ground. "What is this business about Earth refusing to let Eldrinson and Roca go?"

Surprise flickered on her face. "Jon already briefed you?"

I hadn't needed a briefing. My models had predicted their captivity. I just wished I had been wrong. As provided for in the Iceland Treaty, we had sent them to Earth for safety during the war, not only Roca and Eldrinson, but also Kurj's widow, Ami, and her little boy Kurjson. The Allieds had also provided military forces to support ISC in safeguarding the planet Lyshriol, where Roca and Eldrinson had raised their family and where their surviving children still lived.

"I don't know the details," I said. "What happened?"

She picked up the bottle. "Naaj contacted the Allieds to arrange passage home for your family. Earth refused."

"They can't do that."

"No? Well, the vermin-infested fu—"

"Vaz." Noble birth or no, she could swear worse than the proverbial star-sailor when she got going.

"Sorry." Then she poured more whiskey. "The Allieds are keeping them in 'protective custody.' "

"With what justification?"

"They're afraid that if they release your family, you all will build a new psiberweb and restart the war." She drank her Blazer's, but she didn't down it all at once this time. "I believe their comment was, 'The Skolian Imperialate and Trader Empire will destroy human civilization just as they did five thousand years ago.' " She grunted. "Damn Allieds."

Unfortunately, they had a point. But they had missed one "slight" flaw in their argument. "If the Traders build a psiberweb and we can't, we'll all be fodder for their war machine. Including the Allieds."

"Actually, Earth's leaders made that charming comment about us destroying civilization before the Traders broadcast that holo with your husband in slave restraints."

I tried not to think of the holo, but my heart lurched. "And now? Earth can't ignore the danger."

"They hope to negotiate with the Traders."

I stared at her. "Aristos don't *negotiate* with non-Aristos. They think we're dirt."

Her face took on a pensive cast. "Xir looked exhausted on that broadcast. And did you hear all the mistakes he made? He even referred to Lady Roca as your brother. Maybe they're as worn out as we are with this damnable war."

"Maybe." I held little hope for negotiations, but anything was worth a try. "If Earth won't let my family go, Naaj might take it as a hostile act." I could imagine how the hard-line, aristocratic general had taken their refusal. "It could start a war with the Allieds."

Vazar spoke flatly. "Another war will destroy us."

I crossed my arms and rubbed my palms up and down my bare arms. But nothing could warm my chill apprehension. Our future might depend on those four children on Earth. I could reveal my suspicion that they had a link to the Ruby and Qox Dynasties. As farfetched as it sounded, I could probably produce enough evidence to spur an investigation, not only using the lists of their potential parents, but also to ask why ISC's own computer system had covertly blocked my search. It would be interesting to hear ISC's take on that. I wasn't sure I wanted to play that hand, though, at least not yet.

I could just say my models kept converging on the children. ISC also ran models to predict the future, but theirs rarely agreed with mine. They hadn't been able to duplicate my thought processes even before I had neural enhancements. A general had once referred to my brain as an "invaluable interstellar resource." It made me feel strange, as if I were a stockpile rather than a person.

But I hesitated to mention the children. They might have no link to this—or they could be triggers that sent the precarious balance of interstellar power spiraling out of control. As long as a good chance existed that someone else could reach them first, I couldn't risk drawing attention to their existence. Gods only knew what could happen if the wrong people found them. The Traders had reached Jaibriol II first—and it had started the Radiance War, nearly destroying two empires.

Pain stabbed my temples. Wincing, I massaged my head. My mind had jumped into an accelerated mode. Normal brain cells worked much slower than computers. Our minds plodded while our machines whizzed. The nodes we put in our brains worked faster than unaided thought; in a sense, the human mind became a user on the implanted system. It could be unsettling, and difficult to learn, which was one reason not everyone chose to enhance their brains.

I had dealt with the problem in a unique manner, judged from the shock of the neurosurgeons who monitored my brain. I wasn't sure why they became so excited. All I did was have nanomeds in my body redesign my brain so my neurons became part of the implanted system. It accelerated my neural impulses. I thought faster. I didn't use that mode often, though; fiddling with my own brain chemistry gave me a headache. I had discovered the hard way that if I ignored the warning signs, I went into a coma.

According to my chronometer, only three seconds had passed since Vazar made her last comment. I considered her. "Do you know anything about Admiral Rockworth?"

She blinked at me. "What?"

"Seth Rockworth."

"When did we start talking about your ex?"

"I just wondered if you knew anything."

She took on the distant look she got when she accessed her mental files. "He's still on Earth, enjoying his retirement."

"Has he had any contact with the Ruby Dynasty recently?"

"None that I know of." Her focus returned to me. "Why the blazes do you care? He made his position clear when he walked out on you."

"Seth has been around Allied politics longer than anyone else alive. He might have ideas about how we could handle this situation without it blowing up." I could always send a proposal to Earth suggesting Seth and I negotiate. But that might still draw attention to the children.

Don't reveal them. That thought jumped out of the models evolving in my mind. The equations suddenly morphed into pictures, beautiful quantum orbitals. They spun lazily, globes circled by diffuse rings, pale blue, soft gold, the blush of a newly opened rose, the lavender of a desert sky at dawn, all as graceful as delicate ornaments bobbing in a breeze. Math functions. Spherical harmonics.

"Orbitals?" I said. "What the hell?"

Vazar quirked an eyebrow at me. "Orbitals? That makes perfect sense."

"No it doesn't." Why would thinking about Seth make me see mathematical functions? My mind drifted with the images. Spherical harmonics . . .

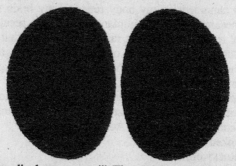

"—medical team now!" The man's voice cut the air in staccato bursts.

"What good will that do?" Vazar demanded. "She's not sick, she's translucent."

I squinted, trying to clear my blurred vision. Medics in gray jumpsuits surrounded the divan, all smelling of the antiseptic nanomeds doctors used to keep their offices sterile. Two were bending over me and several others were working on palmtops, monitoring me apparently, judged from the holos of my body that rotated above their units. They flicked their fingers through the holos, working with sharp, fast motions. One fellow's hand *was* the palmtop; his entire arm was cybernetic. Lights glinted in a circle around his wrist.

Vazar was no longer sitting next to me. She now stood a few steps away, glaring at a man in a green jumpsuit. His uniform identified him as a member of the medical corps in the Pharaoh's Army.

'What are you doing?' I asked the cluster of agitated medics. My words came out like leaves blowing over a distant plain. It didn't even sound as if I were in the room.

A tall man sat on the edge of the divan, leaving enough space so that he was in no danger of touching my body. "Pharaoh Dyhianna? Can you hear me?"

'Yes.' My voice drifted, star dust on an interstellar wind . . .

"Hey." Vazar stepped closer, nudging aside a medic. "Dehya? Are you solid again?"

Her vigorous presence pulled me back into reality, but it was like trying to find purchase on an oiled surface. Without my tenuous connection to her, I might completely disperse into psiberspace.

'Vaz . . . I'm going . . . ,' I whispered.

"Dehya!" She tried to grab my shoulders.

Her hands went through me.

"Don't touch her!" The medic's warning echoed in my ears. The scene smeared as if it were a reflection in a sheen of oil. Vazar's hands swirled, blending with my shoulder.

Dismayed, I tried to inhale. Air sifted through my body. I was a ghost, diaphanous, evaporating. If I became solid, Vazar's hands would be *inside* my body.

"Gods," someone whispered.

The blood drained from Vazar's face. My mind spread throughout the room; I felt her thoughts, knew the blood thundering in her veins, saw what she saw. My body had become almost transparent.

With infinite care, she withdrew her hands from my shoulders. My body rippled like the rings that spread on a lake after a leaf dropped onto its still surface—

Suddenly I snapped back. The room solidified with jarring speed. I slumped on the divan, gulping in air. "Ah . . ."

"Saints al-frigging-mighty." Vazar stared at me. "Dehya, are you all right?"

"I'm . . . fine." I felt as if I had been wrung through a starship drive nozzle.

"Pharaoh Dyhianna?" The medic at my side spoke. "We've never dealt with anything like this. Can you tell us what you're doing?"

Good question. "I'm not sure. I don't think medicine can help, though." I looked up at Vazar. "Your hands disrupted whatever was happening to me."

She paled. "I'm a jackabat on jigs."

I couldn't help but laugh. "What does that mean?"

"I can't say. You told me to clean up my language."

"Vaz, when you grabbed me, it pulled me back."

"It did?" She looked nonplussed.

Some of the medics made entries on palmtops, while others monitored my condition. The one with the cyber-arm was running a calculation that produced holos of my body rippling in the air. The sight made me queasy.

"It's about angular momentum wavefunction expansions," I told them.

"Oh. Well. In that case." Now Vazar sounded more like her usual self. "What the holy hack does 'angular momentum wavefunction expansions' mean?"

Farther back in the room, the medic in the green jumpsuit spoke in a low voice to a man who was studying his palmtop. "Is she going to live?"

The other man glanced up uneasily. "According to this, she was never dying. She just started to—thin out. Like ink diluting in water."

An odd comparison, but apt. "I was going into another reality," I called to them.

They looked around with a start. It seemed odd they wouldn't know I had augmented hearing. Any doctor assigned to my case should have seen my records. Then again, my hearing seemed even more heightened now than usual.

They came closer, joining the medics. The officer in green had a bar on his chest that gave his name as *Bayliron.* "I'm not sure what you mean," he said.

"Spherical harmonics." I rubbed my eyes. "Before Opalite, I was in a Hilbert space spanned by an infinite set of orthonormal angular momentum wavefunctions that used thought as coordinates rather than spatial rotations."

Bayliron rubbed the back of his neck. "Ah . . . spatial rotations."

I could tell he didn't know if I was serious or cracked. Security had cleared my medical team to know what happened, so I tried again. "When the Traders came after us, my husband pushed my son and me into the First Lock. The Lock is—basically it's a pole associated with different Riemann sheets. A branch cut joins the sheets. When Taquinil and I slid through the cut, it took us from this universe into psiberspace. I've only come out part way."

He still had that look. "Uh—part way?"

I searched for better words. "Not all the terms in my partial wave expansion have transformed. They're higher order, so they only contribute to fine details, which is why I look solid. But they're still part of my overall state. Right now, if I don't concentrate, I start to slip back into the Kyle universe. I need a psiberweb to stabilize my transformation so it can finish properly."

I stopped then, mainly because they were all staring as if I had said, "Floobergab miggledy bleck."

"Is it safe for us to examine you?" Bayliron asked.

The thought of being examined made me feel trapped. The concern of all these worried people gathered in one place thickened the air like invisible smoke, gritty against my skin. I needed air. "I will come to sick bay tomorrow."

He didn't look pleased. "Pharaoh Dyhianna—"

"Tomorrow," I said softly. Like most cruisers, this one kept a thirty hour "day."

He started to protest, but when I shook my head, he

stopped. After bowing from the waist, he said, "May you have a pleasant evening, Your Highness." Then he motioned to his people, and they all took their leave.

When we were alone, Vazar shook her head. "You should have let them stay. Admiral Casestar will give them grief."

I sank back into the sofa. The feel of the cushions scratching my skin came as a relief. I was solid. I could feel. "No doctor can cure what's wrong with me."

She sat next on the divan, making the cushions sink. "If you were in Kyle space, why didn't you die when it imploded?"

I wished I knew. Orbitals. They shimmered in my mind. What made me think of them? It had to be important, if it had almost pulled me out of this reality. We had been talking about the Lock. Seth Rockworth. The Allieds. My sister Roca. Her husband Eldrinson.

Orbitals.

I suddenly sat up straight. "Delos."

She blinked. "You survived the implosion of another universe because of a little island on Earth?"

I smiled. "No. We have to go there."

"We can't go to Earth. They'll put you in 'protective custody' too."

"Not that Delos. The planet named after it." Earth had declared Delos a neutral world. Sanctuary. They hoped that Skolians, Traders, and Allieds could meet there in harmony and build bridges among their peoples. It was an inspiring dream, but naïve.

She leaned back, her body turned toward me, one arm on the top of the sofa. "Why Delos? I would have thought you would want to go to a Lock."

"The Locks aren't secure." I rubbed my arms for warmth. "If I hook into one, the Traders might attack me through the one they stole."

"What if you had access to a Triad Command Chair?"

That gave me pause. Normally a Triad member could only use such a chair to operate a psiberweb that already existed. But my mind had been developing for more than a century and a half. I knew Kyle space like no one else. Hell, I had *been* Kyle space. I might be able to do more with the Triad Chair. If we could find one. A few ISC bases had them, and also several battle cruisers, though none of those I had access to now.

"It might help," I said thoughtfully. "But we have to go to Delos first."

She frowned. "How will going to Delos stop you from fading out?"

"It won't."

"Then why go?"

"I don't know," I admitted.

"If you convince Jon Casestar to do this, he will take our entire complement of ships. We also expect to rendezvous with an ISC Fleet Talon from Onyx. It will swell our ranks to several thousand. Moving that many warships to Delos will probably give their authorities collective heart failure." She tapped her long index finger on the top of the sofa. "We had better have a damn good reason."

"I've no desire to give the Allieds collective heart failure." That wasn't completely true, given that they were holding my family hostage. "But we still have to go."

Vazar frowned, somehow making it look regal. She had always been a contradictory mix of aristocrat and hard-living warrior. "Before we take such a large fleet to an Allied world, we will have to notify Naaj."

The last person I wanted to notify was the Majda Matriarch, who had taken the title of Imperator that rightfully belonged in my family. Even worse, she might have enough support within ISC to keep the title. I wondered where Vazar came down on that issue. Majda by blood and Ruby Dynasty by marriage, she could throw her support either way.

I spoke carefully. "We have no web communications. The only way we could inform Naaj would be to send a starship to ISC headquarters. It could take days or even weeks for them to send back an answer."

Vazar considered me. "Jon can make the decision on his own. But for something this big he'll need to justify it. You must have some idea why you think it's important."

"Orbitals."

She made an exasperated noise. "I don't know a kiss in a quasar about your orbitals."

"Yes, you do. You studied quantum theory in school."

"Believe me, Dehya, it's not the way you do it."

"In Kyle space, Taquinil and I became spherical harmonics. How does that connect to Delos?" I spread my hands out, palms up. "He and I are incomplete now. Delos has an answer. I can't define it more clearly even for myself. But we must go there. As fast as possible."

"How can you be sure if you don't understand why you want to go?"

"Calculations."

"What calculations?"

I waved my hand absently. "In my head."

She sighed. "Has anyone ever told you how strange you sound sometimes?"

My mouth quirked up. "You do, periodically."

"The hell of it is, you're usually right."

"I could use your support with Jon."

She lifted her hands in surrender. "All right. I'll talk to him."

13
Primary Inversions

Delos Space Command was not happy.

"We welcome vessels of all worlds." Colonel Yamada's voice crackled over the comm. "However, Admiral Casestar, you have more than a 'few' ships in orbit around Delos."

"Two thousand four hundred and sixty-three," Jon said. He was sitting in a control chair at the end of a robot arm in the center of the bridge. About half a kilometer across, the hemispherical bridge capped the cylinder that formed the main body of the cruiser. Layers of armaments and defensive shields protected it. Consoles studded the inner surface and crew members worked everywhere, some upside down far "above" us, some sideways to the left and right, and others right-side up "beneath" us.

I floated by his chair, holding a cable that stretched to its back. Here in the center of the bridge, we had no gravity even when the hemisphere rotated. Only Jon was visible to Yamada; I remained completely out of sight and sound.

Colonel Yamada was speaking. "What is your intent?"

"Most of my ships are survivors from the war," Jon explained. "I was hoping to give my people a rest, but I realize we can't send down millions at once. Would it be possible to arrange for them to visit in shifts?"

"You're requesting *shore* leave?" Yamada made no attempt to hide his incredulity.

"That is correct," Jon said. He even kept a straight face.

I listened while they hammered out details. Delos was a crux of some kind and I needed time to figure out why. Yamada obviously didn't believe we had brought an entire fleet here for a vacation. He didn't press the point; we outnumbered and outgunned his defenses fifty times over. I suspected he thought we intended to occupy Delos. Given the situation with Earth, such a move made sense, a way to pressure them into releasing their Ruby Dynasty prisoners. Delos wasn't a major world, but it had a symbolic value that could work for our purposes.

I doubted, though, that the Allieds would release their hostages for Delos. With access to a Lock, any of their Rhon prisoners could recreate the psiberweb. So could I. Fortunately, the Allieds didn't know I had survived, which was why I was staying hidden from Yamada. Three empires thought my sister Roca was Pharaoh Presumptive. For that matter, she was also Imperator Presumptive.

In ancient times, the House of Majda had provided our military leaders. They still produced many of our best generals and admirals. Although my father had been titular head of ISC, Naaj Majda's grandmother had been the acting commander. Kurj had wrested the job from Majda, year by year, until he became Imperator in all but name. Then he took the title too—at the bitter price of our father's death. Now we had no Ruby Dynasty Imperator, not my father, Kurj, Soz, Althor, or Kelric.

I kept thinking of my "conversation" with Kelric in Kyle space. What had it meant? He was dead. Maybe I had picked up a sense of him that survived in the mind of his father; Eldrinson and I had a strong link through the Triad. But Eldrinson was also the father of Soz and Althor. If I felt his thoughts about Kelric, I should have felt those about Althor and Soz even more, since we had lost them much more recently. Yet if anything, I had been aware of their *absence*.

Maybe Kelric was alive. Hell, maybe he was a ghost. That made about as much sense. It was hard to see how he could have survived the Trader attack that destroyed his ship eighteen years ago—the debris had been spread all over space—but it wasn't completely impossible that he had lived.

I wanted to search psiberspace again, but I couldn't risk it, not without supporting technology to pull me out if I lost control. A few of the ISC's largest cruisers carried Triad Chairs, those immense command stations a Rhon psion could use to work in Kyle space. But this ship, *Havyrl's Valor,* wasn't one of them.

I opened my eyes and found Jon Casestar watching me. He had apparently finished his negotiations with Colonel Yamada.

Curiosity flickered across his face. "You looked like you were asleep."

"I was thinking."

Now he looked even more intrigued. "Did you come to any conclusions?"

"Kelric Valdoria."

It took him a moment respond. I suspected he was accessing a memory file. Then he said, "Do you mean the Ruby Prince? The one who married Naaj Majda's older sister?"

"Yes." Good gods, of course. That added yet another twist to this convoluted mess. Thirty-five years ago, Kelric had wed Corey Majda, the previous Majda Matriarch, in an arranged marriage. The Traders assassinated her two years later. Naaj, her younger sister, had inherited the bulk of her assets and taken over as head of Majda. Kelric had received a sizable widower's stipend, the Majda palace on Raylicon, and several lucrative enterprises Corey had given him. Now Naaj had *everything,* not only her House and Kelric's assets, but the title of Imperator as well. She stood to lose a great deal if he suddenly showed up from the dead.

"Naaj Majda would be a formidable foe," I said.

Jon blinked. "For whom?"

"Kelric."

"Kelricson Valdoria has been dead for twenty years."

"Eighteen." I was running my models, checking possibilities. New shapes were appearing in the probability landscape. "I need to go to my quarters. I have to think."

Jon studied my face, as if it could reveal answers I didn't have. His gray-eyed gaze seemed to take in all of me. Intent and contained, he could turn fierce in battle, but he never lost his cool, neither in combat nor when dealing at the top-most levels of Imperialate power.

"Coming here to Delos was a good idea," he said. "We can pressure the Allieds without making hostile moves against Earth."

"But there's more." I tried to give definition to what was hardly more than vague impressions in my mind. "I'm finding strange convergences in my models. Soz. Seth Rockworth. Eldrinson. Jaibriol II. Viquara Iquar. Kryx Quaelen. Delos. *Kelric.* I need to figure out what it means."

"Are you sure it means anything? Modeling the future rarely gives reliable results."

"I'm not sure it's the future. Maybe the present . . ." I floated away from his chair, preoccupied.

"Pharaoh Dyhianna."

Looking up, I caught the cable and stopped myself. "Yes?"

Jon was watching me with undisguised curiosity. "Let me know your conclusions."

I smiled. "I will."

His face gentled. "I wish you had reason to do that more often."

"Do what?"

He spoke quietly. "Smile."

I swallowed, aware of the ache inside. "I too."

The sofa shifted, yielding under my back, but not too soft. I put my hands behind my head and stared at the ceiling. In the dim light I could barely see its smooth surface. My hair poured over my arms and torso, onto the floor, a black waterfall, freshly washed, fragrant with soap. My suite also had a pleasant smell, almost imperceptible, like wildflowers in a meadow. The EI was learning my preferences. I had named the EI Laplace, in honor of the Earth-born mathematician who had developed some of my favorite equations.

"Laplace," I said.

"Attending." It had a mellow voice, low and smooth.

"If I reset the security in my neural nodes, can you make a wireless link with them?"

"It should be possible."

"Excellent." Breathing deeply, I concentrated. "Link to my

prime node and project the patterns I've marked there onto the holoscreen in the ceiling."

"Done."

The ceiling directly above me changed to a golden sheet, glowing and thick, as if a deep layer of liquid radiance had been poured across it in defiance of gravity. It gave my suite an antique quality, like an aged picture washed in the sunlight of a lost world.

"Nice," I said.

"It is my translation of your current mood."

Interesting. Laplace equated my mood with warmth and golden light, but darkened with an amber quality. I realized that did fit how I felt right now.

I let my mind drift. A figure formed above me, as Laplace turned the evolving equations in my mind into pictures. Black blobs floated in the gold background.

Then my perception shifted and the gold became the foreground, defined by black blobs. Gold shimmerflies. Lovely and ethereal, they had graceful wings outlined in delicate tracings of black. The black blobs reformed until they were shimmerflies going in the opposite direction, their dark wings veined with gold threads. The black and gold shimmerflies interlocked, making it impossible to say which was foreground and which background. The images gave me a sense of satisfaction, even one of completion.

The gold shimmerflies began moving to the right, their flight making the black ones move left. At the edges of the gold sheet, the figures faded away, while new shimmerflies continually formed in the center of the holo. I liked the effect, but I wasn't sure what it meant.

Foreground and background. Which was which?

The shimmerflies faded, replaced by a series of ruby numbers floating on the gold background:

$$2 \ 1 \ 2 \ 6 \ 4 \ 5 \ 12 \ 9 \ 10 \ 20 \ 16 \ 17 \ldots$$

Fascinated, I tried to figure out what number came next. They could be rearranged in a grid. As soon as I imagined the grid I wanted, Laplace shuffled the numbers on the ceiling:

$$2\ 6\ 12\ 20\ldots$$
$$1\ 4\ \ 9\ 16\ldots$$
$$2\ 5\ 10\ 17\ldots$$

Hah! Each row defined a different series. To figure out what term came next in each, I looked at their "backgrounds"—the numbers you added to each term to obtain the next one.

The background for the first series was even numbers.

The background for the second series was odd numbers.

The background for the third series was prime numbers.

Each of these mini-series had four numbers. So to find the next number in the original series, I needed the fifth term in the 2, 6, 12, 20 group. It had to be 30. That gave me,

$$2\ 1\ 2\ 6\ 4\ 5\ 12\ 9\ 10\ 20\ 16\ 17\ 30\ldots$$

The numbers floating above me gradually became three-dimensional. Each number sat on top a stack of jeweled rings, some large, some small. Studying them, I realized the points within one ring related to those in the ring above or below it according to

$$w = 1/z^*$$

where z^* was the complex conjugate of z. It was a mathematical inversion. The rings sparkled in gem colors: pale sapphire, amethyst, ruby rose, opal, blue diamond. They alternated big and small, thick and thin, layers of jeweled circlets glittering in a gold atmosphere.

Well, fine. It was all lovely. But what the blazes did it mean? Foreground. Background. Inversion.

The foreground for the shimmerflies had started out as dark blobs, with gold in the background. Then the background became foreground, resolving into gold shimmerflies. A similar thing had happened with the series. The numbers were the foreground, but to find what came next I had to look at their background, the numbers added to each term to obtain the next.

What about the rings? Inversion. It meant a reversal, as with words in a sentence, tones in a musical chord, layers of hot and cold air, traits of a person, and more. The physics that described a starship drive involved a mathematical inversion. It was why we called them inversion drives. They made it possible for us to travel to other star systems in a reasonable amount of time. Inversion drives had made interstellar civilization feasible.

Even. Odd. Prime. Foreground. Background. Inversion.

Something was missing. Prime data. What was the primary inversion?

It hit me like the shift of an optical illusion, the way a drawing of normal stairs could suddenly look like an upside-down staircase or the background of a figure could jump into prominence as the foreground. What inversion most defined our lives? We lived in constant fear of the Aristos, even more so now that they might conquer us. Aristos. Anti-empaths. So what was the ultimate inversion? A Rhon psion Aristo.

No.

Gods, no.

An Aristo could never be a psion. It violated the basic traits that defined them. They were fanatical about keeping their genetic bloodlines "pure," which meant no trace of psion genes. None.

Realistically, probably more than one Aristo had tried to pass off an illegitimate child or relative as an Aristo. But a psion couldn't hide among them. Even if she did manage to shield her mind so they didn't guess the truth, it would destroy her. She would need to maintain incredible barriers every moment, never faltering, never letting a chink form in her mental fortress. It would take only one mistake to reveal the truth. She couldn't even risk falling asleep near anyone, for fear her barriers might weaken. To build such defenses took a powerful psion. But the stronger the mind, the more painful the isolation. A psion strong enough to maintain such barriers would go insane among the Aristos or become suicidal . . .

Unless you made her the background.
Made her the background.
Isolated and hid her.
But no. Wait.
Not her.
Him.
Hid *him.*
Jaibriol Qox II.
Primary Inversion.
Soz had met Jaibriol II.
Soz and Jaibriol were Rhon.
This couldn't be. Couldn't be.
Soz and Jaibriol were Rhon.
Soz had met Jaibriol II.
Primary Inversion.
Jaibriol Qox II.
Hid *him.*
Him.
Not him.
Gods no. Rhon.
Isolated and hid him.
Made him the background.
They hid Jaibriol as the background.

My mind jolted out of Kyle space—and everything
snapped into place. It made too damn much sense. Soz had
gone with Jaibriol of her own free will. It was an inversion in
every sense of the word. *And Eldrinson knew.* I was certain
of it. That was why he kept coming up in my models. Gods,
what had he been thinking, to hide it from us? With a Rhon
Emperor and a Lock, the Traders could have built a psiberweb. They wouldn't have needed Eldrin. They had someone
better: their godforsaken emperor.

Except Jaibriol was dead, and he had no heirs.

None we knew about.

And four children lived quietly on Earth, in the background. The oldest was named Jay.

"Laplace! Get me Admiral Casestar *now.*" Pain sparked in
my temples as my mind leapt into an accelerated mode.

Why the hell was my ex-husband taking care of those children? Soz must have gone crazy, if she had been with an Aristo for sixteen years. But she was one of the sanest people I knew. Driven, yes, but stable. Maybe Jaibriol was the one who had gone crockers.

Even. Odd. Even how? Balanced? Everything was *out* of balance. We had four children who just might have been born of both the Skolia and Qox dynasties. If Jaibriol had been a Rhon psion and Soz was their mother, they were also Rhon psions. Skolia, Qox, Rhon. The juxtaposition made my head throb. What would Soz and Jaibriol consider balance?

Saints almighty, had they *married*? It would make their children legitimate heirs to both the Ruby and Qox dynasties. Gods. That boy could be both the emperor and a Ruby heir. He had the proof in his genes.

No. Eube would never accept an emperor without proof of his mother's heritage.

But . . . the Aristos might be desperate. A vibrant emperor could revitalize Eube.

But . . . they would never let a psion sit on the Carnelian Throne. Impossible.

But . . . if any psion had a mind strong enough to hide, it was a Rhon.

But . . . such a life would be utter, unmitigated hell. Insane.

But . . . with the Lock he could join the Triad.

Qox Aristo in the Triad.

A Rhon emperor

Rhon Aristo

Oh, hell.

Never.

Neve.

Nev.

Ne.

N.

n.

e.

.

.

A voice snapped out of my comm, breaking me out of Kyle space. "Jon Casestar here."

I nearly jumped off the sofa. Only two seconds had passed since I had told Laplace to contact the Admiral. I spoke fast, urgency spilling into my voice. "Jon, we have to go to Earth. Four children are there, staying with Admiral Seth Rockworth. We must get them."

Jon was silent a moment. Then he said, "Pharaoh Dyhianna, this fleet had enough resources to take on a minor world like Delos. But we've no chance of coming near Earth, let alone freeing anyone."

"We have to." My heart was pounding. "Before it's too late."

"Staying here makes good sense." He sounded puzzled. "Delos is cut off from Earth and we have control of the system. It gives us a bargaining point to negotiate the release of Lord Eldrinson and Councilor Roca." He paused. "And anyone else we need to free. Who are the children?"

"I think their father is Jaibriol the Second."

Silence.

"Good gods," he finally said. "How did you come to that?"

"Calculations. Models. Intuition. Instinct."

"Do you know for certain they are on Earth?"

Good question. "No," I admitted.

"We have another concern. Yamada is hiding something. He's as nervous as a jumpcat on a hotplate."

Dryly I said, "Well, we do have over two thousand ships in orbit. And I doubt anyone expected us."

"I'm sure they didn't," Jon said. "Until you suggested it, we hadn't considered it either. But having one armed force occupy the territory of another happens in wars. Procedures exist for the situation. It might not make Yamada happy, but it shouldn't create the tension I'm getting from him. We have EIs analyzing his voice; they say he's hiding something. I agree."

Another complication. My temples throbbed. Stay here or go to Earth? I could be wrong about the children. I stared at the numbers floating on the ceiling above me. Three series. Three mysteries, but what were they? Soz. Jaibriol. Seth. Eldrinson. Kelric. *Who?*

A deep chill went through me. We had no Triad right now, only a Dyad: Eldrinson and me. Could Jay Rockworth join the Triad? But no, my models kept coming back to *Kelric*. About one thing I had no doubt: if those children with Seth were Rhon and the Traders captured them, it would be an unmitigated disaster. But how did Delos come in to it all? My calculation-enhanced intuition had driven me here with images of orbitals. Why?

A second had passed since Jon's comment. I had to answer. So I said, "I'm going down to the surface."

He didn't miss a beat with my abrupt topic change. "My apologies, Your Highness, but I can't let you do that."

"Yes, you can. Send Jagernauts with me. Arm them with laser carbines and Jumblers. Turn on my cyberlock. Hell, you can send smart-tanks with me. But I have to go down there. I need to know for certain."

"Know what?"

I took a breath. "Whether or not they have Kelric. I think he's alive—and has become Imperator."

14

Sanctuary

White light filled the docking bay. Electric blue arches made a tunnel down one side. A gold and black shuttle poised at its end, ready to leap down the tube and launch into space. The air tasted sterile and felt cool against my face.

Jagernauts strode through the brightness, indomitable in black uniforms studded with silver, their imposing presence adding to my tense anticipation. Some were checking security on the shuttle while others ran preflight checks. Several carried Lenard K16 laser carbines; others had Jumbler guns, miniature particle accelerators fueled by abitons, the weapons glittering huge and black on their hips. The chief of security, a Jagernaut Secondary, stood with me, working on her palmtop while we waited.

"Heya, Dehya."

Startled, I glanced around. Vazar had come up my other side. "My greetings," I said.

The security chief looked up from her palmtop. She saluted Vazar, crossing her fists at the wrists, the palmtop clenched in one hand. Raising her arms to Vazar, she held them extended straight out from her torso.

"At ease, Secondary Opsister," Vazar said.

As the security chief lowered her arms, I regarded her curiously. "Your name is Opsister?"

She nodded, rustling the short, dark hair that framed her square face. "Jinn Opsister, Your Highness." Her voice had an efficient sound, as if she chose the minimum of words to communicate her response.

"It sounds familiar," I said.

"I've family in the J-Force. Several circle-siblings."

Circle-siblings? A check of my memory files revealed that the term came from the Isobaril region on the planet Metropoli. Isobaril families were related by vocation rather than blood. The Op Circle had distinguished itself in laser and particle science. It tended to make them good with weapons.

"Yes, I remember." It pleased me to make the connection. "You've a niece, Jinn Opdaughter, a weapons expert, quite accomplished I understand."

"Yes, ma'am." Now she sounded carefully neutral. "She died in the Radiance War."

I felt her sorrow. Yet another spark of grief in the flame of our devastation. "My deepest sympathies, Secondary."

Jinn inclined her head to me, her mourning contained but not hidden in her thoughts. "Thank you, Your Highness."

Vazar spoke. "Jinn Opdaughter served with courage and honor. She was part of the ISC raid that captured Jaibriol the Second."

I gazed across the bay to the shuttle. A similar ship had carried Soz and Jaibriol II away from the Trader capital, along with their Jagernaut team—until it exploded. Had Soz brought two empires to their knees in the most brutal war the human race had ever known, all to rescue the father of her children—and then died after she finally achieved her goal?

Then again, Jaibriol and Soz had "died" once before.

"Vaz." I considered her. "Were the remains of the shuttle found?"

"They found pieces of everything. Even the engines."

Hmm. Shuttle explosions could be faked. It seemed unlikely that such a deception would succeed, but this was Soz. Saints only knew what she could come up with. If she and Jaibriol wanted a life together, they had little choice but to go into exile. But as much as I wanted to believe she had survived, I didn't sense her in the Triad. Eldrinson was there. We had tenuous link through whatever remained of psiberspace. But no Soz.

Jon Casestar was coming toward us. He stopped next to Vazar. "Are your preparations complete, Primary?"

"Just about," Vazar said. "We're checking the Pharaoh's cyberlock."

I blinked, startled. They were working on the cyberlock in my brain? I hadn't noticed.

My thought must have been more directed than usual, enough to reach Vazar. Turning to me, she said, "That's because we're just running checks."

Jon gave her an odd look. In the context of his comment, hers didn't make much sense. Jinn Opsister glanced from Vazar to me. As a Jagernaut she had to be a psion, but she had neither Vazar's strength nor family connection with me. I could tell she hadn't caught anything from my mind.

Telepaths didn't usually respond out loud to another telepath's thought when people were with them who couldn't have heard that thought. I didn't think Vazar had offended anyone, but that rule of etiquette gave me a way to distract her. I didn't want her to notice I was guarding my mind more than usual. Although it was unlikely she could pick up anything as well barricaded as my suspicions about Soz and the rest, I could take no chances.

Vaz. I focused my thought on her. *Let's not do that.*

Sorry. Didn't mean to be rude.

Jon was speaking to Opsister. "How are you configuring the cyberlock?"

She showed him her palmtop. "I'm calibrating its field to surround the Pharaoh in two layers. The inner layer will be set on high and the outer on low."

Disconcerted, I looked down at myself. I saw only my blue jumpsuit. If the cyberlock had been active, a faint rainbow glimmer would have overlaid my body like a second skin. On its low setting, the cyberlock field made anyone who penetrated it dizzy. On high, it fatally disrupted the neural structure of the brain. It didn't affect me because as part of my brain, it knew to protect me. Even on high, it only gave me a mild vertigo, but I could identify its setting by minute differences in that sensation. Right now I felt nothing. Although that was fine with me, I knew Jon wouldn't like it.

Vaz, the cyberlock isn't working.

It should be. She spoke to Jinn. "Secondary Opsister, activate the lock."

Jinn studied her palmtop. "According to this, it is activated. But it's not responding normally."

Jon Casestar frowned at me. "Pharaoh Dyhianna, if we have a problem here, I can't send you down to the planet."

Damn. "I don't need the cyberlock," I assured him. "I'm not in danger."

"You can't know that for certain."

"Close to certain. I calculated it."

He shook his head. "I still can't risk it."

"I've been to Delos before. Several times, for diplomatic summits."

"That was during peacetime."

"We've never had peacetime." My voice had an edge of bitterness I hadn't realized I felt so acutely. "We've been at war in some form or another since day one of the Skolian Imperialate."

Jon cracked his knuckles, which made me think he wasn't so sure after all. To Jinn, he said, "Any improvement with the cyberlock?"

She traced her finger over the film-thin screen of her palmtop, her forehead creased with concentration. "I've never seen anything like this."

"What's the problem?" I asked.

"Your cyberlock is—well, incomplete."

Jon shot me a startled glance. "Removing the cyberlock would damage your brain, wouldn't it?"

"A lot." Quickly I added, "And I'm fine. My brain feels great."

Vaz snorted. **Your brain is fried. Otherwise you wouldn't insist on going down to that blasted planet.**

Sometimes I could do without telepathy. *Stop treating me as if I'm helpless.*

You are.

If that were true, I wouldn't have survived Opalite.

All right, yes, that's true. But damn it, Dehya, you look breakable as all hell.

Looks can deceive.

"Could your palmtop be malfunctioning?" Jon asked Jinn Opsister.

"I don't think so." She flicked her finger through another holo, then studied the result. "I've triple-checked it."

"How is my cyberlock incomplete?" I asked her.

"I'm not sure, ma'am." She looked up at me with puzzlement. "It seems to have lost some of the links it makes with your brain."

I rubbed my chin. "It probably hasn't fully transformed back here from Kyle space. The neural threads a cyberlock extends into the brain are only a few molecules thick, so even if only one or two particles are affected, that could disrupt the lock."

Jon had The Look again, the one that made his face seem as if it were cut from granite. "Then I can't approve your leaving the ship."

Exasperated, I said, "I've gone down-planet in touchier situations. During the Carmichael Summit, we met here with Aristos and Allieds both. You didn't protest then. And now we have more ships." Answering his unspoken protest, I softened my voice. "Jon, I won't disappear again."

He responded quietly. "It would be an unmitigated disaster for us to have found you, only to have the Allieds take you prisoner. We've lost too much, Your Highness. I won't be responsible for your loss as well."

"You won't be." I tried my best to look safe and reassuring.

"Stay here. We can send a representative for you."

I wished I could make him see. "As a Rhon, I can pick up things even your best people can't detect."

He studied my face. "Very well. I will accompany you."

I had a taste then of what Jon felt when I insisted on doing things he considered too risky. "The two of us shouldn't go together. If anything happened, we would both be lost."

He snorted. "So. You do acknowledge a danger exists."

"No. I just don't see any use in the two of us going together."

He wasn't buying it. "Why not, if it's safe?"

"You didn't come down with the diplomats during the summit."

"That was then. This is now."

"Jon, please. Trust my intuition."

I expected him to put me off again. But after a pause, he said, "It is true that your predictions, as puzzling as they often first appear, almost always make sense. In hindsight. But they're never exact. Nor can we replicate them." He shifted his weight, watching me with concern. "I deal in concrete facts. This is too uncertain. I don't like it."

"I will be all right." I willed him to believe that.

"You really think Kelricson Valdoria is down there?"

"Yes. I have to go down."

For a long moment he stood thinking. Finally he exhaled a long breath. "Gods help me if I'm wrong. I'm going to trust your instincts, Pharaoh Dyhianna." He fixed Vazar with piercing gaze. "Make sure she doesn't get into trouble."

"That I will, Admiral." To me, she thought, **Even if I have to throw you over my shoulder and haul you out of there.** She made an image in her mind: me being pursued by slavering Aristo monstrosities; me trying to argue math with them, explaining how my calculations showed they couldn't catch me; them grabbing me with barbaric cackles of glee; Vazar appearing in a flash of light; Vazar hefting me over her shoulder and running like the wind.

I smiled. *I promise I won't argue with Traders.*

Jon spoke into his wrist comm. "J-team, Pharaoh Dyhianna is ready to leave."

The Allieds invited us to their embassy in the city of New Athens. Accompanied by ten Jagernauts, with Vazar at my side, I met Colonel Yamada in the spacious lobby of the embassy. Columns bordered the area, all dark pink marble veined with gold. Pink and white tiles covered the floor in diamond mosaics, also veined with gold threads. A groined ceiling arched far above our heads, framing airy spaces, and a large chandelier of rose-hued crystals glittered in its center. It was beautiful, but also cold and formal.

Our footsteps echoed in the lobby. Yamada and his group waited under the chandelier. The colonel was a stocky man with a self-confident presence. His hair had turned gray, but his wide face had almost no lines. So far he had showed himself as skilled, sharp, and savvy; in other words, he wouldn't easily give up information. An Allied dignitary stood with him, Michella Monquou, the Delos Ambassador to Skolia, one of Earth's most respected diplomats.

Yamada had also brought his aid, Lieutenant Jennifer Mason, and ten soldiers. Unlike my retinue, however, his carried no weapons. Although Skolians tended to be more bellicose than Earth's natural-born children, I suspected their discretion now came from enlightened self-interest: we were the occupying force, with far more firepower than they could claim.

Our two groups met with formal nods, a Skolian custom, and with handshakes, an Allied custom. Jon Casestar had identified me as a diplomat, and Yamada treated me as an ambassador. Despite their obvious tension, they didn't seem hostile. I felt unease from their group rather than anger.

After various formalities, Yamada ushered us into a conference room paneled in gold. Swivel chairs of smart-leather surrounded a long, oval table made from a polished red wood. I paused at its head, watching the soldiers and diplomats assemble. Yamada stopped midway between the two ends of the table. The most effective place was actually where he stood rather than my position, but it made no difference. I didn't intend to be here long.

I felt now what Jon had said he suspected; the Allieds were deceiving us. Although the colonel's face remained impassive, his body language showed miniscule, but telling, changes—the tightened jaw and tense shoulders, his tight grip on the back of a chair.

I took a chance and made a guess. "Colonel, we would like to see the Skolian man you have in custody."

His face became even more guarded, and I knew my words

had hit the target. Yamada raked his gaze over the Jagernauts arrayed around me. He had to know that sensors within their uniforms and bodies could pick up the slightest variation in fields within and around the embassy. Using wireless links, they had already deactivated many security systems here. The embassy had monitors, not as good as ours but good enough to know we had neutralized their security.

Yamada spoke as if he were guarding each word. "We don't even know the man's name, Ms. Selei. He refuses to identify himself."

So they did have someone! "I can probably identify him." At least, I could if he was who I believed.

Yamada's grip on the chair tightened, making his tendons stand out. "He may be a member of a noble House. He has an Iotic accent."

No wonder Yamada was so tense, if he had an idea about the importance of his guest. I doubted he had guessed the full extent of it, though. "I will know, when I meet him."

His unease seeped past his mental barriers. He had no way to evaluate whether or not it would be wise to give up their guest to us, but he had no grounds to refuse and plenty of reason to acquiesce. Ten of those reasons had come with me, armed and silent, and another few thousand orbited Delos.

Just when his pause became long enough to grow awkward, he extended his arm toward the door as if offering an invitation. "I will take you to him."

The muscles in my shoulders loosened. "Thank you."

We followed corridors wide enough for six people to walk abreast. The air here felt refined, as if we breathed on a high mountain. The marble walls alternated with floor-to-ceiling holo-panels that showed mountains and lakes on Earth. Their beauty stirred a response deep within me, an instinctual longing blended with sorrow. My people had lost our home world six millennia ago, yet still I responded to those images. But we couldn't return, not now, perhaps never. Our lost home was forbidden to us by the hostilities that had sundered the human cultures spread across the stars.

Yamada and I walked together, with Vazar to my right and

Ambassador Monquou to Yamada's left. Jagernauts and soldiers surrounded us on all sides.

"Our guest may refuse to speak with you," Monquou told me. "He barely says a word, and he went berserk when our doctor tried to examine him."

"A doctor?" I stiffened. "Why? Is he hurt?"

Yamada answered. "He's been a Trader slave, a provider we think."

Provider. The air no longer felt warm, or maybe I felt the chill inside. If the Traders had captured Kelric all those years ago instead of killing him, they would almost certainly have made him one of the psions they tortured to reach their so-called "exalted" transcendence. Had he endured that for eighteen years? No wonder he wouldn't talk to anyone. I would be surprised if he was still sane.

And yet . . . when he had linked to me in Kyle space, if that truly had been him, his thoughts had resonated with strength. It hadn't been the mind of someone who had spent nearly two decades as a provider.

I considered Yamada. "How did you get this man, if he was a Trader?"

The colonel spoke carefully. "It was an exchange."

"Of prisoners?" The Traders must not have realized Kelric's true identity; otherwise, they would never have given him up.

"Not exactly." Sweat beaded his forehead. "One of our people traded himself for the Skolian man."

Unease stirred within me. "Who?"

"A boy. A volunteer with the Dawn Corps. They're a humanitarian group that helps war refugees find their families and return home or relocate."

I stopped in the middle of the hall, my unease building. "Why would the Aristos take him in exchange for a noble-born Skolian provider?"

Yamada had also halted, and everyone else as well, leaving the colonel and me surrounded by soldiers. "We don't know why," he said.

"Who is this boy?" *Please.* I thought. *Let me be wrong.*

Then Yamada spoke my nightmare. "His name is Jay Rockworth."

I felt as if the ground dropped beneath us. "No." *No.*

Vazar was watching my face. "You know him?"

"Not at all." I felt ill. Unable to say more, I went to a marble bench by the wall. I sat down, then put my elbows on my knees and my head in my hands. Somewhere in the distance a cleaning droid whirred.

Why had Jay done it? He might *be* Rhon. He would be insane to go to the Traders. Or did he thirst for the power of the Carnelian Throne? As much as I had hoped to find Kelric alive, now dismay filled me. The universe was forever playing a game with us: *you can't have too much—if life works well in one way, it must suffer in another.* Kelric's miraculous return came at a devastating price.

But this still felt wrong. How had this boy known the Traders had Kelric when ISC had never been able to discover he still lived?

Vazar sat next to me. "What is it?"

I lifted my head. The others had gathered around us, several paces away, watching and waiting. I felt heavy, like lead. I answered in a low voice. "Don't ask, Vaz. Not yet." I needed to know more before I revealed anything, lest I cause more damage than had already been done.

Yamada was watching me with close scrutiny. "Are you all right?"

Rising to my feet, I said. "Yes. I will be fine." I wished it were true.

We continued onward, down wide marble halls. Yamada and Monquou asked questions, trying to understand my reaction. I evaded their inquiries or simply remained silent. I could tell they recognized my Iotic accent. Our noble Houses resembled royal families in countries on Earth, their positions primarily ceremonial and symbolic. However, the Ruby Dynasty and House of Majda still wielded power.

Yamada wondered if I had a link to that power, but he had no idea about the true nature of that connection. Yet. He and his people were sharp; I doubted we could hold them off forever. But my drive to come here had overridden even my preference to remain anonymous.

We turned into a smaller, more private hall. The colonel stopped at a polished wooden door with elegant friezes bordering its frame. I tried to remember what Kelric looked like, but I came up with only a vague image, an unusually tall, well-built man with genetically altered coloring, all metallic gold—his skin, his hair, even his eyes.

As Yamada opened the door, both anticipation and trepidation washed through me. Even knowing they had sent word that we were coming, I still feared we would find an empty room.

Several soldiers and Jagernauts entered, followed by Yamada and Monquou. I went next, with Vazar at my side, and the rest of our retinues came after. We entered a foyer with white walls and abstract holo-art that swirled with pastel color. Beyond the foyer, we followed a white hallway like dark motes in a tunnel of light. The ivory carpet muffled our footfalls, until I felt as if I could almost hear my own heartbeat.

The hall let us out into a spacious living room with white walls and more abstract holo-art. I had an impression of black furniture and glass tables, but that wasn't what riveted my attention.

A man stood across the room with his back to us. He was staring through the floor-to-ceiling window at the gardens outside his room.

He didn't have gold hair. He didn't have gold skin.

He wasn't Kelric.

I whispered his name, the word forming like a miracle on my lips.

"Eldrin."

15
Gabriel's Legacy

He turned from the window and stared at me, his beloved face so welcome that dizziness swept over me, followed by euphoria, then disbelief, then joy, all coming so fast that the emotions tumbled over one another and left me paralyzed, unable to move or speak.

Husband. Consort. Lover. Best friend. Father of my child.

Gods forgive me, but at that moment I was grateful to the son of Jaibriol II. The new Trader emperor might soon conquer Skolia. His decision to claim his throne could have ramifications that shook three civilizations. It could bring about the fall of empires. But in this impossible, incredible moment, I could only be grateful that his trade had brought Eldrin back to me.

My husband looked achingly familiar, with glossy wine-red hair brushing his shoulders and a sprinkle of freckles across his nose. He wore a high-collared shirt of white gilter-velvet. His trousers were dark blue, a color he had always favored. Darker blue boots with soft soles came up to his knees.

Then I comprehended the rest, the darkness under his eyes, the shock in his gaze, the numbed ache in his mind that masked a deeper pain he tried to suppress. He stared at me with no welcome, no joy, no warmth, only suspicion and something close to hatred.

I spoke softly. "Eldrin? Don't you recognize me?"

He simply regarded me, his face cold. Then he turned back to the window and looked out at the landscaped garden beneath the purple-blue sky of Delos. The atmosphere in the room suddenly felt too thin.

I walked over to him, uncertain how to interpret his response. He had closed his mind to me, something he had almost never done, even during a fight. We had argued plenty, but we always worked it out. Now he was a barricaded fortress, battened and dark.

I stood with him and gazed at the garden. I felt more than heard the others behind us: Jagernauts, soldiers, diplomats. Cloth rustled as someone shifted position. Someone else coughed. Vazar's stunned joy at seeing Eldrin swelled against my mind.

After we had remained that way for a while, Eldrin spoke in Iotic. "The depth of your tricks never ceases to amaze me." His voice rasped with laryngitis. I didn't want to think what could have made his throat so raw.

"My tricks?" I asked.

"Cruelty taken to new heights." His face was impassive, but his eyelid twitched.

Moisture filled my eyes. "It's me, Dryni."

No response.

He didn't believe the Traders had released him. They finally had their Lock and Key. They would never give that up. For what? An unknown youth? It was impossible.

His scent drifted to me, familiar, masculine, overlaid with a faint fragrance of soap. On a submerged level, my body reacted to the pheromones that psions naturally produced to attract each other. I wanted to touch him, hold him, welcome him home. But instead we stood in formal, cool silence. I didn't know how to convince him this wasn't a cruel game played by the Aristos, tormenting him with promises of family only to take it all away again.

If my suspicions about Jay Rockworth were true, the trade almost made sense. The Traders had given up Eldrin for a healthy young emperor. Jay could revitalize their empire. With that renewal, they might conquer us without a psibernet. My stomach clenched at the thought. Then they would have all the Rhon psions they wanted, the entire Ruby Dynasty.

The Aristos probably also thought they could control such a young emperor. Hah. If Jay really was Soz's son, they might find him far harder to manipulate than they expected. Soz had possessed an indomitable will and piercing mind. Although I had never seen her as a mother or wife, I suspected she held a deep love for her family. Jaibriol II's personality was anyone's guess, but I had no doubt about one thing: any children of that union would be exceptional. I just wished I knew *how*.

Even if I was right about their parentage, I doubted anyone knew their true identities, except perhaps Eldrinson and Seth. I understood Eldrinson's silence now. Such knowledge could cause political upheavals that would make the Radiance War look mild.

If it became known the Allieds had harbored the Trader emperor—and let him go—the outcry would explode. Jay may have saved their asses by trading himself for Eldrin. Earth could claim they arranged the exchange to stop the Traders from building a psibernet. But whatever they might later say, we knew Jay had set it up himself. I wanted to believe he had done it to free Eldrin, his mother's brother, but that felt more like my own desperate hopes than any reality. I longed for the impossible, an Aristo emperor of compassion. I wanted it so much, it hurt.

Pain stabbed my temples, and I winced. All this accelerated thought might mean nothing. I had been wrong about Kelric. I could be wrong now. I had absolutely no proof. But if I was right and the Aristos learned about Jay's true parentage, his life would be hell. He had *nowhere* to turn. Until I knew more, I couldn't reveal what I suspected. Not now. Maybe never.

Eldrin continued to watch the garden. I didn't know how to reach him. I could bring up a memory only the two of us shared, but he knew he might have revealed it during interrogation and then repressed the experience. I gritted my teeth, wishing the Aristos would suffer the same agony they inflicted on us.

Someone shifted behind us, boots scraping the floor. From Vazar I felt an almost physical pain at seeing Eldrin this way. She had known him for years, first as a family friend, then as her husband's older brother. Not all the Jagernauts knew Eldrin on sight, but they had recognized his name.

The puzzlement from Yamada and his people pressed against my mind. I heard the click of a finger tapping a palmtop. They had Eldrin's name now, so it probably wouldn't take them long to narrow down his identity. No one seemed to know mine yet, but they would soon. Probably the only reason it had taken this long was because they didn't have full access to the interstellar databases, many of which had existed primarily in psiberspace.

Outside, late afternoon sunlight with a bluish tinge slanted across the gardens, blue and lavender flowers laid out in circular beds surrounded by blue gravel paths. In the center of the main bed, bushes sculpted like ships sailed in a sea of blue-green foliage, their bases foamed with white flowers. I let the serenity of the scene calm my mind.

Then I released my mental barriers.

As soon as I let go, I felt Vazar snap to attention, both her mind and body, as if she wanted to protect me mentally as well as physically. Several other Jagernauts responded, coming to a sharper mental alert. I wasn't sure about the Allieds, but I thought Monquou stirred; perhaps she also had empathic ability.

I continued to lower my barriers, layer after layer. My mind spread out, making me truly vulnerable. I reached out with my thoughts, softly, to Eldrin. Our minds began to join, instinctively, the blending only two Rhon psions could know. It was the flip side of our painful empathic sensitivity; we could share an incredible depth of emotion. We rarely lowered our barriers enough to blend this way; the experience was too intense to maintain for long. But when we did, it was glorious.

Eldrin froze. Still staring at the garden, he started to lift his hand, as if to defend himself. Like all natives of his home world, he had only four fingers, all strong and about the same length, with no thumb. His hand could fold in two like in a hinge, letting the two sets of two fingers oppose each other like muscular thumbs. He stood now with his palm facing outward, almost touching the glass, his fingers splayed.

Then he slowly turned to me, lowering his arm. His gaze seemed to drink in every feature of my face. He spoke in a throaty whisper. "Dehya?"

I managed to find my voice. "Welcome home, Dryni."

Horror spread across his face. "It was all for nothing."

"For nothing?" I wanted to draw him to me, to feel the embrace of his muscular arms, but I held back, afraid to push. "What do you mean?"

His voice cracked. "I thought you and Taquinil had escaped."

"We did." I couldn't bear to tell him about Taquinil, not yet. "I came out on Opalite, one of the emergency stations I had set up."

His fist clenched at his side. "When did they catch you?"

I softened my voice. "We aren't with the Traders. We're on Delos."

"It's not possible."

"The Aristos traded you for one of their own."

"That boy?" He raised his hand and almost touched me. Then he stopped himself and lowered his hand, as if he feared to discover I wasn't real. "No. They would not have done this."

"It's true." I took his hand in mine. "You're safe now."

"I'll never be safe," he whispered. "None of us will." Then he pulled me into his arms, drawing me against his body, his motion strained.

I closed my eyes, holding him close. His mind suffused mine, so filled with grief and pain that tears gathered in my eyes.

"Dryni," I murmured.

He ran his hand down my hair. "At least they let us see each other."

"We aren't with the Traders."

"Is that what they told you?" He gave a short, harsh laugh. "Don't believe them. It will only hurt more when you learn the truth."

I knew nothing I said now would convince him. But we had time. For now it was enough to have him in my arms.

So we stood, holding each other. Gradually we relaxed. After a while, Eldrin sighed. He rested his head on top of mine and whispered my name in his ragged voice. Tears rolled down my cheeks.

Sometime later we drew apart. He smiled, not his usual teasing grin, but still a slight curve of his lips. I laughed, unsteady but glad. I felt the stirring of his hope.

A uniform crackled behind us. We turned, holding hands, to find everyone watching us. Eldrin's gaze moved from Yamada to Monquou to the Jagernauts. It stopped at Vazar, and his hand tightened on mine.

Yes, I thought. *It's really her.*

With subdued motions, Secondary Opsister went down on one knee, her carbine in her hand, her head bowed. The other Jagernauts followed suit, including Vazar. Colonel Yamada watched, his hand partially lifted, as if he had started to speak and make a gesture, then stopped when all the Jagernauts moved.

"Please rise," Eldrin said hoarsely, with the burr of laryngitis.

My retinue stood slowly. Vazar spoke to him in a voice husky with emotion. "Welcome home, Your Highness."

Yamada's aide, Jennifer Mason, looked from me to Eldrin. Then she took a deep breath. "You honor us with your presence, Pharaoh Dyhianna and Prince Eldrin."

So they knew now. It didn't matter so much; they couldn't send us to custody on Earth. They had to let us go, given how thoroughly our forces outnumbered theirs.

Yamada glanced at her. Then he turned to Eldrin and me, his expression a mixture of puzzlement, curiosity, and wary astonishment. "Excuse me if this question offends—but are those titles appropriate?"

I spoke quietly. "Yes."

"Good lord." He stared at us. "Should we, ah—kneel?"

"It is not necessary." Eldrin spoke with even more formality than usual. I wasn't sure if his stiffness came from the situation or his shock at seeing me. To the Jagernauts he said, "But we appreciate the honor you give."

We all looked at one another, obviously with the same question. Why the blazes had the Traders given up Eldrin for an unknown teenage boy?

I spoke to Yamada. "Do you have any holos of Jay Rockworth?"

"Several." He gestured to Jennifer Mason. "Lieutenant?"

Mason unrolled her pencil-thin palmtop, laying its screen on her hand. She flicked one of the holicons floating above her palm, a tiny black puma, the symbol of the Trader empire. Then she traced her finger over the screen.

The room darkened. Then one wall lightened with the life-sized image of a youth. I recognized him as the oldest of Seth's foster children. According to the date in its lower corner, this holo had been taken a year later than the other I had seen. The boy's frame had filled out, his shoulders broad, his legs long, his build lean with youth and health. He was laughing and waving at someone. His white sweater had a blue stripe across the chest and he wore those odd "denim" trousers that Earth people had favored for centuries. They called them *jeans*, like their English word *genes*, though as far as I could tell, the trousers had no special connection to DNA.

The youth was, for all appearances, a good-looking high-school boy. But I recognized the classic bone structure of his face. Highton. Unless you were searching for the resemblance, it wasn't obvious, especially with the way he laughed so heartily. Aristos were always reserved.

This image showed his hair better. It wasn't just black; it had gold streaks, as if bleached by the sun. Young people these days were always turning their hair odd colors. I didn't think he had dyed his, though. I had known someone with similar hair.

Soz.

At first glance, his hair bore only a slight resemblance to hers. Soz's had been black, shading into wine-red, then gold at the tips. The gold color wasn't truly blond, though, neither for her nor for this boy. It had a metallic cast, like Kelric's hair. That came from my father, whose skin, hair, and eyes had all been gold. His ancestors had engineered themselves that way to adapt to life on a hot, bright planet.

Eldrin was shaking his head. "That boy isn't the one. The man they traded me for was older, and a Highton Aristo."

"Did you get a good look at him?" I asked.

Eldrin spoke in a low voice. "No." He sent me a private

thought. **I think I was in shock. I had almost no time to look at the other man. And Corbal had told me nothing.**

Corbal? To hear Eldrin call an Aristo by his personal name chilled. *Was he . . . ?* I couldn't finish. I couldn't ask who had owned him.

Eldrin took my hand, his four stocky fingers closing around mine. Then he lifted my hand to the high collar of his shirt. Pulling down the cloth, he brushed my palm against his neck. Except I didn't feel skin. I touched a collar with cold gems.

Corbal Xir put it there, he thought flatly.

I almost flinched. He had been wearing that collar in the Trader news broadcast. He probably had guards on his wrists and ankles as well. Slave restraints.

Dismayed, I lowered my hand. *Can't Yamada's people remove it?*

His face tightened. **The collar extended biothreads through the sockets in my neck. They have intertwined with the bio-mech in my body. The threads are part of my neural system now. It won't be easy to untangle.**

Damn the Traders and their ever-more ingenious methods of controlling people. *We'll find a way to get it off.*

I hope so.

If any of the Jagernauts overheard our conversation, their minds gave no hint. Eldrin and I had learned to guard our privacy well. But everyone had probably guessed what we were doing, given the way he had moved my hand.

I glanced at Yamada. "Do you have a record of the exchange where the Traders released Prince Eldrin?"

"Yes, certainly." Yamada motioned to his lieutenant.

It didn't surprise me they had a record. All of the embassies probably monitored that plaza as a matter of course.

The first holo moved to the right along the wall and a second appeared. It showed a wide plaza with elegant buildings facing in on a quadrangle. Large white and gray diamonds tiled the plaza in tessellated mosaics. Curved benches sat under vine-draped arches along the edges of the spacious area, and fountains on the perimeter sent up spumes of water.

Two figures were walking from the Allied embassy toward the center of the area. A larger group came out of the Eubian embassy across the plaza. As the two groups approached each other, the holo zoomed in on them. The Eubian group consisted of Corbal Xir, four Razers, and Eldrin, who walked with his wrists locked behind his back. The other pair resolved into two men, an Allied teenager and a Highton Aristo.

"Can you zoom on the young Aristo man?" I asked.

"Will do, ma'am," the lieutenant said.

The Aristo grew to life size, filling the image. His face was the epitome of Highton reserve and arrogance, his classic features so perfect they looked sculpted from snow-marble. He wore black trousers and a black shirt, conservative, with an elegant cut. His hair glittered like black diamond, with no trace of any other color. His eyes were as red as blood rubies. Just seeing him made me queasy.

"Gods almighty." Eldrin looked from the icy Aristo to the halo of a laughing Jay Rockworth. "It's the *same* person."

A shudder ran through me. Even knowing both holos showed Jay, I had trouble absorbing it. But more shattering than the difference between the two was a likeness—the youth in those images had an unmistakable resemblance to Jaibríol II, the late Trader emperor.

I picked up nothing from the others in the room to indicate they had made the connection. "Can't you all see who he is?" I asked, incredulous.

"An Aristo." Yamada grimaced. "That kid was here for *days*. We had no idea. He sure as hell didn't look like an Aristo then."

Eldrin was scrutinizing me now. "You see more?"

I rubbed my arms, though nothing would ever warm this cold. "He's the living image of Jaibriol the Second."

A long silence followed my words.

Finally Yamada said, "Jaibriol Two had no heir."

"Neither did his father," I said. "Supposedly. It didn't stop one from showing up."

"Oh hell," Vazar said. "Now we're dead."

16
Dyad

Morale is a chameleon, shifting its purchase on our hearts according to our inconstant moods rather than any absolute truth. Wear down the human soul and the will to live falters. Reality makes no difference; when hearts lose hope, they crumble. But give back that hope, even if reality denies it, and our souls rejoice even when logic gives no cause for optimism.

Eldrin's appearance on the battle cruiser sent spirits soaring. In just a matter of days, two of Skolia's lost symbols had returned. The mood throughout the ship lightened. The long road to renewal had begun.

Then the Traders slammed us again.

An unknown starship hurtled out of inversion with no warning, a Skolian craft, civilian, a small scout vessel. It was broadcasting even as it burst into normal space, blasting its message to any ship within receiving distance. Bound straight for the history texts, its recording came from the Trader capital world.

Eldrin and I stood with Jon Casestar on the observation deck above the spacious bay where I had first greeted the crew. The holo played out on the far wall, its giant figures dominating the room, larger than life. Like the broadcast about Eldrin's capture, this one had been recorded in the Hall of Circles in the Qox palace. Again Corbal Xir stood on the glittering dais surrounded by glittering Aristos, all with perfect bloodless skin, their clothes like woven black crystal, their red eyes the only color in the snow-marble Hall, except for the Carnelian Throne.

At first we didn't understand why the ship had hurled its news so frantically at us. It showed only the memorial service for Jaibriol II, his mother Viquara, and her consort Kryx Quaelen. But after it finished, Xir's voice rumbled through the hall. "Many of you have heard rumors of negotiations between my office and the Allieds." He gave a dramatic pause in the Aristo's overly theatrical style. Then he said, "Those rumors are true."

The Aristos brushed their finger cymbals together, a custom our peoples had once shared, long ago when we and the Traders had been one. Only they had kept the custom. After the susurrations quieted, Xir continued. "The Allieds had in their custody a man. A Highton man. A trade was arranged, this man for a prisoner in my possession." As the cymbals whispered again, he held up his hand. "Eube had triumphed."

Next to me, Eldrin had gone as rigid as steel. He was clenching the rail that bordered the deck so hard, the veins stood out in the back of his hand. The diamond wrist guards Xir had put on him glittered below Eldrin's shirt cuffs. He stared at Xir as if mesmerized by a monster he thought he had conquered, only to find it grown larger than ever. His jagged emotions surged: fear, aversion, anger, shame, self-disgust, echoes of pain, and—

Gratitude?

Yes. Gratitude.

Xir continued. "And so it was agreed between the Allied Worlds and Eube. Our Skolian captive for their Highton captive." His gaze raked the assembled Aristos. "That Skolian was Eldrin Valdoria."

"We *know* that," Eldrin muttered. "Who is the Highton?"

An angry discord of cymbals filled the Aristo hall. Xir remained silent until the tumult quieted. The Aristos watched him with icy faces, waiting to hear what he could possibly offer to atone for his unthinkable misdeed—giving away the Key to their newly gained Lock. Tall and powerfully built, Xir raised his arm to the great arched entrance of the Hall of Circles. He spoke in a deep, rolling voice. "I present to you His Honor, Jaibriol Qox the Third, Emperor of Eube."

Damn.

Jaibriol III entered the Hall. Jay Rockworth. He radiated energy. Even by the Aristo's narcissistic standards, he was handsome. He strode down the aisle with a confidence remarkable in one so young. He was the image of his father, but he stood even taller, with none of the brooding darkness that had accompanied his father's rare broadcasts. If Jaibriol III had been any more radiant, he would have caused a fire.

"For saints' sake," Eldrin said. "Not another Jaibriol Qox. Don't they ever die off?"

"Maybe they cloned Jaibriol Two," Jon Casestar said.

I kept my mind shielded, even from Eldrin. This secret I would hold for as long as it took to unravel Jaibriol III's intentions. I needed to talk with Eldrinson, my father-in-law, to uncover the secrets he had carried all these years. Gods forbid he should take that knowledge to his grave, which was what would happen if the Allieds kept him and Roca in permanent custody.

Jaibriol III spoke with extraordinary self-possession. Seventeen years old. He should have been in school instead of conquering empires. He had a magnificent voice, the kind that could sway hearts with its resonant beauty. The cosmos should have had a law that forbade one human being from possessing so many advantages. Was he enemy or friend? My head throbbed with the many possible conflicting futures.

"I don't understand," Eldrin said. "Why did he set me free?"

"The Allieds claim they set up the trade to rescue you," Jon said.

I spoke dryly. "They could hardly tell the universe, 'So sorry, we had Jaibriol Three all along and we didn't know.' "

Jon shot me a glance. "He was one of those children you wanted to get from Earth, wasn't he?"

"Yes. Seth's foster son." No point existed in hiding that any longer; it was public record. I doubted the Allied authorities were happy with Seth right now.

Jon studied me. " 'Seth' as in Admiral William Seth Rockworth, your former consort?"

Eldrin stiffened.

"Yes." I shifted my weight, uncomfortable. Although Seth had left me years before Eldrin and I married, the Iceland Treaty remained in effect, so neither Seth's government nor mine recognized the divorce. It was awkward.

Jon gave me an incredulous look. "Why would Admiral Rockworth harbor the future Trader emperor?"

"He probably had no idea." I almost meant it; even if Seth knew the truth, I doubt he had expected this. Eldrin continued to stare at the holoscreen, for all appearances not listening to us. But I knew he heard.

Jon was scrutinizing me. "You knew Jay Rockworth's identity. That's why you wanted to get him off Earth."

"I didn't know for certain. But I suspected."

"How? None of us had even an inkling."

Eldrin sighed, turning to us. "Don't ask how, Admiral. She can never explain."

That surprised me. "I talk about my models all the time."

"You talk in equations." Eldrin smiled slightly. "No one understands what you're saying but you. The rest of us only know that it works."

"It didn't with Kelric," I grumbled.

A shadow of old grief crossed Eldrin's face. "You mean my brother?"

"She thinks he is still alive," Jon said.

I hesitated. "Eldrin, I expected to meet Kelric in the embassy."

A surge of hope came from his mind, one he quickly damped. I understood why. It was dangerous to hope. You could be torn apart when fate crushed that dream. But not always; I had feared to hope I would see Eldrin again, yet he had, incredibly, come home.

"You think Kelric has been a Trader prisoner?" Eldrin asked.

"It's possible." But whoever had touched my mind in Kyle space hadn't spent eighteen agonizing years as a provider. His mind had been strong, healthy, vibrant.

Like Eldrin.

My insight came softly, like the wary step of a deer in an open forest clearing. Eldrin was in shock, yes. His time with the Traders had hurt him. But it could have been far worse. Incredibly, he had come back to us whole. Months of providing for an Aristo could have torn him apart, even made him catatonic. If Xir had protected him from the worst of that, I too felt gratitude.

But *why* would Xir make such a choice? The Aristos had never hidden their conviction that they had an exalted right to take pleasure by hurting their providers. They considered empaths a lower form of life, one that supposedly could achieve "elevation" only by providing for Aristos. To them, showing compassion toward a provider was the sign of an abnormal personality.

In the holo, Jaibriol III was turning toward the camera, obviously aware that recordings of his speech would be seen in far more than the Hall of Circles. He spoke with strength. "We have suffered the ravages of our conflicts. Let us now seek to heal. To the people of the Skolian Imperialate and the Allied Worlds, I say this: Meet me at the peace table. Let us lay to rest the hatreds that have sundered our common humanity."

All right, Jaibriol the Third, I thought. *You keep that promise and I will keep your secret.*

I slept alone. Each night Eldrin withdrew into his own suite with no more than the brush of his lips across mine. I caught traces of his emotions: he didn't want me to see him in slave restraints, didn't want to be touched, didn't want to touch. Our nights passed in lonely solitude . . .

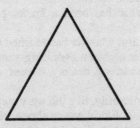

Dyhianna Selei
Eldrinson Valdoria
Kelricson Valdoria

Dyhianna Selei
Kelricson Valdoria

I bolted upright in the night. Sweat soaked the billowy air-quilts on my bed. The images from my nightmare remained vivid.

A triangle. Three Triad names.

A line. Two names.

"Stop it," I whispered.

"Dehya?"

I almost gasped. The voice came out of the darkness somewhere near the bed. Inside the ship, with no light-bars active, the darkness was total. No stray luminance let me see the man who spoke. But it had to be Eldrin; the EI wouldn't let anyone else inside my room without asking me first.

"Dryni? Is that you."

"I had a dream." He sounded strained.

"Laplace, give me night-level lumes," I said.

The room lightened enough so I could see Eldrin standing by the bed, his arms folded around his torso. He had on blue sleep trousers and a loose shirt. The slave collar glinted around his neck, as did the cuffs on his wrists. His ankle cuffs glittered against blue cloth, half covered by his trousers. It gave me an idea of just how much the nightmare had unsettled him, that he came here even though I would see the indications of Corbal Xir's ownership on him.

Doctors had been mapping out the biothreads extended by the restraints into Eldrin's body. They were preparing to untangle the threads from his neural system. Eldrin loathed the restraints, but he hated even more the idea that these reminders of his Trader captivity might leave him with neural damage if they weren't removed properly. So he schooled himself in patience while the doctors worked, day after day, tracing the intruding threads that networked his body, carefully preparing a map of connections that the surgeons could then use to free his body from the web of restraint.

I laid my hand on the bed. "Would you like to sit?"

Eldrin nodded stiffly. He settled on the mattress edge and stared across the dimly lit room at the opposite wall.

After a while he spoke. "My father is ninety-one now."

My heart grew heavy. "I dreamed about your father too."

His voice caught. "Mine was a simple dream, really. He was sitting in his favorite armchair in our home on Lyshriol. Mother was with him. So were my brothers and sisters." A tear ran down his cheek, catching a spark of light. "My father was saying good-bye to them. And to me. He sent a message to me, I don't know how."

Moisture gathered in my eyes. "He had a good life, Dryni. A family he loved. It made him happy."

"Makes," Eldrin whispered. "Not made."

"I'm sorry," I murmured. "I'm so sorry."

"It's just a bad dream."

"Yes. Just a dream." I started to reach for him. Then I stopped, fearing a rebuff, unsure what he needed now.

"Ah, Dehya." He pulled me into his arms, resting my head against his shoulder. With relief, I embraced him. His sleep shirt felt soft against my skin, and his hair brushed my forehead, smelling of the astringent shampoo he favored.

He hinged his hand, cupping it around my cheek, his four fingers firm against my skin. "I wish we could bring Taquinil back." The pain of loss ached in his words.

"He's still alive." I willed it to be true. If only I had the use of a Triad Chair, so I could search better.

Eldrin brushed his hand over my hair, from my head all the way down my back. "My father didn't receive any life-extension treatments until he met my mother. He was already eighteen. And the treatments were less advanced then. But he always said he had a full life, more than he ever expected. Gods know, he loved my mother. And she him."

I splayed my hands on his back, feeling the familiar strength of his muscles. "We need to go to Earth. We have to get him and Roca out of there."

"Yes."

We sat for a while, holding each other, neither saying what we feared, that it would be his father's body we brought home.

After a while Eldrin said, "He's a strange man."

I knew he didn't mean his father. "Jon Casestar?"

"Corbal Xir."

My hands tightened on his back. "Strange how?"

"He could be kind."

Kind? I couldn't believe the word.

Eldrin answered my unspoken protest. "He almost never asked me to provide. Only when the Razers interrogated me—" He took a ragged breath. "Even then, I don't think my pain made him transcend. The Razers did, but not Corbal."

I wasn't sure I had heard right. "You mean Xir left you alone?"

"No. He . . . paid attention. But he tried to control his cruelty." His voice grated. "He didn't always succeed. And he liked having slaves. He used to make me kneel just to see a Ruby prince prostrate before him." His hand clenched my hair. "Nor did the word 'consent' mean anything to him."

My body went rigid in his arms. *I'll strangle him.*

I didn't realize I was gritting my teeth until Eldrin rubbed my jaw. His voice lightened a bit. "Strangulation? Did that come from my gentle wife?"

"I'll put him in the exhaust nozzle of a starship antimatter drive and blast off."

Although he laughed softly, it sounded strained. He bent his head over mine. "It's over now."

"Thank the saints," I murmured.

But I feared the difficulties had only begun.

17

Bloodmark

Over the next few months, two thousand ships joined us at Delos. Many came from the Onyx evacuation. Their crews had delivered the evacuees to freedom, then refitted and set out to find the remains of Skolia's once mighty fleet. Their appearance at Delos didn't reassure the Allied forces.

Then the largest battle cruiser from Onyx arrived, *Pharaoh's Shield*, rumbling through the Delos star system, a star-faring giant attended by ships that were large in their own right, yet dwarfed by the rugged cruiser.

An old friend commanded *Pharaoh's Shield*: Admiral Ragnar Bloodmark. Tall and lean, with long muscles and a rangy frame, he projected a sense of barely controlled power, as if he might uncoil in vehemence without warning. Although his self-assurance, strong features, and dark coloring evoked a lord of the Skolian noble Houses, he had been born in poverty. He wasn't a full Skolian; his grandfather had come from a place called Scandinavia on Earth. But Ragnar was a Skolian citizen and had deeply resented the prejudice he encountered in his youth because of his mixed heritage. Given the high status he had attained in ISC, few dared belittle his lineage now.

We met in the Tactics Room of *Havyrl's Valor*. Ragnar, Jon Casestar, Eldrin, Vazar, Jinn Opsister, and I sat at a table near the luminous white curve of the spherical room. My bodyguards were stationed around the chamber, Ragnar and Jon had brought aides, and Ragnar also had two bodyguards. The sphere seemed too full of uniformed people, like moths clustered within a white flame yet somehow never consumed by its fire.

Ragnar continued his report to Jon. "We lost every space habitat at Onyx. We didn't lose the Orbiter space habitat, but it took serious damage during the Trader raid." He glanced at me, lines creasing his rugged features. "All your bodyguards were killed, Dehya. I'm sorry."

I struggled with that memory. I could still see their crumpled bodies in the coruscating hall that led to the Lock. Here in the Tactics Room, Eldrin was sitting next to me with his palm lying on the transparent table. His hand gripped the surface, his fingertips turning white.

"We must see to their families," I said. "And a memorial service."

"I have people on it." Ragnar watched me with his familiar, dark-eyed gaze. I knew him far better than Jon Casestar. Although Ragnar wasn't always easy to deal with, I valued his loyalty.

"Let us know how it proceeds," Eldrin said.

"Of course, Your Highness," Ragnar answered smoothly. As always, he somehow managed to make his courtesies to Eldrin sound like insults. At best he and Eldrin had a strained relationship; at its worst, their mutual dislike descended into open hostility.

Undaunted by the choppy emotional undercurrents, Vazar spoke to Ragnar. "A man lives on the Orbiter, an artist. He's called Coop."

Ragnar answered curtly. "Your husband is fine, Primary Majda." He had never hidden his distaste for their three-way marriage.

Vazar left it at that, but relief washed out from her mind, swirling over us like warm water from a sun-touched lake. Eldrin's gaze gentled as he watched his sister-in-law. Neither Ragnar nor Jon showed any indication they caught her reaction. The same was true of the woman standing behind Ragnar, one of his aides. Even after so many decades, it bemused me that most people didn't experience the rich tumult of emotions humans produced. Often that tumult became too much and I had to retreat from human contact, except with Eldrin. His mind flowed in strong and deep waves, forming a steady envelope for the faster, entangled oscillations of my own thoughts.

Eldrin had a similar effect on Taquinil, who had a mind much like mine. It was one reason Taquinil and I had such a good relationship; his thoughts, his moods, the way he solved problems and viewed the universe—they all made sense to me. Eldrin sheltered us both from the emotional storms of humanity that raged outside the haven of his love. Even when he was exasperated or annoyed with us, his mind still soothed ours. I'm not sure he understood it, any more than Taquinil and I understood our effect on him. With his songwriter's lyricism, Eldrin called us "spangled life, like dazzling sunlight reflected off waves of the sea, the sparkle that makes me feel alive."

Jon was speaking to Ragnar. "Have we secured the Orbiter?"

Ragnar concentrated his attention on the other admiral. It intrigued me to watch them interact, two of the Imperial Fleet's most influential leaders. Jon's quiet strength and calm efficiency inspired confidence, whereas Ragnar had a dark, brooding aspect that disquieted people.

"We've moved the Orbiter to a new star system." Ragnar turned his keen gaze back to me. "But as long as the First Lock remains operational, the Traders can locate the Orbiter using their stolen Lock."

I glanced at the aide standing behind him.

"She's cleared," Ragnar said.

"I can turn off the First Lock if we return to the Orbiter," I said.

Jon Casestar didn't look the least surprised by my statement, but that didn't make his expression any less stony. "Taking you to the Orbiter right now is too much of a risk."

Eldrin was staring at us, incredulous. No one had ever told him we could deactivate the Locks. But now he had a need to know. The Locks required Rhon psions to operate, and Eldrin and I were the only free Rhon psions. For the Orbiter's safety, we needed to turn off its Lock. But the fact that we could turn them off could also be exploited as a weakness in our defenses and in the Triad. Had Eldrin known before, he might have revealed it to the Traders during interrogation.

A model evolving in the back of my mind suddenly converged. "Of course!" I said. "He turned it off."

Jon blinked at me. Less than a second had passed since his comment about the risk of taking me to the Orbiter.

I clarified my abrupt statement. "Kelric turned off the stolen Lock."

Now they were all giving me odd looks, except Eldrin. "You still think Kelric is alive?" Eldrin asked. He tried to hold in his hope, but it lightened his voice. Even after all these years, I knew he still greatly missed his youngest brother; although Kelric had grown into a huge warrior, towering over his older brother, Eldrin would always remember him as the affectionate little brother who had held so much love for his family.

Ragnar raised his eyebrow at me. "Do you mean Tertiary Kelricson Valdoria? The Ruby Prince?"

"That's right," I said. "Kelric joined the Triad."

Jon spoke. "Pharaoh Dyhianna, I don't understand why you think he is alive."

"*Someone* new is in the Triad," I said.

"How can you tell?" Ragnar asked. "The psiberweb is gone."

"Kyle space is still there. I was in it. So was Kelric."

Ragnar spoke smoothly. "You've been under a lot of strain."

I gave him a dour look. "I'm not imagining it."

"I would never imply such," he assured me. "But what you've been through lately could affect your perceptions."

Eldrin scowled. "Her 'perceptions' are fine, Ragnar."

The admiral answered in an overly courteous voice. "Thank you, Prince Eldrin."

A familiar tension tightened my shoulders. *Not now,* I willed them both, even though I knew Ragnar couldn't hear. They had fought these verbal battles for years.

Eldrin glanced at me. Then he took a breath and answered Ragnar with formal civility. "Very well, Admiral."

When neither of them said anything else, both Jon and I relaxed. I wasn't the only one disquieted by the antipathy between Ragnar and Eldrin. When two people both held such high positions, their antagonism stopped being personal and became political.

Vazar, however, had no hesitation about wading into the fray. "Dehya, could your calculations be connected to Naaj? She was Kelric's sister-in-law."

"I don't think so." My main worry about Naaj Majda concerned what she would do if Kelric showed up, claiming his title and assets. She might decide he should go back to being dead before anyone discovered he lived.

"You think Kelric went to a Lock?" Eldrin asked.

"He would have had to," I said. "If he joined the Triad."

Ragnar didn't look convinced. "No one has been to the Orbiter or the Lock on Raylicon."

"Then he used the one the Traders stole," I said.

Vazar scowled. "How? They crashed the psiberweb with it."

"We don't know for certain they caused the collapse," Jon said.

I sifted through my mental files. "I suspect it was a combination of events. Taquinil and I dropped into Kyle space at the same time the Traders were misusing the Lock. Even without our presence, their activities would have destabilized the Kyle universe. Add Taquinil and me, and it's no wonder it imploded."

"Wouldn't a new one immediately form?" Ragnar's eyes glinted with dark humor. "Sort of a mental Big Bang?"

I quirked my eyebrow at him. "I imagine so, given that I'm not dead."

Jon spoke. "Then the implosion of the psiberspace where we built our webs must have occurred before you and your son fell into the Lock."

"I think so." I prayed I was right, because if I had missed the implosion, Taquinil must have too. Not just him, either. "To join the Triad, Kelric would need entry into Kyle space, but it could be *any* Kyle space. If he has been a Trader prisoner all these years, he might have found a way to reach the Lock." I wondered if he had joined the Triad and then deactivated the Lock.

Ragnar scratched his ear. "I suppose it's possible."

I recognized his look. "No, you don't."

"Well, you have to admit, it's farfetched."

"She doesn't have to admit any damn thing," Eldrin said.

The admiral gave him a sour look. "My apologies if I gave offense."

"It's all right," I said, watching Eldrin. Even with Ragnar, he didn't usually react this sharply, at least not without provocation. Since his return from the Traders, he had been curt with everyone.

Eldrin returned my gaze, his mood a blend of old frustration and new pain. I could tell he didn't want me to trust Ragnar. Even so, I needed the admiral. For all the discords he hit with people, he was an exceptional strategist and strong supporter of our family. But I couldn't fully trust anyone. Majda had a history of loyalty to the Ruby Dynasty that stretched back millennia, yet I had even more misgivings about Naaj. Too many people had too much to gain by controlling the Ruby Dynasty. I wasn't even sure about Vazar. It made me hesitate to mind-speak with Eldrin in her presence.

I abhorred this distrust. The undefined position of the Ruby Dynasty within the political structure of Skolia made it worse. The Assembly governed, but without us they couldn't maintain their power. We were making decisions here that required Assembly approval, but we had no Assembly representative. Technically it wasn't legal. In fact, it could be viewed as an attempted coup by the Ruby Dynasty, with the backing of the Imperial Fleet, the strongest arm of ISC.

Well, hell. What were we supposed to do, sit around until the Assembly let us act? If we had done that, Eldrin would be in custody on Earth now. This was no time to falter. Besides, if I ever did attempt a coup, I would approach the Pharaoh's Army first, rather than the Imperial Fleet. The Army's history of loyalty to the Pharaoh went back five millennia.

Then again, Majda dominated that branch of ISC, with Naaj as General of the Army. I might do better with Jon and Ragnar. Not that I was planning to overthrow the Assembly. But this would be an ideal time for the coup I wasn't contemplating, with the current power structure weakened and communications down everywhere. It was a good thing I wasn't considering it, because before I made such a move, I should have my sister and brother-in-law at my side.

I regarded Jon Casestar. "We need to rescue Roca and Eldrinson from Earth."

He met my gaze. "We've sent ships to confer with HQ and the Assembly. We haven't heard back yet."

"We don't have time to wait," I said.

Ragnar spoke. "We don't have authority to act in a situation as volatile as this." His voice cooled as he glanced at Jon. "The same holds true for the decision to occupy Delos."

Jon was unfazed. "Under the circumstances, I considered it warranted."

Eldrin spoke to Ragnar with barely controlled hostility. "Had they waited for approval, I would be on my way to Earth now."

"So you would," Ragnar murmured.

"Ragnar," I warned.

He turned to me, his gaze intent. "The Imperator wields a great deal of power even in times of peace."

What did that mean? "We've never had a time of peace."

"That calls even more for a strong Imperator." He paused. "A hereditary Imperator, one who isn't hobbled by civilian councils during times of crisis."

Interesting. It almost sounded as if he were putting the Imperator ahead of the Assembly, supporting my family over the current government.

Vazar spoke flatly. "If we make any move on Earth, they could interpret it as an act of war."

"It doesn't have to be that way," I said.

Ragnar tilted his head. "You have a suggestion?"

Before I could respond, Jon spoke carefully. "I can notify HQ of any suggestions you make, Your Highness."

Notify, pah. I tried to glean what lay within the fortress of his mind. I had always had a problem reading him. "We may have to move fast."

Vazar leaned forward, her forearms resting on the table,

her body poised as if she were prepared for battle. Then she dropped her bombshell. "I've been granted authority to speak for Majda."

Everyone fell silent. Her statement left no ambiguity; she had just claimed Naaj appointed her to speak for the acting Imperator. To say it was no small assertion was akin to saying I had worried a bit about Eldrin when the Traders had him. I found her words hard to credit; Naaj had no reason to dilute her power that way. Why had Vazar said nothing before this? The answer was obvious; she had no proof. If her claim proved false, the antediluvian laws of the noble Houses would have her executed for treason. I couldn't imagine her making such an assertion lightly.

Ragnar spoke first. "I assume you have proof?"

"Yes," Vazar said. "Send a message to headquarters."

He snorted. "This discussion started because we need to act faster than we can communicate with headquarters."

I considered. Vazar was a Primary, one of our best. In her youth she had been a top-notch fighter pilot. Now she worked at HQ. It wasn't inconceivable that she and Naaj had discussed this, but had yet to make it official. As Imperator, Naaj Majda was the commanding officer of both Ragnar and Jon. That meant Vazar's claim was tantamount to saying her decisions superseded those of the two admirals. Although she held a rank similar to theirs, she was J-Force and we were on Fleet ships. I didn't think Naaj would give her that authority, but I couldn't be sure. If Naaj *had* charged her with such a duty, it implied she placed great trust in Vazar, enough to make me question Vazar's loyalties.

Or Vazar could be acting on her own. If she moved against Naaj, she would need our protection. If her actions benefited the House of Majda, Naaj might support her anyway; only they knew the truth. But if it came to a confrontation, with the Ruby Dynasty between, that would split the two most powerful factions of the nobility, weakening both Majda and the Ruby Dynasty. It would create a schism that the Assembly could use to wrest away what little power we retained in this modern era.

What a mess. I needed to talk to Vazar in private. I couldn't risk mind-speaking here. I had no problem with Eldrin catching leakage from our thoughts, but my Jagernaut bodyguards were also psions.

Jon Casestar was speaking to Vazar. "We have had no notification from Imperator Majda regarding this matter."

"She made the charge," Vazar said. "I don't have the documentation with me. It is your decision whether or not to accept my word. But if you refuse and my claim turns out to be true, you will have more trouble than you can imagine."

Bold today, aren't we? I thought.

Vazar glanced at me, but didn't answer.

Ragnar was more blunt. "If you're lying, Primary, we could be accused of treason."

"I can't accept a change of command," Jon said. "Not without proof."

"I've no wish to disrupt your chain of command," Vazar said. "However, I can respond for HQ regarding any proposals to move against Earth."

I wished I knew if this came from Vazar or Naaj. Although I didn't sense Vazar lying, she was accomplished at guarding her thoughts.

Ragnar spoke dryly. "It strikes me as premature to discuss how we will execute a plan when we have no plan."

At the word *execute*, Vazar winced.

Watching them negotiate the convolutions of their authority made me uneasy. If Vazar didn't push a change of command, then Jon Casestar held rank here. But Ragnar was an imposing force in the Fleet, as was Vazar in the J-Force. I wanted all their support, but if I became pushed into a corner, I might have to choose.

Whom should I trust?

18
Mists of Loss

I had just pulled on my nightshirt when a bell chimed in the living room of my suite. My hope stirred. I missed Eldrin at night, in the quiet times we used to spend together, before the war had made him withdraw into himself. His responses to Ragnar today had made me wonder if he would come to my quarters tonight, if only to ensure that his claim to the Ruby Pharaoh remained undisputed. I would like to think he would seek me out for more than that, but I would settle for any reason. I longed to see my husband.

"Laplace, who is that?" I asked.

"I don't know," my suite's EI answered. "He's using a shadow maker. I can't penetrate his shroud."

That didn't sound like Eldrin. I went into the living room, to the entrance archway, and touched a small panel at shoulder level. A holoscreen activated by the door, showing the area outside.

Ragnar Bloodmark.

He stood at ease, lanky and lean, exuding casual menace. None of my Jagernaut bodyguards were outside. Although they could be gone because they were changing shifts, I doubted it. Security would never allow such a gap. More likely, Ragnar had dismissed them. I had my neural nodes do an IR check of the suite and verified that the security monitors watching my suite were still operational. Then I spoke coolly into the comm. "Admiral."

"Admiral?" His eyebrow went up. "Since when did we become so formal?"

When indeed. "It's late, Ragnar."

"Are you busy?"

"I was thinking."

His lips quirked. "I thought I felt the ship shaking."

I couldn't help but smile. "Probably the engines."

"May I come in?"

It was an awkward request. Top-level officers didn't visit my private quarters at night. As a family friend, Ragnar could make a personal call, but not under these circumstances. Given the way ISC Security monitored my quarters, they had to be making a record of this exchange. His presumption astonished me. After what Eldrin had been through, and his well-known discomfort with Ragnar, the admiral couldn't have chosen a more ill-judged approach. In fact, it made no sense. Ragnar was too smart for such a mistake.

I turned my voice frosty. "I don't think so, Admiral Bloodmark."

He glanced around the hall. "Dehya, we need to talk. Now that he's back."

What did that mean? He almost made it sound as if he were my lover. It would fit the way he and Eldrin had been at odds this afternoon.

We all knew Security kept constant watch on me. Everyone also knew I could outwit their monitors. Although it warned them that I had something to hide, I often did it anyway, particularly when Eldrin and I used to lie together at night. But if I turned them off while Ragnar was here, especially after today's politically volatile discussion, it would alarm Security. They might fear Ragnar and I were plotting—unless, of course, they assumed we had a more amorous assignation.

So. Ragnar had just given me an excuse to deactivate the monitors without raising too much suspicion. Or his suggestion might actually be as offensive as it looked. If anyone would try such a brazen stunt, it was Ragnar. But as aggressive as he might be, he was never stupid. I suspected he wanted to talk about the issue we had skirted today, the possibility of the Ruby Dynasty maneuvering outside of Assembly bounds. That could shift into talks of a coup, which we certainly couldn't do with ISC monitoring me.

I didn't know if I wanted to consider action against the Assembly. In many ways, they functioned well. In other ways I hated how they worked, particularly in regard to my family. If I ever did move to reassert the reign of the Ruby Dynasty, I would need ISC support. Ragnar could be invaluable. To find out what he wanted now, all I had to do was play his game, turn off the monitors, and let him into my suite.

But such a move would be an implicit betrayal of the trust Eldrin and I shared. Pah. The hell with Ragnar. If he wanted to offer support, he could find a way that didn't make it look as if I had deceived my husband.

I imagined icicles on my words. "I have no idea what you're talking about, Admiral. I will see you tomorrow."

He blew out a gust of air. "Damn it, Dehya. I need to talk to you about Councilor Roca and Web Key Eldrinson."

Fair enough. Given that statement, though, I couldn't turn off the monitors now without making Security paranoid. Nor did I intend to see Ragnar in the middle of the night. But it wouldn't be politic to leave the door shut in his face, either. "Just a moment," I said.

I went to my bedroom for a robe that covered me from shoulder to ankle. Then I returned and released the door. With a blue shimmer, the wall vanished. Ragnar stood there, all in black, from his knee-boots to his sharply creased uniform.

He grinned, a wicked flash of teeth. "My greetings, Pharaoh Dyhianna."

"And mine, Admiral." I didn't invite him in. "I will be happy to meet with you tomorrow."

"We can't waste time." He leaned his arm against the archway, above my head, and looked down at my face. "You need a strong base, Pharaoh. People you can trust."

"And you offer such a base?"

"I think he's offered enough," Eldrin said tightly.

Ragnar turned with lazy insolence, his arm still above my head. As I stepped away from the admiral, Eldrin walked toward us in the corridor outside my suite. His step remained slow, measured, so tightly controlled I almost expected him to explode. He watched Ragnar as if he had found a small, many-legged creature scuttling along in defiance of the robo-sweeps that cleaned the ship.

Ragnar bowed to him. Then he drawled. "My greetings, Prince Eldrin."

Eldrin didn't stop until he stood right in front of the admiral. They were about the same size, Ragnar a bit taller and Eldrin a bit broader in the shoulders.

Then Eldrin said, succinctly, "Fuck you," and swung at him.

He struck at the side of Ragnar's neck with the knife edge of his hand, aiming for below the ear. Ragnar jerked away fast, but the blow still hit his shoulder. He stumbled to the side, out of my doorway. As Eldrin went at him, Ragnar snapped into an enhanced mode. Moving in a blur, he pinned Eldrin against the bulkhead outside my door, pressing his forearm across Eldrin's neck. Although Eldrin possessed greater natural strength, Ragnar's augmentation increased both his strength and speed.

"No!" I shouted. In that instant, Eldrin struck Ragnar's elbows hard with the heels of his hands, breaking his grip. He shoved the admiral away, but they immediately grappled again.

"Security," I said. "Send backup." It was probably a redundant request—the monitors had almost certainly recorded the altercation and dispatched a response—but I had no intention of taking any chances.

I didn't try to interfere with the fight. Even if I could have held one of them back, it would only have given his opponent a chance to hit him harder.

Wrestling hard, they stumbled across the corridor and hit the opposite wall. Ragnar was obviously restraining himself; he could have seriously injured Eldrin by now. With a chill, I realized that if he toggled into full combat mode, he could kill Eldrin before he stopped his programmed reflexes. He would have it all on record, too, that he acted in self-defense.

"Eldrin, don't!" I lunged forward and put myself between them, gambling that their reluctance to hurt me would make them stop. They might knock me over instead, but it was worth the risk if it kept them from killing each other.

They did pause, but only for long enough for Eldrin to push me to the side. Ragnar spoke in an urgent voice. "Dehya, stay back."

Four Jagernauts ran around a corner in the corridor and came toward us. Nozzles had also emerged from the bulkheads. On command, they could disperse a gas that would put us to sleep, but they had done nothing yet. It didn't surprise me that Security sent Jagernauts and only threatened the gas as a backup. I doubted they wanted to be responsible for knocking out any of us. Protecting me and interfering in my private affairs were two very different matters, and the border between the two wasn't at all clear.

Eldrin and Ragnar staggered across the corridor and hit the other bulkhead, dark figures against the white walls. The thud of Ragnar's back against Luminex resounded through the air. His face had the same impassive mask that Jagernauts took on when they switched into combat mode. Sweat dampened Eldrin's blue shirt.

When Eldrin closed his hands around Ragnar's neck, the admiral brought up his arms, fast and hard. He used so much force to break the hold that it threw Eldrin across the corridor into the other wall. The back of Eldrin's head hit the bulkhead and he froze, his eyes glazed.

A husky Jagernaut interposed himself between Eldrin and Ragnar. When Eldrin tried to lunge forward anyway, the Jagernaut caught him in a hold meant to restrain rather than harm. Eldrin's fury seared my mind. His gaze was unfocused as if he saw none of us. His rage beat against my mind like storm-tossed breakers crashing on a rocky shoreline.

Two other Jagernauts were holding Ragnar. It took them both to control him, but within moments he stopped fighting, and his face lost its automated expression. The fourth Jagernaut, a man with red hair, had stopped a few paces from Eldrin, his body positioned between the fighters. Although obviously prepared to help, he hadn't yet touched anyone.

Suddenly Eldrin froze, staring at the fourth Jagernaut. He spoke with a scorching hatred. "You have no right, you goddamned bastard."

Puzzlement washed out from the red-haired man, but he remained poised, ready to act.

Gradually Eldrin's gaze cleared. He finally seemed to see

us. Attuned to Eldrin's mind, the Jagernaut holding him slowly released his grip, but maintained a ready stance.

Eldrin turned to Ragnar, who stood quietly now, flanked by two Jagernauts. "Tread carefully," Eldrin told him softly. Then he strode away from us, down the corridor. His raw fury reverberated even after he left.

I knew then he hadn't been fighting Ragnar or the Jagernauts.

His rage had burned at Corbal Xir.

"Can I enter?" I asked the door.

"Please wait," it responded.

I stood shivering in the remote corridor, facing a blue archway in the Luminex wall, my arms folded across my torso. I wasn't really cold, not physically. It all came from inside.

The Jagernauts who had accompanied me stood a few meters down the corridor, trying to look invisible. I had threatened a court-martial if they didn't go away. They stayed anyway, but at least they had the tact to remain back there instead of looming behind me.

I was about to query the door again when it said, "Please enter." Then it shimmered and vanished, revealing a dimly lit living room beyond.

I glanced at the Jagernauts. One inclined his head to me, but neither came any closer. A wise decision; I might have actually considered the court-martial if they had intruded that far. They would come to the door after I entered, but once the entrance closed, we would have a modicum of privacy inside.

I walked into the suite and the wall reformed behind me. It was almost dark inside; the only light came from holo-panels on the walls. They showed twilight views of the Dalvador Plains on the world Lyshriol. Shadowed grasses rippled in an unseen breeze, and stained-glass bubbles floated through the air, translucent, almost invisible. One popped and showered glitter over the grass. In the distance, mountains raised spindled peaks to a dark sky.

It was Eldrin's childhood home.

As my eyes adjusted, I made out Eldrin sitting on a divan

across the room, his elbow resting on its scrolled arm. Even in this dim light, dark smudges were visible under his eyes.

I spoke awkwardly. "My greetings, Husband."

"What do you want?" His face was unreadable.

"Your company."

"You had plenty of company earlier tonight."

"I didn't ask for it."

"No?" He mimicked Ragnar's gravely voice. " 'Dehya, we need to talk. Now that he's back.' "

"He was out of line. I told him so."

Eldrin snorted. "Right."

Dryni, you know it's true. If I had ever had an affair with Ragnar, you would have seen it in my mind. When he kept his thoughts barricaded, I said, "You ought to know me better than that."

"I thought I did."

"I haven't changed."

He spoke harshly, "He doesn't want to talk strategy with you. He wants to control your power. He wants to control you. And he wants to get under that flimsy little nightshirt you're wearing beneath that robe."

"Eldrin, don't."

"How can you be so brilliant and miss something so obvious?"

I didn't say I missed it.

Yet still you trust him.

Right now I don't trust anyone.

Not even me?

You, I always trust.

Maybe you shouldn't.

Why not?

His thoughts had a clenched feel. **I've been with the Traders.**

I stepped toward him. *Don't let them shame you.*

Now you're going to do the comfort thing, right? I don't want it.

I stopped. *What do you want?*

His hand curled into a fist. The slave cuff glittered on his wrist. **To forget.**

I so much wanted to go to him. *Let me help.*

I don't need help.

All right. I knew if I pushed, it would drive him away.

After a long moment he relented. **Come sit with me.**

I almost closed my eyes with relief. Then I went to the divan and settled near him. "I'm glad to see you, Dryni."

A shadow crossed his face. He lifted his arm as if to touch my face, then let it drop again. In a low voice, he said, "I truly believed I would never . . ." He shook his head as if to throw away a memory.

"We don't have to talk about it."

He didn't answer. But after a moment he thought, **I had an idea that might help free my parents from Earth.**

I would like to know. But maybe you should kiss me first.

He shifted his weight. **Dehya, later.**

I need an excuse to deactivate the monitors.

Ah. He still didn't look comfortable, but he drew me into his arms, his motions stiffly formal. Then he lay on the divan, drawing me underneath him. As we sank into air-cushions, he gave me a perfunctory kiss. It felt familiar and strange at once, the first time we had touched this way since his return.

As we kissed, our hands wandered. At first Eldrin stroked me with a distant formality, only going through motions. But gradually his touch grew more urgent. He hinged his hand around my breast, and my nipple hardened under the nightshirt. He needed no thumb to complete his caresses; what he could do with those four opposing fingers made my body tingle. I pressed against him, distracted from my original intent to discuss Roca and Eldrinson.

After a while, I thought, *Shall I deactivate the monitors now, so we can talk?* I smiled. *We must be raising the blood pressure of everyone in the Security office.*

Eldrin laughed against my neck. **Indeed. Perhaps we should save the talking for later.**

I agreed wholeheartedly. "Suite attend," I murmured.

"Attending," the suite's EI answered.

"Please contact Laplace in my quarters and have it run 'Welcome.' "

'*Welcome*'? Eldrin nuzzled my neck. **What is that?**

It will stymie ISC Security. I paused. *I called it 'welcome' for you.*

He pushed up on his elbows and looked down at me. His face had gentled. **Can Laplace give us privacy?**

For a while. Maybe a couple of hours.

He traced his finger over my lips. **We shouldn't waste our time then.**

I drew him back into my arms, more thankful than I knew how to say that he was returning to himself, bit by bit. I breathed in his scent, and a trace of cologne tickled my nose. It made me wonder if he had come to my quarters earlier tonight for a more intimate evening. Blasted Ragnar. But perhaps this would work out.

I rubbed my cheek against his neck, pushing aside his shirt—and the diamonds of his collar pressed my skin, cold and hard. Startled, I jerked, my hands going still on his back.

The doctors haven't finished mapping the web of biothreads inside me, he thought with brittle anger. **The threads keep growing, using resources from my own body. It's why I tire more easily now.**

Flaming Aristos.

He dragged his wrist across my ribcage, pushing up his sleeve. The gems on his cuff scraped the underside of my breasts.

Does it bother you?

My face flushed. *Actually, it feels good.*

Curiosity flickered in his mind. **What, this?** He pushed his cuff over my breast and my nipple hardened.

I felt myself redden. *Sorry.*

For what?

For my, uh, nipple. You know.

A sense of amusement lightened his darkness. **I won't hold it against it.**

We don't have to do anything.

His lips quirked with his old mischief. **Then again, maybe we do.**

Encouraged, I rubbed the muscles of his back in that way

he liked. After a while he sighed and slid his hands along my sides. We took it slow, relearning each other after our separation. His ragged emotions were like gravel, and he touched me with a rough urgency, as if to prove he had lost nothing. As we came together, his intensity swept us both, no longer rocky, now instead a fire consuming dry tinder.

Later, I drowsed in his arms, Eldrin on his back with me stretched along his side. My palm rested on his muscled chest. I felt the deep satisfaction I had only ever known with him, even more so because I had feared he would never come home.

He stirred, moving his large hand over my arm. "It's always like this with you. Like we're . . . I don't know. Intoxicated with each other."

"Yes," I murmured, drowsy. I tickled his navel. "Beautiful, sexy man."

Fond amusement came from his mind. **Men are handsome, Dehya. Not beautiful.**

I thought of telling him how his eyes reminded me of the twilight sky after a glorious sunset, but I knew it would embarrass him.

Eldrin laughed softly. **Probably. But my eyes thank you for the compliment.** He shifted me in his arms. **Think we're still alone?**

I think so. Laplace would let me know if anyone had breached its systems. Stretching, I added, *You said you had an idea about Roca and Eldrinson.*

I don't know if it can help.

What is it?

Taquinil is still in psiberspace.

Yes. I refused to believe otherwise.

Perhaps we can reach him.

I've tried. I may have made contact. I'm not sure.

If we could, perhaps he could help us make a psiberweb.

I grasped at that thread of hope, as much for the opportunity to draw Taquinil back as for the chance it could help us reach Earth. *By himself, he's probably too isolated. But if I could form a specific enough thought in Kyle space, it might draw him out.* I considered possibilities. *Perhaps he could help us make links with Earth's webs.*

Eldrin ran his hand down my arm. **If only he will come home.** *Yes.* If only. *If only.*

"I don't like it," Jon Casestar said.

He was standing next to the telop control chair where I sat in a Node Room on the battle cruiser. Eldrin stood on my other side, a silent support.

"Jon, this is what I do." I gestured toward the banks of consoles in the room. Operators monitored them, waiting for us to proceed.

"You work in Kyle space," Jon said, intransigent. "Right now Kyle space doesn't exist."

"Of course it exists." I crossed my arms. "I fail to see the point in protecting me from the very thing you all so zealously protect me so I can do."

"You're being deliberately obtuse," he said. "Suppose you phase out again? We can't risk it."

"Everyone says that to me, all the time. 'We can't risk it.' And why?" I thumped my palm on the arm of my control chair. "Because if anything happens to me, you won't have anyone who can do *this*. So let me do my job."

"She's right." The gravelly voice came from behind us.

Eldrin turned with a jerk. Ragnar stood in the entrance of the room, spare and craggy in his black uniform.

"Admiral Bloodmark." Jon nodded, formal and reserved.

"Admiral Casestar." As courteous and correct as Ragnar made his response, he still sounded as if he were poking fun at Jon. He addressed Eldrin in a smooth voice. "You look well this morning, Your Highness. I'm glad you're feeling better today."

Eldrin's expression plainly said, G*o to hell.* But he didn't rise to the bait.

My voice cooled. "Did you want something, Admiral Bloodmark?"

He glanced at me as if taken aback by my unexpected frost. He had his "injured-party" look down to perfection, but

I wasn't fooled. I had seen him pull this act with several truly insufferable officers in ISC, and also with broadcasters who criticized the Ruby Dynasty. In those cases, I had enjoyed his style, even if I couldn't say so in public. But when he turned the sharpened edge of his intellect on Eldrin, I wasn't amused.

"Actually, Pharaoh Dyhianna," he said, "I was offering support." His voice was a subtle parody of my own, but also with humor. He had always been a master at the nuances of human tone and undertone, a talent he had honed in the rough urban landscape of his childhood, parlaying it into personal gain.

I smiled slightly. "Thank you, Admiral. Your support is appreciated."

Jon considered Ragnar, his gray-eyed gaze missing nothing. "You think the Pharaoh should use the telop chair?"

Ragnar joined him at the side of my chair, across from Eldrin. "Her Highness is uniquely qualified to discover what, if anything, remains of the psibernet, and to rebuild it. She is also the one most capable to determine if it is safe to work in psiberspace, and what would make it so if it isn't now."

"And if we lose her?" Jon asked quietly.

"You always run that risk," I said.

Jon shook his head. "These aren't normal times. We don't have normal safeguards."

I leaned forward. "All the more reason for me to investigate the web."

He frowned, then glanced at Ragnar. "And you concur."

Ragnar didn't hesitate. "Yes."

Jon turned to Eldrin. "What do you say?"

Although Eldrin revealed little in his expression, I felt his mood. He feared that instead of recovering Taquinil, he might lose me. He answered with difficulty. "I agree with my wife." Then he spoke to me. "I can anchor you here. If you slip, I'll bring you back."

I touched his hand where it lay on the arm of my chair. Watching us, Ragnar stiffened.

When Jon cracked his knuckles, I felt certain he would refuse. But then he said, "All right, Your Highness. Let's do it."

"Excellent!" I sat up straighter. Finally we were going to act.

He spoke into his wrist comm, and the techs went to work at their consoles. When I activated my chair, its exoskeleton folded around my body, clicking prongs into my neck, spine, wrists, and ankles. Its silvery cage sheathed my body, flickering with lights.

Eldrin walked around my chair to the console on my other side, near the two admirals. Trying to ignore Ragnar, he sat in the command chair of the console, which faced mine at an angle. As he fastened himself into its exoskeleton, the web techs ran tests on the system like a ground crew checking out a spacecraft. Then Eldrin winked at me. When I gave a startled laugh, he grinned.

Ragnar stood on the other side of the console, staring with that brooding gaze of his. Despite his barriers, I picked up his mood. Beneath his sardonic exterior he was actually worried about Eldrin—but he would never admit it, especially after last night. I wished I knew how to smooth the friction between them.

Closing my eyes, I let my mind drift, settling into the receptive state I needed to explore psiberspace. The EI brain of *Havyrl's Valor* rumbled in the background of my thoughts like a great heartbeat. I wondered how Eldrin's brother Havyrl felt about having a battle cruiser named after him. ISC often used Ruby Dynasty names for its big ships. The Pharaoh's Army had one called *Eldrin's Majesty*. It embarrassed Eldrin. He once told me that if they had to use his name, he would have preferred a reference to his prowess as a fighter.

In his youth, Eldrin had been more interested in sword practice than schoolwork. He was very much a son of Lyshriol. During its five thousand years of isolation, the Lyshriol colony had slid back to a more primitive culture, and much of that remained today, seventy-three years after we had rediscovered it. When Eldrin was sixteen, he rode to war and ended up killing several men, one with his bare hands. His people praised his courage, none realizing the experience had scarred him. He became violent at home, fought with men in the village, and trained all day instead of going to school. By Lyshriol standards, he had become a warrior of strength and bravery; by Skolian standards, he had turned into a deadly juvenile delinquent.

Roca and Eldrinson couldn't even agree if he was misbehaving, let alone what to do. But when Eldrin smashed up the school, pulled his sword on his tutor, and fought his own brother, his parents quit arguing. They sent him to a school on the Orbiter, with the hopes that exposure to Skolian culture would help him find balance in the conflicting demands of his life. The school specialized in students with learning disabilities, such as the Lyshriol genetic predisposition to illiteracy that Eldrin had inherited. His inability to read and write well had caused him constant frustration, especially because most of his siblings had no problem learning.

Eldrin and I were married during his first year on the Orbiter. Angry and confused, he rebelled against everything, especially the Assembly. In their inflexible intention to force our marriage, regardless of the cost, they seemed to Eldrin like nightmare authority figures gone berserk.

For a while Eldrin had wanted to take up fencing on the Orbiter, but he couldn't use the standardized swords required in competitions. The Lyshrioli weapons he had trained with were designed for a hand that hinged down the back and had four opposing fingers but no thumb. Most of his siblings had five-fingered hands with a thumb, as did our son, Taquinil. It came from my side of the family. Eldrin had inherited his father's hands.

Then he discovered that his teachers valued his magnificent singing voice. The opposite had been true on Lyshriol, where the culture had survived for thousands of years on the prowess of its warriors rather than the voices of the bards who recorded its history. He had suppressed his interest in singing there, but on the Orbiter he plunged into voice studies. Always fascinated with music and its mathematical beauty, I loved to listen to him practice. It was one of the first times I had seen him truly happy.

I still remembered his puzzlement at how Skolians treated him. He came from a culture with well-defined roles for men and women. Although it descended from a colony established by the matriarchal Ruby Empire, it had changed over its millennia of isolation. Aspects of the matriarchy survived, but they had become subsumed in the male-dominated culture, with the role of warrior shifted from women to men. In contrast, modern Skolia had never lost its origins. The overriding culture was egalitarian, for the most part, but the surviving remnants of its early history were solidly matriarchal, especially among the noble Houses, including a sexist tendency to value and objectify physical beauty in men above all other qualities. It had bewildered Eldrin that people praised his handsome face and well-built body yet never mentioned his martial skills.

But regardless of anything else in the rest of his life, he had been a wonderful father to Taquinil. It had always pleased Eldrin that he, who couldn't even read or write until he was seventeen, had sired such a genius.

My thoughts intensified with the affection stirred by my memories. Now, as an adult, Eldrin had a sophistication that contrasted with the wild, brash innocence of his youth.

Brash innocence? Picking up the tail end of my thought, Eldrin sent a mental snort. *I was an insufferable, arrogant kid with only one thing on my mind.*

No, you weren't. I smiled *At least not insufferable or arrogant.*

He sighed. **Dehya, you see me through a rosy filter.**

I do not. I'm very pragmatic.

Logical, yes. But you are, and always have been, a dreamer. His mood softened. **I hope you never change.**

I watched him in his command chair, encased now in an exoskeleton, with a visor ready to lower over his face. *You look like a starfighter pilot.*

He gave a mental laugh. **Are you ready to go in?**

All set. Then I thought, *Ship attend.*

ATTENDING. The answer rumbled, coming from the EI that controlled the massive brain of the battle cruiser.

Activate psi-gate.
ACTIVATED.

A psicon appeared, an elegant script ψ, like a computer icon except that it formed in my mind. Then it vanished. In its place—

Nothing.

Silvery mist filled the universe. My alarm surged, but I pushed it down. This wasn't nonexistence. It was only my interpretation of Kyle space without the structure of the web.

I could so easily disperse into that nothingness, become no more than an echo in a nether universe . . .

Dehya? Eldrin's thought came like the tendril of a vine reaching through the ψ gate.

I'm here.

What is there?

Just mist. I floated, trying to find definition with its swirling veils. *Taquinil? Are you here?*

No response.

Dryni, can you call him too? It may give him a tether through the gate into real spacetime.

I will try. His thoughts flowed past me, swirling. I felt rather than heard him call to our son.

Still no response.

I let go and drifted farther. Mist suffused my mind . . .

Flowing . . .

Rolling . . .

Mother?

Taquinil! Is that you?

He formed out of the mist, my miracle child. Then he was standing there in his familiar gray pullover and dark trousers. He lifted his hand and the fog re-formed, creating the wooded valley where Eldrin and I lived on the Orbiter. Misty trees swayed in a breeze and blurred mountains rose behind them.

My greetings, Mother.

My greetings, Taquinil. Your father is here too. My joy surged, but I held it in check, lest it swamp Taquinil, making us lose him again. *Dryni? Can you reach us?*

I'm here. Eldrin's thought caught with emotion. *Taquinil, come home.*

My greetings, Hoshpa. Taquinil answered gently, as if to spare Eldrin and me pain. *I am home. I'm free for the first time.*

How can you be free? Eldrin asked. *You're a thought.*

True, Taquinil answered amiably.

Eldrin tried another tack. *You're alone here.*

All my life I've been crushed by emotions, Taquinil thought. *I've learned to cope, to avoid people, see my doctors, withdraw when I'm overwhelmed. But I don't want to cope. I want freedom.* He spread his arms. *I have it here! I can let my thoughts encompass an entire universe and never be crushed. I feel like a man dying of thirst who has suddenly found an oasis.*

His joy filled the universe. The mist drew me. Freedom. No more onslaught of emotions. No more forever guarding my mind. No more politics. No more constraints. *Freedom . . .*

```
                              . . .
                 spin         spin
              spinning           spinning
             freedom               freedom
            spinning               spinning
           spiraling               spiraling
           flowing                 flowing
           out free                out free
          spin free       .        spin free
           around        o         around
            flowing      o         flowing
             spiraling  oo        spiraling
              spinning  ooo spinning
                 freedom      .
                  spinning
                   freedom
                    free . . .
                       free . . .
                          fr . . .
                            f . . .
```

Dehya? Eldrin's words reverberated. *Where are you?*

Somehow I managed to pull my mind back. *Here.*

Taquinil's thoughts came softly. *Can you understand?*

I can. Sorrow diffused my thoughts. *It is incredible.*

Yes.

Will you never return home? Eldrin's sadness filled space.

Perhaps someday. I'm not really gone. I will always be here. I can help you, too.

How do you mean? Eldrin asked.

I can weave threads here. He waved his hands and the mist braided into cords. *I can't make a psiberweb, but I may be able to help build one.*

Can you reach any nodes on Earth? I asked.

Why Earth?

Eldrin answered. *We want to infiltrate their systems. So we can rescue your grandparents.*

I can help you do that.

My hope surged. *How?*

I'm mist. An irreverent gleam came into his gaze. *I can fog up their systems. I have no firm links to any place in your universe, so I can't do anything specific. But I can cause more generalized distortions. If I make enough trouble for the Allied networks, you might be able to sneak past some of their security.*

It's worth a try.

Let me know . . . when you're reeeeadyyyyyyyy . . .

Taquinil?

After a painful silence, Eldrin thought, *I think he's gone.* He paused. *I'm getting a signal on my console. The telops want us to pull out.*

I didn't want to go. We had a rare privacy now; none of the others could follow us here. Had the psiberweb still existed, the telops could have used it to reach us, but they couldn't exist in psiberspace without support. Although Eldrin couldn't either, he could link to me through the ψ gate.

It also meant he could pull me out. The mist changed bit by bit. Blurred lines became visible and thickened into consoles. Ever so slowly, the Node Room took substance.

I became aware of aches all over my body. Doctors surrounded my chair, conferring in low tones. A similar group was gathered around Eldrin's console. He looked half man, half machine, with control panels still sheathing his body. As I watched, they lifted his visor and his eyes slowly opened. He peered around with a bleary gaze.

You look like I feel, I thought to him.

I feel like hell, he grumbled.

"Pharaoh Dyhianna, can you understand me?" A medic was at my side, an older woman with gray hair.

I focused on her. "Why so many people here . . ." My voice rustled eerily, like dried leaves.

"We had to pull you and Prince Eldrin out of—wherever you went."

I concentrated on her. "Why? We had only just started."

Another medic spoke, a slender man. "It's been thirty hours, ma'am. You became, well—translucent."

I shivered, wondering if that would keep happening for the rest of my life, until one day I faded away altogether. "He found what he needed," I murmured. Taquinil could finally be at peace. But even knowing that, I grieved, afraid he would attenuate in that strange place until he became indistinguishable from the mist that gave him freedom.

In the other console, Eldrin sat while the medics worked on him. *We need to trust that he knows what he is doing.*

I know. But it is so hard. I tried to smile. A muscle in my cheek twitched and I ended up grimacing.

Laughter came from his mind. *That was lovely.*

Bah. I glared at him.

The slender man was speaking to me. "He? Do you mean you found someone?"

"Taquinil . . ." I lifted my arm, bemused by how heavy it felt. Shifting my gaze to the doctor, I spoke in a stronger voice. "I need to talk to Admiral Casestar."

But as I watched him contact Jon on his wrist comm, disquiet spread over me. I knew we would soon face choices that challenged the power structure of our civilization.

19
Diffraction

We strode down a corridor with cobalt blue walls, darker blue hatchways, and white light-bars embedded in the ceiling. Eldrin and I walked together, with Jon to Eldrin's right, Ragnar to my left, and Vazar on Ragnar's other side. A slew of aides went before and behind us, as well as my infernal bodyguards.

"We can't assume Prince Taquinil will always be able to help," Ragnar continued. "If we wait, we might lose this opportunity."

I made myself speak. "The longer we take, the more uncertain his help becomes." It hurt to acknowledge a day might come when we could no longer reach him, but denying that possibility wouldn't make it disappear.

Jon shook his head. "How could a human mind become a waveform? I can't even imagine it."

"Have you ever seen the diffraction pattern from a circular aperture?" I asked.

He motioned at the aide on his other side. "Lieutenant."

She unrolled her palmtop and worked on it until a holo formed, floating above the screen, glowing soft green.

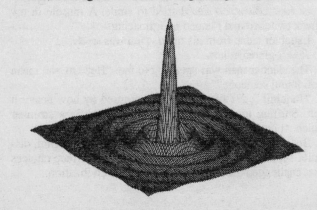

Jon peered at the image, then gave me an incredulous look. "Your son has become *that*?"

"Yes." A strange answer, but I had to give it. "His actual form is probably more complicated, but that gives you the basic shape. The peak is the main part of his personality. The ripples are satellite thoughts, the sort that tug the edges of your mind. The farther away from the peak, the less direct the thought." Before now, I had always found that waveform a thing of beauty, its shape evoking a graceful, perfectly symmetrical mountain. Now it only conjured sorrow.

Jon considered the holo doubtfully. "It's hard to imagine."

"He can help us beat the defense systems at Earth," Eldrin said.

On my other side, Ragnar snorted. "How? He's a credit-counter. Not a security expert."

"Not a credit-counter," I said. "An economist. He develops models to predict economic futures." Taquinil had become so adept at it, the dismayed Office of Finance had passed a law forbidding him to work financial markets, lest he destabilize the economy of some world.

"No one doubts his abilities," Jon said. "But they aren't in military intelligence or security."

"Normally, no." I had no doubt Taquinil could do what he claimed, but given that I was his mother, they might not consider me the most objective judge. "However, he has all of psiberspace to work with. So he has its power at his disposal as well."

Vazar spoke. "Even if he could help us infiltrate Earth's defenses, it wouldn't be enough. We have to get a ship to the planet, do our rescue, and get out again."

"We have four thousand ships," I pointed out.

"Earth has prodigious defenses," Jon answered. "They can easily withstand our measly four thousand ships."

"We're not going in to fight," I said. "Just put on a show."

He gave me a dour look. "We will never get into the system to put on anything."

I smiled. "Ah, but Admiral, they can only stop us if they find us."

"You plan on hiding four thousand ships?"

"ISC hid the Radiance Fleet."

He wasn't buying it. "And no one knows what happened to them."

"That's because the webs are down," I said. "But we've picked up enough messages from scout ships to know the Radiance Fleet destroyed the Trader capital. That means they penetrated Trader space the way we want to penetrate Allied space."

Jon shook his head. "You need the psiberweb to hide ships that way."

I knew he was right. To conceal the ships, we would have to deal with three strange universes: psiberspace, Haver-Klein space, and superluminal space. In psiberspace, thoughts defined existence. In Haver-Klein space, charge took on an imaginary part, which made it possible to store more antimatter in the fuel bottles. To reach superluminal space, we added an imaginary part to our velocity, circumventing light speed. The Radiance Fleet had used all three: they put most of their ships in giant fuel bottles and twisted them into Haver-Klein space; they used the psiberweb to communicate with the hidden ships; and they traveled at superluminal speeds to reach Trader territory.

"We need to rebuild the psiberweb," I said.

"We can only do that if you have access to a Lock," Vazar said. "Or maybe a Triad Chair. We have neither."

At the word *Triad,* Eldrin's pace slowed. I understood. My links to the Triad were . . . drifting. No pain, just a gentle *ending.* An ache filled me. I couldn't forget Eldrin's nightmare or my dream of a triangle that became a line. Had Eldrin's father left the Triad? I couldn't imagine life without him. He had been more like a brother to me than a father-in-law. I had to accept that he would die someday, but what my logic knew, my emotions denied.

"The point is moot," Jon was saying. "We haven't the go-ahead to invade Earth."

With no warning, I stopped. Everyone else halted, their response delayed by a few seconds, so aides and Jagernauts surged around me like water around a rock in a river. I regarded Jon with a steady gaze. "You have my go-ahead."

The silence stretched out. Jon watched me, his mind shielded.

Then Ragnar spoke in his gravelly voice. "That should be sufficient."

That should be sufficient. With those four words, spoken in public, he gave his support to the Ruby Dynasty—over the Assembly and ISC.

Jon raked him with an appraising stare. Then he turned to me. "I must consider this."

He continued down the corridor, his face closed and unreadable.

"He won't do it," Eldrin said.

I paced the living room of my suite. "We can't be sure."

Ragnar was leaning against a console by the wall. Eldrin stood across the room, leaving plenty of space between them. I had refused to let my Jagernaut bodyguards enter. I had no idea where their loyalties lay.

Vazar was standing by one wall, her body a dark figure against a bright holo-panel of Parthonia, the world where I had spent my childhood. The image showed Selei City, which had been named for my mother. Elegant manor houses were set far back from boulevards, screened by trees with graceful, curving branches hung with pale green streamer-leaves and white blossoms. Vazar blocked the center of the holo, where the gold spire of the capitol building rose into a lavender sky.

"Jon Casestar never deviates from established procedure," Ragnar said, actually agreeing with Eldrin for once. "You have to decide, Dehya. Remove him or forget about going to Earth without Assembly approval."

"Jon came to Delos." I continued to pace, lost in thought.

"For Delos, you weren't suggesting a hostile raid on a major power," Vazar said. "Hell, Dehya, if we move on Earth, we could end up at war with the Allieds and the Traders at the same time."

"We won't." I sorted through models in my mind. "With their Lock deactivated, the Traders can't make a psiberweb."

It wasn't until everyone had been quiet for a while that I realized they were all giving me that odd look again. I stopped pacing. "What?"

Ragnar quirked his eyebrow. "How can you know their Lock is off?"

"I'm a Triad member."

Eldrin was watching me thoughtfully. "Did you pick up something about Kelric and the Lock when we looked for Taquinil?"

"I'm not sure." I sifted through my memories. "The loss of the web is such a big difference, it swamps out everything else." I turned to Vazar. "You say you speak for General Majda."

She met my gaze squarely. "If you're asking me to override Jon Casestar, I think it is unwise."

"You supported coming to Delos."

"It was a good idea." As she glanced at Eldrin, her intractable posture softened. "An excellent idea." To us both, she said, "I believe General Majda would have agreed. But this is different."

General Majda. Not Naaj. When Vazar called her cousin by her formal title, she meant business. I did notice, however, that she said "General" rather than "Imperator."

The console behind Ragnar beeped.

"Laplace, who is it?" I asked.

"Admiral Casestar," my EI answered.

"Put him through."

After a pause, Jon spoke. "My greetings, Pharaoh Dyhianna."

"Admiral." I kept my voice neutral. "What can I do for you?"

"I would like to speak with you in private."

Ragnar narrowed his gaze. Eldrin came forward, standing at my side as if to offer protection against Jon's request.

What was Jon up to? He tended to be more direct than Ragnar, also more conservative. Although he didn't enjoy politics, he was perfectly capable of playing them. If he wanted me in custody, to stop me from stirring up trouble, he could have sent his soldiers here for me. On his ship, in his domain, in space, I had few options to resist. Requesting that I come to his quarters could be a diplomatic way of achieving the same end, one less humiliating for me than having armed guards take me from my quarters. Or maybe he wanted to offer support, but not as openly as Ragnar, in front of witnesses. I doubted it, though. More likely, he wanted to continue our discussion without so many high-ranking people listening.

I had my own security running now, shrouding my suite from his monitors, but he had to know I had people in here. Witnesses. That he had made his request in front of them was a reasonably positive sign. Then again, given my prominence on his ship, it would be impossible for him to keep it secret if I suddenly disappeared. He might see no point in being covert about our meeting.

Don't go alone, Eldrin thought.

I turned and ran my knuckles down his arm, considering my options.

Then I went to the console, stepping past Ragnar, who was studying us with a laser-like intensity. Leaning over the console, I said, "Admiral Casestar, Prince Eldrin and I will meet with you."

Jon's suite resembled mine, except with sharper lines. The furnishings were glass Luminex, and leather upholstery. Holos with vivid, detailed depictions of ancient battles paneled the walls.

When Eldrin and I entered the living room, Jon gave Eldrin an appraising stare. He made no attempt to hide his displeasure that I hadn't come alone.

Eldrin spoke flatly. "I'm not leaving her alone with you, Admiral."

His bluntness startled me. It wasn't typical of Eldrin, but he had a point. If I forced the issue of Earth, Jon would have to choose: Ruby Dynasty or Assembly. His answer would have greater ramifications than one mission. Ragnar had already offered me his support. If Jon did as well, I would have backing from two of the Fleet's most powerful commanders. Given that the Fleet was the largest branch of ISC, it would give me a large portion of the military. Naaj Majda would then be the deciding factor: if she pledged her loyalty, the Assembly was history. But if Naaj supported the Assembly, it would sunder ISC in two, with the Pharaoh's Army in opposition to the Pharaoh.

Jon regarded Eldrin with a neutral expression. "I intend no harm to your wife, Prince Eldrin." He motioned to a white air-sofa that curved around an oval table made from glossy black Luminex. "Please, be comfortable."

We sat stiffly, none of us the least bit comfortable. Jon's mood leaked past his defenses: he hadn't asked Eldrin to accompany me here because he feared *Eldrin* posed a threat to me. He wondered if the Traders had tampered with Eldrin's mind, planting a psychological bomb that could turn him into a weapon.

My throat felt tight. I resisted believing the Traders could have changed Eldrin at that basic a level without my detecting *any* hint of it. I didn't know if Jon genuinely believed otherwise or if he had let that thought leak deliberately, to undermine my confidence in my husband. Although it did make me think, it made me fear for Eldrin rather than myself. If I suddenly became widowed, it offered a prime opportunity to whoever supported me. Such machinations were Ragnar's style rather than Jon's, but I could be sure of no one. More than once during the Ruby Empire, a military leader had gained power by marrying a member of the Ruby Dynasty who had lost a spouse. In those cases, the military leader had been a woman who wed the surviving husband of a dead Pharaoh. I doubted the ancient Ruby matriarchs could even have envisioned this situation.

Pain throbbed in my head. Dropping out of accelerated mode, I realized Jon had only paused for a second. He continued, cautiously neutral. "I have to decide what to write in my report for HQ regarding your proposal about Earth."

So. He hadn't sent a report yet. Interesting. "We need to act now. We can't wait for HQ to respond, especially if we want Taquinil's help."

"Neither you nor Prince Taquinil is trained for such work." Jon hesitated. "Prince Taquinil isn't even alive. Exactly."

"Jon, we can do this." I knew he wouldn't be impressed by assurances he thought were unrealistic. "My calculations only give probabilities," I acknowledged. "But they're good ones. We have a good chance to pull this off."

Jon sat back, his face pensive. "I served under Kurj Skolia for almost twenty years and Sauscony Valdoria for two. Both were leaders of vision. I was honored to give them my loyalty."

I held my breath. He could go either way, adding a "But much to my regret . . ." or an "And so I continue . . ."

He did neither. Instead he said, "We have no proof of Primary Majda's claim that Imperator Majda gave her authority to make decisions in her absence, but it also seems an unlikely lie."

I didn't miss the title he gave Naaj. My voice cooled. "Neither Primary Majda nor General Majda speak for the Ruby Dynasty."

"Were Imperators Kurj Skolia or Sauscony Valdoria still alive, they would consult with you on this decision about Earth." He didn't make it a question.

"That's right."

"You aren't currently available to consult with Imperator Majda."

I didn't like where he was going with this. "And?"

"Primary Majda claims to speak for the Imperator. And she has reservations about taking any ships to Earth."

Pah. He was lying; that came through despite his defenses. Vazar hadn't told him about her doubts. The more Jon and I talked, the more certain I became that he intended this as prelude to putting me in custody. Given that Eldrin had come with me, he would probably lock us both up.

My impression also, Eldrin thought.

He hasn't committed himself yet.

True. But it isn't promising.

I considered Jon. "So you asked us here to discuss Primary Majda's reservations?" I could call his bluff by telling him Vazar agreed with my idea, but he might call *my* bluff and really ask Vazar. She would tell him exactly what he wanted to hear.

"I'm concerned about your safety," Jon hedged.

"On your own ship?" Eldrin asked. To me, he thought, *Here it comes.*

"These are difficult times," Jon said. "My loyalty to your family demands I ensure that conflicting loyalties endanger neither you nor the Imperialate."

Right. Lock me up for my own good. I wondered at his use of *Imperialate,* though. The word had become controversial; the Assembly consisted primarily of elected representatives, whereas *Imperial* implied a hereditary power base. The Ruby Dynasty.

Some felt that calling ourselves an Imperialate was tantamount to agreeing with the Allied detractors who dubbed us "imperialistic warmongers." The Allied Worlds had the only truly elected governments. The Traders practiced tyranny; they could call themselves benevolent all they wanted and it wouldn't change the fact that they enslaved over a trillion people. Both we and the Allieds believed all humans had the right to freedom. Given the way ISC occupied planets, though, Skolia had a ways to go before we reached that ideal. As long as we and the Traders kept fighting each other, we left the Allieds alone. But if one side ever won a decisive victory, the Allieds knew the winners would come after them next. Now they had a chance to neutralize us when both sides were weakened.

I dropped into normal-speed thought, but I wondered if it was the accelerated mode that made my head ache this time. In my more honest moments, I had to admit the galaxy would probably be a far more peaceful place if the Allied Worlds were in charge.

Amusement came from Eldrin. *If you really want to shock the Assembly, tell them that.*

Hah. Not a chance. To Jon, I said, "I value your loyalty immensely. Your support would mean a great deal."

His control eased, revealing the depth of his concern. "Then I entreat you, Your Highness. Don't split loyalties within the Imperialate. This is the time we can *least* afford such rifts."

"The rifts already exist," Eldrin said. "We must make the best of the situation."

Jon glanced at him. "That's what I'm trying to do."

I spoke quietly. "Then we *must* retrieve my family from Earth."

"I wish I could agree with you." Reaching forward, he touched a panel in the table. "But I'm afraid I can't."

A door whispered open elsewhere in the suite, followed by the tread of booted feet. Damn. Even knowing that Jon probably wouldn't back us, it still came as a disappointment.

They've never given us freedom, Eldrin thought tiredly. *This just makes it explicit.*

The soldiers entered like fog: gray uniforms, gray boots, gray eyes, gray gauntlets threaded with glittering conduits. We all stood up as they surrounded the sofa. I didn't know how my expression looked, but when I turned to Jon, he had the decency to appear ill-at-ease. I spoke with deceptive softness. "I would never have expected a betrayal from you."

For all his disquiet, he showed no sign of relenting. "I regret that you see this as a betrayal, Your Highness. But I must do what I believe is best for the Skolian Imperialate."

Imperialate again. It sounded incongruous from him, given that he had just implicitly pledged his loyalty to the Assembly.

It is the name of our civilization, Eldrin pointed out. *Jon does everything by the rules.*

The guards escorted us out of the suite and along empty, secured corridors. Our trek ended at an entrance hidden deep within a maze of tunnels. The suite beyond had soft carpets. Gilded furniture. Soothing holo-panels on the walls. Blue. Gold. Crystal. Genuine wood. Amazing that they could provide such plush quarters on a battle cruiser.

But making the brig attractive made it no less a prison.

20

Interlude

Eldrin paced the living room, restless and edgy. Despite his mental shields, I could tell this reminded him of being a Trader captive. Again I wondered if they had tampered with his mind. What better way to reach the Ruby Pharaoh than to sabotage the one person she was willing to trust?

Eldrin froze and stared at me. *I would never hurt you.*

I know.

Do you? Do I? He pushed his hand through his hair. **I've no guarantee you're any safer with me than with anyone else.**

I don't believe you would do anything.

That's your heart speaking. Not your intellect.

Sometimes the heart knows more.

I hope you're right. He looked around the elegant room. "You can't even see the spy monitors."

We both knew security would be monitoring everything we did. I smiled wryly. "I hope we're entertaining."

Can you do anything about them?

Maybe. I sat at a console near the wall. Then I went to work.

First I dumped the security blocks Jon's people had put on the console to stop me from using it. They could have removed the console and it would have done no good; with computers ingrained in everything we used, even ourselves, no way existed to cut off an experienced telop from a ship's networks.

Within an hour I had infiltrated the security that guarded the suite. Although it was well set-up, I managed to turn off the monitors. But I didn't believe it; Jon knew what I could do. They had created this "security" as camouflage for the real systems.

It took the rest of the night for me to find the real monitors. They had systems watching us I had never even heard of. Jon's security people had done a superb job. Fortunately, it wasn't good enough.

Eldrin slept a few hours, then returned to the living room. He leaned on the back of the console, facing me, his arms folded on a ledge that jutted up to chest height. As he watched me work, he spoke musingly. "On Lyshriol, we didn't have these consoles in every room. When I was young, our only computers were in a console room my mother had installed in my father's castle, and those in the school." He grimaced. "I didn't like them then."

"Then?" I looked up. "I didn't know you ever started liking them."

"Ah, well." He gave me a rueful smile. "One gets used to how easy all this tech makes our lives."

"But some things it can never replace." I stood up and stretched, long and languorously, working the kinks out of my back. Then I went around to him and put my arms around his waist.

He drew me close. *Do we have privacy now?*

It should be all right. I have the spy monitors running a fake program of us in bed sleeping. I continue to mindspeak, just in case. *I couldn't finagle a direct line to anyone outside, but at least we have privacy. And I did manage to send some hidden messages to some of our supporters.*

Won't Security find them?

I hope not. I was discreet. I shifted my weight. *I just, uh, twiddled some accounts.*

Twiddled? He laughed. *Dehya, what did you do?*

I had Laplace send them cartoons from the erotica databases.

He grinned. *Why those?*

They're the easiest to hack. Dryly I added, *It seems they're the most accessed databases on this ship.*

Now he looked intrigued. *And what did you do with these pleasing holos?*

I encoded them with directions to this suite. It had been the best way I had found to minimize the chance of alerting Security. Given how often people accessed those databases, the spike in activity due to my fiddling wasn't likely to draw attention. *Jon's security is good. It won't be long before they figure out what I've done. If we're going to get out of here, we have to go soon.* I unlocked the door.

Escaping won't help unless we have support. Otherwise Jon's guards will just put us back.

Then we'll try again.

As long as it doesn't involve you getting hurt.

I almost groaned. *Don't you start too.*

Dehya, what do you expect us all to say? 'Sure, go take all the chances you want with your life.' I don't think so.

The door beeped.

"That was fast," I said.

Eldrin raised his voice. "Computer, who is it?"

"I don't know," it answered. "The Pharaoh turned off my spy monitors."

I went to the entrance. "Activate the viewing panel."

"I can't," it said. "You have another program running on it."

Ah well. Caught by my own intrigues. "All right. Open the door."

The wall shimmered and faded. In the corridor outside, soldiers waited in rows, a metallic sea of silver and gray warriors. A man in a crisp black uniform stood at their front.

"My greetings," Ragnar said pleasantly.

21
Mutiny

Ragnar bowed from the waist. "My honor at your presence, Pharaoh Dyhianna." Next he bowed to Eldrin, somehow making exactly the same motion seem less respectful. Then he lifted his hand, inviting us to leave the suite. "At your pleasure."

I considered all the human firepower he had brought. His soldiers stood like a wall of cybernetic muscle. He couldn't have organized them so fast; he must have prepared this before tonight. It made me uneasy. Just what had he planned? With this much backup, he could do whatever he wanted with us.

Eldrin crossed his arms. "How do we know we won't just become your prisoners instead of Jon Casestar's?"

Ragnar looked exasperated. "Your Highness, we're rescuing you."

With no warning, a shot came from the side. Ragnar lunged forward with the eerily smooth motion of someone controlled by physical augmentations rather than by his own conscious thought. A soldier behind him stumbled and fell, his shoulder soaked where a melting ice bullet had impacted him. The unexpected bullet had missed Ragnar, apparently because his internal system had detected its firing and thrust him out of its path with enhanced speed.

Everyone burst into action. As Ragnar grabbed me, his soldiers blurred, moving with extraordinary speed, like a machine with many human components. Even using my extra optics, I couldn't follow their movements. It happened in eerie silence; they communicated by implants in their brains rather than by voice.

Ragnar yanked me into the corridor, away from Eldrin, and pushed me toward a small tunnel with a shadowed entrance. Two of his cyberthugs helped him drag me away from the mêleé.

Straining to look back, I saw a blur of moving people, not only silver and gray, but with black mixed in now as well. Black. Damn. That meant Jagernauts. A flash of wine-red hair and blue trousers surfaced in the scuffle. Either the Jagernauts were rescuing Eldrin from his rescuers or else Ragnar's people were stopping him from following us.

Ragnar strode at my right side with his left arm around my waist and his right hand clenched on my upper right arm. I had never realized how strong a grip he had with all those augmentations of his. I struggled to pull free. "Let me go."

"Dehya, come on," he said. "This is our only chance."

We were almost running now. "Damn it, Ragnar, kidnapping the Ruby Pharaoh in the middle of a mutiny is stupid."

"I'm not kidnapping you. I'm saving your royal razoo." He maneuvered me into the side corridor. The two husky soldiers he had brought, a woman and a man, strode on either side of us.

"What the hell is a 'razoo'?" I said. When my language files supplied the image of a shapely posterior, I muttered, "Never mind."

As we ran down the dim tunnel, the tumult behind us faded. Then Ragnar drew me into an even narrower access tube. We were in a maintenance area now, one used mostly by robots. He pushed me into a niche barely big enough for the two of us to stand together.

Glancing at his soldiers, who waited outside the niche, he said, "What happened back there?"

The woman tapped a comm on her gauntlet. It glittered in a familiar pattern; it was sending data to implants in her ears. "Those were Primary Majda's people."

I narrowed my gaze at Ragnar. "Why would Vazar's people attack yours?"

"She doesn't agree with me."

"Agree how?"

"I told you. I'm taking command of this fleet." His gaze was so intense I thought it might burn off my skin. "For you, Dehya."

I wanted to move back, away from him, but he had me

pinned against the wall. "And that explains why you dragged me away from my husband."

His mouth twisted, almost a snarl. "It astonishes me that a woman with your intelligence can be so blind about men. He was never good enough for you, even before the Traders ruined him. He's been their prisoner, damn it. You have no idea what they did to him, besides torture. They could have redesigned his brain. Someday you'll give the trigger—a word, gesture, thought—who knows. I'm trying to stop your barbarian from murdering you."

"Eldrin isn't going to hurt me."

"He hurts you just by being married to you." He leaned closer, his palms flat against the wall on either side of my shoulders. Bending his head, he brushed his lips across mine. "You need a man with strength."

I turned my head aside. "You will not touch me."

Ragnar lifted his head. His desire cloaked us darkly; seeing me backed up against the wall with no escape aroused him. He trailed his finger along my jaw, keeping the tip just above my skin so he didn't touch me. "Think of the ISC forces I can bring to your command. The knowledge of ISC politics. The secured data. All yours. I can give you what you want." His voice deepened as he leaned closer. "In all ways."

"I'm not going to betray my husband."

He kissed me again. "Fifty years," he murmured. "Gods, you must be sick of him."

I pushed him away. "Stop it, Ragnar. This isn't worthy of you."

"I feel your heartbeat." He touched his fingertip to my cheek. "You can play the ice queen all you want, but your body betrays you."

Telling him that my pulse had sped up because I feared him didn't seem a good idea. He knew I didn't have the strength to stop him. But I doubted he would force me; he had too much to lose. Had I been other than the Ruby Pharaoh, he might not have worried, but he probably wouldn't have been interested either. If he wanted only rough sex, he could find it elsewhere. The idea of controlling *power* excited him. I needed his support, but not at the price of my husband or self-respect. This entire business was about family: Roca, Eldrinson, those unnamed children, the rest of the Ruby Dynasty. I had no intention of betraying them to free them from betrayal.

"You need my help," Ragnar said. Menace simmered beneath his smooth exterior.

"I welcome your loyalty." I crossed my arms, making a bulwark between our bodies. "But not in my bed."

A dangerous edge honed his thoughts. "Perhaps not tonight."

"Not ever, Ragnar."

He glanced back at his warriors, who were trying to look alert without appearing to eavesdrop. "What's the situation?"

"We've secured most of the ship," the man said. "Casestar's people still hold the bridge."

Ragnar's gaze darkened. "We can't finish this if we can't reach the bridge."

I swallowed, understanding the implication of his words. If this operation failed, Jon Casestar would have no choice but to execute Ragnar for mutiny. By supporting the Ruby Dynasty, Ragnar might have signed his own death warrant.

"You've put a lot on the line for this." I said.

He turned back to me. "It's a calculated risk."

I saw another aspect of the "kidnapping" now. Although it didn't lessen the threat Ragnar exuded, it reminded me that he had other sides as well. "You grabbed me this way because you don't want it to look as if I'm involved with the mutiny. In case you get caught."

"You aren't involved." He leaned closer, cupping my chin with his hand. "Unless you change your mind."

I pushed him away, my hands against his shoulders. "I won't." Quietly I added, "But I won't forget your loyalty or what you've risked. Be assured of it."

"Good," he murmured.

"What happened with Vazar?"

"Her people attacked us outside your quarters."

"Then she has thrown in with Jon?"

His voice grated. "She refused to listen to reason."

I couldn't hold back my sense of betrayal. I thought of her leaning her head against mine while we wept for the loved ones we had lost. *Vaz, don't do this.* But she had made her choice. At least it meant Eldrin was safe; even in my most cynical moments, I couldn't believe she would let harm come to her late husband's brother.

Ragnar drummed his fingers on the wall. "We need control of the bridge. Until we have it, I can't claim to be in charge of this fleet."

My mood lifted. "I can get you to the bridge."

"How?"

I swirled my hand in the air as if stirring a liquid. "I know these ships. Find me a good console, one where I don't have to fight layers of security, and I'll get you bridge access."

He grinned. "You've got it, Pharaoh."

The lights in the main office of the Security Division stayed dim; nothing the mutineers tried would bring them back up. The bridge crew had cut power to every system we needed. It didn't matter. Ragnar had stockpiled portable generators, another indication he had spent more effort planning this than he could have done in the short time it had taken him to find Eldrin and me after Jon put us in custody.

With the generators, we rigged enough power to run Security Major, the main console. Other machines loomed around us, cloaked in shadow. Stray light from the rod-lamps carried by Ragnar's people trickled here and there, or caught the edge of some hulking machine.

I settled in the control chair and it enfolded me, bringing panels to my fingertips and plugging prongs into my body. I submerged into the virtual reality it created. Darkness spread around me, filled with flickers, not that different from the actual physical room where I sat, except these defined computer networks. I followed a bright thread as it wove through a velvety black mist. Gradually the line thickened, until I was speeding along a silver tunnel, plunging ever deeper into the mind of the ship.

I knew my impressions resulted from the way my mind interpreted the data flooding it. But I still felt vertigo, as if I were plummeting down a long chute. The light intensified until it hurt my eyes, except I wasn't looking at anything. I tried to slow the onslaught of data, and my brain translated that as if I were braking against the chute.

INTRUDER IDENTIFY. The words rumbled like thunder.

Dyhianna Selei. I encoded my identifications into the name.

VERIFIED. ATTENDING.

I released the virtual breath I had been holding, making blue condensation swirl around me. Although I had worked for decades with ISC networks, it was always possible someone would discover my twiddling and remove some of the backdoors I had hidden in their systems, like this one.

I need access to the bridge systems.

ACCESS DENIED.

Override.

OVERRIDE REFUSED.

Why?

YOU DO NOT HAVE AUTHORIZATION.

I have authorization for anything. It wasn't true, but it was worth a try.

NEGATIVE.

What do I have authorization to do?

COMMUNICATE.

Interesting. Did Jon *want* me to contact them? *Open comm channel.* I deliberately didn't specify which one. I wanted to see what it would do.

The light faded into darkness. I became aware of more flickers. At first I thought they were the ship's networks again. Then I realized this was actual light. Focusing outward, I saw Ragnar and his soldiers clustered around the console.

I spoke to Ragnar. "Have you talked with Jon Casestar since the uprising started?"

He started at my voice. "I thought you were going into the system."

"I've already been in and out."

"Excellent." He leaned forward, one hand on the back of the console, his posture evoking the poise of a wild animal ready to strike. "Casestar has refused contact. But it's been less than an hour since we showed up at your suite."

I paused, thinking. Jon could have done a lot with the bridge systems in one hour. "Ship attend."

"ATTENDING." Its voice rumbled in speech as well as in my mind.

Now we would see what *communicate* had meant. "Put me through to Admiral Casestar."

"WORKING."

Then we waited. Ragnar was standing in front of the console now, leaning against the back of another, facing me with his arms crossed. Everyone else stood ramrod straight. I felt like a dust mote dwarfed by asteroids.

The comm on my console crackled. "Casestar here."

"My greetings, Admiral," I said.

Ragnar stepped forward and put his hands against the back of my console, listening.

"Are you all right?" Jon asked. "Prince Eldrin said Ragnar Bloodmark dragged you out of your suite."

"Is Eldrin with you?" I asked.

Eldrin's deeper voice came over the comm. "I'm here. Where the hell did that bastard take you?"

Ragnar raised his eyebrows as if to say, *Civilized, isn't he?* I ignored him.

"I'm all right," I told Eldrin.

Ragnar leaned over the console and spoke into the comm. "She's fine for now, Your Highness. What happens to her depends on what you and Casestar do."

I switched off *transmit,* leaving only the comm's *receive* function active. That way, Eldrin and Jon couldn't hear us. To Ragnar I said, "What, now I'm a hostage after all?"

He braced his hands on the back of the console. "You aren't my hostage, Dehya. But as long as they think you are, this remains a mutiny. Give your agreement and it becomes a coup."

I snorted. "No one will believe otherwise. Why would you mutiny except to help me challenge the Assembly?"

"They can speculate all they want." He gave a dry laugh. "If I say you're a hostage, what are they going to do? Accuse me of lying? They aren't stupid."

"What's going on?" Eldrin's voice came out of the comm with a snap. "Bloodmark, if you've harmed her—"

Ragnar flicked on the transmit panel. "If you would be so kind as to put Admiral Casestar back on, we can commence with negotiations."

Jon answered. "What negotiations?"

"Release this ship to me, and I will release the Pharaoh to you."

Jon said, simply, "No."

I gave Ragnar a dour look. He was right, Jon Casestar wasn't stupid. Jon knew I was no hostage. He wasn't going to negotiate terms that would leave me in charge of his fleet.

I closed my eyes and submerged again into the virtual darkness. Silver comm threads curled around me in the velvety-black mist. I followed the line of Jon's words to their source, slinking through the networks, analyzing as I went, leaving behind fragments of my own code intruding on theirs. His security people had guarded this bridge channel with remarkable locks. Truly brilliant.

Ragnar's drawl echoed in the misty darkness around me. "I won't release her until you release the ship. But I might have other plans."

I could almost feel Eldrin losing his temper. Opening my eyes, I scowled at Ragnar and mouthed, *Don't overdo it.*

Trust me, he mouthed back.

Like hell, I answered. I was half in and half out of the simulation, and the virtual effects continued, curling threads of light around his dark form, outlining him in silver.

Jon's voice came over the comm. "Pharaoh Dyhianna, you have my protection. But not my ship."

"Don't be so sure," I said.

A pause. Then Jon spoke with a hint of humor. "With you, I am never sure of anything."

"A wise man," I murmured. Then I cut the connection.

Ragnar thumped the console with his palm. "Damn it, Dehya. How am I going to shield you if you insist on making it sound like you're doing this of your own choice?"

"Because I am." I smirked. "And I'm protecting your admiralic razoo."

He gave a startled laugh. "My razoo thanks you." His face took on a sensual look. "We would make one hell of a team. You picked the wrong man."

He knew perfectly well I hadn't "picked" anyone. But that changed nothing. "We do make a good team, Ragnar. As allies. Not lovers."

"Perhaps. Unfortunately, right now that team is going nowhere." He tapped the console. "We still can't break the bridge defense."

"You think so?" Sitting back, I closed my eyes and let threads of light brighten around me, in particular those I had marked during our communication with Jon. I examined the systems his security team had erected to defend the bridge. They were excellent. Amazing.

Then I activated all the intruder code I had put into their security—and crashed the entire bridge defense system.

22
Radiance

Havyrl's Valor was one of ISC's largest battle cruisers, several kilometers in length. Its bridge alone was larger than many ships, over half a kilometer across. Ragnar and I entered the great hemisphere together, sailing through the air with a formation of his commandos. Many of his soldiers were already here, having secured the bridge. Jon still sat in his chair at the terminus of the robot arm, but Ragnar's people surrounded him.

The holoscreens that covered the surface of the hemisphere all showed space, in every direction, as if we floated in the void itself. Delos rotated "below" us relative to Jon's chair, a magnificent orb of blue, green, and swirling white, like an extraordinary jewel set against a backdrop studded with gem-stars and nebulae.

Ragnar's soldiers were relieving Jon's officers of command, replacing them at consoles set into the surface of the hemisphere. Then I realized Ragnar's people weren't the only ones on guard. Members of Jon's crew had joined the mutineers. The ramifications were sobering. If this failed, these people would pay the price of their loyalty to me with their lives.

As we headed toward Jon's chair, the guards around it shifted and I saw Eldrin floating there, gripping a cable. The mutineers had him surrounded too. I didn't like it. Regardless of what Ragnar wanted to be true, Eldrin wasn't an enemy.

Ragnar and I skimmed up to Jon's chair, using cables that stretched across the bridge. Jon watched us approach, his face unreadable. When we reached the chair, the guards moved aside so I could come in closer.

No one tried to stop me as I took hold of the cable near Eldrin. He didn't speak, but I felt the brief touch of his mind, a moment of reassurance. Then he moved back, leaving me with Jon.

I spoke quietly. "I regret that it came to this, Admiral Casestar. But I must relieve you of command."

"I also regret it, Your Highness." He pushed out of the chair wearily, as if he felt heavy despite the lack of gravity. The guards took his arms and moved away with him.

It gave me no satisfaction to see them escort Jon and his officers off the bridge. I hated having to treat a long-time ally as an enemy.

Ragnar watched them with triumph in his dark gaze.

Eldrin floated closer to me, holding the cable. He glanced at Ragnar, who had moved to the other side of the command chair to confer with several officers. Then Eldrin followed my gaze to the hatchway at the back of the hemisphere, where the guards had taken out Jon. *No regrets, Dehya. Casestar is the one who locked us up.*

I pulled myself into the command chair, then paused while it readjusted to my size. *He thought he was doing the right thing.*

He was wrong. Anger edged his thought, pure and direct.

Where Ragnar exuded dark intrigue, Eldrin reminded me of open fields and mountains; where Ragnar had sophistication, Eldrin was rustic simplicity overlaid with his years in the Imperial Court. Yes, Eldrin could move easily now among the powers of Skolia, speak their arcane language, and use their manners, always watching his behavior. But beneath that veneer, he was still the farm boy I had fallen in love with.

He came closer, grasping the armrest on the command chair. I brushed my fingers over his knuckles, and relief gentled his face. Although he didn't look at Ragnar, we were both aware of the admiral's presence—and how much we needed him. An uneasy alliance.

Ragnar was speaking into his wrist comm, directing his people as they secured the ship. Although technically I was in command, he was the ranking officer. I had no intention of taking his loyalty for granted. I couldn't give him what he wanted, the title of Pharaoh's consort, but other rewards existed. While we laid our plans, I would find out what else he sought.

The comm on the armrest hummed. Touching it, I said, "Selei here."

"This is Lieutenant Qahot, Your Highness," a woman said. "I'm picking up a ship entering the Delos system."

"Do you have an ID?"

"Not yet, ma'am."

Ragnar glanced at me, his face puzzled. I put my hand over the transmit panel and spoke to him. "It could be from Earth. Colonel Yamada may have slipped a message past our blockade."

His expression turned wry. "We've been so involved with our affairs here, I'd almost forgotten Delos."

Qahot spoke again. "Pharaoh Dyhianna, the ship is one of ours. An ISC scout."

"Are you expecting anyone?" I asked Ragnar.

He shook his head, pulling himself closer along a cable. Leaning over the comm, he said, "Lieutenant Qahot, this is Admiral Bloodmark. Escort the scout in. As soon as you know why they're here, let me know."

"Aye, sir."

As I turned off the comm, Ragnar said, "It might be from HQ, perhaps even from General Majda."

"Is Primary Majda still in the brig?"

"That's right. I gave her the option of joining us." His eyes glinted. "She declined."

Eldrin spoke tightly. "Were Althor alive, she wouldn't have gone against us."

Ragnar shrugged. "If Prince Althor were here, he would be Imperator. That would release Primary Majda from her loyalty conflict between the Ruby Dynasty and the Imperator."

Lieutenant Qahot's voice crackled on the comm. "Pharaoh Dyhianna, we have two more ships coming in, a Jag starfighter and a Jackhammer."

"Anything further on the scout?" I asked.

"Nothing yet—make that *six* more ships, another Jag, a destroyer, two more frigates—no, that's two destroyers—" Qahot drew in a sharp breath. "Gods, they're dropping out of inversion like pop-jacks. We have forty-three on scan. Forty-four."

I gripped the armrests. "Lieutenant, find out where they're from. Report to Admiral Bloodmark."

"Yes, ma'am. Sixty-eight ships now. Seventy."

"Are they Fleet?" Ragnar asked. "Army? ASC? J-force?"

"All of those, sir," Qahot said. "They're evading our questions."

Eldrin spoke uneasily. "Jag fighters often accompany army Talons."

"To Delos?" Ragnar snorted. "For what?"

"You brought your ships here," I said.

"I received word of Jon's fleet. We were cut off from HQ, so I came to rendezvous with Casestar."

I exhaled. "Pray these are doing the same."

Ragnar regarded me evenly. "Jon Casestar or Vazar Majda may have managed to send messengers to HQ asking for backup."

"This couldn't be a response to that," I said, hoping I was right. "How could Naaj mobilize the few forces we have left and get them here so fast? Even if anyone did slip out a message, it probably hasn't reached HQ yet."

Lieutenant Qahot's voice snapped out of the comm. "Admiral Bloodmark, I have that ID on the ships now."

"Who are they?"

She took an audible breath. Then she said, "It's the Radiance Fleet."

They came in waves: tens, hundreds, thousands, then tens of thousands, all that remained of the greatest fleet we had ever assembled. They had invaded Eube's Glory, the heart of the Trader Empire and broken the Trader military, but to do it they paid an almost unimaginable price. Eight hundred thousand ships had gone into Eube, hundreds of billions if you counted the smart missiles, drones and dust.

Seventy thousand returned.

They streamed through space, some damaged, some whole, all intent on one goal. Delos. They came in every form: bristling destroyers, frigates with deadly aplomb, Jag starfighters brilliant and fast; stinging Wasps and Scorpions; razor-edged Scythes; Bolts, Masts, Rafts, Tugs, Booms, Blades, Fists, and hundreds of even smaller vessels darting through the fleet. Ram stealth tanks appeared on our sensors and then disappeared, camouflaged even in plain view. Needle Spacewings soared alongside the unfolding Jackknives. Leos, Asps, and Cobras cut through the advancing fleet, as deadly as their namesakes. Thunderbolts and Starslammers rumbled with power. Then came the Firestorm battle cruisers, star-faring cities, massive and rugged, dwarfing the other ships that hurtled by them.

The vessels raced, lumbered, sprinted, or limped. Some barely made it in tow. Others blasted their exhaust with triumphant energy. They swelled in a colossal wave of living, thinking ships, filling the star system. From all directions they kept coming, in the plane of the ecliptic where the planets orbited their parent star, "below" the ecliptic according to the southern hemisphere of Delos, and above it. The fleet moved steadily onward, stretching from the outreaches of the star system all the way into its inner planets.

More ships continued to drop out of inversion, rank after rank of the armada that had turned the tide of the Radiance War. They had done the impossible, breaking the backbone of Traders' brutal military machine, and in doing so, they made it possible for the rest of us to remain free. It may not have been the largest fleet ever gathered in the history of the human race, but as far as we were concerned, it was without doubt the greatest.

Colonel Yamada was not sanguine.

"We're registering over seventy *thousand* ships." His alarmed voice crackled out of Ragnar's wrist comm. "Admiral Bloodmark, we are a peaceful world dedicated to sanctuary, a diplomatic outpost."

Ragnar was floating by my chair, holding a cable. "We appreciate your situation, Colonel."

"Admiral Casestar gave me reason to believe no actions would be taken against Delos beyond the occupation."

Ragnar's gaze darkened. "Admiral Casestar has been relieved of command."

A silence followed his words. Then Yamada said, "I see."

I had no doubt he did see, probably all too well. One admiral wouldn't relieve another during an occupation unless major changes were taking place, changes that might signal
political upheavals Yamada probably didn't even want to be
near, let alone caught in without backup.

Lieutenant Qahot's voice came over the comm on my
command chair. "Ma'am, I have a Lieutenant Garr on six.
He's an aide to Rear Admiral Chad Barzun, who is now in
command of the Radiance Fleet."

We were building up a regular plethora of admirals here.
"Route it to Admiral Bloodmark." I kept my channels open
and listened while Lieutenant Qahot and Lieutenant Garr
arranged for Barzun and Ragnar to talk.

As a full admiral, Ragnar outranked Barzun, but that
wouldn't mean squat if Naaj Majda had sent Barzun and his
seventy thousand ships to stop our mutiny. Where had the
Radiance Fleet come from? How did they find us?

When ships jumped into inversion, for superluminal travel,
they couldn't communicate by conventional methods. It did
no good to shoot photons at one another if you were traveling
faster than light. Using superluminal particles wasn't much
better; the uncertainty in their time and location made signals
unreliable. Superluminal ships communicated through the
psiberweb; without it, Barzun had no way to maintain contact within his fleet during inversion. The longer they spent in
inversion without communications, the more the ships would
be spread out in space and time when they dropped into normal space.

And yet, for all that Barzun's fleet stretched throughout the
system, and despite how long it took them all to arrive, their
formation was remarkably organized. To keep anything resembling a coherent formation, Barzun must have regularly
dropped the ships out of inversion, then used hours or even
days to regroup. Proceeding that way, it would take the Radi-

ance Fleet *months* to reach any major ISC center. They certainly couldn't have already made it to headquarters and then back out here to a distant volume of space where Trader, Allied, and Skolian territory abutted.

This made no sense, unless the fleet had come straight here from their battle with the Traders. It had only been several months since the invasion of the Trader capital; the Radiance Fleet could conceivably make it to Delos in that time. But *why*? What did they know?

It was possible that, before Jon and Vazar were confined, one or both had managed to send messenger ships to HQ asking for reinforcements. The Radiance Fleet might well have intercepted one, with its own ships dropping in and out of inversion so much. And they were a formidable force. Against them, our four thousand ships had no chance.

When the lengthy protocols finished, Chad Barzun's voice came out of the comm. I didn't activate any visuals; we had no idea how much Barzun knew. If he didn't realize I was alive, that could work in our favor.

"Admiral Bloodmark," Chad said, following the ISC protocol that required the lower ranked officer to speak first.

"Rear Admiral Barzun," Ragnar acknowledged.

Chad spoke simply, with no preamble. "Request permission to speak to Pharaoh Dyhianna."

I silently swore. Ragnar glanced up at me, the question in his gaze.

Pushing back the long tendrils of hair that had escaped my braid, I nodded. Then I said, "This is Pharaoh Dyhianna."

A sharp intake of breath came over the comm. When Chad spoke again, his voice sounded uneven. "My honor at your presence, Your Highness." Then, more softly, he added, "Gods almighty, it really is you."

"Yes." I couldn't say more until I knew why he had come.

Chad continued wthout hesitation. "It is the honor of the Radiance Fleet to serve the Ruby Pharaoh."

23
Majda Quandary

Virtual simulations of Admiral Bloodmark, Rear Admiral Barzun, Admiral Casestar, Primary Majda, Eldrin, and myself stood clustered in a virtual conference room on *Roca's Pride,* the battle cruiser commanded by Chad Barzun. We were all actually sitting at computer consoles in VR suits on our respective ships. In the sim, no one wanted to sit down, a position we all apparently associated with a weakening of status. So here we stood in a room with no furniture, just white marble walls veined with gold. The starburst emblem of Skolia was emblazoned on one wall in a flare of crimson and gold.

I had brought all my advisors together in the sim, current and former, including Jon and Vazar, who were still in custody. I had long ago learned that the only way to maximize my chances of receiving strong, thorough advice was to include everyone's opinion regardless of whether or not they agreed with me.

"You're suggesting treason." An uncharacteristic anger honed Jon's words as he faced Chad Barzun in the center of the room. "Take the Radiance Fleet to Earth? Are you insane? It's a blatant declaration of hostilities."

Chad showed no sign of relenting. "Earth made that declaration when they refused to release Web Key Eldrinson and Councilor Roca." His square chin, beak of a nose, and bushy eyebrows, iron-gray like his hair, made a sharp contrast to Jon's even-featured face.

Jon Casestar's frustration sparked, creating red flashes around his simulated body. "What about your loyalty to ISC and the Assembly? Are you going to throw that away?"

"Don't question my loyalty," Chad said harshly. "I commanded the fleet that took out the Traders. I saw our ships go down, over *ninety* percent of them." His voice roughened. "I saw the shuttle with Imperator Skolia and her brother Prince

Althor explode. Damn it, Jon! I won't turn against the Ruby Dynasty."

Jon met his gaze. "More people will die if we go to Earth."

"We aren't going to attack," I said. Although I was standing near the wall, the sim carried my words as if I were right next to them. "A show of force may be all we need." Even though Eldrin's dream had put his father on Lyshriol, Eldrin remained convinced that his parents, if still alive, were on Earth, not Lyshriol. My models agreed. Nor had the Allieds notified ISC that they had moved any members of the Ruby Dynasty.

Ragnar was pacing back and forth. "We don't know that we won't have to fight." He had darkened his clothes and hair in the sim, giving him a shadowed quality. "And we have to decide what to do about Lyshriol." He stalked over to me. "Even if we rescue your sister and her husband, their children are still imprisoned on the planet Lyshriol. The Allieds are using our own defenses at Lyshriol to keep us out."

"And it's a damn good system," Vazar said. She was leaning against the wall across from me. "It's just as good when used *against* us as by us. The Allieds also have their own forces there. They could do serious damage if we engaged them." She strode forward to where Jon and Chad stood, her body shedding fiery light. Stopping with an admiral on either side, she glared between them straight at me. "I want it on record that I protest any such plans."

"No one has suggested we attack Lyshriol," I said mildly. *Vazar, we need your support,* I thought, even knowing she was too far away to pick it up. Although she was no longer in the brig, she remained confined to her quarters on *Havyrl's Valor* just as Jon Casestar was confined to his.

"Something is going on with Lyshriol," Chad Barzun said.

"You've had word?" Vazar asked.

"A lot," Chad said. "Almost every time the Radiance Fleet dropped out of inversion, we picked up reports from ships we encountered. One of the Ruby princes—Havyrl Valdoria—has organized some sort of continent-wide act of nonviolent civil disobedience. ISC managed to slip in a Jagernaut team to help him. It's been going on for weeks."

Jon spoke dryly. "I would hardly call on Jagernauts for a nonviolent protest."

Ragnar shrugged. "I don't see the point. What can a crowd of planet-bound rustics armed with swords and bows do against Allied Space Command?"

"They aren't armed," Chad said. "That's the whole point. They're fighting this battle with social opinion. Somehow the J-team is sending footage of the protest to one of our ships, the *Ascendant*. The PR people on the *Ascendant* put together reports and send them to the holo-news broadcasters: Skolian, Allied, even Trader. Without the psiberweb, it takes days, even weeks, to spread the news to so many worlds, but the media still loves it. The image of these helpless natives and their noble, rustic prince holding a valiant protest against the mighty invading army. It's one hell of a good story."

"Rustic prince?" Eldrin quirked his eyebrow at that description of his brother Havyrl. He was standing against a nearby wall. "Vyrl has a doctorate in agriculture from one of the top universities in the Skolian Imperialate."

"Well, yes," Chad acknowledged. "The reports don't mention that."

I thought of Havyrl, one of Eldrin's younger brothers. He and Eldrin resembled each other, both with violet eyes and those handsome Valdoria features women loved. Vyrl was taller, with a curly, red-gold mane of hair. Unlike Eldrin, Vyrl had never had any problem reading and writing, or dealing with Skolian culture. Yet he was the one who had opted to stay on Lyshriol, as a farmer, rather than live a more modern life offworld, as Eldrin had done.

"Is the protest having any effect?" Jon asked.

"How could it?" Ragnar demanded, incredulous.

"It's making the Allieds look like a bunch of warmongers." Chad turned to Eldrin. "Your brother is brilliant. He's brought together almost the entire population of the Rillian subcontinent. Two hundred thousand people. They've gathered at that small starport near your village on the Dalvador Plains. They plan to stay until the Allieds withdraw from Lyshriol."

"It's a noble sentiment," Eldrin said. "But I don't see how it can do any good."

Chad beamed at him. "Lyshriol has become a symbol. The longer the Allieds refuse to withdraw, the more bellicose they look. And now they have three interstellar civilizations watching everything they do."

I couldn't resist a smirk. "That's a switch for Earth. Usually they're the saints, we're the sinners, and the Traders are the devils."

"So." Vazar bestowed on us an implacable stare. "What a great help it will be to Prince Havyrl when we show up at Earth with seventy thousand war ships. What shall we say? 'Greetings, Allieds. Would you care for tea?' "

"She's right," Jon said. "Our moving on Earth in full force could weaken what they're trying to do at Lyshriol."

"Not if we make a lot of noise about our friendly intentions," I said. "We tell them we've just come to pick up Roca, Eldrinson, and the others, and we thank them for giving protection. Then we make sure the media gets reports of everything."

Jon wasn't buying it. "No one will believe we come in peace with a fleet this large."

Chad looked thoughtful. "I'm not sure about that. It's big enough now to be a respectable deterrent, but not so large as to form an overt threat. Sure, they could defeat us if they attacked, but it would be a brutal battle. Do you really think they want that, especially if we come claiming peace?"

"Ah, hell," Vazar said. "They may be right, Admiral Casestar. Everyone knows the Allieds are holding their Ruby Dynasty 'guests' prisoner. Of course we would bring ships to defend ourselves. But with a fleet this size, we look careful rather than belligerent."

Chad grinned. "*Roca's Pride* should be our flagship. It's great symbolism, given that they're holding Roca Skolia prisoner."

Vazar grunted. "Pah."

Ragnar paced over to her. "I thought you agreed with us."

She met his aggressive stare without a twitch. "I said it makes sense. It also makes sense that you will all be tried and executed for treason."

I spoke softly. "By whom, Primary Majda?"

Everyone went silent. Who indeed. The Assembly couldn't make their censure into policy without military backing. We had the major share of ISC forces now.

Unfortunately, Naaj Majda had the rest.

As Vazar watched me, her body went hazy. I did a quick check. No tech problem existed. She had blurred herself on purpose, a protest against the conflicting loyalties we had forced on her.

"Admiral Bloodmark." Lieutenant Qahot's voice snapped in the air. "We have an incoming ship. Civilian this time. It's from the Orbiter."

"What the hell," Ragnar said. "Now what?"

"Is it alone?" Jon asked.

"Yes, sir." Then realizing she had answered Jon instead of Ragnar, Qahot quickly added, "Admiral Bloodmark."

"What idiot would leave the safety of the Orbiter now?" Ragnar demanded. "Is she suicidal?"

"Not she, sir. He." From the sound of Qahot's voice she might have been preparing for an explosion rather than reporting a ship. "It's Primary Majda's husband and son."

"I'll throttle him!" Vazar strode at my side, her long legs eating up distance. Her guards came with us, as well as my bodyguards, and Ragnar and his aides. She was going so fast that even they had to work to keep up.

"What was he thinking?" She exuded fury, but I knew it was a shield. Vazar was terrified, knowing her husband and son could easily have been killed or captured. "I swear, I'll throw him in the brig for this."

"You're already in the brig," I said. Actually, she was still confined to quarters, but it had the same effect.

"Damn crazy man," Vazar muttered. "They had better be all right."

We took an elevator to the docking tube. Vazar set the car

speed at maximum, and the rapid change to microgravity almost made me lose my last meal.

We exited into a ring that circled the docking tube like a giant donut. Floating around its bend, we came into sight of the the decon chamber where the incoming ship had docked. The chamber was in use when we arrived, so we waited around the entrance, a blue portal bordered by light-bars and conduits. I didn't envy the two people inside. They would come out into a cluster of Jagernauts, including one furious Primary.

The hatch hissed. Then it swung open, framing a man in the entrance.

Even after fifteen years, it still took my breath away every time I saw Coop. He had an angel's face, eyes as blue as Earth's legendary sky, and a dancer's lithe build. At thirty-nine he still looked like a boy. His golden curls shone. He was as stunning now as the day Althor and Vazar had met him. At the moment he also looked scared to death, and it wasn't of the Jagernauts, at least not most of them. His gaze was riveted on only one.

"Are you out of your mind?" Vazar growled. "You came here in a single, unarmed ship? With *Ryder*? Are you crazy?"

"My greetings, Vaz." Coop's voice seduced the ear, like music, deep and inviting in a way that came naturally to him, with an innocence that all the guile in the universe couldn't have reproduced. I had seen both Althor and Vazar, two of the most formidable warriors I knew, turned to putty by that voice. It didn't work today, though. Vazar still wanted to throttle him.

A fourteen-year-old boy appeared behind Coop. He resembled his father, with the same blue eyes and slightly darker gold hair, but his face had traces of the Majda bone structure, giving him stronger features. Ryder was also taller than his father, and growing fast, with broader shoulders and a more muscular physique.

"I wouldn't let him go without me," Ryder said. His voice had changed since the last time I saw him. It was deeper now than his father's voice.

Vazar gripped the edge of the hatchway. "I could have lost

you both." Her words were all the more compelling for being so quiet. "*Both*. After we lost—" She drew in a ragged breath and said no more. The name she left unspoken almost seemed to hang in the air. Althor.

"That's why we came." Coop drifted closer to her. She started to lean toward him, then pulled back. He touched her shoulder, and she put out a hand to steady him so he didn't float away. "Whatever happens," he said, "we want to be with you. Security on the Orbiter wouldn't let us leave. So we, uh—avoided them."

She glowered. "You stole a ship and made an illegal launch? It's bad enough you do that yourself, Coop. But Ryder too?"

"He said I couldn't come." Ryder moved out of the chamber. "I told him that if he didn't let me, I would steal another ship and follow."

"What if you had been hurt?" Vazar growled at her son. "I ought to ground you—for the rest of your life."

I cleared my throat. "Perhaps we should take our guests to more comfortable quarters."

Vazar glanced around with a start, as if just remembering their sentimental reunion was taking place in public. It disconcerted me to see her so unsettled. I had watched her face Trader commandos without a flinch, but seeing her family undefended shook her in a way she never showed in battle.

So we headed back, with Coop and Ryder. Vazar now had an even worse conflict; if our fleet ended up in combat, her husband and son could die.

Coop and Ryder entered Vazar's quarters as if they were visiting a stranger. Given the way Vazar was seething, it didn't surprise me. She motioned curtly at the aide who had brought their belongings from the ship, and he sent a robot carrier to unload their bags. As it trundled off, Vazar crossed her arms and glared at Coop.

"I'll help the robot unload my bags," Ryder said, his glance darting between his parents. Then he made a fast retreat, headed for the safety of his guest room.

Coop stood self-consciously in the center of the living room, watching Vazar with those large blue eyes that could melt steel. He resembled a concubine more than a husband. And indeed, when Althor had first set up Coop in an apartment and given him an art studio, everyone assumed Coop was little more than a male courtesan. That he turned out to be a remarkably gifted artist had caused surprise; few people had actually believed Althor had any interest in becoming a patron of the arts.

Coop obviously wished to please his patron, though, and did whatever Althor wanted, like turning his hair from gold to red and then back to gold again on Althor's whim. He spent his days working on his holo sculptures and his nights doing who-knew-what with Althor and Vazar, and no one of the noble Houses said a word, just smiled with glee at the beautiful if rather kinky toy Althor and Vazar had acquired.

Then Althor and Vazar married him.

The irony never stopped amazing me, that the Houses accepted with salacious delight the idea that the Imperial Heir and a Majda Primary would share a male concubine, but exploded with outrage when Althor did the honorable thing and offered a legal contract that gave Coop the full rights of a spouse.

I understood why Vazar and Althor loved Coop. Not only was he a strong empath, but his mind also shone like an idyllic harbor filled with light. He gave off a golden aura.

A prickle went up my spine. Puzzled, I glanced around and saw Ragnar by the wall. He was watching Vazar and Coop with unabashed fascination. I recognized that look, the hunter studying his prey. Damn. Given Ragnar's hunger for power, it made too much sense. Amazing how his distaste for unconventional marriages could evaporate if it involved gain for him. Not only was Vazar a high-ranking member of the House of Majda, she had a similarly high status within ISC. Add to that her connections to the Ruby Dynasty, and she wielded great power. And here she was, a blazingly sensual widow desired by many men, with a bereaved husband who loved her more as a sister than a wife, leaving a gaping hole in their marriage.

Enter Ragnar.

Vazar stalked over to Coop, her arms crossed, her hair disheveled about her face. "I ought to take you over my knee and thrash you."

His lips curved upward with an unconscious seductive appeal that I had long ago realized he had no idea he projected. "Such promises."

"It's not funny." She waved her hand at the room, but the gesture seemed to encompass the entire fleet. "If we send you back with a full escort, it will deplete our forces. We can't afford that right now."

"We could go back alone." He didn't sound worried; everyone knew Vazar would battle a Trader squadron single-handedly before she would let Coop put himself or Ryder in more danger.

"What if we go to war with the Allieds?" Vazar demanded. "This fleet is the front line of defense now. How can I shake sense into your beautiful head? You and Ryder shouldn't *be* here."

"Well, we are," he said mildly. "Vazar, being safe means nothing if we never see you again."

I moved away quietly, not wanting to intrude. Security would monitor Vazar's quarters as long as she remained in custody, but we could at least give her and Coop the privacy of being alone.

I paused by Ragnar and spoke in a low voice. "We can talk to her later."

He was still watching them with that hungry look. "I should stay. In case they need help."

"You will leave."

He glanced at me. "What's wrong?"

"Nothing," I murmured. "As long as you stay away from my sister-in-law and brother-in-law."

"I don't know what you're talking about."

"I'm glad." I motioned toward the entrance. "Shall we go?"

He paused as if to say more. Then he gave me a sour look. "Of course."

So we left. I tried not to dwell on the fact that I now had even less reason to trust Ragnar.

24
Dawn

Thunder rolled in the night. I bolted upright in bed, jerked awake by the noise. Although the air-mattress next to me was still warm, Eldrin had gone. A pounding came from somewhere in the suite. I scrambled out of bed, pulling on my robe, and ran into the living room.

Eldrin had gone mad. I had heard tales of his bloodlust in battle, when he was sixteen, but it had never sounded real. Now I better understood. He threw himself against the walls, his face twisted with fury, his fist pounding the unyielding surface, as if he would tear down the panels and crush the bulkheads beneath them. His rage flooded my mind.

"Eldrin!" I started forward, then stopped. In this state, he could kill me without realizing it. With alarm, I remembered my Security-busting programs. I had set them up earlier to make the monitors see Eldrin and me sleeping when we had been otherwise occupied.

"Laplace," I said. "End 'Welcome' program."

Eldrin whirled to me, his hair swinging around his face, his eyes huge and his gaze wild. He started forward, his fists clenched.

I backed into the bedroom. "Dryni, it's Dehya. Don't you recognize me?" I tried to reach his mind, but his thoughts flared like wildfire.

He kept coming. As I stumbled, he strode into the bedroom. I regained my balance, but I had nowhere to run. He caught my upper arm and flung me against the wall. I put up my hands to cushion the impact and barely managed to turn my head in time to keep from breaking my nose when I hit. I couldn't believe this. Not Eldrin—

"Father, don't."

The voice came from behind us. Eldrin's grip on my arm jerked and dropped away. I looked over my shoulder to see him facing me, his hand raised, the fingers spasmed into a claw. Then he lowered his arm and turned around.

Taquinil stood in the doorway to the living room. He wasn't as tall as Eldrin, nor did he have his father's broad shoulders or muscular frame. But he showed no fear. Eldrin started toward him, making what sounded like a snarl.

Taquinil faded into mist.

Eldrin faltered, raising his fists as if to defend against an unseen foe. Then he swung around, his gaze raking the room. I didn't feel his rage as much now; it was fading into confusion.

"Dehya?" He dropped his arms and slowly opened his fists, looking at his hands as if he didn't recognize them.

"Are you all right?" I asked. Now that he was rational, the reaction set in and I began to shake. I gulped and sat down hard on the floor.

"What happened?" He came over, then stopped when I flinched. "I won't hurt you."

I took a ragged breath. "Are you sure?"

"Yes." Moving more slowly, he sat next to me. "What did I do?"

I tried not to shake, wishing I could be more hardened, a warrior like Vazar. But with Eldrin, I had no defenses. A tear ran down my cheek.

"Ah, love." He pulled me closer, drawing me sideways against him, between his legs, his muscular arms around my body. I should have felt threatened, being held so close by a former warrior who had just gone berserk, but I couldn't fear Eldrin. Logic told me to run; intuition said stay.

I laid my head against his chest and closed my eyes. Eldrin had been the only one I could trust. I needed him. Without the sanctuary of the man I loved, I didn't know if I could keep going. Somehow I had to rebuild the psiberweb out of nothing. And I knew too many secrets. Soz. Jaibriol. Eldrinson. Seth. The children. I understood why Taquinil wanted to stay in Kyle space; I wished I could retreat myself.

Laplace suddenly spoke. "I have Jagernauts outside. Shall I let them in?"

"No." My voice caught, trembling. "Not now."

"Dehya, don't cry." Eldrin brushed his hand down my hair.

I swallowed. "I've no right to cry. You're the one they did this to."

"No. Gods, no." He laid his head against mine. "Don't tell me the Traders did something to me. I couldn't bear it if I hurt you. I would rather die."

"You didn't recognize me."

Bitterness darkened his voice. "On Lyshriol, my going berserk was considered bravery, especially after I crushed a man in combat with my bare hands." He shook his head. "When I went to the Orbiter, the doctors said my brain had a problem, that in the midst of battle I had experienced a convulsion caused by a neural overload."

The memory trickled into my mind. The extra neural structures that made Eldrin such a powerful empath also made his mind susceptible to overloads, sending him into a convulsion. It wasn't epilepsy; during an episode he could continue what he was doing but he lost control of himself. At Eldrin's request, the doctors had treated him so he no longer had seizures.

"Your mind was always that way," I said. "This may have nothing to do with the Traders."

"Unless whatever they did to me triggered it."

"But why tonight?"

"I had another dream." His voice quieted. "About my father. That he died several months ago."

"I'm so sorry, love." I had felt it too, a drifting apart of the Triad.

"Before now, I was certain he went peacefully, surrounded by family." The tensed muscles in his arms felt like steel cords. "Tonight I dreamed ISC buried him alive in space. I was him, trapped in orbit, inside a coffin."

No wonder he had lost control. "Could the Traders have planted the image?"

"Perhaps." He spoke softly. "I only know you aren't safe with me."

"No." I didn't want to lose the haven of his presence. "If

your father's death triggered that, why did it happen now instead of when he died?

"Something about our debate today with Chad and Jon stirred it up." He bent his head over mine, his voice strained. "Until we know more, you can't risk being alone with me. Taquinil might not stop me next time."

A tear slid down my face. "We've lost so much, Dryni. I can't lose you, too."

His voice caught. "We have no choice."

The residential parks of *Havyrl's Valor* had a serenity at odds with the cruiser's purpose. The ship was so large, it could maintain a self-sufficient biosphere. Security chief Jinn Opsister and several of our bodyguards led the way along a graveled path between several gardens. Other guards accompanied us, but they stayed far enough away to give the illusion of privacy.

Eldrin and I walked on either side of Tania Merzon, one of the cruiser's doctors. She continued in a subdued voice. "I can't find any tampering to your mind, Prince Eldrin, but that doesn't mean nothing was done. Are you certain the nightmare set it off?"

"Yes." New lines furrowed Eldrin's forehead. "It felt like I had been buried alive. No sight, touch, sound, smell. Not even taste, because a med-line was cycling nutrients into my body." He shuddered. "Nor could I reach anyone with my mind. I was in space, not underground."

It sounds like sensory deprivation, I thought.

Yes. His thought had a hollow feel.

Tania considered. "It could be a subconscious reaction to your captivity with the Traders."

He didn't look convinced. "Yes, I hated being Corbal's slave. But this nightmare felt like an echo of someone else's memory."

"If someone imprinted it on your mind," Tania said, "it would probably feel as if it didn't belong to you."

I pushed aside a curling tendril that had escaped the hair piled on my head. "But what triggered it?"

Tania glanced at Eldrin. "Anything unusual happen yesterday?"

He answered dryly. "Just a bit. Ragnar Bloodmark mutinied and relieved Jon Casestar of command. The Radiance Fleet showed up. Chad Barzun pledged his loyalty to the Ruby Dynasty. Vazar's husband and son arrived."

Tania smiled. "I guess that qualifies as an unusual day."

"Maybe the Radiance Fleet did it," I said. "They've certainly stirred up the rest of us, and we weren't even Trader prisoners."

Darkness came into Eldrin's gaze. "Thank the saints for that."

"Yes." Tania's mood blended many emotions: relief that Eldrin and I were safe; gratitude that the surviving Radiance soldiers hadn't ended up as Trader slaves; fear for the future; and a wary hope. "If yesterday's events triggered your outbreak, it may happen again. Pharaoh Dyhianna shouldn't be alone with you until we understand what happened."

I knew she was right, but it added to the isolation already parching our lives.

Jinn Opsister paused ahead of us. As we stopped, she turned to me. "A message is coming in, ma'am." She indicated her gauntlet comm. "Shall I route it through to you?"

"Yes, please do." Then I thought, *Activate receiver.*

My neural nodes responded. Using wireless signals, they sent my message to Jinn's comm, which then sent it to Vazar's computer. That machine communicated with Vazar and sent her response back to Jinn's comm, which relayed it to my nodes. It wasn't telepathy; I had no sense of Vazar's emotions or thoughts, only her words. But it felt similar.

=Dehya, I need to talk to you,= Vazar said. =It's important.=

This isn't a good time. Can it wait?

=I don't think so.=

Vazar wouldn't make such a request without good reason.

Very well. I will come now.

=Can you bring Eldrin also? He needs to hear this.=

I glanced at Eldrin. *Vazar wants to talk to us. She says it is important.*

I will come. If these Jagernauts do also.

I sent a message to Vazar. *We will be there soon.*
=Please hurry.=

Vazar ushered us into her living room. Its holo-panels swirled in washes of color: pale green, blue, ivory. Diffuse, golden light softened the room. The air smelled like a fresh mountain glade. It was soothing. Too soothing. Vazar never decorated her quarters this way, not unless she thought she needed a calming mood. It didn't bode well.

Our bodyguards took positions along the walls, black-uniformed monoliths silhouetted against pale swaths of shifting color. As Eldrin and I exchanged stiff greetings with Vazar, standing awkwardly in the center of the room, Coop and Ryder entered from an inner archway. They greeted us with courtesy, their faces unreadable, so carefully neutral. If I hadn't already been uneasy, that alone would have been enough to alarm me. Both Coop and his son had a cornucopia of moods, but neutral wasn't one of them.

Vazar motioned us to molded armchairs set around a rounded table, all the furniture made with holo-surfaces that were also bestowing us with pleasant washes of color rather than the sharper primary hues Vazar preferred.

Coop and Ryder sat on the sofa across the table. Ryder was losing his shield of neutrality. He had the least experience guarding his thoughts, and his agitation was coming through now. It peppered us like hail. He was a strong psion, rated at nine. Coop was five, Vazar also nine. A child's ability usually tended toward the parent with the lower rating, because psion genes were recessive. But Coop had some of the genes unmatched, which meant he didn't express their traits. Apparently those had paired with Vazar's genes, giving their son a rating closer to his mother.

As we settled into our chairs, the furniture readjusted, trying to make us comfortable. I didn't think any of us relaxed. Ryder's agitation spiked.

"Are you all right?" I asked him.

He regarded me with his large eyes. "Earlier today, they told me what they're about to tell you."

Eldrin spoke quietly. "And that is—?"

Vazar started to answer, but she stopped before any words came out. She started again and stopped again. Finally she said, "I don't know how to do this with finesse. So I'll just say it. I'm not Ryder's mother."

"That's not true!" Ryder thumped the arm of his chair. "You're my mother in every way that matters."

Her face softened. "And you are my son, always."

I glanced at Eldrin. He returned my puzzled gaze and shook his head. To Vazar, I said, "I've seen the DNA records. They say Ryder is your son."

Coop answered. "We set it up that way." He sounded tired. "The uproar about Althor marrying a commoner had already drained us. I had no titles, no rank, no status, nothing. This would have made it even worse, especially since Majda expected Vazar to produce heirs."

"But then who is Ryder's biological mother?" Eldrin asked.

Vazar shifted her weight. "He doesn't have one. Exactly."

"Yes, I do." Ryder's voice rumbled, deeper than Coop's had ever been. "You carried me. You gave birth to me. It was your egg."

"Vaz's egg?" I had a good idea what was coming. "But the nucleus didn't contain her DNA, did it?" I turned to Coop. "You and Althor?"

He flushed, then cleared his throat. "Yes."

"Good gods." I blinked at Ryder. "You're Althor's son."

Eldrin stiffened. "What?"

"He has two fathers," I said.

Eldrin's face turned red. "That's absurd."

"Not with modern biotech," Vazar said.

"I may not know molecular biology," Eldrin retorted. "But I'm not stupid. You need a man and a woman to make a child."

"Not if you splice the genes you want," Coop said. "We used Althor's DNA and mine."

I could see it, to an extent. Ryder's height, his muscular build, and his high psi rating all suggested Althor's heritage. But he had no trace of Althor's metallic gold coloring. And I still thought he looked like Vazar. "You have Majda genes too, don't you?" I asked him.

"A little." He glanced at his mother. "My face? And skin?"

"Yes." Vazar's voice when she spoke to Ryder and Coop had far more warmth than when she spoke to the rest of us. Turning to me, she became businesslike. "I wanted Majda to accept Ryder as my heir. And we didn't want a furor. So we used enough of my DNA to give him a visible Majda heredity."

"Then you *are* his genetic mother," I said.

"A little." Tenderness gentled her expression as she turned to Ryder. "You are a miracle. With all of us psions, we didn't know if it would work, given the genetic complications."

Eldrin made an incredulous noise. "This can't be. It's wrong."

Coop bristled. "It isn't wrong to want a child born out of love."

Eldrin stared at him as if he had lost his mind. "Not out of two *men*."

I spoke. "Eldrin, your grandmother was created in a Trader lab. Does that make your birth wrong?"

"That's different."

Ryder watched him with large eyes. Blue eyes. Like Coop. "Do you think I'm abnormal, Uncle Eldrin?"

Eldrin looked startled. Then he spoke more quietly. "No. No, I didn't mean that." He paused. "I really am your uncle, aren't I? By blood, I mean." He glanced at Vazar, his gaze darkening. "He has Ruby Dynasty genes. That makes him almost as valuable to the Traders as a Rhon psion."

She answered with difficulty. "That was why Althor had the knowledge about Ryder, Coop, and me set to erase from his brain if the Traders captured him."

Coop spoke in a subdued voice. "It must have worked. The Traders ignored Ryder when they raided the Orbiter."

"That's why you left the Orbiter, isn't it?" I asked. "You feared they might still locate it using their stolen Lock."

"In part," Coop said. When he looked at his wife, the affection on his angelic face could have melted stone. "But it's also true what we said, that we wanted to be with Vaz."

Vazar made a gruff noise, but I knew she wasn't angry. Coop knew it too. His mind warmed like sunlight, luminous and affectionate.

Vazar started to lean toward her husband. Then she seemed to remember the rest of us were there. She turned to me, edgy again. "Before you take this fleet to Earth, you should know you're carrying another member of the Ruby Dynasty."

Well, hell. What could I say? I had an impossible conflict. We didn't dare leave members of the Ruby Dynasty out here with only a few ships to protect them. Normally I wouldn't go to retrieve political prisoners either. But our plans couldn't succeed without my psiberspace links, and we were safer with seventy-five thousand ships than if we stayed behind with only a few. Nor could we risk depleting our fleet by leaving a larger force. But taking Ryder and Coop with us also put them in danger.

No matter what I chose, the Ruby Dynasty would bear the brunt of that decision. However, if Earth continued to hold Roca and the others, all the people of Skolia would suffer the consequences. We needed all of the Rhon if we were to regain our strength; Eldrin and I couldn't do it alone.

I hesitated, hating what I had to say. "I am truly sorry. But we still have to go." All the threads led to Earth—and if we didn't unravel them, they would strangle us.

Webs of every kind networked the cruiser; nothing was free of them. Most were simple systems with specific purposes. Only a select few consoles had control chairs that allowed a human user to link in as an operator on the ship webs. The captain's command chair was unique in that it could boost his mind straight into the brain of the ship.

Those paled next to the Triad Chairs.

Three battle cruisers orbited Delos now: *Havyrl's Valor,* *Roca's Pride,* and *Pharaoh's Shield.* Among those powerhouses, only *Roca's Pride* carried a Triad Chair. Most telops couldn't use it without brain damage. Although in theory any member of my family could operate such a chair, only Triad members dared. The fluxes of power were too great even for most of the Rhon.

A Spark racer took us to *Roca's Pride.* I rode with Ragnar and his aides. Eldrin stayed on *Havyrl's Valor* at the recommendation of the doctors, who were investigating what had happened during his nightmare. No one wanted to take risks with either of us. But I did so miss him.

On *Roca's Pride,* we went straight to the Triad Chamber. Its domed ceiling showed a panoramic view of interstellar dust clouds made brilliant with the birth of new stars blazing in blue, yellow, red, and white. Interstellar space in the neighborhood of Delos was hardly the "black void" of poets. But this spectacular view was fake, a holograph. Given that gravity pointed outward from the ship's rotation axis, an actual window to the stars would have been under our feet.

The Triad Chair formed the terminus of a massive robot arm. Rank upon rank of panels surrounded the giant chair, glittering. More controls were embedded in the blocky armrests and hood. I *felt* the chair. Nor was I the only one; an aide in Ragnar's retinue winced and several of my Jagernaut bodyguards paled. One of the strongest psions actually stepped back, his face drawn. But I found the Chair's presence exhilarating, like rushing up a mountain in a ski-racer with its cockpit open and air streaming past your face.

Come to me, I coaxed.

The great chair descended. Its hum filled the chamber, as if it were purring in its huge, biomechanical heart.

Come.

It moved toward us, conduits glowing green, white, blue. Beads of light ran like linked cars along the massive throne.

Its exoskeleton gleamed silver. With a deep-toned hum, it settled in front of me, looming. The lights in the chamber dimmed until only the controls on the Chair and the holostars above us gave any illumination.

Ragnar walked to the Chair and stopped by its side, his face lit from beneath by its panels, his gaze covetous. Watching him, I felt even more isolated. I had been separated from the people I wanted to trust: Jon, Vazar, Eldrin, Taquinil. My strongest ally, Ragnar, was an old family friend, yes, but I knew all too well his sharp-edged ambition.

The Triad Chair thundered in my mind: **ATTENDING.**

Prepare to commence.

PREPARED.

I settled into the throne. Panels readjusted, forming a cage around my body. I could see my reflection in the robot arms, a slender woman, waif-like, her face dominated by large green eyes, her body bathed in the eerie light from a chair so powerful it became a living entity. The Triad Chair had intelligence, but it was unlike anything we understood. It rarely communicated with humans beyond the barest minimum required to carry out its purpose, and it showed no other interest in us.

The techs went to work, running tests much as a pilot ran preflight checks on a spacecraft. As the exoskeleton clicked prongs into my body, I closed my eyes. The Chair hummed around and within me. My mind became attuned to everyone in the room, my reception of them magnified. Although the Jagernauts had enough mental strength to feel energy flow through the Chair, they didn't revel in its presence. They knew its power but none of the joy.

Initiate.

DONE. The Chair's hum surged.

I dropped into nothing.

Kyle space existed everywhere and nowhere. Without a web, it had no organization the human mind recognized. Even my perception of light and dark ceased. This was nothing . . .

Nothiiiing . . .
Nothiiing . . .
Nothiing . . .
Nothing . . .
Fading . . .
Fade . . .
Fad . . .
Fa . . .
F . . .
. . .
. .
.

I concentrated, taking the mental equivalent of a step back
from a cliff. No precipice existed here, but I embraced the
metaphor. *Cliff. Ocean.*

A promontory appeared out of the nothing. I was standing
on its edge, far above a wild seascape. An ocean of silver and
green surged powerfully against the cliff, spraying up fountains of water. Exhilaration swept through me.

WEB NODE ARCHITECTURE ESTABLISHED.

Good. I gazed across the primitive sea. Raising my arm, I
gathered the Rhon power I had honed with over a century of
experience and swung my hand in a great arc, palm facing
upward. A sky suddenly appeared, boiling with swollen
clouds, dark and lowering, torn by gales. Sapphire lightening
cracked across the thunderheads.

Activate node.

DONE.

The clouds exploded apart. Shafts of diamond-bright sunlight burst through, turning the sea into a sparkling tumult of
water. The waves cascaded ever higher, sending arches of
star-bright spray into the streaming light.

So a new psiberweb was born.

BOOK THREE

Transformation

25

The Roaring Tide

They renamed our armada the *Pharaoh's Fleet* in the hope of redefining its purpose as well, from war to a new beginning. We prepared a communiqué to send to Parthonia, the capital world of Skolia, and to Diesha, where ISC had its headquarters. In the communiqué, I relieved Barcala Tikal of his position as First Councilor and Naaj Majda of her position as Imperator.

However, we didn't send it yet. We had another operation to carry out first, and I didn't want Barcala or Naaj warned until absolutely necessary. The less time they had to gather forces, the better. But I did want Barcala in custody soon, not only to stop him from building support, but also to make sure no overzealous Ruby loyalist decided to kill him.

Barcala and I had been friends for decades. I tried not to dwell on how few options I would have if this rebellion succeeded. He would become the deposed leader, a symbol that posed too much danger.

Although Naaj Majda and I had a more distant relationship, I didn't want her assassinated either. Her loyalty to the Houses and her conservatism, steeped in tradition, suggested she might accept a shift of power to the Ruby Dynasty. But she would lose the title of Imperator. I had made Ragnar acting Imperator until further notice, taking that authority away from Vazar, if she had ever really had it. Given her support of Jon Casestar, I had no choice but to leave them in custody, as much as I disliked the situation. Coop and Ryder stayed with Vazar.

Right now we were racing through superluminal space, where mass, energy, length, and even time became imaginary. We were also rotated into Haver-Klein space, hiding our ships in gigantic bottles made from fields that twisted out of the real universe. The only way to hold the ships in formation was to link through the psiberweb, but the fledgling web was too new to handle such a gargantuan job. It needed a central node to hold it together. We had only one node capable of managing the huge fluxes that poured through the web from seventy-five thousand ships.

So I became part of the psiberweb.

Using the web had always been humbling, but this was like nothing I had experienced before. I had no support, no buffers, no other nodes to siphon off the power. *Nothing.* The fleet thundered through my mind like hurricane-driven breakers smashing against cliffs. Power burst through the sky and flooded the mindscape. Seventy-five thousand ships linked through me. Their combined power roared, filling the universe until I knew only an agonizing joy that came in wave after wave of streaming, booming energy.

Booming on the roaring tides of the mind! Booming on the roaring tides of the mind!

A trillion energies, trillion thoughts. A trillion energies, trillion thoughts.

Exquisite, shimmering orbitals. Exquisite, shimmering orbitals.

One energy, one thought. One energy, one thought.

Spherical harmonics. Spherical harmonics.

Thought orbitals. Thought orbitals.

All orbitals. All orbitals.

Orbitals. Orbitals.

Orbs. Orbs.

Orb. Orb.

Or Or

O O

o o

o

.

.

Rebirth

A thread glowed among the harmonics. I oriented on it, trying to decipher its meaning. *My greetings, Taquinil.*

Greetings, Mother. We have done good work here, eh?

We have indeed.

The Allied defense systems are a bit more complex than I expected.

A bit.

Nothing too much.

No. Nothing too much . . .

Dispersing

Free . . .

Mother, they are calling you.

Ah, Taquinil, it is as beautiful as you said.

Truly it is. But they are calling you.

An intruding thought rumbled among the orbitals. **Dehya?**

Who was that? Not Eldrin.

A different thought came, vital and warm. **Dehya, come back.**

That was Eldrin. I sighed, longing to drift here forever. But his thoughts pulled. I followed, slowly coalescing into real space.

As I coalesced, so did our fleet.

We dropped out of superluminal space at close to the speed of light. The ships were still in their fuel bottles, hidden in Haver-Klein space. We shot past the outer defenses of the solar system. Long hours seemed like seconds as I absorbed endless, endless data from seventy-five thousand EI ship brains. We passed Pluto's erratic orbit, then Neptune, Uranus, and Saturn. At the orbit of Jupiter, we rotated into normal space.

To the Allieds, our entire fleet suddenly just appeared.

So the Pharaoh's Fleet entered the solar system, birthplace to the humans spread across the stars. Our people came in every size, shape, color, creed, and culture, including many varieties of human that our long distant ancestors could never have imagined.

Earth's lost children had finally come home, after six thousand years.

26

Dialogue of Illusions

The hazy chamber came into focus. Despite my disorientation, I didn't feel the jarring dislocation that had troubled me the other times I returned from psiberspace.

Eldrin? I thought.

You're back. Relief suffused his thought.

Yes. The haze resolved into misty people. Holographic starlight poured into the darkened chamber from the dome overhead. A blur was leaning on the armrest to my right. I focused and it formed into Eldrin.

Greetings, Husband.

Greetings, Wife. I'm glad you decided to exist again.

I smiled. *I too.* I lifted my arm, feeling unreal. Starlight reflected in the silver mesh that sheathed my limbs. I touched Eldrin's cheek with a dreaming brush of my fingers.

"Pharaoh Dyhianna." That came from far away, blowing across an endless plain. I turned my head slowly, floating between realities. A woman stood on the other side of the chair. Jinn Opsister. Good officer, Opsister. A man hovered next to her. Bayliron. The doctor from *Havyrl's Valor.* A fine doctor. I tried to speak, but the words blew away like wind.

Bayliron paled. "Can you bring more of yourself here, Your Highness? We're only reading about fifty percent of your body."

Fifty percent? How odd. If Eldrin hadn't been here, I would have drifted back into the web. But I couldn't; I had too many responsibilities.

Focus.

Coalesce.

"My greetings," I whispered. The words still sounded far away, but understandable now.

"Greetings, Your Highness." Jinn also seemed disquieted. "Our honor at your presence."

Another oddity. Usually people only said the honor business when I first appeared somewhere. But I had been in this chamber for days according to my neural chronometer. Then again, maybe I hadn't been here. I didn't know exactly what happened when I dispersed into psiberspace.

The honor is mine, I murmured, whispers on the wind.

"Can she be taken out of the chair?" a man asked.

I recognized that voice. Turning my head, I perceived another blur. It stood about a meter in front of the chair, which was as close as anything could come with all the control panels in the way.

"My greetings, Chad," I said.

The blur resolved into Chad Barzun. "My greetings, Pharaoh Dyhianna."

"Have we arrived at Earth?"

"We're passing the asteroid belt now, above the plane of the ecliptic."

My mind drifted. "How do you know we aren't under the ecliptic?"

He blinked. "Well, yes, it could be either. We're 'above' as Earth defines its northern hemisphere."

"Does Earth know we're here?"

"Very much so. We've an escort. One hundred thousand Allied ships."

I jolted out of my dreamy contentment. *End session.*

DISENGAGING, the chair thought. Its exoskeleton unfolded from my body.

I leaned forward, pushing at panels. As the techs helped free me from the chair, I spoke to Chad. "How have the Allieds taken our appearance?"

"Calm. But stunned." He came around to where Eldrin stood, so I could hear him better. Their proximity created an eerie effect, a slight rippling of their bodies, as if he and Eldrin interfered like waves. Caught in my dream-like state, I felt only a mild curiosity, no alarm at all.

"I saw the record of your communications with Yamada at Delos," Chad said. "Imagine that reaction, multiplied many times."

What I remembered most was Yamada's relief when we left. Enough of our fleet had remained to occupy Delos, though. That way, if this failed, we would still have a negotiating point, albeit a small one. But a great difference existed in our situation here, compared to Delos.

"We're outnumbered," I said.

"To some extent." Chad paused. "The Allied fleets are stretched thin, though. They're spread across Skolian as well as Allied space, helping clean up after the Radiance War." His hawk-like visage blurred. "We've revealed a weakness in their defenses. They thought it was impossible for a fleet to come in the way we did."

"It is impossible," Eldrin said.

Impossible? And why did Eldrin sound so odd? *It wasn't hard. It was glorious.*

For you, yes. It would kill anyone else. Eldrin touched my face, tracing his fingertip from my temple to my cheek. As he lowered his arm, his finger rippled like water. **It is so strange, Dehya, that you are so fragile and yet so strong at the same time.**

My lips curved upward. *I'm a fierce one.*

Chad was watching us. I caught his wistful thought; he wondered what it was like to converse as a telepath.

"Do you think the Allieds will attack us?" I asked him.

Chad shook his head. "So far, they have shown no inclination to do so, but they've given us no response about your family, either."

That didn't sound promising. "Do we have news from Prince Havyrl on Lyshriol?"

Incongruously, Eldrin suddenly grinned. "He got married."

I blinked. "What?"

"He married a young woman, an empath who has helped him heal."

"Heal?" I was growing confused. "From what?"

"The nightmares," Eldrin said. "The sensory deprivation."

This conversation felt oddly languid. Out of place. And where was Ragnar? It wasn't like him to be out the loop if anything happened.

Good gods. Why was *Eldrin* here? What happened to everyone's fear that his convulsive rage would explode again, endangering my life?

Chad vanished.

Eldrin vanished.

The Chair vanished.

The chamber vanished.

I plunged into dark mist.

What——?

Dehya. The thought rumbled. **Come back.**

Who was that?

Mother, go back.

Taquinil?

The mist cleared and the Triad Chamber reformed. The Chair had taken me back up in the dome.

Dehya, can you hear me? Eldrin asked.

Drrrrynnnni? My thought was muffled. Reverberating.

Focus.

Who the blazes had thought that?

A comm on the Chair lit up. An annoyed voice came out of it. *Mother, I'm a grown man now. I don't need you to coddle me.*

Taquinil. Why did his thought come out of the comm? That was impossible. *I don't coddle you.*

Well, this isn't the time to start.

I don't understand what you mean.

You don't need to stay here. I'm fine.

Stay here?

In psiberspace.

I'm not in psiberspace.

The universe rippled.

The universe rippled.

The universe rippled.

Dehya, focus.

Who are you? Psiberspace was turning into a regular Starport Central.

No techs were bringing down the chair. No recovery team was taking me out of it. I hung here in the starlight, alone except for impossible thought-voices on the comm.

Mist silvered the chair until I could no longer see it. A great stillness surrounded me.

?
F.
Fo.
Foc.
Focus.
Focusing . . .
Fading, fade, fade . . .
No fading, fading, no fade.
Concentrate thoughts, tight focus.
Whispers scrape edges of my mind.
Concentrate thoughts, tight focus.
No fading, fading, no fade.
Fading, fade, fade . . .
Focusing . . .
Focus.
Foc.
Fo.
F.
?

Whispers grew. Louder. Not whispers. Distant shouts. Far away. Curious, I opened my eyes, though I hadn't realized they were closed, or even that I had eyes.

The Triad Chair had descended to the floor again. I could see all of it below me, as if I were separated from my body. Techs swarmed over the chair, unfastening a limp form from its heart. Dr. Bayliron gently pulled robot arms away from the body. Chad Barzun and Jinn Opsister stood back while the techs and medics worked. Ragnar was striding back and forth, more agitated than I had ever seen him before.

Interesting. That was my body.

I concentrated, and the shouting became louder. *Her heart's stopped!*

Ragnar stopped pacing, his face contorted. *Flaming hell, do something!*

Apparently I was dying.

I preferred that didn't happen.

I concentrated, trying to collect back into my body.

Vertigo hit me like a fist. *Ah, no.* My chest hurt, hurt, *hurt*—

"*Stat,*" someone shouted. "Get a shocker in here!"

Forcing my eyes open, I found myself in the chair. Techs were working all around, fast and expert as they disengaged me from the chair's mechanical embrace. My nausea surged. So much pain. How long had I been here, my chest hurting, my body on fire?

Pain . . .

Then they had me out and onto an air-stretcher. With my last desperate threads of conscious thought, I wondered if we would reach the hospital before or after I died.

27
World of Legends

Virtual reality had advantages. It wasn't the same as being with a real person, but it came close. In a good system, even touch felt so authentic, you couldn't tell the difference between that and the real thing.

But you knew; your loved one wasn't really there.

So Eldrin came to visit while I was dying.

"Dehya, you can't do this," he told me, sitting by my bed in a dark blue chair. "You escaped the Traders. You survived Opalite. You can't die now."

Opalite wasn't so bad. I meant to speak, but only thoughts came. This was a computer-generated simulacrum; Eldrin was actually on *Havyrl's Valor* and couldn't pick up my thoughts. It was a good sim, though. He came across as real even to me, who had been married to him for fifty-seven years.

He leaned forward. "Damn it, Dehya, don't you die. We haven't finished our argument."

"Argument . . . ?" I asked.

Eldrin froze, his eyes widening. Softly he said, "Thank the saints." He hinged his hand around mine, his touch warm. Almost real.

Then it hit me: Why would doctors put a dying Pharaoh in a virtual sim? Ah, hell. This was another weird Kyle space creation.

His voice caught. "Welcome back, Wife."

"What argument?" I asked.

He laughed shakily. "I don't know. We're always having one. I figured that might stir you up."

Hmmm. That sounded authentic.

A voice spoke somewhere, indistinct.

Eldrin turned to someone I couldn't see. "I think so."

"You think what?" I asked, confused.

The room faded. Eldrin went too, which saddened me. Instead of one of those nightmare Triad Chamber scenes, though, this time a normal hospital room took shape. I was lying in bed wearing a white sim-suit that covered my body like a supple velvet skin. Dr. Bayliron leaned over me, his face concerned. Two robot medics, humanoid in shape, were checking the many monitors arrayed around my bed.

I peered at Bayliron, wondering if this was another illusion. "Did you have me in a VR simulation?"

"Yes. Your husband wanted to talk to you." He spoke with a doctor's comforting tones, but strain underlay his words. "How do you feel?"

"A little tired." His drawn expression puzzled me. "Doctor, did I phase out in the Triad Chair?"

He spoke quietly. "For three days. We couldn't see you, except a silver outline every now and then."

Three days? Good gods. No wonder he seemed upset. "How did you know I was still there?"

He set his hands on the rail that kept me from rolling out of bed. "The communications in the fleet continued to work, with all the new psiberspace links. And the chair sensors registered your presence."

"Couldn't you pull me out?"

He shook his head. "We might have disrupted your state and lost you for good."

So strange. What had the chair been doing? Its intelligence was so different, it was hard to fathom even when I was joined with its mind.

I pulled myself up into a sitting position. "I need to check the Chair's records."

He lifted his hand as if he meant to lay it on my shoulder, stopping me. Then he paused. People never touched me unless absolutely necessary. Otherwise, my bodyguards became upset, both the human and mechanical ones.

He sighed, lowering his arm. "Your Highness, you must rest."

"I've been nonexistent for three days," I grumbled. "I need exercise."

He gave a soft laugh. "Perhaps so. But humor me."

I bestowed him with my curmudgeon look. "Oh, all right."

"The techs tried to download the Chair's records. But it won't cooperate."

I stretched my arms, assuring myself I really was solid. "Cooperation is a human attribute. Triad Chairs don't have those."

He regarded me uneasily. "Do you think the Chair caused your problems?"

"Not with intention." I searched for words to describe what I only understood on a subconscious, instinctual level. "The Chair is alive, but it isn't even remotely human. It coexists with us when we work in it. If we have a full Triad, that stabilizes the interaction. But with just me, it's less—" I hesitated to say *less stable*. Instability was a human concept defined by what made humans comfortable. "It's less attuned to its human partners. So it is less likely to interact in ways we understand."

His forehead furrowed. "Isn't Web Key Eldrinson also in the Triad?"

My mood dimmed, like the shadow cast on the sun by the moon during an eclipse. If Eldrinson had truly died, the Allieds had probably told his family and ISC Headquarters by now. We may have heard nothing simply because we were cut off from them. But if the family wanted to make it public, I suspected we would have at least picked up rumors. Or perhaps he still lived, saints willing. Neither Eldrin nor I wanted to start another wave of grief among our people until we knew the full situation.

All I said was, "The Triad has two people, I'm fairly certain. But we haven't been working with the Chairs for some time now. The longer we go without interaction, the less attuned to us they become." Sorrow tinged my thoughts. We needed the anchor of the late Imperator, Kurj, with his massive, muscular mind. To say the Chairs had mourned his death these past few years would be giving them human traits they didn't possess. But in their own way, they experienced his loss.

The hum of an opening hatchway came from across the room, followed by the quiet tread of booted feet. Then Chad appeared at Bayliron's elbow. "Pharaoh Dyhianna. It is good to see you." Although he appeared unruffled, the relief in his mind was sharp and vivid.

"My greetings, Admiral." The EI for this room had probably notified him when I regained consciousness. "I'm glad to be back."

His rugged face gentled. "Your husband sends his greetings."

The memory of Eldrin's touch warmed me. "Was that really him in the VR sim?"

"Very much so," Bayliron said. "He was with you, in VR, the entire time you were unconscious. About four hours."

Eldrin, you thaw my life. I thought. I couldn't speak such personal sentiment here, though. Instead I asked, "So we've been in the solar system four hours?"

"About," Chad said.

Odd. That was when the chair was supposed to have released me. I thought back to my strange "dialogue" with it, which had consisted of it submerging me in illusions. "Did you only manage about a fifty percent recovery when you tried to bring me out of the chair at the appointed time?"

Chad started. "Yes. How did you know?"

"You told me."

He paused, and I could tell he didn't want to contradict me. Finally he said, "We didn't speak, Your Highness. You weren't even solid."

Well, being translucent did put a damper on conversation. I remembered so much, though. "You said we were passing the asteroid belt. You also said we had an escort of about one hundred thousand Allied ships, but that the Allied fleet was stretched thin."

"It's all true." He pushed his hand over the iron-gray stubble of his hair. "But I didn't tell you."

I considered. "I think our 'conversation' was the Triad Chair's way of letting me know the situation." I thought back over the experience. "Eldrin was there, too."

"He never left *Havyrl's Valor*," Chad said. "He is still on channel two, though. Shall I put him through?"

My mood picked up. "Yes. I would like that."

Chad touched a button on the rail of my bed, and it morphed into a comm mesh. Then he said, "Prince Eldrin, your wife is on two."

"Thank you, Admiral." Although Eldrin spoke with the formality he used around people we didn't know well, I heard his relief. His voice brightened the hospital room, at least to me.

"Greetings, Husband," I said.

"I'm glad you're back, Dehya."

I grinned. "It was that handsome face of yours. It revived me."

Amusement lightened his voice. "You sound a lot better now."

"I am." I thought back to my "conversation" with him. "Dryni, did Vyrl recently marry a young woman? An empath?"

"Actually, yes. How did you know? I just heard."

"I had an episode in the Triad Chair when I thought you and I were talking. You said his marriage helped him heal from nightmares. From sensory deprivation. It sounded like your nightmare."

"But I dreamed I was my father. Not Vyrl."

"It must be connected." I pushed down the rail of my bed and swung my legs over the edge.

Bayliron moved to block my departure. "Your Highness," he said, using the overly respectful tone people invoked whenever they were about to say something they knew I didn't want to hear. "You must stay in bed."

"I'm fine." I tried to push him aside. He was a lot bigger, which made him rather akin to a rock. "Please remove yourself."

"I can't do that, ma'am."

"Doctor Bayliron." I pulled myself up as tall as possible, which meant the top of my head came to his shoulder. Looking up, I said, "I don't have time to be sick."

He sighed. "Your Highness, if I give you clearance to get

up, you must stop pushing yourself so hard. One of these days you will collapse."

I sensed his resistance weakening. "I'll be careful."

He gave me a doubtful look, but he did move aside and let me slide off the bed. The white Luminex floor felt cool and smooth under my bare feet.

After various formalities, Bayliron took his leave with the robot medics. The gold one paused at the door and pulled out a soft-chair with laundered clothes on it. I recognized the blue jumpsuit I had worn in the Triad Chair.

I sent a wireless message to the robot's EI brain: *Thank you.*
You are welcome, Your Highness. Its tone felt metallic.

Chad was watching me. "Your bodyguards are outside. I'll be on the bridge. When you're ready, they can bring you up."

"Very well." I rubbed my arms, feeling the cool air through the sim-suit. "Thank you, Admiral."

"It is my honor, Your Highness." His mood washed over me like clear notes rising above a mutter. His lack of misgivings about our actions contrasted sharply with Vazar and Jon's doubts. Even I had doubts, but I couldn't let them show.

When I was alone, I changed my clothes. I had a sort of privacy; my nodes detected no visual sensors watching the room. But monitors kept track of my physiological functions. The whole room was one big sensor.

I sometimes daydreamed I lived in a place where no one cared what I did, where I never had to worry about privacy with my husband, and no one wanted to assassinate, use, kidnap, assault, or be afraid of me. I thought of Eldrin's words about his childhood on Lyshriol, where they didn't even have consoles in most rooms and the children had run free in the fields.

I mourned a freedom I had never known.

The holoscreens on the bridge projected huge figures. An Allied officer filled the view, Raymond MacLane, a craggy five-star general with gray hair and deep lines engraved on his face. The Allieds had a reverse cultural dynamic than ours when it came to aging; their men tended to ignore its signs more than their women, whereas Skolian men disguised its advance more than our women. MacLane's hazel eyes were deeply set under thick eyebrows. He commanded one of the Allieds' great flagships, the *Tricia Andreque*, named for one of Earth's most renowned authors. MacLane was Chad's counterpart among the Allied fleet escorting us to Earth, since I had promoted Chad to full admiral.

"Our intent is peaceful," Chad continued. With firm purpose, he added, "We look forward to seeing Councilor Roca, Web Key Eldrinson, Lady Ami, and Kurjson."

"Of course." MacLane remained noncommittal.

MacLane's responses set off my mental alarms. Despite Eldrin's dream of his father on Lyshriol, Eldrin remained convinced his parents were here, or at least his mother. We needed Roca, who was my heir now that Taquinil had left, and also best suited to take over as Imperator. So we had come to Earth, where the Allieds claimed their "guests" resided. I hoped they were telling the truth.

Even if they had sent Eldrinson to Lyshriol, I doubted they would have let Kurj's widow Ami and her young son accompany him. She had no blood relation to that branch of the family, and the Allieds wouldn't want too much of the Ruby Dynasty in one place. I couldn't imagine they would separate Roca from Eldrinson, but if both had gone to Lyshriol, the Allieds had to tell us soon. Moving the Ruby Dynasty could be interpreted as a hostile act, and they knew ISC responded vehemently when challenged. If Eldrinson had died, they were probably having collective heart failure right now, given our request for his return. Our presence put them in a hellacious position.

The Allieds had always seen us as belligerent and uncivilized, just as we saw them as weak and naïve. And yet . . . I sometimes thought their approach to life might be better for humanity, even though such a government would strip the Ruby Dynasty of all power. I had never revealed that to anyone, of course, except Eldrin.

As Chad parried with MacLane, I floated a few meters away, holding a cable, with Ragnar at my side. Chad's channel to the *Tricia Andreque* showed no more than his command chair. Both Ragnar and I outranked MacLane, so Skolian hierarchal protocols required we not appear unless MacLane acknowledged us as the ranking dignitaries. Given that we didn't know yet how the Allieds would respond to the new political landscape of Skolia, we hadn't revealed we were in the middle of a coup or that I had accompanied the fleet.

After Chad and MacLane closed the connection, Ragnar and I moved to the command chair. Chad spoke dryly. "He ought to win the prize for responses that say nothing."

"Maybe Roca and Eldrinson aren't here," I said.

Ragnar scowled. "Then where the blazes are they?"

Good question. "I think it's time I spoke with the Allied President."

"No," Ragnar stated, forgetting protocol.

Chad spoke more carefully. "Pharaoh Dyhianna, I don't think we should reveal your presence."

"Why not?" I asked. "If they know I'm on this cruiser, they will be far less likely to attack it."

Ragnar snorted. "That's right. They'll do their damnedest to capture it instead."

Copying one of his favorite expressions, I raised my eyebrow. "With seventy-five thousand of our ships in attendance?"

"They have over one hundred thousand pacing us," Chad said.

"They don't want to fight." I hooked my arm around the cable, then took floating lengths of my hair and began to twine them into a braid. "We don't want them to assume this fleet represents the Assembly. I *can't* hide now, not if I intend to establish my claim. We have to preempt the Assembly. If the Allieds recognize me as the leader of Skolia, not just in name but in fact, it strengthens our position."

"I don't like the risk involved," Ragnar said.

"It's not a risk," Chad said. "They have nothing to gain and everything to lose if they harm a Skolian leader. They know if they do, ISC will retaliate regardless of our internal affairs."

I knew what he meant. Skolian politics were like family upheavals; you might argue within the family, but you tolerated no outside attacks against your kin. "The Allieds don't want war any more than we do."

Ragnar glanced from Chad to me, scrutinizing us with his legendary intensity. Finally he said, "Very well. Admiral Barzun, set up the link to their president from here."

The protocols required when two interstellar leaders spoke to each other were interminable. Different procedures existed for opening a dialogue between the Allied president and the Imperialate's civilian leader than for the Allied president and Ruby Pharaoh. Chad combined the two procedures, making it implicit that I now held both Imperialate titles. We would see what the Allieds made of that.

They had a new president: Hanna Loughten. It could work in our favor that she had assumed office only a month ago, giving her a lack of experience, but it also could work against us because we knew so little about her. One particularly tricky aspect of protocol involved who appeared first: Loughten or me. We and the Traders had procedures dating back to the Ruby Empire. The person who requested the communication spoke first. However, in a case such as this, where we came with a show of strength, the "request" took on more force. I had no intention of appearing first. It would be tantamount to conceding that the Allieds had the dominant position. From their point of view, we had entered their system uninvited and had no business making demands. We also had fewer ships. So Loughten shouldn't want to appear first either.

The problem was, you could never tell with the Allieds. They had this penchant for fairness. They preferred timing these things so both leaders appeared simultaneously. It exasperated our protocol officers no end, who insisted on strict adherence to procedure. We usually prevailed because we were the stronger power, but that didn't faze the Allieds. They did their best to oblige the customs of all peoples. I had long harbored a suspicion they would quietly and courteously take over the universe without the rest of us noticing, busy as we were with all our posturing and metaphorical shield-banging.

Right now, I had no intention of relinquishing advantage. Ragnar and I stayed out of sight while Chad went through lengthy greetings with various Allied officials. They hid their disquiet, but as an empath I had become proficient at associating body language with emotions, and after a century and a half of practice I could interpret the way most people moved down to small nuances.

Our fleet was well out from Earth, between its orbit and that of Mars, and some distance above the ecliptic. We still weren't admitting we had a new psiberweb, so communications could only go at light speed, with a built-in lag of several minutes. It flustered some of the Allieds. Given that they were probably used to such delays, their disconcerted response hinted at how much we had rattled them. In the past ten years I hadn't even made any public broadcasts, let alone arrived unannounced in anyone's star system.

A senior official appeared, a distinguished man of indeterminate age. After a formal greeting, he finally spoke the words we had been waiting for: "Her Honor, President Hanna Loughten."

The holoscreens went dark. Then a new image formed, a woman with dark hair going silver at the temples. She sat behind a large desk of glossy red-brown wood. The flag of the Allied Worlds hung on a pole behind her, its design simple: blue concentric circles on a white background.

We weren't sending an image yet, so she appeared first. Hard-edged satisfaction emanated from Ragnar, and Chad gave off relief; they assumed the Allieds had acquiesced to us, acknowledging Skolia as the greater power. I supposed they had, but I didn't think Loughten really cared. From experience, I knew the Allieds would respect our hierarchal modes of interaction if that was what it took to get to business, but afterward they would go their way with no difference in how they viewed the universe. It could be annoying, especially when they were right.

Chad beckoned to me, then pushed out of his chair. As he moved past me and grasped a line, I slid into the massive seat. Its panels adjusted to my smaller size and plugged in prongs, connecting my mind to *Roca's Pride*.

Activate image, I thought.

ACTIVATED, the cruiser rumbled.

I knew when President Loughten saw me. She sat straighter, her shift in position almost undetectable. Then she spoke in Iotic, my language, using the minimalist Skolian form of address: "Pharaoh Dyhianna."

I responded in kind. "President Loughten."

"Welcome to the solar system."

"We appreciate your hospitality." Stock replies. I knew what I would really want to say if I were in her position: *How the hell did you get past our defenses?*

Loughten paused. "Your Highness, I am unsure of the proper titles in this situation. Do you prefer your Assembly title or a dynastic address?"

That was tactful—better than asking point blank if I had deposed First Councilor Tikal and stolen his job.

"Pharaoh will do," I told her. "The position of First Councilor no longer exists."

"I see." The tension in those two words spoke volumes.

I waited, keeping my face neutral. How she responded now could make or break our relations with the Allieds. She had to decide whether or not to acknowledge me as head of the Skolian government. Declining to do so would be an implicit statement of support for the Assembly, which meant she had better hope the Assembly defeated my forces. But if she accepted me as the ruler of Skolia, and my side lost, it would also deepen hostilities between her government and ours. I didn't envy her the decision.

After a delay longer than that due to distance, Loughten said, "The President of the Allied Worlds of Earth acknowledges the Ruby Pharaoh of the Skolian Imperialate."

Ragnar's exultation surged from his mind with such force I was surprised he didn't shout his triumph. Chad's satisfaction rolled through it. I had to hold myself back from giving the arm-rest a satisfied thump. Loughten had even used the ancient Ruby form of address for a fully invested pharaoh.

I managed to stay calm, outwardly. "The Imperial Dynasty acknowledges the ascension of Hanna Loughten to the office of Allied president." It didn't have the same ring as "ascension to the throne," but it fit Skolian protocol for a leader who had newly assumed her title.

Loughten inclined her head to me, the gesture controlled. I thought she was uneasy, but I wasn't sure. She guarded her body language well. I wished Eldrin were here to give me his impressions.

"It would be our great honor to have you visit Earth," Loughten said. "To show you the birthplace of our species."

We both knew perfectly well that if the Allieds got me on-planet, they wouldn't let me go. "Your invitation is gracious," I said. "I regret that I must decline. Certain matters cannot be delayed." The time had come to do business. "President Loughten, my people appreciate the generous protection that Earth has provided in guarding my family. It means a great deal to us that they were safe during the war. Their return home now will cause great rejoicing. If you will have Web Key Eldrinson, Councilor Roca, Lady Ami, and Prince Kurjson escorted to us, we will trouble you no further."

Despite her control, Loughten paled. "I greatly regret that we cannot accommodate your request, Your Highness."

Request, hell. "Aren't they here?"

Her strain showed now in her rigid posture. "Yes, certainly. They are our guests in an Allied United Centre."

I decided to push harder and see what happened. "I would like to speak with Web Key Eldrinson."

Again her answer took longer than it needed to go from Earth to here. "I am truly, deeply sorry, Your Highness. But I'm afraid that isn't possible."

In a deceptively soft voice, I said, "Why not?"

Her answer had great gentleness. "He passed away several months ago."

As much as I had expected those words, they hit hard. So hard. I bit my cheek to hold back my tears. I couldn't weep in front of Loughten. Not now. Gods please, not now.

I remembered the last time I had seen Eldrinson, sitting in

a starlit chamber with a panoramic view of the stars. It had been just minutes before he left for Earth. *Take care, my sister,* he told me. I had answered, *And you, my brother.* We were always arguing about one thing or another, often with gusto, but on that day we had parted without hiding our familial affection.

A tear ran down my cheek. I rubbed it away with my palm, acutely aware of everyone watching.

Loughten spoke with kindness. "Please accept our deepest sympathies."

"Thank you." My response came out stiff and formal. I glanced at Jinn Opsister, who floated behind Chad. In a low voice I said, "Please notify Prince Eldrin."

She nodded and withdrew a short distance. As she spoke into her gauntlet comm, I turned back to Loughten. "Did Web Key Eldrinson pass away on Lyshriol?"

Her body language betrayed shock. She hadn't expected us to know. After a moment, she said, "Yes. He wanted to go home. Councilor Roca went with him." She leaned forward, her hands folded on her desk. "However, Lady Roca has since returned to Earth."

Relief flowed over me; to have come this far and then find out Roca wasn't here would have been a great blow. From the Allied view, it made sense to split up the Ruby Dynasty, lest we get together and hatch plans the rest of the universe didn't like, such as, say, deposing the Assembly. I wondered if it had occurred to all these politicians and military leaders, both within and without Skolia, that if they had just left us alone, we might have minded our own business and stayed out of interstellar politics.

I thought of Eldrin. He would want to pay his respects to his father, even if he could only go home in a virtual simulation. "Was Lord Eldrinson buried on his farm?" I asked Loughten.

She shook her head. "His dying wish was that we launch his coffin into orbit around the planet."

I stared at her. What the blazes? Eldrinson would never ask such a thing. He loathed space. His love had been for the land, especially his farm and the crops he tilled. He had eventually made a truce with the technology Roca had brought into his life, but I could never imagine him asking for a burial in space.

Suddenly I thought of Eldrin's nightmare about his father in a coffin. Saints almighty, had they buried Eldrinson *alive*?

Somehow I kept my voice cool. "And my sister allowed this burial?"

Sympathy touched Loughten's face. "After her husband's death, Councilor Roca asked that we reconsider. It upset her to think of his body in orbit. We arranged with ISC to have one of your ships pick it up."

My dismay eased. Eldrinson couldn't have been alive when they launched that coffin; he would have been in utter terror. Both Eldrin and I had felt the peaceful release of his life. He had gone gently, surrounded by his family. The Allieds had shown compassion in letting him return home, but the matter of this strange burial remained.

It hit me like ice. A living man *had* been in that coffin. Of course. It was a way to slip someone off-planet, gruesome yes, but effective. In my Triad Chair–induced "conversation" with Eldrin, he had said Vyrl needed to heal from a nightmarish sensory deprivation. Had *Vyrl* been the one in that coffin? He was taller than his father by a good half foot, but with enough planning they might have fooled the Allieds' sensors.

Only two seconds had passed since Loughten finished speaking. I replied quietly. "The Ruby Dynasty thanks you for the sensitivity your people have shown in this matter." I paused for effect. "His death comes as a surprise. He had been in good health when he left for Earth." Let her sweat that one. Regardless of how sensitive they had been, Eldrinson had still died in their custody. "We expect to take up orbit around Earth soon."

She met my gaze. "We await your arrival."

So we began the final approach to our lost home.

28
Starfall Dreams

We believe we've located Councilor Roca." Jinn Opsister set holosheets on the table before us in the Tactics Room. "She's in Sweden. We're less certain about Lady Ami and her son, but we think they are there too."

Ragnar and Chad were also at the table. "What about Rockworth's three foster children?" Ragnar asked.

"We've found no trace of them at all." Jinn glanced at me. "But we aren't sure what to look for."

"I don't know much," I admitted. "Just that Jaibriol the Third lived with them."

"I don't like it," Chad said. "When we asked the Allieds, they went into one of their we-have-no-idea modes."

Ragnar snorted. "That means they know exactly what we're talking about and they're scared to death."

"What about Seth Rockworth?" I asked. "Anything on him?"

"Plenty, ma'am." Jinn tapped another holosheet. "He's in custody at a military base on the Atlantic coast of North America."

Ragnar shrugged. "They must know by now he fostered Jaibriol the Third."

Seth, what are you hiding? At least now we had a valid reason to ask about the children; of course we would want to make sure no other Aristo time bombs were walking around on Earth. Our inquiries gave no one reason to suspect the children might be the Rhon offspring—perhaps even legitimate heirs—of Soz and Jaibriol II.

"We need to act," I said. "The longer we wait, the more strained this becomes."

Jinn leaned forward. "We can send a drop team into the Allied United Centre in Sweden."

"What are the chances of success?"

She stacked her holosheets together. "Earth can probably

shoot down any craft we send in. Their defenses are too strong. We can't evade them."

"Can't we hide the racer?" I asked. "If we can sneak an entire fleet into this star system, we should be able to get one racer down to the planet."

Chad answered. "Traveling through interstellar space with ships in fuel bottles is one thing. Space may not be a true vacuum, but it's close enough. I wouldn't want to try it on a planet. The ship could twist out of the bottle right into a tree or mountain."

"So bring it out above ground," Ragnar said.

"We don't know how the atmosphere will affect it," Jinn said. Dryly she added, "And Earth has more junk in orbit than ten colonies combined."

"Which is the greater danger?" I asked. "Hiding the ship in a bottle or the Allieds shooting it down if we don't?"

Jinn lifted another of her holosheets, its surface catching prismatic glints of light. "We estimate the risks are about the same."

"Even if they could fire on the racer," I mused, "I wonder if they would." I could imagine the questions the Allied military was asking itself now. "They don't know if or how we would retaliate. With the size of our fleet, we could do a lot of damage to Earth before they stopped us."

Chad gave me an incredulous look, clearly aghast at the idea of firing on humanity's home world. Ragnar's approval of the idea leaked from his mind. Jinn immediately began considering how to solve the tactical problems in such an engagement.

I regarded them with exasperation. "I'm not suggesting we attack Earth. Just that the *Allieds* must fear we might."

"We could bluff," Jinn suggested. "Tell them that if they don't return the Ruby Dynasty we'll have to take action."

Chad shook his head. "The moment we threaten them, we lose. Any response they make then becomes self-defense. It will also weaken what Prince Havyrl is doing on Lyshriol. His attempts to force out Earth's occupying forces depend entirely on censure of the Allieds by the rest of humanity.

Right now, the Allied Worlds of Earth are the villains. If we threaten to attack *Earth,* we lose the high ground Prince Havyrl and his people have fought so hard to gain."

I smiled slightly. "I wonder how the Allieds feel, cast in the role of Nefarious Evil. Quite a change, eh?"

Ragnar waved his hand as if to dismiss Earth, the home of his own grandfather. "They're just like anyone else. They want power and wealth. They could pretend to the high ground when they were the weaker power because they had no other options. Now that we and the Traders are weakened, what do the Allieds do? Grab for power, using your family."

I knew most Skolians shared his view. Our propaganda wizards were working overtime to portray the Allieds in the worst possible light. But I couldn't deny the other side, not when our success depended on how well we judged the situation. I spoke quietly. "Our animosity with the Traders and their progenitors has followed us through six millennia. The wars that brought down the Ruby Empire almost destroyed humanity. More than politics drives the Allieds; they genuinely fear that if they let my family free, we will destroy civilization again, on a much bigger scale, including Earth this time."

They stared at me. The last person they expected to express that argument was the Ruby Pharaoh.

I splayed my hands on the table as if to support myself. "We need to acknowledge their fear. If their only interest is power, they will respond differently than if they genuinely believe they're the only bulwark against humanity's destruction."

"If you follow that to its logical conclusion," Chad said, "then either way, they lose. If they keep the Ruby Dynasty, we may turn on them and bring about what they fear anyway."

Bitterness scraped my thoughts. My family had never asked for this power. But the rest of humanity could never leave us alone, not as long as whoever controlled us controlled interstellar civilization. Nor could we refuse the responsibility, not when it could mean the difference between a universe subject to the Traders and one where humans lived free. Somehow, some way, we had to find accommodation with those who wished to control us.

I glanced at Jinn. "Do you have the latest news holo about Lyshriol?"

"We picked a new one up from a ship coming into the solar system about ten hours ago." She spoke in a louder voice. "Tactics Room, attend. Engage Lyshriol A-nine-gee."

"Working," the Tactics Room said.

The chamber faded to darkness. Then the light came up again—and we were standing in a hip-high field of slender tubes, silvery and green, swaying in a breeze. Little bubbles tipped many of the tubes. I touched one and it floated into the air. Then it burst, spraying me with glitter. The simulation was so well done, I felt the powder on my wrists, below the sleeves of my jumpsuit. Had I not known the Tactics Room was sending wireless signals to a node in my body, I might have believed I actually stood on the Dalvador Plains of Lyshriol.

Bracing air filled my lungs, crisp and pure. I gazed around, thrilled by the energy of the place. Beyond our small patch of tubes, an ocean of people spread out in all directions: Lyshrioli men in blue, purple, or gray trousers, laced shirts with belled sleeves, and soft knee-boots; Lyshrioli women in bright dresses with slits in the swirling skirts and laces everywhere. Children ran all over, laughing, enjoying themselves. Tents covered the trampled plain, with irrigation canals running between them. Smoke rose from campfires as cooks prepared meals in big metal pots. In a nearby camp, people were digging furrows and planting seeds; in another they were building a pen for horned animals with shaggy blue coats.

Ragnar, Chad, and Jinn were standing with me on the plain. Chad beamed. "Amazing, isn't it?"

"Indeed." I inhaled deeply, with satisfaction. "Can you link to the Tactics on *Havyrl's Valor*? I'd like to bring Eldrin into the simulation."

Ragnar bestowed me with one of his dark looks. "We still

don't know what the Traders did to him. Revealing our tactics discussions to him could be dangerous."

"His nightmare had nothing to do with the Traders." I wasn't actually certain about that, but Ragnar's response annoyed me.

It was Jinn who answered. "Are you sure we should chance it, ma'am? He still has the restraints."

I understood her implication. Although the neurologists had made great strides in mapping the web created in Eldrin's body by the biothreads from his cuffs and collar, and in stopping the growth of new threads, the process wasn't complete enough yet to risk removing the restraints. But it was almost done, and no one had found any indication the Traders had tried to make Eldrin a weapon. Such an act of human sabotage would have taken a great deal of planning and technical work, and I doubted they had had time after Jaibriol III contacted them to arrange the trade.

I regarded Jinn steadily. "Yes, I'm sure."

She activated her comm and arranged for the link. I felt all their doubts, but they also knew the advantage of calling in Eldrin. He had grown up here.

After several minutes, the air flickered. Eldrin's body formed in front of Ragnar, the ranking ISC officer, and took on solidity. Eldrin stood for a moment, reorienting to his surroundings. He greeted Ragnar stiffly, but loosened up with the others. Then he turned that grin of his on me, the one that blazed with unstated mischief. Gods, I missed him.

"This is a gorgeous simulation," he said, wistful. "I feel like I'm really home."

A cluster of women was strolling toward us. I blinked as they walked through me, like vivid, chattering ghosts. When Eldrin laughed, I said, "They look like they're having a good time."

He bowed as if to acknowledge a compliment. "We've raised the process of having a festival to an art."

Chad chuckled and Ragnar watched Eldrin with his brooding gaze. Jinn spoke to the air. "Run news sim."

We suddenly became wind blowing over the plain, racing across the tent nation toward a cluster of buildings. At first I thought it was a village of whitewashed, circular houses. They had bright, turreted roofs in purple and blue, like upside-down blossoms, an incongruous image for this world that had no flowers unless you counted the bubbles.

As we touched down near the buildings, I realized it wasn't a village, but a starport designed to blend with the pastoral countryside. Beyond it, a small tarmac stretched out. An empty tarmac; no spacecraft waited there. The entire port looked deserted. It didn't surprise me. I would have evacuated, too, if two hundred thousand people had come to call.

The sky suddenly roared. I glanced up with a start, to see a silver flier arrow above us, the Allied insignia in blue on its hull. Many fliers were criss-crossing above the plain—

Good gods. They were *bombing* the tent nation. The good-natured, wholesome Lyshrioli were no longer having a festival. They staggered through the fumes, gasping, falling down, lying still. I would have thought they were dying, except I recognized the gas; it only put you to sleep.

The theatrical voice of a reporter overlaid the simulation. "The assault of Earth's forces on the helpless natives continues on this, the forty-fourth day of the protest. Not a single native has made a hostile move against the occupying forces, yet the Allieds continue with their merciless attack."

"My, my," I murmured. The Allieds must hate these melodramatic broadcasts. They had to be desperate, if they were willing to go this far.

Eldrin swore. "This is an outrage."

"It certainly looks that way." Ragnar sounded positively gleeful.

The scene shifted; now we were watching Earth soldiers in gas masks carry sleeping Lyshrioli natives to a flier. Other Lyshrioli clambered over the flier, yelled, jumped in front of the soldiers, and otherwise made a nuisance of themselves. They held wet cloths over their faces, and a few had makeshift gas masks. Several young fellows glanced at us, which meant they were looking at the Jagernauts making this recording. One scrambled on top the flier, posturing for the cameras, and yelled zestfully at the Allieds.

The soldiers continued their work, carefully avoiding the rambunctious Lyshrioli as they loaded the unconscious ones onto their aircraft. One youth holding a cloth over his mouth stumbled into the flier. He stepped away, then sat heavily in the trampled grass. With a sigh, he lay down and closed his eyes, succumbing to the gas.

"And so the Allieds continue to transgress against the innocent people of Skyfall," the narrator said dramatically.

"I really wish they would stop that," Eldrin muttered. "The name of the planet is Lyshriol. Not Skyfall."

Chad glanced at him. "I thought Lyshriol meant Skyfall in your language."

"It does. But we call it Lyshriol. Do you translate your name into whatever language you happen to be speaking?"

"Well, no." Chad diplomatically left it at that, without mentioning that the general public loved the name Skyfall, which everyone seemed to remember better than Lyshriol.

The narrator continued. "For days the Allied forces have been drugging people, hauling them off without their consent, and leaving them senseless in distant villages, with only the old and infirm to care for them." The image shifted to a crying child desperately gripping the hand of a sleeping woman. "How much longer will this go on?" the narrator cried.

The scene shifted again. Now we were at the edges of the tent nation. In the distance, Lyshrioli natives were riding across the plains toward us on graceful silver and blue animals with crystalline horns that splintered the sunlight like prisms. The narrator's voice surged with enthusiasm. "Despite the outrages perpetrated against them by the occupying force, the people of Skyfall refused to be cowed! As fast as Earth's soldiers can ferry them out, they are returning, bringing fresh supplies for their beleaguered brethren."

"This is incredible," Eldrin said. "I don't think anything like this has ever happened before in the history of my people."

"It certainly makes a theatrical broadcast," Chad said.

We were moving slowly now, while soft music played as

background for the melodious greetings called out among the Lyshrioli. A distant man and a woman were standing together, surrounded by people. As we drew nearer, the broadcast focused on the man, heartily extolling his bravery and heroism. He was healthy and well-built, with long legs and a mane of red-gold curls. Metallic gold lashes framed his large violet eyes. Very hologenic. He resembled Eldrin, but was taller. I had always thought Eldrin the handsomer man, but I supposed I was biased. Most people considered Havyrl Valdoria among the best-looking of the Valdoria sons.

I didn't recognize the woman with Vyrl. She had great hair, curly black tresses that tumbled to her waist. Her face was exotic, with a heart shape and dusky skin. Her large eyes had vertical rather than circular pupils.

"Saints above," Eldrin said. "Who is that gorgeous creature?"

I scowled at him. "Your brother's wife."

He looked inordinately pleased. "You're jealous."

"I am not."

Eldrin laughed. "You are. I'm flattered."

"Pah."

"She can't be native to Lyshriol," he said.

Chad and the others, who had been pretending not to notice our exchange, started paying attention again. "She has to be from here," Chad said. "No one has been able to get onto the planet."

Eldrin indicated his own hair. "The first colonists here fiddled with their DNA. Whatever their intent, we ended up losing the genes for black hair."

I remembered Eldrin's fascination with my hair when we had first met. He and his brother had similar taste in women. Vyrl's wife also had other traits that didn't belong to this world. I recognized her vertical pupils; they were an adaptation designed for worlds that received low levels of visible light. That certainly didn't apply to Lyshriol.

I drew Eldrin away from the others. In our respective Tactics Rooms, we remained in our chairs, of course. To make our conversation private, my neural nodes sent my thoughts to *Roca's Pride,* which transmitted them to *Havyrl's Valor,* which then communicated with the nodes in Eldrin's brain.

He regarded me with a warmth he had rarely shown since his return from the Traders. Lyshriol seemed to agree with him. "What is it, Wife?"

I pretended to glower at him. "What, I only get 'Wife'? Not 'gorgeous creature'?"

Eldrin gave me his experienced-husband grin, "To me, you are utterly gorgeous." He brushed his knuckles down my cheek. "But I know you, Dehya. You didn't pull me over here to extract compliments."

"I'm wondering about the Allieds." I indicated the fliers circling in the sky. "Why can't they stop Vyrl from broadcasting these scenes off Lyshriol?"

Eldrin shrugged. "We have better technology."

"They're using our orbital defense system. That's our tech."

"You have an idea, don't you?"

I spoke carefully, aware I was about to breach security. "It's possible to access the orbital defense system from down here." I indicated a distant blur at the foot of the mountains. "The control center is under the Stained Glass Forest."

He went rigid. "ISC buried a base under our *home*?"

"They didn't build the installation. It's from the Ruby Empire, over five thousand years ago. They've only managed to restore a few functions."

His voice tightened. "And never told us."

I spoke quietly. "You didn't have a need to know."

"Then how would my brother Vyrl know?"

"I think he left Lyshriol."

"Vyrl?" He made an incredulous sound. "He would never leave home."

"For something this important, he might." I felt almost certain. My models were converging again. "ISC got him off Lyshriol, told him what he needed to know, planned all this, and snuck him back in with Jagernauts."

Eldrin didn't look convinced. "Yes, a few Jagernauts might have slipped in, if they took no substantial equipment and settled for a one-way trip. ISC knows enough about the orbital system to evade it. But even if a team made it in, they wouldn't be able to get out again. The Allieds' primary concern is keeping us confined to the planet. I don't see how *anyone* could have left, let alone Vyrl."

I swallowed, hating what I had to say. "Dryni, I think he escaped in your father's coffin. Your nightmare came from him. You had it right after Chad told us about Vyrl's actions on Lyshriol."

He stared at me. "That's an appalling suggestion."

"They were desperate." I touched his arm. "If that's true, the Traders had nothing to do with your going berserk. I can return to *Havyrl's Valor*."

Concern shaded his face. "You can't be sure. I still might hurt you."

"You won't."

"That's your emotions speaking. Not your logic."

"They're both part of the same thing."

He took my shoulders, gazing into my face. "I would like you to come back. I have missed you. But we can't chance it."

Although I wanted to insist no danger existed, I couldn't be certain. However, I had confidence in my models, and they predicted my safety with Eldrin. "My bodyguards will be with us. Dryni, listen. You and I need to present a united front, to the Allieds and Assembly, and for all the people who have risked so much to support us."

He rubbed his palms up and down my arms. "I don't see how my presence will help."

I put my hands on his upper arms and he slid his behind my back. "Your brother Vyrl is a hero. And you're the firstborn son, the head of the family now. If you appear, entreating the Allieds to release your grieving mother, whose husband died in Allied custody, how can the Allieds refuse? They'll look like monsters."

A gleam came into his eyes. "It would make it that much harder, politically, for them to shoot down any racer we send in to Earth."

"That's right. And good gods, you're on a ship called

Havyrl's Valor. We would be crazy not to take advantage of that."

His grin flashed wickedly. "You have to appear in the broadcast with me."

"Me?" I tried to step back, but he kept his hands around my back, holding me in place. "I hate broadcasts."

"Ah, but Dehya, just look at yourself." He cupped his hand under my chin. "Can you imagine it? On their broadcasts, the Allieds describe Skolia as a massive, truculent, imperialistic empire. Our leaders are blood-thirsty dictators. And then who appears as our leader? You, the Imperial Waif. Lady Vulnerability. You look about as bellicose as a holomovie ingénue."

I crossed my arms and glowered at him. "I am not a waif."

He gave me an innocent look. "We could call you massive, truculent, and blood-thirsty."

I couldn't help but smile. "Maybe not."

A virtual comm appeared on my wrist and beeped. I touched it. "Yes?"

Ragnar's voice crackled. "Shall we return to the Tactics Room?"

"Very well." I glanced at Eldrin. "I will see you soon." Softly I added, "In person."

The mischief glinted in his gaze again. "Try not to depose anyone else before then."

"Deal."

But I couldn't laugh at the joke. Eldrin didn't yet see the full ramifications of what I had done. I thought of Barcala Tikal, the First Councilor of the Assembly. *Former* First Councilor. He and I had known each other for decades. I had supported his bid to head the Assembly ten years ago. But I would soon have to face him as the leader of the faction that deposed him.

I dreaded what we would have to do then.

ISC recorded the broadcast in the observation bay on *Havyrl's Valor.* Eldrin and I stood together at the rail above the bay while media globes whirred above us, recording the scene from every possible angle. The public relations office on the cruiser would decide what footage to use.

In his speech, Eldrin made a heartfelt appeal for the release of his mother and family. The PR people had him wear his native Lyshriol clothes: blue trousers that clung to his muscled legs, darker knee boots with silver buckles, and a white shirt with long, belled sleeves and a high collar. He hardly looked the way the Allieds described him in their counter-propaganda, as a militant agitator who had seduced the Imperialate's tyrannical Ruby Pharaoh to satisfy his unbridled ambition.

His shirt had beautiful embroidered designs. In the "news" that accompanied the speech, the reporter implied Eldrin's mother had stitched them. In truth, Roca knew zero about embroidery. Her expertise was politics, which was why she had become the Foreign Affairs Assembly Councilor, a position she won by election, not heredity. But the broadcast portrayed her as a rural woman hand-making shirts for her beloved sons. Of course the holocast showed images of her. She made great press, with her gold skin, huge eyes, and angel's face. She had the body of a holomovie goddess and a sensual appeal mixed with innocence. She wore her gold hair piled high on her head, woven with exquisite pearls. Never mind that rustic farmer's wives didn't wear pearls, exquisite or otherwise.

So here was Eldrin, urging the Allieds to let his bereaved mother return to her grieving children and people. The media ran it after a dramatic piece on Lyshriol that showed Allied soldiers hauling big-eyed Lyshrioli children back to their villages. Even knowing the broadcast was choreographed for effect, I still found myself affected by it.

They called Eldrin the King of Skyfall. No such title actually existed. Eldrin had inherited his father's position as Dalvador Bard, but that didn't make him king of anything, let alone an entire planet. The Dalvador Bard served as historian for the province of Dalvador. He recorded the lives of his people in ballads. Although the Bard also had some governing duties, he didn't lead the province. But our PR people thought the King of Skyfall had "rockets," whatever that meant, so my husband became King Eldrin.

They fussed over my clothes too. They wanted me to wear heels, so I didn't look short next to Eldrin. I didn't care, but PR did, so finally I offered to don some black shoes with my black jumpsuit. This went over like compressed neutron matter. The fashion-ware systems analyst, whatever that title meant, didn't think it would project the right image for me to appear in a black catsuit with stiletto heels. I didn't know where she came up with cats, but I told her to do whatever she thought best. Eldrin got a gleam in his eyes when the computer imaged me in the cat outfit, so I decided to keep that one for a private showing.

The outfit they came up with was beyond reason. A long white dress? I never wore such clothes. They tangled around your legs and made you trip. Jumpsuits were more practical. But the fashion-ware person said I should wear the dress, so I wore it. I had to admit, it draped gracefully. It also fit snugly around my torso, giving me a "classic silhouette," whatever that meant. The analyst put a gold chain around my neck. Then she added a gold cord around my hips like the belts worn in images they had dug up of medieval clothes on Earth, with the tasseled ends of the belt hanging down the woman's front and the cord forming a V in front of her pelvis. It made me look curvier. The whole business was absurd. I came from a long line of ancient warrior queens, fierce and violent, who had led great armies into battle, owned their men, and towered over everyone. All right, so I didn't tower. But this dress was too much.

After I put on the white heels they gave me, which the dress hid, the PR fiends put me next to Eldrin in his King-of-Skyfall clothes. When it came time for me to speak, I conveniently "forgot" the speech the PR team had written. I just spoke the truth, in my own words: I didn't want war, I wanted to live in harmony with Earth and the rest of humanity. I wanted to reunite my family and begin the talks that would give all our peoples a new era of peace.

It was a dream I had always cherished, even fearing it was an unreal bubble of hope too high to reach, too fragile to hold.

The Allieds said no.

I shouldn't have been surprised, given how they had steadfastly evaded our inquiries, requests, and veiled demands that they return Roca and the others. But I had still hoped. Even on Earth, the outcry grew in volume, fueled by the broadcast Eldrin and I had made, and those from Lyshriol. Over the next few days, as express messenger ships ferried the news, it reached other star systems and the Allieds came under an increasing barrage of censure for their perceived intransigence.

Finally I gave the go ahead for Jinn Opsister to send a racer to Earth. By then we had a substantial portion of our fleet in orbit around Earth, accompanied by an escort of Earth's ships. We constantly reiterated to them how we didn't want trouble, and they constantly reiterated their agreement, but we all knew everyone was in full combat readiness.

We decided to send the racer in a fuel bottle made from containment fields and rotate it back into normal space in the atmosphere. It could be a suicide mission, given how little we knew about how the fields for such a large bottle would behave near a planet. Yet when we asked for volunteers, hundreds offered. Jinn Opsister put together a crack team: two Jagernauts, including herself; an army major with experience in on-planet operations; a special operations expert from the Fleet; and five Advance Services Corps commandos.

I also went, in telepresence.

The techs strapped, plugged, and fastened me into the Triad Chair. Both Ragnar and Chad watched. None of us had forgotten what happened last time. I didn't have to stay in as long this time, and I only had to maintain a link with one ship, but I knew the siren call of freedom would come. I would never be free of its lure.

This time when I submerged into Kyle space, it had form.

The silver mist still swirled, but it had thinned, part of it having condensed into a silver mesh. So far it supported only a few nodes. I wove another strand and threaded it into the racer, which waited in its docking bay.

Lightning attend, I thought.

ATTENDING, the racer answered.

Communications between *Lightning* and *Roca's Pride* whispered in the background of my mind. The racer prepared to launch—and we were off! I lost contact with most of its systems when it rotated into the fuel bottle, but I still had the psiberspace link.

Jinn, How are you all in there? I asked.

Everything looks good, she answered.

The racer shot toward Earth, hidden in a space where charges took on both real and imaginary parts. What that meant this close to a planet, we weren't sure. I thought unlikely the racer could go through solid matter even when it was only partially real. Imaginary numbers behaved like waves, which meant the ship might interact like a wave with an object in real space. When ships stored antimatter in fuel bottles, the bottles always experienced a loss of fuel, as interference effects caused the antiparticles to annihilate particles. Energy produced by the annihilations went into Haver-Klein space, so it didn't endanger people. But when we rotated the fuel out of the bottle, we had less than when we put it in. The effects increased in an atmosphere. Of course, a ship wasn't antimatter; with the proper shielding, it could travel in an atmosphere. We should be all right as long as we didn't try to go through anything solid. But I still worried.

Secondary Opsister, I asked. *What is the status of your ship?*

Staaaaabllllle. Her words rippled like liquid.

I sent out tendrils of thought, forming extra links to *Lightning*. *Opsister, you're wavering.*

Caaaaannnn't staaaabaaaliiiize. Her words phased in and out of my mind.

I added a filter to compensate for the effect, so I could understand her words better. *Secondary, what do you see?*

Some odd effects here, she answered. *The ship is rippling.*

I didn't like it. *If you come out now, you have almost no chance of reaching the surface undetected. The Allieds might shoot you down. If you stay in the bottle, your ship will lose coherence. You may not be able to come out.*

Jinn's answer was indecipherable, even with my filters. It gave me an impression, though: disintegration.

Opsister, rotate back into normal space! Don't wait any longer.

Nothing.

Jinn, now!

The racer rippled back into existence like liquid metal taking solid form. It was far down in the atmosphere and plunging ever closer to Earth.

An Allied voice crackled over Jinn's comm. "What the hell is *that?*"

"Imperial racer, identify yourself!" a second voice snapped out.

"You are violating the EuroConfed airspace," another voice said, hard and crisp. "Send your ID codes immediately."

I jumped from *Lightning* to *Roca's Pride*. The cruiser's bridge formed around me, a swirl of colors that rapidly took on definition. Silver tinted the scene, a reminder I was actually still in Kyle space.

"Can their satellites hit *Lightning?*" Chad was speaking into the comm on his command chair.

"They could hit the racer with any of fourteen systems," a voice said.

I spoke. "Any of those could have fired by now." My words also came out of Chad's comm, on a different channel.

Chad looked around. "Pharaoh Dyhianna? Where are you?"

"In the Triad Chair."

"Are you still linked to the racer?"

"Yes." I switched nodes and the display changed; I was in the racer, submerged in the flux of communication between Jinn and the ship. I jumped back to the bridge on *Roca's Pride*. "All its systems are green."

A new voice came out of Chad's comm. "Admiral Barzun,

this is Lieutenant Garr. I have General MacLane from the Allied battle cruiser *Tricia Andreque* on four."

"Got it." Chad switched to channel four. "Barzun here."

MacLane's words rumbled. "Admiral, your racer is violating our airspace."

Chad answered in a guarded voice. "They're going to pick up Councilor Roca, Lady Ami, and Prince Kurjson. Their intent is peaceful."

"Then we will take them into custody," MacLane said. "Pending an investigation. I must warn you, however, that if that racer makes any hostile moves, attempts to evade us, or resists an escort, it will force us into more direct action."

Chad remained unruffled. "Check your sensors. It has no weapons."

I could almost feel MacLane swear. In volunteering to take an unarmed craft, Jinn and her team had left themselves defenseless. The court of public opinion was already grinding Earth's forces into metaphorical pieces. Although Earth might fire on the racer anyway, this would make it even harder.

Chad switched channels. "Secondary Opsister?"

Jinn's voice came out of the comm. "Here, sir."

"Any after-effects from the bottle?"

"One disposal unit is out. Otherwise, we're fine."

"Good." Chad spoke to the air. "Pharaoh Dyhianna?"

"Here," I said.

"Do you detect any problems with the racer?"

"Nothing it can't handle." Then I said, "Switching to *Lightning*."

"Good luck," Chad said.

My mind flowed through the racer in a current of thought, spinning around circuit loops and swirling in molecular stews. The ship was hurtling through the lower atmosphere now, toward Sweden.

The Allieds hadn't fired.

Jinn sat ensconced in the pilot's chair, the lights on her gauntlets glittering blue, green, and amber. "Prepare for landing."

The rest of her team settled in. I submerged in a web made by repair nanobots in the structure of the ship. Jinn's commands flowed through my conduits. I felt the deceleration, the hull heating, and its flexing as it adjusted to optimize the racer's speed. Jinn clenched the arm of her chair.

Still the Allieds hadn't fired.

The racer shuddered as if a great hand had shaken it. But instead of fragmenting, the ship kept tearing through the atmosphere. I flexed my hull with relief as data flooded Jinn's nodes: the shaking came from a storm that raged in the thunderclouds surrounding the ship. We hadn't been hit.

The racer burst through the cloud cover. Land spread below in a patchwork of emerald green forests, dense with foliage, and pristine snow that draped the forest in every direction. The scene struck me at an instinctual level. I felt a deep longing, and with it a profound sense of loss. This was no longer home; we came here as interlopers rather than siblings.

The racer kept dropping, headed toward a rugged coastline with crashing waves and jagged spears of rock. Trees rushed toward us, a forest that appeared untouched by human hand. Jinn was holding her breath, though I didn't think she realized it. Still no attack. I could imagine the heated debates among the Allieds now, as they decided on a course of action.

We shot over a clearing, then skimmed more forest. We had to land soon; the racer couldn't slow much more without going into hover mode, which would make it even more vulnerable.

A long, open area came into view below. A road. Jinn angled so we were flying along it. Racers usually took off and landed vertically, but Jinn used this winding ribbon of asphalt as a runway, bringing us down until we were gliding over it like a hovercar. I doubted the Allieds could shoot now without endangering people in the area, not to mention destroying this spectacular countryside.

The road arrowed into a cluster of buildings rounded with snow. Needled trees heavy with more snow crowded around gabled houses. Jinn brought the racer down without even a bump, settling it in front of a large building.

Her team disembarked with smooth efficiency. According to the ship's computer, we were on the eastern edge of the Allied United Centre. Given the armaments ISC intelligence had listed for this AUC, not to mention everything we didn't know about, it was a miracle we had made it down in one piece. The Allieds must have disarmed their own defense systems to allow us passage.

As Jinn left the cockpit, I jumped into the biomech web within her body. It was normally impossible to maintain such a tenuous link over such a long distance. But the psiberweb boosted my mind, which already had a Rhon's unusual mental reach, and my decades of experience helped me optimize the link. So I held the connection, though just barely.

A group of people in heavy jackets and trousers were approaching us from the building. Another group had come out of the forest and was walking toward the racer. Jinn and her team waited with the ship. Most of them carried sedative air guns that could put a person to sleep, but no one had anything more threatening.

Jinn accessed her language nodes, drawing on their libraries to augment her fluency in Earth languages. She spoke three: Spanish, English, and Mandarin Chinese. She also knew something called *Pig Latin,* though for the life of me I couldn't see the point of that one. Maybe it was a code.

A man in a heavy jacket with a fur-lined hood led the group from the house. When they reached Jinn, he spoke to her in Skolian Flag, a language designed by our linguistic experts to provide a common tongue for our many peoples. It was one of the first languages our own diplomats learned.

"You're on these grounds illegally." He sounded polite but firm. "We will have to take you and the rest of your people into custody until we straighten this out."

"We will be happy to leave," Jinn said. "As soon as Councilor Roca, Lady Ami, and Prince Kurjson are aboard."

She didn't mention the three children; we had thought they were across the ocean in a country called *America,* but none of our sensors had found any trace of them. Nothing. Judging from the agitation that the Allieds tried to hide every time we mentioned the children, I suspected they couldn't find them either. If those children had a relation to Jaibriol III, he might have arranged for them to leave Earth before he appeared in that heart-whamming broadcast and declared himself Emperor of Eube.

"We would be happy to discuss the situation," the Allied man said. He indicated the house as if inviting Jinn and her commandos to tea. "If you will please come with me."

"Thank you." Jinn could actually be diplomatic when she wanted, though I suspected she preferred a good blast on an EM pulse rifle to negotiation. She sent a message into the link shared by her team: *Employ program C.*

Four of the team joined her and the others remained with the ship. The Allied soldiers from the forest had surrounded the racer and were keeping watch on the ISC team. They tried to look neutral, but their expressions and body language revealed both wariness and curiosity. The situation intrigued them. Although everyone was armed, no one seemed inclined to shoot.

Jinn and her people accompanied the Allieds into the house. Inside, plush rugs and elegant paneling complimented wooden furniture upholstered in rich burgundy cloth. The Allied soldier pushed back his hood and invited Jinn to sit with him at a glossy table of deep red wood. As they settled into their chairs, he introduced himself as Mikael Fjeldssen.

Jinn spoke plainly. "Major Fjeldssen, the longer your people keep the Ruby Dynasty imprisoned, the less options you leave us."

"We have no wish to antagonize Imperial Space Command." He regarded her steadily. "However, we have concerns in regards to the intent of your fleet."

"Release your prisoners to us and we will leave," Jinn said.

"We have the matter of the psiberweb to consider."

Shall I tell him? Jinn asked.

Go ahead, I thought.

She met Mikael's gaze. "We already have a psiberweb, Major."

Although his body language subtly revealed the increase

in his tension, he didn't show any surprise. "With the Pharaoh, yes? But can one person maintain the Triad that supports the web? I was under the impression that even with three people in the powerlink, the job was difficult."

So. He had done his security work. ISC kept very quiet about the need for a full Triad. It had worked well with El-drinson, Kurj, and me; Kurj had strength, I had finesse, and Eldrinson had flexibility. After Kurj's death, Soz had joined the Triad. She had also had strength, a bit less than Kurj, but with more finesse. I needed them.

Jinn flooded Mikael with verbiage, trying to disguise how close he had come to the truth. "The previous web spanned billions of trillions of nodes, if you include the electro-optical, quantum, biomechanical, nano, and picowebs linked into it. Whether or not a web of that size could be maintained with less than a Triad is irrelevant. A new web can and has been created. So it serves no purpose to hold the Ruby Dynasty, either here or on Lyshriol."

His expression gave away nothing. "Certainly I will relay your message to my commanding officers."

Jinn leaned forward. "Our messages have been relayed for days now. We have come to take our people home."

"It isn't in my power to make such a decision." Mikael paused. "However, if you continue to flout our laws and security, you will force us to take steps we prefer to avoid."

Although his response made sense, his tone had an odd nuance. He was hiding something. It agitated him. He covered well, but not well enough. He didn't want us to make a certain discovery. But what?

Jinn parried with him a while longer, until finally they brought the negotiations to a close. Jinn even let Mikael convince her that it would be best if her team returned to our ships in orbit. His people would let her go if she left immediately, with an escort of Allied fighters. He gave her a cube with messages from various officials meant to mollify us. It even included a note from my sister Roca telling me that she, Ami, and Kurjson were fine.

The Allieds escorted Jinn and her people to the racer, and

the entire ISC team climbed back inside. Allied fighters
roared overhead, a subtle reminder that we should vacate the
premises. The ISC team settled into their seats and Jinn took
the cockpit.

Pharaoh Dyhianna? she asked. *Are you there?*

I shifted into the racer's computer system. *Right here. Do
you have a fix on my sister?*

*Negative, ma'am. But we know she isn't in these buildings.
My people scanned the area while I spoke with Major
Fjeldssen.*

I'll double-check. Using the racer's sensors, I extended my
awareness. I kept nudging Allied stealth shrouds. They were
well designed. Effective. A few even required a good bit of fi-
nagling before I slipped past them. *I'm not picking her up either.*

We don't have time to search, Jinn said. *We're already
inviting trouble by taking these few moments to leave.*

Damn. I was almost certain Roca was on the AUC. But
where? The Centre covered hundreds of square kilometers.
Jinn, I'm going to extend into Kyle space and look for my sister that way.

Got it, ma'am. Jinn linked the nav controls into the central
processor where I resided now, directly connecting my
search to the ship's navigation system.

LAUNCHING, the racer thought.

As we took off, I extended my mind, reaching for Roca.
Had I actually been on Earth, it probably would have worked.
But I was too far away, up in orbit on *Roca's Pride*. I couldn't
find her even with the psiberweb magnifying my strength.

Our escort of Allied fighters continued to patrol the sky.
When Jinn paused, hovering only a few meters above the
trees, someone warned her to continue her ascent.

Then, faintly, I caught of sense of golden power.

Roca? It didn't feel right. But we could delay no longer. I
wove a thread from that distant mind into the racer's nav system. *Go.*

The racer leapt into action, sheering above the forest. My
extended senses detected one of the Allied fighters powering
up a laser. Trees bent underneath us—and then we were
dropping back down through them. The leafy canopy

whipped us like a thunderstorm. We landed with a crash of
falling branches—

And the Allieds finally fired.

They could have pulverized the racer. Instead they seared
the forest around us, starting fires, blocking our escape. And
guess what?

ISC had lied about the racer having no weapons.

They had disguised the system so well, even I had missed
it. Jinn fired an Annihilator, a high-flux beam of anti-protons.
Designed for space combat, it annihilated protons—with
drastic results. In space, it could gut a large ship and demol-
ish a smaller one. Fighters rarely used them in an atmosphere. The anti-protons interacted with air molecules,
attenuating the beam while showering the ground with radiation and particle cascades.

The beam stabbed the sky in a brilliant column of white
light, bending slightly due to the Earth's magnetic field.
When the main flux of the anti-protons slowed enough to interact with the air, they reacted in a great burst of energy. The
resulting annihilations created an intense ball of fire at the
end of the beam. It dazzled the sky, blazing like a miniature
artificial sun above the forest of Sweden.

High-energy particles and radiation rained out of the sky.
The gamma radiation attenuated fast and the energetic
mesons underwent rapid decay into other particles, including muons, electrons, positrons, neutrinos, and fast neu-
trons. Enough of it survived to reach the racer, but the
composite armored hull and magnetic shields protected the
crew inside.

Jinn aimed to warn rather than destroy. She could have
easily brought down the fighters; turning an Annihilator on
them was like using nuclear weapons to fumigate a house.

"Holy mother!" The voice exploded out of Jinn's comm.
"ISC racer, cease fire!"

Opsister! I mentally shouted. *Back off! You'll kill the people we
came to rescue.*

*I won't hit them. I can choose my targets with millimeter
precision.* Then she added, *Someone is coming to us, ma'am.*

Using the ship's cameras, I located several people running through the forest. The fighters in the sky had to make a decision. They could target the racer with surgical precision using lasers or smart missiles, but if they waited any longer to attack, they risked hitting the people running toward us.

The Allieds were jamming our sensors, and I couldn't make a clear ID on the runners. I didn't think the Annihilator shot had produced enough fallout to pose them a serious danger, but to reach us they would have to run through the area around the ship that had taken the worst of it. I hoped they had good health nanomeds patrolling their bodies.

The muscles in Jinn's face tightened. The runners were close enough now that if the Allieds fired, they would probably kill everyone. Was Roca with them? Ami? Kurjson? If they died, ISC would take it as an indisputable act of war, but the Allieds would achieve their purpose of keeping us from building a full psiberweb. Given that Jinn had fired an Annihilator, on-planet, from a supposedly unarmed craft that had violated who knew how many laws, the Allied response was obviously provoked. Had the situation been reversed, ISC would have crushed the intruding racer. For all that we portrayed the Allieds as the offenders, they had so far acted with a far more peaceful intent than we would have shown.

But we may have pushed them too far. They could kill my sister.

The runners had reached the ship. *Open!* I thought. In the same instant, Jinn shouted, *"Open airlock."*

The airlock whipped open like the shutter on a high-speed camera. A woman scrambled through and threw herself across the deck, out of the way of those coming behind her.

Roca! Without a telepresence link such as I had with Jinn, I couldn't reach my sister's mind from so far away. But I called her anyway, in instinct. My sister, Skolia's golden goddess, my heir, lay on the deck in rumpled blue leggings and an over-sized blue sweater, her face flushed.

I didn't recognize the older woman who clambered in after Roca, her white hair tousled, her lined face pale. Ami came next, a younger woman with brown hair. Kurj's widow. She held tight to her child, Kurjson, a strapping toddler with gold curls.

Then I saw the man.

He came last, jumping inside just before the airlock snapped closed. As the racer leapt into the sky, I had a good, clear view of him. He filled the cabin with his size and massive physique. Gray lined his metallic gold hair. He had inherited his mother's gold skin and classic features, but with a strong-jawed, masculine power. His thought thundered in my mind, booming and ragged, roughened with mental scar tissue, its massive force unparalleled, yet, incredibly, also gentle:

My greetings, Aunt Dehya.

Kelric had come home.

30

Never Home

This time I dropped out of the web fast and clean. I was un-fastening myself from the Chair even before it finished descending to the floor. By the time the techs reached me, I had pushed out, past the control panels. Standing on my own, I barely managed to hold still while they did medical checks. As soon as one of them indicated they had finished, I took off running, my bodyguards striding with me.

Chad Barzun joined us at the entrance to the Triad Chamber. Ragnar was nowhere in sight, but I knew where we would find him. As I jogged down the ship's corridors, Chad asked questions, but I could only shake my head, too wound up to answer.

By the time we reached the decon chamber outside the bay where Jinn had docked the racer, my heart was pounding. Ragnar had already arrived with his aides. They greeted us with nods. Floating outside the chamber, clenching a grip, I waited.

Waiting.

Waiting.

Waiting—

The decon chamber opened.

When the woman first appeared in the entrance, I didn't recognize her. Her presence hit me too hard; I couldn't take it in. Then my mind caught up with my sight, and I propelled myself forward. As I reached her, she let go of the bulkhead and threw her arms around me. My momentum sent us back into the decon chamber, slowly spinning, but we paid no heed.

So I embraced my sister.

We hugged in silence, unable to speak. It wasn't until we bumped the opposite wall of the chamber that we separated, each of us giving a self-conscious laugh. I was aware of other people around us, but I could only see Roca. She caught a grip in the wall and put out a hand to keep me from floating away.

"Dehya." Her voice caught. "It's good to see you." Despite her smile, she lacked her usual glow. Dark circles under her eyes gave her a hollow look.

I spoke softly. "I am so, so sorry about your husband."

"People can't live forever." A tear slid down her cheek. She wiped it away quickly, as if embarrassed I should see her cry.

"Ah, Roca," I murmured. I pulled her into my arms again and made comforting noises. She cried more then, her emotions a heart-breaking blend formed from the unexpected joy of our reunion and a deep, abiding grief.

A commotion finally made us separate. Looking past Roca, I saw that Eldrin had arrived. He was embracing a big, gold man in the center of the chamber. Kelric. His "little" brother. They drew apart, and Kelric thumped Eldrin heartily on the arm, sending his older brother spinning away.

Eldrin laughed and caught a grip on the wall. "You're remarkably strong for a dead man."

Kelric laughed too. But his appearance stunned me. White streaked his hair, lines showed around his eyes, and his face had a weathered quality, as if he had seen too much life. A worn pouch hung from his belt. He was still huge, with the broad shoulders and well-built physique that had flustered generations of women. In his youth, he had been a stunningly handsome man. Age had added a depth. Now he looked like an Imperator.

"It really is you," I said, floating forward.

Kelric grinned, his teeth flashing against his golden face. It still caught me off guard how much he looked like a powerful, male version of Roca.

"Tummy hurts," a young, disgruntled voice announced in Iotic.

Startled, I looked around. Ami was floating nearby, gently holding her son. He seemed uncertain what to think about all these people hugging and crying around him. I smiled at him, and he hid his face in his mother's arms, then peered out at me.

I still didn't recognize the older woman who floated near Ami. She resembled a Majda matriarch, with strong features, high cheekbones, and a square chin. But her face had a rugged, weathered aspect that suggested years of hard work with no treatments to delay aging. I estimated her age at about sixty, though she had the lean, fit body of someone younger. Her nose had been broken sometime and never fixed.

She kept glancing at Kelric. I wondered if she was an employee from the AUC in Sweden. It wouldn't surprise me if she had helped Kelric escape. He had always charmed women out of their good reason, an appeal that came from more than his good looks. He worked an empathic magic, picking up their attraction and giving it back to them multiplied. I didn't think he realized he did it, but it made people fall in love with him. I hoped she wouldn't be disappointed when she realized how many others wanted him.

Kelric floated toward me, bringing the woman with him. Her unease washed out as they came up to me.

"My greetings, Kelric." I glanced at his companion.

"My greetings." Kelric drew the woman forward. "I would like to present my wife, Jeejon." He turned to her. "Jeejon, this is my Aunt Dehya."

Wife? I had no idea how to respond. And Kelric had spoken in Eubic, a Trader language.

Jeejon gulped. "I am muchly honored by your presence, Pharaoh Dyhianna."

"I am pleased to meet you." Good gods. She spoke Eubic like a taskmaker. She had been a Trader slave. And Kelric had made her the Imperator's Consort. Hah! I would love to see the Trader reaction to this.

I beamed at her. "Please call me Dehya. You're my sister-in-law now."

She murmured an appropriate response, but her puzzlement showed. I supposed I should have said niece-in-law, given Kelric's introduction. I hoped she didn't ask about our convoluted family relationships. This didn't seem the best time for explanations.

Ragnar and Chad were also in the decon chamber, greeting everyone. For all their obvious gratification at the success of Jinn's mission, they exuded an almost visible tension. We didn't have much time; the longer we hulked around Earth, the more abrasive our presence became.

We may have already stayed too long.

"Del-Kurj?" I lowered my mug of kava and stared at Roca. "Your son?" If I remembered correctly, Del-Kurj was the third oldest of her children, a rangy man with lean muscles and a wild, hard edge. He had been born a few minutes prior to his twin sister, Chaniece.

We were seated around a table in my suite: Roca, Eldrin, Kelric, Ragnar, Chad, Jeejon, Jinn, and myself. My bodyguards stood around the walls, silent and discreet. Ami had taken Kurjson into my bedroom for his nap.

Ragnar spoke to Roca. "Why would the Allieds take one of your sons from Lyshriol to Earth?" A scowl creased his narrow face. "Haven't they done enough to your family already?"

"You would think," Roca said tiredly. She warmed her hands on her mug. "They wanted to split up the power centers of the Ruby Dynasty. They brought me and Del-Kurj to Earth because I'm one of the highest-ranking members of the Rhon and Del-Kurj was the eldest of my children on Lyshriol. They took us away from our home only a few months after . . ." Her face was shadowed. "After my husband died."

Ragnar swore under his breath. "Bastards."

As much as I wanted to agree with him, I saw why the Allieds had done it. Put too many of the Ruby Dynasty together and we could cause Earth all sorts of problems, at least from their point of view. With care, I asked, "And they also separated you and Prince Del-Kurj on Earth?"

"Yes." Roca rubbed her eyes. "Del is in America. They wanted him to help in questioning Seth Rockworth. They had me try it before Del. They were going to send Kelric next."

I stiffened. "Question Seth about what?"

"Those foster children of his that disappeared."

I leaned forward. "Then they don't have the children?"

Roca shook her head. "No one knows where they are. Or who."

"What did Seth say?" I asked.

Instead of answering, Roca glanced at Eldrin. The subject of Seth had always been awkward for him, given the unresolved situation.

Eldrin didn't look uncomfortable, though. He himself asked, "Did Seth know his foster son was Jaibriol the Third?"

"He says no." Roca swirled her kava. "The Allieds wanted me to talk with him because they know my expertise in reading people."

It made sense. As Rhon psions, we had an almost unmatched talent at discerning what people thought. Roca's years as an Assembly Councilor had honed that ability.

"Do you think he's telling the truth?" I asked.

She spoke quietly. "Yes."

Her answer disquieted me. I felt as if a handful of gold dust were trickling between my fingers, dispersing in the wind, impossible to call back. My models all pointed to Eldrinson and Seth as the ones who knew the truth about the children. Eldrinson had taken his secrets to the grave. Roca read people better than most anyone I knew . . . and yet, I didn't believe Seth. I *knew* him. He might fool even Roca. Of all the people alive, I was the only one with both the Rhon strength and personal familiarity to go beyond his defenses. And I had less chance than a kiss in a quasar of convincing the Allieds to let me see him.

I turned to Ragnar. "What are our chances of pulling out Seth and Del-Kurj? And the children, if we can find them?"

He grimaced. "We've already pushed the Allieds too far. If we try again, I'm almost certain they will attack."

"Earth has been recalling her forces from other star systems," Chad said. "Reinforcements arrive every day. We're painfully outnumbered now. And they're starting to break the security on our computer networks. The longer we stay here, the worse it gets."

Damn. We had pulled out more of the Ruby Dynasty than we expected, but we still didn't have all the answers—or the people—that we should have retrieved. "How much longer can we stay?"

"It's already been too long," Ragnar said. "Our security is compromised. The sooner we leave, the better."

Kelric was watching me, listening intently. He sat with confidence in his chair, one long leg extended under the table, the other bent at the knee. More than his size dominated the room; he had an aura of authority now that he hadn't possessed in his youth.

The edges of wrist guards showed below the cuffs of his shirt. Although his trousers covered his ankles, the outline of guards showed through the dark cloth. It puzzled me. They resembled Trader slave restraints, less gaudy than most, works of art in fact, but still restraints. Why not take them off? It seemed unlikely he had the same problem as Eldrin, that the picotech of the restraints had to be deciphered and neutralized before the surgeons could risk tampering with them. These looked too old to be that sophisticated. In fact, they looked ancient.

Every now and then he touched the pouch that hung from his belt. It apparently contained jeweled game pieces he used to play a type of solitaire game, which he refused to teach anyone or even play much around other people.

As I considered Kelric, he considered me. Then he asked, "What do you know about those children?"

"Not much," I admitted. "I think they have some Qox heritage. Jaibriol the Third probably arranged for them to leave Earth."

"Probably?" Chad Barzun asked.

I rubbed the back of my neck, wishing I could better ease the aching muscles. "We can never be sure until we find them." And find them I would, even if it took me the next fifty years.

Kelric was still watching me. "What do you think of this new emperor?"

I answered carefully. "I would like to believe he wants peace."

"And do you believe that?"

"I'm not sure." I had no sense of Jaibriol III. He might be a Rhon psion. Even worse, the Triad had an empty space now. It belonged to Eldrin, but without the Third Lock we couldn't support three people in the powerlink. Jaibriol III had that Lock. Gods, what a nightmare: the Trader emperor in the Triad. Even if he had sympathy for the Ruby Dynasty, I didn't want him in our minds.

I sent a private, guarded thought to Kelric. *You deactivated the Lock.*

Yes.

That is good.

Maybe not. Jaibriol Qox witnessed it.

I swore silently. *No.*

He can't turn it back on. Only a Rhon psion can.

I wasn't reassured. *What do you know about him?*

He let me go when he found me deactivating the Lock. Kelric paused. **I had an odd sense.**

Yes?

That he was a psion.

Ah, hell.

Roca glanced from Kelric to me. "What is it?"

I took a mental step back. Although Kelric and I had guarded our thoughts from them, Roca was too savvy not to realize we were communicating even if she couldn't pick up our thoughts. I had to be careful. If rumors spread that Jaibriol III was a psion, few would believe them. But someone might investigate. Even worse than the nightmare of Jaibriol III in the Triad of his own free will was Jaibriol III forced into the Triad by the Aristos.

I chose a story close to the truth. "I think Jaibriol the Third might have loved that girl Seth fostered." She could be his sister, after all.

Ragnar looked intrigued. "For the emperor to love a woman who isn't an Aristo would be considered an abomination by his people."

"It would make him vulnerable to censure," I said. "If he

really means to negotiate peace with us, we want him in power. Not weakened."

You don't want them to know what I suspect? Kelric asked.

I'd rather not. We can talk in private. Kelric probably already knew what I had to say; if Jaibriol III was a psion, he had more reason than any other Aristo to negotiate with us. We wanted him on the Carnelian Throne. That meant we had to protect him. Keep his secret.

A strange prospect, that the Ruby Dynasty would shield a Trader emperor.

31

Queen's Gamble

In the end, we had no choice but to leave Earth without Del-Kurj or Seth. We still had no idea what had happened to the three children. I didn't care how long it took; someday I would find them. Someday I would learn what Seth knew. And someday we would bring Del-Kurj home. But for now we had an explosive interstellar situation on our hands.

By the time the Pharaoh's Fleet reached Parthonia, the capital world of the Skolian Imperialate, we had accumulated most of Imperial Space Command's remaining forces. They rallied when the news spread that Skolia had its Pharaoh and a new Imperator. Ships gathered to us like starved travelers offered an unexpected sanctuary. I had previously wondered at the Assembly's conviction that the Ruby Dynasty provided symbols of morale, but now it became clear they were right, probably far more than they had ever wanted to know.

It caused a scandal that Kelric had chosen to seek asylum on Earth, even knowing they would hold him prisoner. Apparently I wasn't the only one who had feared his assassination. When we took up orbit around Parthonia, we came with the majority of ISC's forces and overwhelming public opinion on our side. The Assembly had little choice but to surrender. But it wasn't enough to have their surrender; we needed the symbol that represented them.

I dreaded this. Of all the actions I had ever had to take as Pharaoh, this was one of the worst. But if we intended to establish our authority as a government, then according to every tradition of the Ruby Empire, this had to be done.

So I sent my generals to imprison my friend and colleague, Barcala Tikal, the deposed First Councilor of the Skolian Assembly.

The Hall of Chambers stood in Selei City. In this great vaulted cathedral, with its spacious hall and polished columns, our founders had declared the birth of the Skolian Imperialate. Blue sunlight filtered through leaded glass windows. Dust motes drifted in the slanting rays. Soaring arches reached far above our heads, and birds flew through the upper spaces of the groined ceiling.

Kelric and I walked with four columns of military personnel, two on each side of us. Jinn Opsister led them, and Ragnar Bloodmark and Chad Barzun walked with us. Media techs came as well, recording everything. No part of these proceedings would be broadcast live, though; we knew too little about how it would go.

I felt acutely the absence of Jon Casestar and Vazar Majda. However, another Majda had come to the great Hall of Chambers.

The Majda.

Naaj waited on a dais at the end of the spacious hall. Multicolored light from stained glass windows bathed her tall figure. A retinue surrounded her: officers from the Pharaoh's Army, high-ranking members of her House, and her Jagernaut bodyguards. She stood in their center, watching us approach.

Kelric and I climbed the dais together, and the general's retinue parted to let us approach Naaj. At six-foot-five, she towered. Narrow gold bars glinted on the shoulders of her dark green uniform, and a stripe of darker green ran down her trousers, disappearing into her knee-boots. Her dark belt had the Majda insignia tooled into it, a hawk with wings spread. Close to seventy, she still had lean, muscled limbs and excellent health. Iron-gray streaks showed in her close-cropped hair.

Kelric faced her like a statue of aged gold. He wore dark gold trousers and a darker gold pullover, reminiscent of a uniform. His pouch hung from his belt. He had a different quality now than that of the beautiful young man who had wed Naaj's elder sister. His understated quality of authority compelled attention.

No one moved. No one spoke.

My unease grew. Too much time had passed without

Naaj's acceptance of Kelric as Imperator. At best, further delays would weaken his support among those loyal to Majda; at worst, we might have to imprison Naaj and her followers. I had no wish to depose the Majda Matriarch as well as the First Councilor. It would further destabilize an already depleted Skolia.

Naaj glanced at me, her gaze unreadable. Then she turned to Kelric. With formality, she performed the ancient salute given by the General of the Pharaoh's Army to its commander, a salute descended from the only branch of our military that dated back to the Ruby Empire. Clenching her fists, she crossed her wrists and extended her arms out straight. Her voice carried in the hall. "The Pharaoh's Army welcomes you home, Imperator Skolia. Our oath of fealty is yours, now and for as long as Majda may serve the Ruby Dynasty."

An almost visible exhalation of relief came from my retinue. But watching Naaj, I finally knew the truth. She guarded herself well, but I knew. She hadn't wanted to acknowledge Kelric. Today she had chosen the path laid down by her ancestors, but if she had believed she could have kept the title of Imperator, she would have fought for it. I doubted I would ever fully unravel how she viewed Kelric's ascendance; she had too much expertise in shielding her thoughts, gestures, and words. This I also knew, however: when Majda gave an oath, it became a matter of honor. She would keep her word.

Kelric's voice rumbled like slow thunder. "You honor the Ruby Dynasty with your fealty." He had an odd look, as if the oath ceremony jarred him. But he nodded to Naaj, accepting her as the General of the Pharaoh's Army.

When Naaj turned to me, I became even more aware of her imposing presence. I wondered what she saw when she looked at her pharaoh. Did I seem lacking, a pale remnant of the warrior queens from our past? Nowadays, the pharaoh's duties were more involved with the mind than with battles. Whatever she felt, she revealed only the dignity of her position. With regal grace, she went down on one knee and bent her head.

I didn't expect her words.

"Majda honors the Ruby Pharaoh," she said. "For Skolia and the Ruby Dynasty, I enter this circle to give my oath. I swear to hold your House above all else, as you hold the future of Skolia in your mind and hands. On penalty of my life, I swear that my loyalty is to the House of Skolia, only to Skolia, and completely to Skolia." Then she raised her head. "May your reign be long and glorious, Pharaoh Dyhianna."

Good Gods. The House of Skolia. No one used that title for the Ruby Dynasty now. In this modern age, the General of the Pharaoh's Army gave her allegiance by swearing the Army would perform for the glory of Skolia, in honor of the Assembly. Naaj had given me an oath that no one had spoken for thousands of years.

"You honor me, General Majda." I touched her shoulder. "Please rise."

Naaj stood. Then she turned to one of her officers, a colonel in dark green. She said, simply, "Bring him."

My stomach felt as if it dropped. I didn't want this.

Guards brought the prisoner out through an arched doorway behind the dais. Long and angular, with a piercing gaze and dark hair, the man stared straight ahead. He wore simple clothes: dark slacks, a gray shirt with a high collar, and dark shoes. Prison cuffs circled his arms, the modern equivalent of chains, lights blinking within them to indicate they were active. They would inject a neural blocker if he tried to escape. To me, they were an ugly reminder of Trader restraints. I wanted to take them off and crush them under my boot. But if I intended to overthrow the Assembly, I had to finish this.

The guards brought him up the dais. As the group stopped in front of me, the hall became silent.

With motions slow and stiff, the prisoner went down on one knee and bowed his head. Then Barcala Tikal spoke in the resonant voice that had made him such a renowned orator. "The Skolian Assembly acknowledges Dyhianna Selei as Pharaoh of Skolia." He raised his head and finished in a numb voice. "I surrender to your authority. May your reign be long and glorious."

"I accept your surrender." With painful formality, I touched his shoulder. "Rise. Please."

He stood slowly, as if pressed by a weight. In my side vision, I saw Ragnar watching with vindictive satisfaction. I had never fully realized how much he wanted to see the powers of Skolia humbled. Yet Barcala had never been an arrogant man. He governed well, with far less intrigues than the noble Houses. If Ragnar wanted this for Barcala, how must he feel about the Houses? I couldn't help but wish that Jon Casestar stood at my side, rather than Ragnar.

The techs would prepare a news holo about this ceremony. For now, Naaj spoke to her officers, arranging Barcala's transfer to *Roca's Pride*. She kept her voice neutral, but I felt her anger. She wouldn't soon forget that we had forced her to bring Barcala here in chains.

So began my reign.

Roca and I met in her suite. I told my bodyguards to wait outside, and I deactivated the visual and audio sensors inside. Had I also disengaged the physiological monitors that let Security know we were alive and well, they probably would have ordered my bodyguards back in. This way, we at least had a modicum of privacy.

I sank into a molded chair. Roca sat in another at right angles to me, drinking wine from a goblet, her long legs crossed, her hair tumbling in great shining lengths over her body and the chair. Despite her subdued mood, she radiated vitality.

The difference in our ages meant I had been well into adulthood when she was born. For years I had felt more like her aunt than sister. Then one day I realized my "baby" sister had become a grown woman with her own job and family. Soon she was an interstellar celebrity, renowned for her ability as a dancer. Over the years her political work within the Assembly had taken on more importance, until she earned election to one of its most coveted posts, the Councilor for Foreign Affairs.

Roca and I had grown even closer during those decades, as

we weathered the storms of our family and the Imperialate, through wars and the loss of loved ones, but also in joy, when good came into our lives. We didn't always agree, having our arguments like any siblings. But most of all we loved each other. After Eldrin and Taquinil, I was closer to her than anyone else. Seeing her now, safe and alive, I felt a gratitude so deep I couldn't find words to express it. If I turned sentimental on her, though, it would probably embarrass us both.

"You're pensive tonight," she said.

I slanted her a wry look. "I just overthrew the government. I'm allowed to be pensive."

A fierce pride came into her gaze. "Never doubt your choices, Dehya. The Assembly has manipulated, controlled, and condemned us for centuries. Yet despite all that, the Ruby Dynasty has risen again. It is our right. They took it from us, but we have overcome them."

I blinked at her vehemence. From past discussions, I knew generally what she thought, but we had never talked about this situation, at least not in the concrete terms we now faced. "I hadn't realized you felt that strongly about it."

"Until now, we had no choices." She swirled the wine in her goblet. "Politics, diplomacy, foreign affairs—it fascinates me. I could no more step back from it than I could stop breathing."

I spoke quietly. "Perhaps you would make a better Pharaoh."

"Why? Because I enjoy governing and you don't? The desire for power is no guarantee a person will make good use of it."

Would I? A good use of power wasn't enough. It had to be the best possible use; otherwise the Traders would conquer us. Then all humanity would lose. If we fell, the Allieds would be next. That was probably why, in the end, they hadn't fired on the racer; we needed them and they needed us.

"Why do you doubt yourself?" Roca asked.

"I don't."

"Dehya, I know you."

I paused, knowing I couldn't put her off with platitudes. So I spoke frankly. "I'm not sure the mindset of the Ruby Dynasty is a good model for leadership."

"You want perfection." She took a swallow of wine. "Every government has flaws. I've no doubt about your fitness to rule."

I leaned forward. "I know I can do well as Pharaoh. It's the position itself I doubt. Aristocracies are outdated. Why does humanity need another?"

"Because we can do a better job than the Assembly."

"They weren't doing a bad job."

"No?" Anger edged her voice. "Skolia needs the Ruby Dynasty to survive. The Assembly was destroying us. The more desperate they became, the worse we suffered."

I thought of my son. "You know about Taquinil?"

A shadow came over her expression. "I am sorry, Dehya."

I swallowed against the lump in my throat. "He's happy. That's what matters." I doubted I could ever really accept losing him from our lives, but it did help to know he had chosen what he wanted.

"You are once again my heir," I told Roca.

She started. "I've no desire for your title."

"That isn't how you sounded a few moments ago."

"Dehya, listen." She set down her goblet. "Being Pharaoh and being the Councilor for Foreign Affairs are two very different things. If the time comes and you have no heir, I will accept the title. But I don't crave it." She spoke quietly. "You have nothing to fear from me."

It hadn't occurred to me to fear my own sister. "I know." I spoke with difficulty. "Eldrin and I don't know if we should try to have more children. Even with modern genetic medicine, the baby still has a good chance of being born with severe deformities or the extreme mental sensitivity that nearly destroyed Taquinil."

Her voice softened. "At least now the Assembly can no longer force you to have them against your will."

"Yes. No longer." I wondered if the universe was laughing

at us. For in the end, when Eldrin and I discovered just how much we longed for children, we couldn't have them.

The living room was empty when I entered the suite. Someone had to be here, though, or the EI wouldn't have let me inside. An open doorway arched in the opposite wall. It was dark beyond, and at first I didn't see the woman there. But I felt the nuances of her mind: wariness, curiosity, restraint, anger, even relief.

Vazar walked through the archway. She stopped several paces away from me, a larger distance than social convention dictated. "Have you come to say your revolution is done? I already know. I saw the news holo."

I had too much respect for her to evade the central issue. "I wanted to let you know I've spoken to Naaj."

Her posture became even more guarded. "And?"

"She verified that you had authority to speak for her." I doubted I would ever know if Naaj had made that decision before or after Vazar made her claim, but whatever the truth, Naaj had backed her cousin. Vazar wouldn't face execution. That meant more to me than I knew how to express. Whatever else I thought of Naaj Majda, I would always be grateful to her for supporting Vazar, who in many ways had become like a cousin to me as well.

Vazar let out a breath. Her posture eased, almost imperceptibly, but the tension still showed. "I understand Naaj accepted you as Pharaoh."

"Yes." I paused, afraid to ask. But I had to know. "And you?"

Her throaty voice was low. "I honor the Majda oath to the Ruby Dynasty."

Relief washed over me. Her response hardly qualified as a ringing endorsement, though. I tried to decipher her mood. Conflicting loyalties tore at her. She had many misgivings about the changes I had wrought. "Vaz, I value your support. But why the doubts? The mission to Earth succeeded, better even than we expected in one respect. They had Kelric."

"Aye, it worked. And it is good to have your family back." She came closer. "But are you certain about the rest? Is this really what you believe best for Skolia?"

"I have no doubt I can rule in the best interest of Skolia." I knew it was an evasive answer. I glanced back at the shadowed archway, aware now of someone else beyond it listening to us. "Your son is a Ruby Dynasty heir. He has a right to his full heritage."

She turned her head slightly, toward the archway. Then she returned her gaze to me. "Does that mean the Ruby Dynasty will acknowledge him?" Her tension almost crackled in the air.

I spoke quietly. "Yes."

She closed her eyes for a moment. When she opened them again the chill had left her gaze. "I thank you." With an edge, she added, "Majda has disowned him."

Alhtough it shouldn't have surprised me, I had hoped that for Ryder, might be willing to bend. But Naaj could be hard. "Majda has been known to re-evaluate."

Vazar snorted. "Right. And the Traders would love to make peace with us."

I managed a smile. "We can always hope." In both cases. "But regardless, your son will be recognized by the House of Skolia in a formal ceremony when we return to the Imperial court." Let Naaj chew on that.

If Vazar realized I had evaded her original question, she gave no indication of it in either word or thought. Was I certain that absolute rule by the Ruby Dynasty was the best choice now? Ironic that a Majda warrior, of all people, should ask me that. If I intended to keep the confidence of Skolia, I could never give her my true answer.

No. I wasn't certain it was the best choice.

Chad Barzun was in the Tactics Room. Its luminous walls had depth, as if you could walk into them, on and on, until the deep, viscous light swallowed you up. Today the sphere had absorbed all furniture and ledges, so only one break showed in its smoothness—this hatchway, where I had entered on the sphere's equator. The air felt cool on my face, without character or scent. It offered a metaphor for life on ships that made me long to run in open fields under an open sky.

Chad was in the bottom of the sphere, down a slope of many meters from where I stood. He called up to me. "Would you like to join me, Your Highness?" Despite his distance, the good acoustics in the chamber made it sound as if he were right next to me.

"Yes, thank you," I said.

Tactics molded a staircase for me. I went down and joined Chad at the bottom.

Enthusiasm warmed his voice. "Wait until you see this." Raising his voice, he said, "Tactics, run number six."

The sphere plunged into blackness. When it lightened, we were again standing on the Dalvador Plains of Eldrin's home on Lyshriol. Strange, how the Tactics Room that symbolized for me a sterile life on the ship could also offer the open sky and fields I craved.

The Lyshrioli people were still camped out at the starport. Their tent nation stretched around us in every direction. An exuberant hum of life filled the air: voices murmuring, livestock snorting, all the clicks, thumps, rattles, and rumbles that such a large assembly made. We weren't far from the port. Someone had erected a stage there, and my nephew Vyrl stood on it with his wife and siblings. A globe floated above his head, twirling with iridescent colors as it transmitted his voice to thousands of other spheres floating over the encampment. His words flowed over us, resonant, deep, musical.

Chad raised his hand, indicating the scene as if he were offering me a gift. At first I didn't understand. It didn't matter; the sheer beauty of Vyrl's voice thrilled me. He spoke in Trillian, the harmonious tongue of his people. I had libraries for it in my neural nodes, along with translation programs. As my mind processed his speech, I began to understand. Yet even then, it took time to absorb. I heard him, yet I feared to hope.

Over the past months, the outcry against the Allied occupation of Lyshriol had risen in intensity. It came from all over settled space, not only from Skolians, but from the Allieds and even the Traders. The criticism against Earth for holding the Ruby Dynasty prisoner had turned excoriating, especially after it became public knowledge that Eldrinson had died in Allied custody. Then Eldrin and I made our plea for the release of our family and peace among our peoples. The war of public censure had heated into a star-spanning verbal conflagration.

The Allieds had finally had enough. They pulled out of Lyshriol.

"Saints above." I gave a startled laugh. "We *won*."

Chad inhaled deeply, filling his virtual lungs with the oxygen-rich air of Lyshriol. "That we did, Your Highness. May your reign continue with even greater successes than those you have already achieved."

His positive take on my new position should have gratified me. "Do you really think what we've done with the Assembly is such a success?"

"Of course."

"Why?"

"Because you are the Pharaoh." He regarded me evenly. "We have always been the Ruby Empire, even if for a few hundred years we called ourselves something else."

I understood what he meant; our identity was linked inextricably to our history. Skolia had started as the Ruby Empire. We had *no* other history, nothing more than legends of a place called Earth. No one had even believed those stories anymore, at least not until our siblings from Earth actually showed up.

"What you say is true," I answered. "But I find myself questioning whether or not what we've always done is the best choice now."

He indicated the tent nation around us. "What happened here is unlike anything we've done before. War has been our way for so long. It is auspicious that we found a peaceful alternative."

"And if the Allieds had been as warlike in their recent history as we still are?" I shook my head. "Peace has to come from two sides. This would never have worked with the Traders."

He spoke dryly. "Perhaps someday they will change."

I could tell he didn't believe it would ever happen. Even if Jaibriol III genuinely wanted to improve our relations, one person couldn't change the ingrained traditions of millennia, not without years of work. Decades. Centuries.

Suddenly I thought: *half a century. Fifty years.* For some reason I recalled the racer that Jinn Opsister had taken to Earth: *Lightning.* Yet when I thought of it, I didn't envision a racer. I saw a Jag starfighter. Then I thought of Viquara Iquar, or maybe not Viquara, but another Iquar.

Jags, lightning, Iquar: it made no sense. But I didn't dismiss it. I had long ago realized such images could come from models in my mind that evolved below conscious thought. This image was too far in the future to offer anything definitive, but it must refer to powerful events if it registered even now. Maybe in fifty years we would finally find accommodation with the Traders. Or perhaps we would face our destruction.

Chad was watching me. "Pharaoh Dyhianna, I have no doubt that you will build a greater Skolia."

"I value your loyalty. It means a great deal to me." It was the reason I had promoted him.

Chad moved slightly, straightening his spine. I felt his satisfaction. Unlike Ragnar Bloodmark, who had ulterior motives everywhere, Chad genuinely believed we had made the right choice. His confidence came like a balm on blistered skin.

I needed that, to help prepare myself for the next person I had to face.

Jon Casestar's suite hadn't changed, but a great deal had happened since the last time I had been here. We sat at the same table as before. Instead of Eldrin, this time I came with bodyguards, Jagernauts loyal to the Ruby Dynasty. Jon no longer wore his uniform; today he had on gray trousers and a gray tunic. His face was drawn, his manner wary.

He spoke the requisite ceremonial words in a neutral voice, with no emotion. "My honor at your presence, Pharaoh Dyhianna."

I almost winced. He sounded as honored as a soldier facing execution. And indeed, during the Ruby Empire, that would have been his sentence for acting against the Pharaoh. I didn't want him to die. He had been a loyal and valued advisor to the last two Imperators, Kurj and Soz. I had no doubt he could have done the same for Kelric. But I couldn't let him go now, not after he had defied the authority of the Ruby Throne.

"Ah, Jon." I pushed my hand through my hair. "What will we do?"

I felt him tense. Although he wasn't any more ready to trust me than I him, he understood the implicit message in my question—I wanted to negotiate.

He spoke carefully. "We have options."

"Perhaps we should explore them."

"I would agree, yes."

Good. If he recanted his opposition to my reign, I wouldn't have to do anything drastic. "Perhaps you might make a public statement. A pledge of support to our future. To Skolia." I paused. "To the Ruby Dynasty." Then I waited, willing him to say yes.

Resignation leaked past his mental barriers, and the fear that he was about to sign his death warrant. "I cannot lie, Your Highness."

I should have known he wouldn't go that far. As much as I admired his integrity, it wouldn't help him in his grave. "Surely a middle ground exists." I tried to think of what he might say that would mollify those who wanted his death. "Most people will understand your misgivings about our move against Earth. You feared to start a war. But perhaps you are gratified by its success and encouraged by the peaceful resolution at Lyshriol."

"Yes, I could say that." His unspoken question seemed to hang in the air: *What is the catch?*

I didn't hedge. "You must never speak against the Ruby Dynasty."

He didn't answer immediately. Again I willed him not to refuse. Although he would probably never regain his authority as a top-ranked ISC admiral, he had many other options for a career. Most of all, I wouldn't have to order his blasted execution.

Although he remained silent, his mood came to me. He had grave concerns about the rule of the Ruby Dynasty. The concentration of so much power with so few people troubled him. But given the choice between death and a measured support of the new government, he remained silent about his doubts. I had offered him an out: if he stopped opposing us, I wouldn't ask that he recant his objections. He didn't have to lie, he only had to keep quiet.

I spoke softly. "Silence requires less compromise that denial."

Regret touched his voice. "One learns to live with compromises." He took a tired breath. "I will make the speech, as you say."

The hard knot in my stomach loosened. "I am glad, Jon. Truly glad."

Yet still a part of me knew only regret. Even with his pardon, the Ruby Dynasty had lost one of its strongest military leaders.

Sprawled in his command chair, Ragnar Bloodmark waved at the holoscreens that curved around the bridge of his cruiser, *Pharaoh's Shield*. A panorama of stars surrounded us. Bridge consoles studded the surface of the hemisphere like ledges floating in the vast expanse of stars.

He spoke with fierce exultation. "This is all yours—your triumph."

I tried to feel his euphoria. "Apparently so."

He turned his dark gaze on me. "It is worth whatever price it exacts."

"Why?"

He made an incredulous noise. "What kind of question is that for the winner to ask?"

"And you think that is what matters: the winning."

"You didn't start this hoping to lose." His smile had a hard, vicious edge. "Dehya, you think too much. Enjoy your triumph."

I wondered what he truly supported: me, or the power his loyalty would bring him. What did it matter? He had chosen the Ruby Dynasty. "You led the Fleet well."

"That is what you need. People who serve you well." The edge deepened in his voice. "People who understand the intricacies of power."

Meaning you. Not Eldrin. He wouldn't say it today or tomorrow, but it would come. Ragnar wanted more. He wanted the Ruby Throne. I couldn't deny the truth.

I could never trust him.

The holo-panel in Naaj's living room showed the Majda home planet, Raylicon, the world that had birthed our ancestors after we lost the green hills and blue seas of Earth. In the holo, violent winds hurled the sands of a red desert against gaunt red cliffs, like an ocean of sand breaking against a primordial shoreline. High on the cliffs, modern towers rose in mirrored needles, their metallic surfaces sharp against a pale blue sky. Naaj stood in front of the panel, her imposing figure dark against the fiery background.

"You must speak to the Skolian people as soon as possible," she said. "They must hear from their Pharaoh." Her eyes glinted.

The chill air made me wish I had worn clothes with a heating system. Or maybe facing Naaj was what made me cold. "The Office of Public Affairs is arranging for Kelric and me to appear in a broadcast."

"Astonishing that he survived all these years," she said, her tone guarded.

"He hasn't talked much about it."

"It disquiets me. Nineteen years is a long time."

It disquieted me too, though I suspected for different reasons. No one found it surprising that he declined to talk about his experiences as a slave. But he wasn't just restrained, he was utterly silent on the matter. Often he refused to talk at all.

"He is always building structures with those jewels," I said. "I think it's more than a game."

Naaj shrugged. "He puts them away whenever I come near."

I walked around the room, studying its holo-panels, haunting views of Raylicon, including the Majda palace, an exotic cascade of domes and towers aglow in a rosy dawn. It belonged to Kelric now. "He speaks with fondness of the wedding present your sister gave him. He will be glad to see the palace again." I had no doubt she knew exactly what I meant; we expected her House to honor Kelric's claim to his Majda assets.

Naaj spoke with a formal tone, as one matriarch to another discussing the men under their responsibility. "Majda will see to his well-being."

Although I doubted Kelric would appreciate that Majda felt obligated to look after his well-being, her answer made sense. Naaj coveted the title of Imperator the way a powerful matriarch in the Ruby Empire would have sought to expand her influence. She engaged her adversaries in an honorable manner. The Ruby queens had constantly fought such battles. The winner kept all, including the loser's men.

Had Kelric been female, Naaj would have challenged him for the Majda assets. But even now, when he had become Imperator, I wasn't sure she could see him as fully independent. In her view, he belonged to the winner, the House of Skolia, to which she had pledged her oath. She would always be entrenched in the Majda conservatism, but if it meant she wouldn't seek his assassination, that was all that mattered.

"It pleases me that you venerate your sister's widower," I said.

"As we venerate your House." She raised her head. "I have always known the Houses would rise again. The Ruby Dynasty is where it belongs."

"You honor us with your fealty." Not that she had had much choice.

"As it should be."

"Why?"

"Why honor you with fealty?" She snorted, letting go of her formality. "Dehya, what kind of absurd question is that?"

I held back my smile. "You should indeed honor us," I agreed. "But why should we rule?"

"I can't believe you have to ask."

"Humor me."

"The Houses are better fit to do it than the common people." She spoke as if that were obvious and universally accepted, rather than one of the most controversial debates of our time.

"Not everyone feels that way," I said.

"Not everyone deserves a voice."

Well, Majda certainly hadn't lost her arrogance. I had the approval of the people now, but if Naaj started talking this way in public, I would lose support fast. My ascendance was already going to create trouble in exactly those circles she was most likely to offend. I frowned at her. "That many nobles among the Houses feel as you do is one reason the rule of the Ruby Dynasty will be controversial in certain groups."

"Then those groups need 'reeducation.'"

"*Lése majesté,*" I said. "That's what you want."

She tilted her head. "What language is that?"

"French. From Earth. It means a crime against the sovereign of a realm. The punishment could be severe."

"As it should be." Surprise trickled past her mental barriers. "I wouldn't have expected the Allieds to be so sensible."

Sensible depended on your point of view. "They no longer support that attitude. They long ago chose to govern through elected representatives."

She waved her hand in dismissal. "Which is why they are weak."

I didn't believe she actually had that narrow a view. She hadn't risen so high in the treacherous seas of political intrigue by ignoring reality. "Or it could be that we simply happened to be here first and had longer to build our power base."

She refused to relent. "It doesn't matter, Dehya. The Allieds aren't strong enough to deal with the situation. You must be firm now, both with the Allieds and with your 'certain groups.' "

Firm, yes. But with whom remained to be seen.

I expected the clink of gems to stop when the bodyguards ushered me into Kelric's study. He looked up as I entered, his hand poised over a tower of playing pieces. A ruby ball sparkled in his hand. Setting it down, he rose to his feet.

"My greetings, Dehya." He motioned at a chair. "Please join me."

"My greetings." I sat with him at the table.

Instead of putting his jewels back into his pouch, this time he left them out: diamond polyhedrons, sapphire disks, emerald rods, opal rings, gold cubes, and more. I had come to discuss our impending public appearance, but I couldn't pass up this opportunity. He had steadfastly refused to let anyone watch his games.

I studied the structure. "These are beautiful gems."

"Dice."

I looked up at him. "They're dice?"

He watched me intently from across the table. "Yes."

"You're gambling then?"

"No." His gaze never wavered. "You must learn to play."

"Why me?" I asked, intrigued.

"Who more appropriate?" He indicated the lustrous tower. It had an amethyst cube as its base. A seven-sided sapphire polyhedron sat on top of the cube. An emerald octahedron balanced on the sapphire, held in place by a small emerald ring. The tower continued with a nine-sided green-yellow gem, a ten-sided yellow gem, an eleven-sided topaz, and a twelve-sided bronze die. He had found ingenious ways to balance them, using rings and small cups. The room lights glittered off the gems.

"It is called a queen's spectrum." He considered the tower. "Actually, this would be a queen's gamble."

"What is the difference?" I asked.

"A gamble is any structure built with great risk but substantial potential payoff." He balanced the ruby ball on the top, within a diamond ring.

"Shouldn't you have put a ruby with thirteen sides there?"

Kelric gave me an approving glance. "You're fast. But the highest ranked polyhedron is the dodecahedron. None have more than twelve sides." He indicated the ruby. "Unless you consider a sphere a polyhedron with an infinite number of sides."

"Clever. But that isn't a sphere. It's a ball."

He laughed. "True. A sphere is hollow. Surely our highest-ranking piece must be solid."

Possibilities swirled in my mind, tantalizing. "It's more than a game, isn't it?"

"That depends on how you play." He shrugged. "Most people gamble."

"But you don't?" I had forgotten how hard it could be to converse with Kelric. He had never been talkative, and the last nineteen years had intensified his taciturn inclinations.

"No." He gathered up the pieces and put them in his pouch, but instead of tying it on his belt, he offered it to me. "You must have copies made."

Stunned, I took the pouch. No one had ever seen him part with it. "Are you certain you want me to take this?"

"Yes." He shifted his weight. "Return them soon."

"I will." I knew he could have had his console do a holo-scan of the dice and transmit the results to my jewelers, who could make them without the originals. This was a deliberate gesture of trust. "Thank you."

"When you have your own set, we will play Quis."

"Is that what you call the game?"

"Yes. It means 'influence.'"

"Literally?" My neural nodes sifted through language bases, trying to find a match for the word *Quis*. If I could narrow down the language, it might provide a clue about where Kelric had been all these years. Most people accepted that he had been with the Traders, but I didn't believe it.

Quis sounded like *keys* in Earth English. In Earth Latin, *quis* meant "who," and in the language of the Topolo people on the world Metropoli, *keez* meant "rebirth." None of those fit with places that it made any sense for Kelric to have been all these years.

"The literal translation is 'resurrection,'" he said. "But Quis gives influence if you play well. You plan with it, analyze, tell tales."

"It sounds fascinating." My nodes came up with *kuxel* for resurrection and *kux* for "come back to life," both ancient Mayan words. But that didn't help much, either, given that all our languages derived in part from ancient Mesoamerican tongues.

"You must learn Quis." Kelric was studying me with his gold gaze. "No other person will play it like you."

Who could resist a pitch like this? "All right. But why won't you teach anyone else?"

"They don't have my oath."

"Your oath?"

He spoke quietly, not in our modern tongue, but in classical Iotic, a language over five thousand years old. "For Skolia and the Ruby Dynasty, I come to your Circle to give my Oath. I swear to hold your Estate above all else, as I hold the future of Skolia in my mind and hands. I swear, on penalty of my life, that my loyalty is to the House of Skolia, only to Skolia, and completely to Skolia."

I stared at him, stunned. He had repeated the ancient oath Naaj Majda had given me in the Hall of Chambers. But it wasn't identical. Where did his version come from? And how did it relate to Quis? I was certain it did, somehow.

"You honor me with your oath," I said. "And I give you mine in return."

He nodded, apparently satisfied with my response.

An image formed in my mind:

$$l\,m$$

The *l* was dark purple and three-dimensional, like a plum, but polished and smooth, almost reflective. The *m* looked similar, except with a bluer hue. Those two letters could mean anything, but to me, in that font, they referred to the quantum numbers that defined a spherical harmonic wave.

The letters suddenly morphed into spherical harmonic orbitals.

They shimmered in my mind, glistening blue, violet, rose, and lavender.

"They're *us*," I sudddenly stated.

Kelric blinked. "The Quis dice?"

"Not your gems. Spherical harmonics. They're us. The Rhon." His dice had prodded my thoughts. The way he built with them, their beauty . . . an idea hovered at the edges of my mind, if I could only catch the thought.

"Spherical harmonics as the Rhon." Kelric smiled. "The idea has a certain symmetry."

I laughed, tickled by his humor. Our bodyguards exuded bafflement. I supposed the joke wasn't that funny unless you liked to play with the symmetry properties of spherical harmonics. I had forgotten this side of Kelric, the way he and I used to talk in math puns. The rest of the family had thought us strange, but we enjoyed ourselves.

"A Rhon psion is an orbital in Kyle space," I said. The orbitals continued to glimmer in my thoughts. Some resembled Kelric's round Quis dice. "They're made from spherical harmonics."

"Orbitals of thought." Kelric tilted his head. "But spherical harmonics give only the angular dependence. It's like saying the Rhon only goes *around* a center. Nothing takes us *out* of that center."

More puzzlement came from our guards: They wondered if we were talking in code.

"You're still missing something," Kelric said. "The radial extent."

The idea suddenly coalesced in my mind. Just as his Quis dice formed individual balls or rings, symmetric about their centers, so spherical harmonics built up the mind of a Rhon psion in Kyle space, symmetric about our mental center of being. But a spherical harmonic had only angular dependence; it only described how a shape varied *around* a central point. It had no radial dependence. It didn't tell how a shape varied as we moved *into* or *away* from that center.

I saw the problem now. It was obvious. A Rhon psion could exist in Kyle space, but only in isolation. We were complete with respect to our own centers, but we couldn't reach out.

I spoke slowly. "When the Rhon make the psiberweb, we link our minds with the minds of many others. Those links radiate out from our centers. The web takes us out of ourselves. Without it, we can exist, but we are cut off from humanity." I paused, uncomfortable. "If we want to be truly human, we need those links."

"Do you think we are truly human?"

Gods. What a question. I thought of Taquinil. The waveform I had used to describe Taquinil's existence in Kyle space had come from my impression of my son. It included radial as well as angular dependence, which made me think he wasn't ready yet to completely shed his humanity. We had the ability within ourselves to reach out, if we wished. What we did with that ability depended on us. "Perhaps we each have to make that choice."

He regarded me curiously. "What made you think of all this?"

I indicated his dice pouch of gems. "They remind me of spherical harmonics. All those colors."

"You see mathematical functions in color?"

"Always. Texture, too. Even music." I chuckled. "Spin is more frivolous than angular momentum."

"I should enjoy hearing more about it." Kelric rested his elbow on the table and his chin on his knuckles. It pulled down his shirt cuff, uncovering his wrist guard. Intricate hieroglyphs were engraved in the gold. Intrigued, I tried to decipher the language. It had a faint resemblance to Iotic, but I couldn't be sure without a closer look.

Following my gaze, he glanced down. Then he lowered his arm and pulled down his cuff.

"They're marriage guards," I said. Almost no one wore them anymore, not even among the most conservative Houses. They looked too much like Trader slave restraints. That resemblance had destroyed a tradition with a five-thousand-year history among our people. At one time, the giving of such guards had been an expression of love.

"Dehya, don't ask." He paused. "There is Jeejon. My wife."

I knew Jeejon hadn't given him the guards. Perhaps he was protecting a former wife. Children? Given the current turmoil in the Imperialate, he had reason for caution. And he obviously loved Jeejon, as unlikely a pair as they seemed.

I didn't push. When he was ready, if ever, he would talk about it. Instead I said, "I like your wife."

Kelric grinned, his teeth bright against his gold skin. "So do I."

My breath caught at his smile. I was no more immune to his beauty than anyone else. But more had changed than the gray in his hair or the lines around his eyes. Nineteen years ago, he had often let a woman's physical appearance dazzle him, sometimes to his detriment. He had also tended to prefer women from the noble Houses. Jeejon came from a background so different from his, she had almost no overlap with his previous life.

"I wonder, though, how she will survive the Imperial court," I said.

"She is my consort. She can do whatever she wants."

"Well, yes." I could just imagine how that would fit Naaj's ideas of nobility and *lèse majesté*. "But the Imperial court won't go easy on her."

"Then forget the Imperial court." His face relaxed. "I love her, Dehya. And if the noble Houses have a problem with that, tough."

"Well. Good." I liked this new Kelric more and more. He had also given me a valuable insight.

I thought of his ruby ball, which resembled an orbital. By itself, the ball meant little. It took meaning only as part of a Quis structure. So it was with my mind in Kyle space: the psiberweb gave it meaning. Kyle space formed another aspect of human existence. It deepened our humanity by creating an alternate reality out of the sum total of human thought. The Rhon could open portals to it, but those gates went nowhere without the rest of humanity to give structure to that mental universe.

Only a short time remained before the shuttle took Kelric and me from *Roca's Pride* down to Parthonia for our speech, which would be broadcast to all the settled worlds. Before we could leave, one visit remained to be made. So I walked with Jinn Opsister and my bodyguards, my heart heavy.

We paused at a large hatch guarded by more Jagernauts, who unlocked and opened the heavy portal. When my bodyguards started to follow me through the hatchway, I shook my head. "Please wait out here."

Jinn didn't look happy, but this time she didn't argue. Perhaps she understood.

I continued on alone and closed the hatch behind me.

The observation dome curved out from the hull, a transparent bubble of dichromesh glass. The stars blazed outside; ruby, sapphire, emerald, topaz, and diamond. Interstellar Quis dice. Nurseries of interstellar dust filled with hot, newly-born stars spewed through space like impossibly huge fountains frozen for millennia. The aft end of the battle cruiser curved away from the bubble in both directions, huge, its hull gnarled and massive. Far down the curve, the maw of thrusters dwarfed this bubble, but they were quiescent, making the bay safe for now.

A man stood across the chamber, looking out at the spectacular panorama. The transparent floors, walls, and ceiling made it appear as if he were standing in open space. His hands rested on a waist-high rail.

I went to stand with him. For a long time we both gazed at space.

Then he spoke. "How long until you go down to Parthonia?"

I looked at him. "As soon as you and I finish here."

"So." The First Councilor continued to watch the stars, his face drawn. Prison cuffs glittered on his wrists.

"Barcala," I said softly.

Finally he turned, pain in his gaze. "Must my final view of another human be my executioner?"

I felt as if were dying inside. "I'm sorry."

He looked as if he had aged years. "How long do I have?"

"A few hours." Gods, I hated this. But unlike as with Jon Casestar, no leeway existed here. The noble Houses, our supporters, ISC—all demanded the deposed leader die. Never mind that Barcala and I had been friends for years or that he had done a good job as First Councilor. Unless we executed him, he would be a constant shadow over the new government.

He was watching my face. "Did you get what you wanted?"

"No." My voice caught. "I don't want this."

"I won't beg for my life." He spoke quietly. "The Assembly has always done what it believes best for our people, Dehya. No, it hasn't been pretty, what the Ruby Dynasty has endured. But the alternatives were even worse."

" 'Hasn't been pretty?' " My anger stirred. "My father and mother died from 'not pretty.' Kurj gave up his peace of mind, his ability to love, and finally his life. Soz died. The

Assembly drugged Eldrin and me, threatened and imprisoned us. For what? A son who almost went insane because we should never have had children? What benefit to Skolia was Taquinil's misery? The Traders tortured Althor for two years. They tortured Eldrin." I took a deep breath, stunned at the depth of the rage I had suppressed. "My son, husband, mother, father, Soz, Kurj, Althor, Kelric—how *long* must the list go on? When will we have lived enough hells to satisfy you all?"

Deep lines were etched his face. "I grieve for your losses. But what is more important? What is best for your family or for human survival?"

"That's a cheap shot."

"It is a valid question, Dehya."

"It doesn't have to be an either-or question. The Assembly never gave us a chance to find a better way."

"And you think you can."

I couldn't evade his question, not when he would soon die because of its answer. I spoke slowly. "This much I know: I can best decide myself how I serve Skolia. As long as the Assembly controls my life, everyone loses. Why must we always have a loser and a winner? A way must exist for both to win."

"It isn't this." He pushed his hand slowly through his hair, that one motion telling of a deep-seated fatigue beyond physical exhaustion. "You unnerve people. Gods know, none of us can claim to understand how you think. How did you know Kelric Valdoria still lived? That Delos was important? Or about those foster children on Earth? Then there are the webs. You go anywhere. We've never found a security system that could stop you. As much as you take that for granted, no one else can do it. Saints only know what else you've concluded that you're telling no one."

I froze. *What else you've concluded.* I kept the name Jaibriol III shrouded in my mind. "Barcala, recant your opposition to my government. Go in public and give your support to the Ruby Dynasty. Exhort the former Assembly Councilors to support us. Damn it, let me let you *live*."

He spoke mildly. "Even if I did all that, you still couldn't let me live. ISC and the noble Houses will demand the execution."

"I don't care. I won't order it. But you have to give me a reason I can support. Otherwise my rule is undermined before it starts."

"I won't dishonor my principles." He took a deep breath. "Not even to live."

The hatch hummed behind us. As we turned, it opened. Kelric filled the entrance. He glanced from Barcala to me. "The shuttle is waiting."

Turning to Barcala, I mentally beseeched him one last time. Aloud I said, "Come with us. Make the statement."

He spoke with regret, and also fear, but his voice remained strong. "I can't do what you want. I couldn't live with myself if I did."

My eyes felt hot. "Then we must, each of us, do what is necessary."

Softly he said, "Farewell, Dehya."

I swallowed. "Good-bye, Barcala."

Then I had to leave, to face the unforgiving future.

32

Light and Air

Golden light bathed the Hall of Chambers, gilding it in antique hues. Media teams surrounded the dais, setting up consoles, arranging holocams, and checking lamps. They would broadcast our speech to Parthonia and also to ships in orbit, which would carry it to other worlds. Telops also prepared to use the newly-birthed psiberweb to send the broadcast. Jagernaut bodyguards paced the hall. Less visible, but more deadly, EI-controlled defense systems kept track of everyone.

Kelric and I stood in an alcove. Techs moved around us, attaching mikes that would carry our voices to whatever recording devices wanted them. I felt numb. Kelric watched me in silence, his gaze questioning, but I couldn't answer.

I thought of Colonel Yamada on Delos, who had dealt with us in honor, yes, but also in fear that we, Earth's bellicose siblings, would lay waste to an innocent world in retaliation for an offense against the Ruby Dynasty. And the Allieds, who had chosen to hold their fire on the racer. Would I have let an Allied racer go free in a similar circumstance? Then I thought of Soz, Jaibriol II, Jaibriol III, of three children who had vanished. Soz had to have died for a reason. I couldn't believe the Radiance War had been in vain.

A tech adjusted a micro-monitor on my collar. It would analyze anyone who came near me and relay data to my bodyguards. I wore a simple blue jumpsuit and had my hair piled on my head. No ostentation. Not today.

The tech spoke into the comm on her wrist. "We're ready here."

"Good." The voice came out of her comm. "Have Pharaoh Dyhianna and Imperator Skolia come out after we finish the anthem."

"Will do," the tech said.

Kelric spoke to me in a low voice. "Are you sure about this? I can still speak."

"It's all right. I don't mind." It didn't surprise me that he had asked that only I speak during the ceremony. He had always loathed public oration.

Our bittersweet anthem floated from the airy Hall, painfully beautiful. Its notes flashed like water in the sun, yet they also sang of pain and loss. When the anthem finished, Kelric and I left the alcove, escorted by techs and bodyguards. The holocams followed our progress through the golden light, which the techs were no doubt enhancing. As we mounted the dais, the media crews moved back so they wouldn't block the cameras. Our bodyguards continued with us to the center of the great disk. Then we waited, gazing at the holocams, aware we were also looking out at billions, even trillions of people.

A low voice sounded in my ear, coming from a commbutton the techs had put there. "We're ready to start, Your Highness."

So. It was time. I took a breath. Then I began. "My people, I greet you. I come before you today with great hope. It has been five thousand years since the height of the Ruby Empire, almost six thousand since the Ruby Dynasty first rose to power. Throughout our history, Skolia has been our heart. Now, today, we honor that heart with the advent of a new and greater era."

I stopped, the words of the speech in my mind, poised like spears ready to fall. The next sentence would start simply: *With a smooth transition to the new government* . . . Those eight words had caused more debate among my speech writers than the rest of the address. It was the closest I would come in this broadcast to mentioning Barcala's execution.

"With a smooth transition to the new government," I began. The rest waited on my tongue: *The Ruby Dynasty again assumes full sovereignty of the Skolian Imperialate.*

I looked past the techs, consoles, and holocams to the people around the edges of the Hall. Eldrin was there, leaning against a column, his arms crossed. He wore normal clothes today, no fairy-tale king for the Allieds, just a normal man in gray slacks and a gray pullover.

You are the sea that carries my ship, I thought to him. *The currents of wind I ride above the mountains, the air that lets me breathe.* The love he and I shared, it had been enough to pull me across the stars to him at Delos. Harmonics of love. He and I, we existed together, complete in ourselves, but isolated from the rest of humanity. Someday we would have to decide: remain as we were or relinquish our humanity and become something else. Taquinil had made his decision, completing the evolution he and I had started. A day might come when I also took that journey.

But not today.

I still wanted my humanity. I wanted Skolia. But I couldn't do it alone. Just as Kelric's Quis dice needed structures to give them meaning, or spherical harmonics needed physics to define them as more than pleasing shapes, so the Rhon needed the rest of humanity to achieve our full potential. Kelric's dice were exquisite jewels. Spherical harmonics were lovely functions. But what did you do with gems in geometric shapes? What did you do with beautiful functions? They could exist in isolation or they could be more. Kelric's dice created Quis. Spherical harmonics described the physical universe. The Rhon wove the psiberweb.

Less than a second had gone by while I paused. So I spoke again, letting the acoustics of the hall amplify my voice. "We will meld an alliance unlike any Skolia has known before."

Throughout the hall, the techs and media people looked up from whatever they were doing. This wasn't the script.

"Several tendays ago," I continued, extemporizing, "the government of Skolia shifted from the Assembly to the Ruby Dynasty. I stand before you now as full sovereign. During the Ruby Empire, the rule of the Dynasty was absolute."

Techs were talking into comms now, agitated, intent on my words, and also on whatever protests were coming over their comms.

"Skolia identified itself for six millennia through the Ruby Empire," I said. "Yet in this modern day, in the complexities of human life, we chose a representative government instead." I paused for many seconds this time, giving myself one last chance to reconsider. Then I said, "And so it should be."

The techs froze, their comms forgotten. Beyond them, Eldrin lowered his arms and stood upright.

I searched for the right words. Although I had planned none of this, the thoughts had long been in my mind. "The uneasy meld of modern politics with ancient tradition has often rent our civilization. We think of ourselves as an ancient race from Raylicon, yet compared to humanity on Earth, we are incredibly young. We have no history prior to six thousand years ago, only distant memories of our birth world. We are new. Raw. At this crucial time in our growth, we dare not destabilize Skolia. We need *both* the Ruby Dynasty and Assembly."

The techs were moving fast now, making sure they caught every word as I continued. "For that reason, the new government will join old and new." I was guessing now; I had spoken of this with no one. "The Ruby Dynasty and the Assembly will share the governance of Skolia."

If the Assembly accepted my proposal, they would never again control us. But neither would we control them. It wasn't an ideal solution; the traditions of the Ruby Empire didn't allow for partial pharaohs. But if sharing power could give the Ruby Dynasty the freedom to control our lives, I could live with my title being called honorary. The reality mattered, not the names applied by history and tradition.

The noble Houses wouldn't like it. Yet Vazar's responses through all this made me wonder if even some of them would prefer this to a complete overthrow of the Assembly. The new relationship wouldn't be easy, but maybe, just maybe, it would be better.

"So begins our new future." I turned to another holocam, shifting my focus as I had been asked to do at the end of the speech. I was supposed to finish with a rousing tribute to Skolia. But I had a different conclusion in mind, one that had been turning in my thoughts ever since I had heard Jaibriol III speak these words: *We have suffered the ravages of our conflicts. Let us now seek to heal. To the people of the Skolian*

Imperialate and the Allied Worlds of Earth, I say this: Meet me at the peace table. Let us lay to rest the hatreds that have sundered our common humanity.

I had neither the eloquence nor planning that had gone into his speech, but I did have the authority to respond. All settled space would hear my words, but they were meant for one person. Perhaps he was my nephew, perhaps not, but he still extended the bittersweet promise of hope.

I spoke to the camera. "I accept the offer of Jaibriol the Third, Emperor of Eube, to meet at the peace table. Let us work together—Skolian, Trader, and Allied—to heal the rifts that have divided our common humanity."

So finished my first—and last address—as a full Ruby sovereign.

We strode down a goldstone corridor, Kelric, Eldrin, and I, in a flurry of motion and a crowd of people, all headed away from the Hall of Chambers. The elevator at the end of the corridor would whisk us to the roof, where we would board a racer and return to *Roca's Pride.* Holocasters sped along with us, both human and robot, keeping up a barrage of questions. Jagernauts surrounded us in a bulwark. Actually, Kelric made a good portion of that bulwark. Although his face remained impassive, I could tell he was enjoying himself.

Harried techs ran with us, giving the same answer over and over to the holocasters: Details would be forthcoming. It was fortunate we hadn't planned to take questions after the speech anyway, because we had no answers. I didn't know if Barcala would consent to my idea. But even if he refused, no one could execute him now. I had become part of a coalition government, one that *included* the Assembly. If Barcala said no, the Assembly could vote him out and pick a new First Councilor.

No reporters managed to shove into the elevator with us, but when we reached the roof, many more were there, shouting. With our bodyguards clearing a path, we ran through the crowd to the racer. Even after we boarded the ship and were closing the hatch, the reporters continued to call out questions. As we strapped into our seats, the comms in the cockpit lit up like a festival tree. The racer engines rumbled and the people outside scattered. Then the ship leap off the roof and soared into the sky, headed for orbit.

Messages flooded in as we traveled to *Roca's Pride*. Ragnar and Naaj hated my idea, an odd alliance given Ragnar's antipathy toward the Houses and Naaj's arrogance toward anyone not of them. Chad Barzun pledged support. And so, of all people, did Vazar Majda.

Then the pilot said, "Pharaoh Dyhianna, I'm receiving a message through Secondary Jinn Opsister." She paused. "It comes from Barcala Tikal."

I sat up straighter. "What does he say?"

Her voice quieted. "Three words. 'Yes, I agree.' "

Relief flooded over me and I sat back in my seat, my breath coming out in a long exhalation. For the first time since I had awoken on Opalite, I felt hope for the future.

The darkness in my quarters gave a much-needed respite. The day had seemed endless, while Barcala Tikal and his Assembly councilors met with me and my people. We had debated for hours, trying to hammer out a compromise. It was going to take time, and Kelric and I were in for some riproaring fights—but saints almighty, it looked like it would work.

Footsteps entered the room. "Dehya?"

I turned onto my side. "My greetings, Dryni."

Eldrin sat on the bed, a silhouette in the dark. "A long day."

"Truly." I tugged playfully on his sleeve. "Come, Husband."

He gave a low laugh. "You come, Wife." Then he slid under the covers and pulled me into his arms.

I touched the bare skin of his neck. "When did the doctors operate?" No one had told me they had finished mapping the intruding web within his body and could remove the restraints.

"Today. We didn't want to distract you." He settled me in

his arms. "It is true that Jaibriol the Third has responded to your speech?"

I nodded, my head on his shoulder. "He will meet with us."

"Gods," he murmured. "It's incredible."

"I hope so. But we've so far to go. It may take decades. I ran models on it."

"I didn't think you could predict that far ahead."

"I can't tell much, only that the next fifty years will be rocky." I thought back to the sessions today. "But we have the separation of powers formalized now."

"It was good what you did."

I winced. "Not everyone agrees. And I wish people would stop acting so shocked."

Amusement lightened his voice. "The Ruby Dynasty isn't known for a willingness to compromise."

"I suppose." That intransigence had started wars in ancient times. "Many Aristos don't want peace either. My models predict the Aristo line of Iquar will resist any treaties between Skolia and the Traders."

"Iquar? That's the line of the late Empress?"

"Yes." ISC had been responsible for her death. Their vengeance would culminate in fifty years, though I had no idea how. Nor did I know yet how Seth and his vanished foster children came into it, but they too were in the models. I would discover why and how even if it took me the next five decades to solve the mystery.

Eldrin was playing with a tendril of my hair, twining it around his four fingers. "Do you remember those black shoes the computer imaged for you when the PR people were deciding what you should wear for the holocast we made at Earth?"

"The high heels?"

"Yes." He spoke in a low voice near my ear. "You should get those. Just to wear for me."

I laughed softly. "All right." I had asked my personal EI why Eldrin liked those shoes, given that they made me taller and he preferred small women. The EI gave me a dreary discourse about how raised heels changed human female posture in a way that inspired human males to think of reproduction. I supposed it made sense, but at a gut level I still couldn't fathom why stiletto heels would make Eldrin want to make babies.

"Eldrin?"

He kissed the ridges in my ear. "Hmmmm . . . ?"

"My models predict something else."

He sighed. "Dehya, you need to stop thinking about math and concentrate on your husband."

"I am."

He raised his head, looking a bit alarmed. "You are?"

"Dryni . . . what if we had another child? A son?"

He laid his forehead against mine. "Dehya, love, we don't dare."

"Maybe we could find a way."

"I wish it could be true. But you know the risks."

"Medicine is always advancing."

His voice softened. "We can always hope." His thoughts carried a bittersweet ache, remembering both joy and anguish with Taquinil.

I touched his cheek. "If we do ever have another son, I would like to name him Althor. For your brother."

"Yes. I would like that." He pulled me closer.

So we loved each other, at the dawn of this new era we had entered. The future still held many unknowns. It wouldn't be easy to solve the problems that plagued humanity. But hope had come.

Perhaps we could find a way, after six millennia, to reunite the sundered children of Earth.

Author's Note: Science in Science Fiction

I
THOUGHT HARMONICS

Spheres of Art

Spherical harmonics are among the most beautiful functions in physics. In this essay I will describe what they are and try to give a feel for how and why they inspired this book.

Spherical harmonics can be used to form spheres, rings, teardrops, and other rounded shapes. They appear in many areas of physics, including quantum theory, electromagnetism, and optics. When I do physics, I tend to associate mathematical terms with colors, textures, and other traits. I envision spherical harmonics in shimmering hues: rose, lavender, blue, silver. My doctoral thesis brims with them, a pleasant set of equations to work out given the lovely images they create in my mind.

I've also always liked the name, in part because of the musical associations it evokes. Music has played a big part in my life; I've studied both ballet and piano, and to a lesser extent voice. The word harmonic simultaneously makes me think of melodic harmonies and pleasing equations.

The spark of creativity I feel when choreographing a dance is similar to what I feel when solving an equation, and the meditative quality of ballet class reminds me of working on a satisfying derivation. I first combined the two in a ballet called *Spherical Harmonic* that I choreographed for several students in a dance program I directed while in grad school at Harvard. Spherical harmonics often describe waves, so the ballet evoked wave motions as the dancers wove in and out of spherical patterns. The colors of their skirts, leotards, and tights matched the colors I see for spherical harmonics. I set the ballet to a Gymnopedie by Eric Satie, which has a delicate beauty that fits the way I imagine the functions.

That ballet became the seeds of this story.

Spanning Space

When I was choreographing the dance, I couldn't resist playing with some science fiction "What if?" questions. I wondered what a universe spanned by spherical harmonics would be like if you could actually visit there.

What do I mean by *spanned*? Let's talk about coordinates. Imagine you are sitting in a room. The top of your head is two feet from the wall in front of you, three feet from the wall at your right, and seven feet from the ceiling. Those three distances define your coordinates: (2, 3, 7). They specify your location. We need three to specify your position completely because we live in three dimensions.

If we imagine arrows pointing from the two walls and the ceiling to your location, we have one arrow that is two feet long, one three feet long, and one seven feet long. We call them *vectors,* and they define three directions. When we say those vectors *span* our three-dimensional universe, it means we can specify the location of *any* point in the universe by using those three vectors, if we make them long or short enough. For example, if you stand up, the top of your head moves closer to the ceiling, until it is only, say, four feet away. The same three directions that specified your position before do now as well, but the vector that points from the ceiling to your head shortens to four feet, making your coordinates (2,3,4).

Now let's look at some really odd vectors. The solutions to certain equations are functions that act in an analogous manner to vectors. However, they span a universe with infinite dimensions! To specify a point requires an infinite number of them. The functions don't point anywhere; they are shapes or curves. But mathematically they can be treated like vectors. Such universes are called Hilbert spaces, and the infinite set of functions that span them are called eigenfunctions.

Many eigenfunctions are named after the people who figured them out, like Bessel or Legendre functions. In the book *Spherical Harmonic,* the Selei eigenfunctions refer to the fictional functions discovered by Dehya Selei, the main character.

In our real universe, the three vectors we use to specify our position are mutually perpendicular, that is, they intersect at right angles. We say they are orthogonal. Eigenfunctions are also orthogonal, but here the meaning is more complicated. Roughly speaking, two functions are orthogonal if they have no overlap. This is a simplification because it doesn't actually mean that no parts of the two functions overlap; rather, when certain math operations are perpetrated on them, they cancel each other out.

On the other hand, if we have two copies of the same eigenfunction, they will overlap. We can scale that overlap so it equals one; then we say our functions are *normalized* as well as orthogonal; in other words, they are *orthonormal.* Now we have a wonderfully arcane description of our new universe; it is a Hilbert space spanned by an infinite set of orthonormal eigenfunctions.

Spherical harmonics form such a set.

Figuring a Good Angle

To understand what these eigenfunctions mean, recall how we specified our position in a room. Our location depends on our distance from the walls and ceiling, so we say it varies with distance. Other quantities can depend on other coordinates. For example, if you keep track of your temperature during the day, you would say your temperature *varies with* or *depends on* time. If I keep track of how my weight varies during a diet, I can say my weight depends on what I eat. I could also say it depends on time, since it changes during the diet (hopefully!). Likewise, a function must depend on something, such as time, distance, energy, momentum, or any other physical quantity.

Spherical harmonics depend on angles. Imagine you stick a fork in the center of a pie (so much for the diet). Next you lay a knife flat on the pie with the end of its handle against the fork. Then you rotate the knife around so its end stays against the fork and its tip moves in a circle. If you rotate the knife one quarter of the way around the pie, we say it makes an angle of 90 degrees with its original position. Halfway around is an angle of 180 degrees and the full circle is 360 degrees.

Of course if we just push our knife around on top the pie, we will never cut out a tasty piece. Suppose we stick the knife in the pie right next to the fork. When the two are straight up and down together, the angle between them is zero. As we bring the knife down, the angle it makes with the fork increases. When the knife reaches the pie, it makes an angle of 90 degrees with the fork. If we cut through the pie (and the pie dish) and continue the knife down until it is opposite the fork, the angle between them is 180 degrees. If we bring the knife all the way around, cutting through the other side of the pie (and the beleaguered dish), the knife has gone through 360 degrees.

Now we've described two angles; one is measured around the surface of the pie and the other is measured on a circle that cuts through the pie. The knife in both cases makes a circle, either on the pie or cutting through it. The two circles are perpendicular to each other, just as were the directions that gave our location from the walls and ceiling.

But wait! We've only defined two angles. Space has three dimensions, so we need a third coordinate. That's easy; we let the length of the knife vary—it can be as short or as long as we want. This is called the radial coordinate; together with the two angles, it can completely specify any point in space. These three coordinates define a *spherical* coordinate system; the three vectors we talked about earlier define a *Cartesian* coordinate system.

Spherical harmonics depend only on the two angles; to add the third dimension, we need to multiply them by some function that has radial dependence. This is what Kelric meant in chapter XXXII when he told Dehya she was missing the "radial extent" from her model of psiberspace.

Thought Space

Now comes a central extrapolation in the book: the fictional Selei functions span a Hilbert space, but instead of its functions depending on any of the usual coordinates, they depend on thought.

Well, what does that mean? To start with, we need to decide how to define a thought. We can't really isolate a single thought completely; they blend into one another and we can think about more than one thing at once. One way to specify a thought might be according to how long it takes to complete an idea, whether it is a single thought about going to the store, or a mingled thought about fixing the car and feeding the cat. More complicated thoughts could be broken into individual components, such as the ideas that go through your mind when you read an essay about the science in science fiction.

You could think of your brain, at any moment, as being in a "slice" of a thought. Sum up the slices over the time it takes to complete the idea, from an approximate start to finish, and you have the whole thought.

The size and structure of our brains are reasonably fixed, but the brain isn't identical from moment to moment. As we think, neurons fire and other chemical reactions take place. At each instant, everything in the brain from its structure to its chemical processes can be described by what we call a quantum wavefunction. We don't need to understand details about the wavefunction, only that it exists and that physicists know (in theory) how to calculate it. Then a thought could be described as the sum over the wavefunctions for all the slices of the thought, from start to finish. Voila! We have a mathematical description of a thought.

In theory, we know how to calculate a wavefunction for the entire brain; in practice, it would require computer memory and speed far beyond our current technology. But given the theory, we can jump to a science fictional "What if?"; suppose we let the thoughts act as coordinates and have our eigenfunctions depend on them? These are the Selei eigenfunctions in the story. They span psiberspace.

Transformations

In physics we often use *transforms*. These are mathematical procedures that transform a function depending on one type of coordinate into a function that depends on a different type of coordinate. It is like a caterpillar turning into a butterfly; the cocoon acts as the transform, causing the change. Just as the appearance and other characteristics of the caterpillar determine those of the butterfly, so do the characteristics of the original function determine those of the transformed function.

A big difference exists between the caterpillars and functions, though: you can do an inverse transform on the transformed function and go back to the original type. Imagine if the butterfly could return to the cocoon and come out as a caterpillar again. The new caterpillar wouldn't be exactly like the original because the butterfly wouldn't be exactly the same when it transformed back as when it emerged from its cocoon.

Fourier transforms are used extensively in science, math, and engineering. They take a function that depends on time and change it into one that depends on energy. In the time "universe," the function has a fixed energy and varies with time. If the time function is transformed into the energy "universe," the new function has a fixed time and varies with energy.

Now consider our wavefunction for a thought. It depends on many things, mainly the position of all the particles in the brain (spatial coordinates) and how long it takes to have the thought (time coordinates). In this book, the fictional Selei transform takes a wavefunction for a fixed thought, which varies with space-time coordinates, and transforms it into a wavefunction for fixed space-time coordinates that varies with thoughts. However, just as a thought isn't precisely defined in this universe, so the spacetime coordinates aren't precisely defined in the "thought" universe. Some degree of uncertainty exists in both.

In the book, I called the thought universe by several names: Selei space, because the character Dyhianna (Dehya) Selei derived much of the theory to describe it; psiberspace, because it's fun; and Kyle space, after a character who helped the Ruby Dynasty in the early days, before the Skolian Imperialate existed.

The fictional part of all this is the transform that can convert a spacetime wavefunction describing a thought into a universe defined by thoughts. However, if we assume that "psiberspace" behaves like a Hilbert space, then we can apply all the rules of mathematical physics to its behavior, keeping in mind that we are playing a math game now.

The (real) wavefunction for a thought has a shape, probably curved around the brain. If we imagine the wavefunction as a hill, its peak would probably center on our brain in space for however long it takes to think the thought. In thought space, the hill would correspond to a specific thought, and as you move down its slopes you would sample related thoughts. Say the central peak is your thought of your next-door neighbor. As you move down the slope, your thoughts might turn to other people with a close association to your neighbor. Far down the slope, the thoughts become less distinct and refer to subjects with only a distant relation to your neighbor.

In quantum mechanics, wavefunctions can be built out of eigenfunctions. We add up the eigenfunctions, weighting each by a value that determines how much it contributes to the overall shape of the wavefunction. You can think of it as making a dish for a meal. We add ingredients together, varying the amounts depending on what type of dish we're making.

Now imagine you have an infinite number of ingredients. With that many, you can make any dish in the universe. For many dishes, the amount you add of some ingredients will be zero or very tiny (say a pinch of salt). So it is with eigenfunctions. To build a wavefunction, we might add in major amounts of some eigenfunctions and lesser amounts of others. The number of eigenfunctions needed to make the wavefunction may be infinite, but for higher order terms we are probably adding only pinches.

A wavefunction can be made from any set of eigenfunctions. Two well-known sets are Bessel and Laguerre functions. We could build a wavefunction out of either type, but the amount we use of each eigenfunction would differ from set to set, because the shape of the eigenfunctions vary from set to set. Usually an optimum set of eigenfunctions exists for making a particular a wavefunction. It's roughly equivalent to finding a recipe that requires the fewest possible ingredients.

In *Spherical Harmonic,* Dehya becomes a thought wavefunction when she goes in psiberspace. As she reverse transforms back to our universe, she fragments into the individual eigenfunctions used to make her in the thought universe. Those eigenfunctions are the spherical harmonics, chosen on the soundly scientific principle that the author thinks they are gorgeous. Given that Selei eigenfunctions have thoughts as coordinates, they would be wickedly messy conglomerations of math. Remarkably, in psiberspace they reduce to a beautiful simplicity, because I'm the author, so I get to make up the rules.

II
WORLD BUILDING

Star Makers

One aspect of science fiction I'm often asked to talk about at workshops is world building. Over the years I've accumulated many folders full of notes and equations about the various worlds in my books. I've also put each system in a spreadsheet that calculates many properties of the worlds and their stars. In the three-body system of the moon Opalite, the gas giant Slowcoal, and their parent star, for example, I worked out the size of each, their orbital motions, their relative distances, temperatures and luminosities, densities, gravity, the albedo of Opalite, how close Opalite can get to Slowcoal without being torn apart, the angular extent of Slowcoal in the sky as seen from Opalite, and many other details. It is fun to create such systems, like solving a puzzle.

Since so many readers have asked about the world building, I decided to write these essays at the end of the books. For those interested in creating their own systems, I recommend the Writer's Digest series edited by Ben Bova, including *Alien and Alien Societies,* by Stanley Schmidt, and *World-Building,* by Stephen L. Gillett.

All in a Word

In this essay I've picked an area I've been asked about on convention panels and in interviews: planning languages.

To develop languages for the Ruby Dynasty universe, I first needed its history. The background: an unknown race took humans from Earth about a thousand years ago, from Mesoamerica, North Africa, and India. The aliens not only moved humans in space, they also shifted them in time, dumping them on another planet about six thousand years in our past. Then they vanished, stranding the confused humans.

Earth's lost children eventually developed star travel and built the Ruby Empire. Unfortunately, it collapsed after a few centuries, leaving its colonies isolated for five millennia, until humanity made its way back to the stars and built the Skolian Imperialate. For me as a writer, this offers great possibilities. I have a slew of colonies that evolve for five thousand years on their own, so I can experiment with many ideas for their cultures as long as they remain true to the roots of the situation.

Modern Iotic, Dehya's first tongue, is spoken by only a few people in modern Skolia: the Ruby Dynasty, people who interact regularly with them, descendants of the ancient noble Houses, and scholars. Modern Iotic descends from Classical Iotic, a language no one speaks any more. All Skolian languages, including Classical Iotic, derive from the languages humans brought from Earth from Mesoamerica, India, and North Africa.

The resource I most often use is *The Great Tzotzil Dictionary of Santa Domingo Zinacantan,* compiled by Robert M. Laughlin with John B. Haviland, Smithsonian Institution Press. It describes the language of the Tzotzil Maya. For the Shay language in the book *Spherical Harmonic,* for example, I use variations of Tzotzil words. The language schemes in *The Last Hawk* and *The Quantum Rose* are even more detailed, so I will also talk about those.

Hawks

The Last Hawk takes place on the world Coba, one of the lost Ruby colonies. The Coban settlers included descendants from all the areas on Earth where humans were taken from. The name Coba comes from Mesoamerica, but other words in the book have North African or Indian roots. Languages evolve, of course, so the words shouldn't be identical to those on Earth now. So I used Ahl Majeb River (Al Maghrib/Morocco) and Raajastan Cliffs (Rajasthan, India). Mesoamerican influence shows in the Teotec Mountains, Jatec River, and Olamec Desert.

When writing science fiction, you get to pick what language the story is told in. For *The Last Hawk,* I decided on the modern language of the Coban people. If you imagine that an SF writer translates the language of the characters into that of the reader, then words in the modern Coban language would read as English, like Forest of the Mists or Lake of Tears.

A language scheme needs a consistent basis. However, if it derives from too narrow a base, the words will all sound the same and the design may lack depth. When I started *The Last Hawk,* I had Dahl, Khal, Kehsa, Vahl, Kiesa . . . (yawn). As I developed the culture and its languages, a richer tapestry took form.

In real life, we use words from many languages, such as Sierra Nevada or Lafayette in the United States; in *The Last Hawk,* I had words for ancient customs derive from their older languages, such as the word *Calanya* for the elite dice players. Just as we combine English and other languages for some names, like New Mexico, so Cobans have names like Little Jatec River. Different geographic areas on Coba have different schemes: Estates in the western desert draw more on languages of North Africa and India, those in the upper mountains of the northwest use modern Coban, those in central areas mix Mesoamerican influences with modern Coban, and so on.

Roses

In *Spherical Harmonic* and *The Quantum Rose* I draw primarily on Mayan. Four main languages appear in *The Quantum Rose:* Bridge, spoken on the world Balumil; classical Iotic; modern Iotic; and Iotaca, an altered version of classical Iotic that evolved on Balumil during its isolation.

To complicate matters, many names in *The Quantum Rose*

refer to physics, because the story is an analogy to quantum scattering theory. Mayan languages from one thousand years ago had no words for many of those concepts. In such cases, an author has two options: have the people in the story create new words or have them give new meanings to words already in their language. That also left me with two constraints; I wanted to distinguish those two cases, and I also didn't want nuances of the quantum analogy to be lost in the linguistics.

I'll start with the case of words already in the language. For example, I needed the name of the main character in *Rose* to refer to a quantum-mechanical bound state. I found "ak'il tz'i," which means "leash" in Tzotzil Mayan, changed it into akil tz'i, which the fictional characters used to mean "bound," then further evolved it into Argali. It needed at least two stages (or more) of changes because the original language of the settlers couldn't start out identical to Tzotzil Mayan. It then had to undergo further changes because five thousand years have passed and the original language has evolved into a new one.

For words intended to be completely new to the language, I used a different method. Since we're imagining that an SF writer translates the language of the characters into that of the reader, it makes sense to put the new words into the reader's language, given that they are modern rather than derived from the older languages. So we get the name Lyode in *Rose,* contracted from "light emitting dyode." The characters shorten it because for them the name is ancient, though it is modern compared to the Mayan that formed the basis for Classical Iotic.

Another advantage of the above method is that I didn't have to keep explaining word origins, as I did with words like Argali. Without such explanations for the unusual words, the quantum scattering analogy wouldn't have made sense, but constantly stopping to expound on names would have been tedious. This allowed me the flexibility I needed to make the story work. I had that situation in *Spherical Harmonic,* too, but to a much lesser extent because Dehya knows so many languages.

I've been impressed by how my readers pick up on even the subtlest aspects of the world building. I will leave readers with a puzzle. Many of my books also include references to Greek mythology, not as part of any linguistic scheme, but as allusions. A cipher appears in *The Last Hawk* that has significance to the story. Can you find and solve it?

Family Tree: RUBY DYNASTY

Boldface names refer to members of the Rhon. The Selei name denotes the direct line of the Ruby P
All children of Roca and Eldrinson take Valdoria as their third name. All members of the Rhon within
Dynasty have the right to use Skolia as their last name. "Del" in front of a name means "in honor of."

= marriage

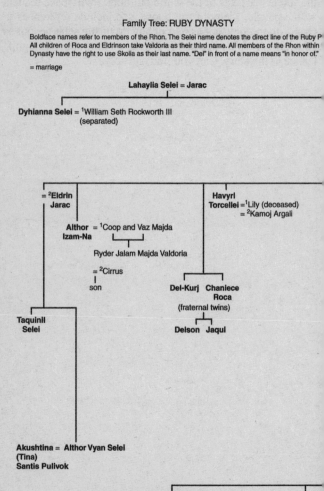

Lahaylia Selei = Jarac

Dyhianna Selei = [1]**William Seth Rockworth III**
(separated)

= [2]**Eldrin
Jarac**

**Havyrl
Torcellei** = [1]Lily (deceased)
= [2]Kamoj Argali

**Althor
Izam-Na** = [1]Coop and Vaz Majda

Ryder Jalam Majda Valdoria

= [2]Cirrus
son

**Del-Kurj Chaniece
Roca**
(fraternal twins)

Delson Jaqui

**Taquinil
Selei**

Akushtina = **Althor Vyan Selei**
(Tina)
Santis Pulivok

Jaibriol III   **Rocalisa**

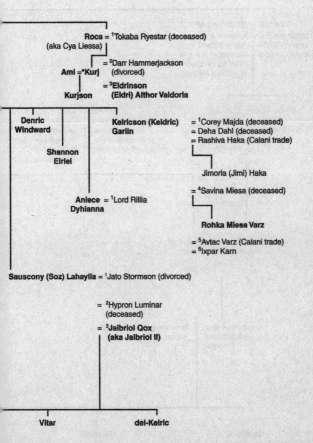

Roca = [1]Tokaba Ryestar (deceased)
(aka Cya Liessa)

= [2]Darr Hammerjackson
(divorced)

Ami =*Kurj

= [3]Eldrinson
(Eldri) Althor Valdoria

Kurjson

Denric
Windward

Kelricson (Keldric) = [1]Corey Majda (deceased)
Garlin

= Deha Dahl (deceased)

= Rashiva Haka (Calani trade)

Shannon
Eirlei

Jimorla (Jimi) Haka

= [4]Savina Miesa (deceased)

Aniece = [1]Lord Rillia
Dyhianna

Rohka Miesa Varz

= [5]Avtac Varz (Calani trade)

= [6]Ixpar Karn

Sauscony (Soz) Lahaylia = [1]Jato Stormson (divorced)

= [2]Hypron Luminar
(deceased)

= [3]Jaibriol Qox
(aka Jaibriol II)

Vitar   **del-Keiric**

*Genetically, Kurj carries Jarac's DNA

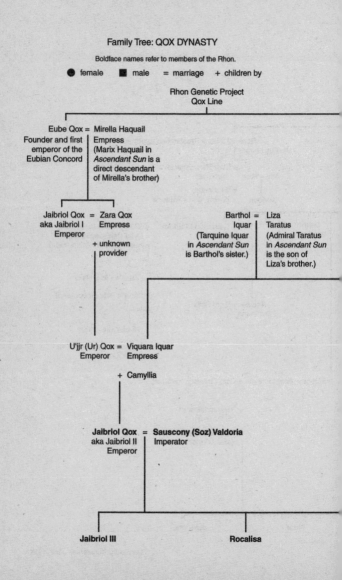

Family Tree: QOX DYNASTY

Boldface names refer to members of the Rhon.

● female ■ male = marriage + children by

Rhon Genetic Project
Qox Line

Eube Qox = Mirella Haquail
Founder and first
emperor of the
Eubian Concord

Mirella Haquail
Empress
(Marix Haquail in
Ascendant Sun is a
direct descendant
of Mirella's brother)

Jaibriol Qox = Zara Qox
aka Jaibriol I
Emperor

Zara Qox
Empress

+ unknown
provider

Barthol = Liza
Iquar   Taratus
(Tarquine Iquar   (Admiral Taratus
in *Ascendant Sun*   in *Ascendant Sun*
is Barthol's sister.)   is the son of
Liza's brother.)

U'jjr (Ur) Qox = Viquara Iquar
Emperor

Viquara Iquar
Empress

+ Camyllia

Jaibriol Qox = **Sauscony (Soz) Valdoria**
aka Jaibriol II   Imperator
Emperor

Jaibriol III   **Rocalisa**

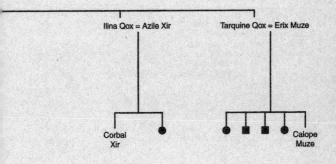

Ilina Qox = Azile Xir

Tarquine Qox = Erix Muze

Corbal
Xir

Calope
Muze

Barthol II

(The great-grandson of Barthol II
is Kryx Iquar, the Eubian Trade
Minister in *Catch the Lightning*.)

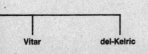

Vitar

del-Kelric

Characters and Family History

Boldface names refer to the Rhon. All members of the Rhon within the Ruby Dynasty use *Skolia* as a last name. The *Selei* name indicates the direct line of the Ruby Pharaoh. Children of *Roca* and *Eldrinson* take Valdoria as a third name. The "del" prefix means "in honor of" (it is capitalized if the person honored was a Triad member). Names are based on world-building systems drawn from Mayan, North African, and Indian (India) cultures.

= marriage

Lahaylia Selei (Ruby Pharaoh: deceased) = *Jarac* (Imperator: deceased)

Lahaylia and *Jarac* founded the modern-day Ruby Dynasty. *Lahaylia* was created in the Rhon genetic project. Her lineage traced back to the ancient Ruby Dynasty that founded the Ruby Empire. *Lahaylia* and *Jarac* had two daughters, *Dyhianna Selei* and *Roca*.

Dyhianna (Dehya) Selei = (1) William Seth Rockworth III (separated)
= (2) *Eldrin Jarac Valdoria.*

Dehya is the Ruby Pharaoh. She married William Seth Rockworth III as part of the Iceland Treaty between the Skolian Imperialate and Allied Worlds of Earth. They had no children and later separated. The dissolution of their marriage would have negated the treaty, so neither the Allieds nor the Imperialate recognized Seth's divorce. Both Seth and Dehya eventually remarried anyway. *Spherical Harmonic* tells the story of what happened to *Dehya* after the Radiance War. She and *Eldrin* have two children, *Taquinil Selei* and *Althor Vyan Selei*.

Althor Vyan Selei = '*Akushtina (Tina) Santis Pulivok*

The story of *Althor* and *Tina* appears in *Catch the Lightning*. *Althor Vyan Selei* was named after his uncle/cousin, *Althor Izam-Na Valdoria*.

Roca = *(1)* Tokaba Ryestar (deceased)
     = *(2)* Darr Hammerjack (divorced)
     = *(3) Eldrinson Althor Valdoria*

Roca and Tokaba had one child, *Kurj* (Imperator and former Jagernaut), who married Ami when he was about a century old. *Kurj* and Ami had a son named Kurjson.

Although no records exist of *Eldrinson*'s lineage, it is believed he also descends from the ancient Ruby Dynasty. He and *Roca* have ten children:

Eldrin (Dryni) Jarac (bard, consort to Ruby Pharaoh, warrior)
Althor Izam-Na (engineer, Jagernaut, Imperial Heir)
Del-Kurj (Del) (singer, warrior, twin to *Chaniece*)
Chaniece Roca (runs Valdoria family household, twin to *Del-Kurj*)
Havyrl (Vyrl) Torcellei (farmer, doctorate in agriculture)
Sauscony (Soz) Lahaylia (military scientist, Jagernaut, Imperator)
Denric Windward (teacher, doctorate in literature)
Shannon Eirlei (Blue Dale archer)
Aniece Dyhianna (accountant, Rillian queen)
Kelricson (Kelric) Garlin (mathematician, Jagernaut, Imperator)

Eldrin appears in *The Radiant Seas* and *Spherical Harmonic*. He married *Dyhianna Selei*. They have two children (see *Dyhianna*).

Althor Izam-Na = *(1)* Coop and Vaz
= *(2)* Cirrus

Althor has a daughter, Eristia Leirol Valdoria, with Syreen Leirol, an actress turned linguist. Coop and Vaz have a son, Ryder Jalam Majda Valdoria, with ***Althor*** as co-parent. ***Althor*** and Cirrus have a son. ***Althor*** and Coop appear in *The Radiant Seas*. The novelette "Soul of Light" tells how ***Althor*** and Vaz met Coop ("Soul of Light" appears in the erotica anthology *Sextopia*, from Circlet Press). Vaz and Coop also appear in *Spherical Harmonic*.

Havyrl (Vyrl) Torcellei = *(1)* Lilliara (Lily) Opaline (deceased)
= *(2)* Kamoj Quanta Argali

The story of ***Vyrl*** and Kamoj is in *The Quantum Rose*. An early version of the first half was serialized in *Analog*, May 1999–July/August 1999.

Sauscony (Soz) Lahaylia = *(1)* Jato Stormson (divorced)
= *(2)* Hypron Luminar (deceased)
= *(3)* ***Jaibriol Qox*** (aka ***Jaibriol II***)

The story of ***Vyrl*** and Lily appears in the novella "Stained Glass Heart," in the anthology *Irresistable Forces*.

The story of how ***Soz*** and Jato met appears in the novella "Aurora in Four Voices" (*Analog*, December 1998). ***Soz*** and ***Jaibriol's*** stories appear in *Primary Inversion* and *The Radiant Seas*. They have four children, all of whom use Qox-Skolia as their last name: ***Jaibriol III, Rocalisa, Vitar,*** and ***del-Kelric. Jaibriol III*** becomes Emperor of Eube.

Aniece = Lord Rillia

Lord Rillia rules Rillia, a province on the planet Lyshriol, which consists of the Rillian Vales, Dalvador Plains, Backbone Mountains, and Stained Glass Forest.

Kelricson (Kelric) Garlin = *(1)* Corey Majda (deceased)
                      = *(2)* Deha Dahl (deceased)
                      = *(3)* Rashiva Haka (Calani trade)
                      = *(4)* Savina Miesa (deceased)
                      = *(5)* Avtac Varz (Calani trade)
                      = *(6)* Ixpar Karn (closure)
                      = *(7)* Jeejon

Kelric's stories are told in *The Last Hawk, Ascendant Sun, Spherical Harmonic,* the novella "A Roll of the Dice" (*Analog,* July/August 2000), and the novelette "Light and Shadow" (*Analog,* April 1994). ***Kelric*** and Rashiva have one son, Jimorla (Jimi) Haka, who becomes a renowned Calani. ***Kelric*** and Savina have one daughter, ***Rohka Miesa Varz,*** who becomes the Ministry Successor in line to rule the Twelve Estates on Coba.

Timeline

circa 4000 BC	Group of humans moved from Earth to Raylicon
circa 3600 BC	Ruby Dynasty begins
circa 3100 BC	Raylicans launch first interstellar flights Rise of Ruby Empire
circa 2900 BC	Ruby Empire begins decline
circa 2800 BC	Last interstellar flights; Ruby Empire collapses
circa AD 1300	Raylicans begin attempts to regain lost knowledge and colonies
1843	Raylicans regain interstellar flight
1871	Aristos found Eubian Concord (a.k.a. Trader Empire)
1881	Lahaylia Selei born
1904	Lahaylia Selei founds Skolian Imperialate and takes Skolia name
2005	Jarac born
2111	Lahaylia Selei marries Jarac
2119	Dyhianna Selei born
2122	Earth achieves interstellar flight
2132	Earth founds Allied Worlds
2144	Roca born
2169	Kurj born
2203	Roca marries Eldrinson Althor Valdoria
2204	Eldrin Jarac Valdoria born Jarac dies and Kurj becomes Imperator Lahaylia dies
2206	Althor Izam-Na Valdoria born
2207	Del-Kurj and Chaniece Roca Valdoria born
2209	Havyrl (Vyrl) Torcellei Valdoria born
2210	Sauscony (Soz) Lahaylia Valdoria born
2211	Denric Winward Valdoria born
2213	Shannon Eirlei Valdoria born
2215	Aniece Dyhianna Valdoria born
2219	Kelricson (Kelric) Garlin Valdoria born
2223	Vyrl marries Lily ("Stained Glass Heart")

2237	Jaibriol II born
2240	Soz meets Jato Stormson ("Aurora in Four Voices")
2241	Kelric marries Admiral Corey Majda
2243	Corey assassinated ("Light and Shadow")
2258	Kelric crashes on Coba *(The Last Hawk)*
early 2259	Soz meets Jaibriol *(Primary Inversion)*
late 2259	Soz and Jaibriol go into exile *(The Radiant Seas)*
2260	Jaibriol III born (aka Jaibriol Qox Skolia)
2263	Rocalisa Qox Skolia born; Althor Izam-Na Valdoria meets Coop ("Soul of Light")
2268	Vitar Qox Skolia born
2273	del-Kelric Qox Skolia born
2274	Radiance War begins (also called Domino War)
	Kurj marries Ami
2276	Traders capture Eldrin. Radiance War ends
2277–8	Kelric returns home *(Ascendant Sun)*
	Jaibriol III becomes emperor *(The Moon's Shadow)*
	Dehya coalesces *(Spherical Harmonic)*
	Kamoj and Vyrl meet *(The Quantum Rose)*
2279	Althor Vyan Selei born
2287	Jeremiah Coltman trapped on Coba ("A Roll of the Dice")
2328	Althor Vyan Selei meets Tina Santis Pulivok *(Catch the Lightning)*

About the Author

Catherine Asaro grew up near Berkeley, California. She earned her Ph.D. in Chemical Physics and her M.A. in Physics, both from Harvard, and a B.S. with Highest Honors in Chemistry from UCLA. Among the places she has done research are the University of Toronto, the Max Planck Institut für Astrophysik in Germany, and the Harvard-Smithsonian Center for Astrophysics. She currently runs Molecudyne Research and lives in Maryland with her husband and daughter. A former ballet and jazz dancer, she founded the Mainly Jazz Dance program at Harvard and now teaches at various ballet schools, including the School of the Ballet Theatre of Maryland.

She has also written *Primary Inversion, Catch the Lightning, The Last Hawk, The Radiant Seas, The Quantum Rose,* and *Ascendant Sun,* all part of the Skolian Saga, and *The Veiled Web* and *The Phoenix Code,* near-future science fiction thrillers. Her work has won numerous awards, including the Nebula, the *Analog* Readers Poll (the AnLab), the Homer, and the Sapphire Award. Her short fiction has appeared in *Analog* and anthologies. She can be reached on the Web at http://www.sff.net/people/asaro/.